ANGELIC & BLACK
CONTEMPORARY GREEK SHORT STORIES

A<small>NGELIC</small> & B<small>LACK</small>

C<small>ONTEMPORARY</small> G<small>REEK</small> S<small>HORT</small> S<small>TORIES</small>

Edited and Translated by
D<small>AVID</small> C<small>ONNOLLY</small>

With an Introduction by
V<small>ANGELIS</small> H<small>ATZIVASSILEIOU</small>

COSMOS PUBLISHING

Copyright © 2006 by Cosmos Publishing Co., Inc.

All rights reserved.

No part of this book may be reproduced in any form or by any electronic or mechanical means, including storage and retrieval systems, without permission in writing from the publisher, except by a reviewer, who may quote brief passages in a review.

Book design by Mary A. Wirth
Cover painting by Yorgos Rorris; "Sun Glasses," 2000, oil on canvas, 45x35 cm.
Reproduced courtesy of the painter.

Library of Congress Cataloging-in-Publication Data

Angelic & black : contemporary Greek short stories / edited and translated by David Connolly; with an introduction by Vangelis Hatzivassileiou.
   p. cm.
Includes bibliographical references.
10 digit ISBN 1-932455-11-6 (pbk.: alk. paper)
13 digit ISBN 978-1-932455-11-3
  1. Short stories, Greek (Modern)—Translations into English. 2. Greek fiction, Modern—20th century—Translations into English. 3. Greek fiction, Modern—21st century—Translations into English. I. Title: Angelic and black. II. Connolly, David, 1954-

PA5296.E5A56 2006
889'.30108—dc22

2006004248

First published in 2006 by:
COSMOS PUBLISHING CO., INC.
P.O. Box 2255
River Vale, NJ 07675
Phone: 201-664-3494
Fax: 201-664-3402
E-mail: info@greeceinprint.com
Website: www.greeceinprint.com

THE GREEK EXPERIENCE
Books, Music, Video, Art
www.GreeceInPrint.com
262 Rivervale Rd, River Vale, N.J. 07675
Tel 201-664-3494 Email info@GreeceInPrint.com

Printed in Greece and in the USA

*This translation
was made possible thanks to
the generous support
of
Sotiris A. Felios
&
Lary Chanou*

"Light, angelic and black . . ."
GEORGE SEFERIS, *Thrush III*

CONTENTS

INTRODUCTION BY VANGELIS HATZIVASSILEIOU:
The Mosaic of Greek Prose in the Last Quarter of the 20th Century — xi

EVYENIOS ARANITSIS
Jesus Aged Twelve in the Temple — 3

SOTIRIS DIMITRIOU
The Plunderer — 7

MARO DOUKA
Carré Fix — 12

MICHEL FAÏS
Halima, Desdemona, Bubu — 19

RHEA GALANAKI
An Almost-Blue Arm — 33

E. H. GONATAS
The Preparation — 36

TASSOS GOUDELIS
Afternoon with Alcoholic View — 44

VASSILIS GOUROYANNIS
The Cock's Crowing — 48

CHRISTOS HOMENIDIS
Not All Fingers Are Equal — 50

NIKOS HOULIARAS
The Body — 57

YANNIS KAISARIDIS
    The Old Man and the Tree   70

DIMITRIS KALOKYRIS
    Militsa or Mid-August Reverie   77

IOANNA KARYSTIANI
    Mrs. Cataki   82

MENIS KOUMANDAREAS
    Seraphim   93

ACHILLEAS KYRIAKIDIS
    Nebraska   106

PAVLOS MATESIS
    Murder's Singular Taste   116

AMANDA MICHALOPOULOU
    Lermontov   121

CHRISTOPHOROS MILIONIS
    The Find   131

DIMITRIS MINGAS
    Memory   141

MARIA MITSORA
    Halfpastdoom   148

CLAIRE MITSOTAKI
    Pink and Black   159

SOPHIA NIKOLAÏDOU
    How the Sting Hurts and It's in Deep   165

DIMITRIS NOLLAS
    The Old Enemy   169

NIKOS PANAYOTOPOULOS
    The Strength of Materials   175

ALEXIS PANSELINOS
    Arrogance   191

I. H. PAPADIMITRAKOPOULOS
    Rosamund   199

DIMITRIS PETSETIDIS
    Away Ground   203

YORGOS SKABARDONIS
    Mussels in the Flower Vase   207

ERSI SOTIROPOULOU
    The Assistants   211

ANTONIS SOUROUNIS
    His Last Role   217

PETROS TATSOPOULOS
    A Smelly Weakness   223

VASSILIS TSIABOUSSIS
    The Doll   228

THANASSIS VALTINOS
    Addiction to Nicotine   233

ZYRANNA ZATELLI
    The Ivory Buttons   245

BIOGRAPHICAL NOTES   253

ABOUT THE TRANSLATOR   263

INTRODUCTION

The Mosaic of Greek Prose in the Last Quarter of the 20th Century

The authors presented in this anthology are representative of contemporary Greek literature in some of its most fundamental and characteristic trends. Coming from all generations and age-groups and covering a wide range of stylistic experimentation and thematic concerns, they reveal the way in which Greek authors in the 21st century are seeking to find their path, while orienting and also adapting themselves to the requirements of an age which more and more appears to regard the local as being inseparable from the universal and the national as being inevitably linked with the intercultural.

Of the older authors, mention must be made of four in particular: Thanassis Valtinos, Christophoros Milionis, I.H. Papadimitrakopoulos and Menis Koumandareas. All four first appeared in Greek letters during the sixties, dissociating (at least in part) prose fiction from the political and historical concerns bequeathed to it by the Second World War and the Greek Civil War and turning it towards more personal and everyday concerns. The connection with politics and history becomes indirect and fragmented in the novels and short stories by Valtinos and Milionis. The violence and bloodshed that for a long time characterized the whole of Europe during the postwar period is by no means absent from their work since they attempt to convey the corresponding Greek experience (particularly strained because of the Civil War in Greece). However, this experience emerges through the memories of childhood and adolescence—through things heard and through visual and physical encounters. And the main element in such a setting is not the savagery and inhumanity of war, but the longing and fear that a child has for the object of his desire or of his abhorrence—an object that introduces the political and historical enormity into the game through the back door in order to emphasize it in even more striking and lucid colors. On the contrary, this approach appears not to suit Papadimitrakopoulos. Having traveled for many years throughout Greece because of his military background, he endeavors to retain in his narrative the everyday, yet eminently revealing sketches of life in the provinces—in a time that is *de facto* fixed and ahistorical and in a space that is *ab initio* limited and static, whose changes are countable on the fingers of one hand and constantly recycled. Also far from the bloodshed of politics and history is the work of Koumandareas, who prefers, like Papadimitrakopoulos, to focus his lens on daily life, though shifting the center of his narration from the familiar provincial community to the urban world of the big city and the anonymous crowds that inhabit it. Here, the emphasis is on personal relationships and often insurmountable communication problems on the one hand, and, on the other, on the individual's ceaseless endeavor to stand out from the crowd, seeking a path that will correspond to his deeper desires, inclinations and needs. Before leaving this older generation of authors, I should mention the very special position occupied by E. H. Gonatas in postwar Greek prose. Influenced by the allegorical content and inscrutable language of prewar German expressionism, Gonatas imbues his narrative material (which cannot easily be categorized as novel, novella, short story or poetry) with a strongly poetical and mythical dimension, through cryptic references to a variety of inner questions relating to human existence—ranging from the fear of death and the desire for freedom to loneliness and the actual possibility of communication and coexistence with the other.

In moving from one generation and age group to another, we also note a marked change in climate. The prose writers who appeared in Greek literature at the beginning or in the middle of the seventies find themselves in a peculiar and undoubtedly transitional stage. As a result of Greece's transition from the troubled postwar years and the gloom of the seven-year military dictatorship (1967-1974) to a parliamentary system and constitutional democracy, politics gradually becomes disassociated from daily life after over a century during which the country had been more or less obliged to accept this situation. Nevertheless, at the same time, new political agendas are created: from terrorism and its far-reaching activity to corruption in authority and the numerous ideological changes at both ends of the spectrum. Prose writers such as Maro Douka, Alexis Panselinos and Dimitris Nollas enlist a wide variety of means in order to confront this new reality. Douka delves deep into politics (often publishing wholly political novels, at other times entering into a dialogue with the social or historical novel, though always from a political perspective), without, however, forgetting even for one moment the peculiar characteristics of the women who feature in her works (the women are as a rule Douka's strongest narrative characters). Their link with the collective landscape is in each case rooted in the need to present a plainly visible personal world, within which the most crucial developments are fermented. It is to the elements of history and fantasy that Alexis Panselinos has recourse in order to depict Greek politics and society from the end of the Second World War to the beginning of the 21st century. The plots constructed by Panselinos in his novels and short stories usually force his heroes out of their shells in order, willingly or unwillingly, to come into contact with others, exploring and realizing their capacities only through confrontation with these others. External events, the writer whispers to us, are never without effect on individuality, which is always, in some way, linked with them. And this is equally true for the artists and policemen as for the femmes fatales or restless adolescents who are driven action in his books. Dimitris Nollas, on the other hand, goes off on a different tack in order to cover the same ground. In writing novels and short stories about terrorism, politics and the spectacular social and economic upheavals in Greece since 1974, Nollas follows an elliptical orbit, with the faces of his heroes deliberately indistinct, with a centrifugal plot, and with an imperceptibly ironic language, which, making use of the most harrowing subject matter, attempts to show the ludicrous nature of any self-seeking politics or social involvement. And because, in such a field, it is impossible for any ideologist to prevail, those of his characters who struggle to defend their integrity are in the end utterly defeated. A far cry from all of this are the novels and short stories of Nikos Houliaras, who has recourse to the elixir of the solitary life, but also of the solace provided by distance from any active convention: dream and personal transcendence as an antidote to the pain of a reality that has difficulty in legitimizing its values.

When Greek society begins to approach the modernizing goals set by the political change of 1974 and when the country begins to come noticeably closer to the more developed countries of Europe on every level (economic, social and cultural), thereby entering a long period of peace at home and abroad, the literary system changes once again. Free once and for all from political obligations and historical concerns, with its attention turned to the literary developments in Europe and North America and nurtured by the most disparate domestic and foreign sources, prose writing in Greece during the last quarter of the 20th century is transformed into an enormous mosaic, the surface of which depicts the most heterogeneous forms and scenes, in countless combinations and in a plethora of connections and conjunctions.

A very strong trend during this period (one which has lost nothing of its vitality or energy even today) is the novel or short story that parodies or satirizes everyday life. Pavlos Matesis, Antonis Sourounis, Petros Tatsopoulos, Ersi Sotiropoulou and Christos Homenidis may be considered, both in their novels and short stories, as leading representatives of the genre and as self-confessed advocates of it. Drawing on the celebrated tradition of surrealism, Matesis fashions his characters from the most outrageous materials, creating paranoiac conflicts and compromises that completely disorient the heroes, shattering their integrity and their credibility. Less frenzied though in an equally violent and cruel world, Sourounis employs sarcasm in his dry comedies as a dynamic counterbalance to their unbearably oppressive and dramatic content. With Tatsopoulos, we enter a world where nothing is left standing: politics, public life, daily routine, professional and literary circles are distorted in the extreme, not only revealing their corrosion and decay, but also underlining (and herein lies the essence) their exceptionally limited significance. Moving along similar paths, but with subtler nuances of a more introspective type, Sotiropoulou takes care to sever her heroes from all forms of prettified transcendence, endowing them with successive degradations and breakdowns, which lead them to the verge of ridiculousness, and also of panic. With Christos Homenidis, we are back to the spirit of Tatsopoulos: continual ironic reversals of the action, characters who in the blink of an eye lose their outwardly good regard and their dignity and situations that quickly turn into devastating, black humor.

Socially oriented, though without any intention to parody or ridicule, is the group constituted in terms of their novels and short stories by Dimitris Petsetidis, Dimitris Mingas, Sotiris Dimitriou, Ioanna Karystiani and Vassilis Tsiaboussis. Petsetidis focuses on everyday life in the provinces, which he records often in connection with historical memory in a subdued and unadorned language. Mingas concentrates more on the inner universe of his characters in order to show their gradual alienation from and eventual break with their depressing environment, though he always retains a large part of the contemporary social fabric in the setting. Dimitriou turns to more clear-cut and sometimes purely external phenomena: immigrants, the financially helpless and socially wretched often constitute the main axes of his subject-matter, into which the specter of Evil that afflicts his characters constantly infiltrates. Karystiani should most properly be regarded as an out and out social writer. She deals each time with matters that reside in the heart of the collective: from the position of women in traditional and also contemporary communities to the question of the Cretan vendetta and the grim sexual loneliness in today's huge and impersonal cities. Tsiaboussis, too, is concerned with collective daily life. By means of a catalytic irony, he makes his characters realize what it is exactly that alienates them from their environment, and with what painful consequences.

It cannot be claimed that Greek prose-writing has been greatly influenced during the last quarter of the 20th century by the dynamism of magical realism in the same way that this spread throughout Latin America and other continents. Nevertheless, nor can it be claimed that Greek literature remained completely uninfluenced by its manifold presence and diffusion. Three of the authors anthologized here confirm this in the most exuberant way. Zyranna Zateli, Yorgos Skabardonis and Vassilis Gouroyannis imbue their narrative with a markedly magical function, without, however, rending its realistic framework and also without ever having recourse to dream narrative. Zateli, who is preeminently a novelist, seeks the settings for her stories in northern Greece at the turn of the 20th century and takes her symbols from the local myths and legends, which she cleverly interweaves into her impressive plots, calling upon readers to find their own explanations for the plot's absurdities. Skabardonis, whose forte lies in his short stories, repeatedly pits his heroes against the inexplicable and the unexpected, temporarily creating, both for themselves and for the observer of their actions, a kind of parallel reality—a reality that wishes to underline the imaginary possibility of an alternative world. Alongside his novels, Gouroyannis has also written interesting short stories, finding his magical refuge in nature and the external setting, often creating thereby an unquestionably animistic and pantheistic atmosphere.

Recourse to dream and also to what is played out in the deeper levels of the self is what links the writings of Rhea Galanaki, Maria Mitsora and Yannis Kaisaridis. Galanaki is one of the pioneers in the resurgence of the historical novel in Greece: a trend that began in the early nineties and continues even today. Nevertheless, her stories are regularly infused with a markedly poetical and dreamlike quality, which detaches the characters from the space and time of history and surrenders them, in clearly fateful circumstances, to their inner experiences and concerns. We also find dreamlike and transcendent elements in the short stories by Kaisaridis, with the difference that what unites and directs them in this case is contact with the dead: a conversation with dear ones no longer alive and the constant transformation of their quasi-presence. Both in her novels and in her short stories, Mitsora brings us back to the harsh present, only to immediately distance herself from this, however, through delusion, illusion and hallucination. *Attempts to deaden the pain* is what Cavafy would call the actions of her characters and this would not be far from the truth: substances are what always determine the luck of the game in Mitsora's stories and what, in clear yet harsh lines, sketch their dramatic outcome.

The circle comes to a close with a group of writers whose work (novels, short stories and novellas) belongs to the constellation of intense stylistic and genre experimentation and of postmodernism. I am referring here to Dimitris Kalokyris, Achilleas Kyriakidis, Evyenios Aranitsis, Claire Mitsotaki, Tassos Goudelis, Michel Faïs, Nikos Panayotopoulos, Amanda Michalopoulou and Sophia Nikolaïdou. Under the strong influence of Borges, and also of the European and Greek surrealist traditions, Kalokyris boldly removes the divisions between prose, essay and poetry, holding the most unexpected turns in store in his openly ironic mythology. Kyriakidis, too, engages in intertextual chitchat, influenced both by the older French lettrism and by contemporary magical realism and by the language of the cinema. His stories can be read in many different ways and it is this, of course, that determines their meaning. An insatiable experimenter with literary genres is Aranitsis, who has the ability on the one hand to dismantle his sources right down to the very last screw and, on the other, to continually emphasize to the reader that literature, whatever lighting or stage direction is applied to it, never loses its fascination. Mitsotaki resorts to a combination of learned, analytical language and the paratactic, oral and idiomatic tradition in order to create her fictional universe, which not for one moment ceases to remind us of its contrived character. For his part, Goudelis prefers the short form. A minimum of action, character outlines, deliberate confusion between inner and outer reality and an intentional vagueness of feelings and situations constitute the basic elements of his work. A dialogue with the literature of documentation is opened by Faïs, who deals equally with autobiography, fictional biography and theater in a world where the dominant rule is the constitution and defense of solitary individuality from the moment that its ties with others can only be created on the basis either of the deeply traumatic or the wholly circumstantial and fortuitous. Panayotopoulos begins his own journey from the literature of futurology and science fiction and continues with the epistolary novel, with the local saga, and also with the popular and historical or encomiastic legendary, using an anthropogeography that is founded totally on delusion and deceit. Michalopoulou, for her part, has no difficulty in conversing with the political and social novel, or opening accounts with the jargon of the kitchen and gastronomy, at the same time making use of elements from the human sciences and also from music and the visual arts, in a world in which everything is judged by the way in which loves and friendships are arranged and regulated. Finally, Nikolaïdou devises an ironic disruption of the campus novel, at the same time paying due to both science fiction and the medieval romance, in a landscape where the heroes are obliged to survive through constant clashes and violent shifts in position.

These, then, are some of the general characteristics of contemporary Greek literature, at least as it appears in the present anthology. It goes without saying that the literary reality is far more expansive and far more varied than the anthology—as is the case with any literary reality in relation to any anthology. Nevertheless no one would deny that the work of any anthologist is precisely to locate and underline from a multiform, multifaceted and multilevel reality whatever best and most clearly represents it. And this is certainly the case in the pages that follow.

VANGELIS HATZIVASSILEIOU

Angelic & Black
CONTEMPORARY GREEK SHORT STORIES

Evyenios Aranitsis

Jesus Aged Twelve in the Temple

On entering the Temple on the Sabbath day Jesus felt that his radiance was no different than childhood's mystery itself nevertheless he adopted a less meek expression more in keeping with the idiosyncrasy of someone respectful of the law because otherwise the elders would not listen to him and he was aware of this so at first they gave him their undivided attention because the boy spoke like an orator but then they began yawning and of all of them only two suspected that the boy was not just any boy and that perhaps at long last they had before them the one to whom the prophets had alluded though hardly alluded given that they had actually been more than explicit and of course these were the two that Jesus immediately singled out and closely observed before saying to the first one you the tall one back there with the wound on your brow why don't you come closer but he replied I am not sure if I should and Jesus said to him approach don't be afraid you have God's blessing for he has given you the gift of being able to express yourself like a poet so step forward and don't give it another thought to which he replied I'm afraid to come close to you Lord lest all the flowers suddenly bloom together and your darkness blots out nature's resplendent mask whose music entwines the power of good deeds and apart from anything else I suffer from heart trouble and as you can imagine my doctor advised me to avoid every active force in nature particularly anything centrifugal or centripetal and it's for this reason that I don't know how I can bear for you to be the son of God and man at the same time and Jesus said to him quite simply my Father forgives you for your honesty therefore your descendents' shadows will be nurtured by caresses alone and when the dampness spreads their children will sing in the spirit of the Lord beneath a shower of love's kites what more do you want he asked him do you want anything else and if so say it don't hesitate but he didn't want anything else so it seemed and said no I want nothing more and then asked will you permit me at least to fall on my knees but to this Jesus answered no for knees are not of the heart knees are of the mind if the truth be told the things of the heart are the eyes and the fingers that caress your neighbor's skin the very thing that became so desirable after the Fall and the other one protested saying surely not desirable and added now you're getting us confused but Jesus cut him short replying you've still a long way to go my friend anyhow off with you now and then he turned to the others saying to them and each of you each with your mind your so-called brain that likes lots of cherries stop grumbling because your heart carries a little basket and limps on its way to the fruit besides you shouldn't be fooled by the fact that I am still a child for time is standing still and will go on standing still until further orders so let the next one come forward and the other man actually did begin to approach muttering I'm coming Lord if you mean me but how can I know given the way you look at me and everything else at the same time and Jesus said to him I mean you Gadelon you are my beloved so come up if you don't mind and he replied if you do mean me it is as if I have already come and Jesus answered it is as you said except that I must touch you or there can be no miracle whereupon the man asked if some miracle was indeed going to happen now and what kind it might be because he wanted he said proceeding logically from the form to the content of the matter to provide a dowry for his sister who was thirty years old and still unmarried and Jesus said to him your faith has saved you my friend so return home and beneath the bed of your grandson Rubin you will find a chest with one hundred thousand sesterces that I hope will suffice for the first payment and the man said it will more than suffice and then he kept on asking what he should do to thank his benefactor and Jesus said first you might pray that the trees might hearken and might blossom three auxiliaries in succession a major stylistic infelicity but never mind provided the trees blossom in accordance with divine economy secondly when you stoop to take the money from under the bed take care not to wake the boy because otherwise our labors will have been in vain then upon hearing these words half the elders began applauding and the other half began banging their feet on the floor in a show of disapproval and the noise lasted a few seconds but in the space of these few seconds or rather in the cracks between them an invisible chorus of angels glided in and arrayed itself in the loft and immediately there was heard a psalmody so unusual that one by one the elders began to faint apart from the two who had been benefited for they left on tiptoe quietly closing the door behind them whereupon Jesus asked the angels to sing something more joyful as it was a day of gladness and glory and the angels did indeed sing in a different tone and manner and cascades of hyacinths began to pour from the ceiling at which those referred to by most people as sages gradually began to recover because of the strong scent and felt that the Temple was hovering at the center of the universe which had shrunk like a lentil bean and in which everything but everything had temporarily become united through the bonds of universal attraction with the result that they were astonished and so that they wouldn't be afraid Jesus described this attraction as the absolute lack of fear which is the mode of existence of the Father the Son and the Holy Spirit whether this appears in the form of a dove or in the form of passionate concern on the part of the younger brother for the successes of the elder yet the sages were now playing with their worry beads and fidgeting and shaking the flower petals from their clothes and generally were all doing whatever any sage would do in the face of such a scandalous questioning of the foundations of the Roman-Jewish ethicopolitical axis when at that moment Mary ran into the Temple crossing the dimly lit hall and opening a path through the angels who meanwhile had become visible and were sitting in large groups listening to and commenting on the boy's sermon but who now fell silent and watched her going up to her son and gently taking hold of him by the wrist in order to take him outside and so realizing that they themselves no longer had any business there they one by one transformed themselves into musical notes and vanished in swirls around the tall pillars which were made out of ivory and agate and for which Solomon had spent a fortune most probably not his while the sages remained undecided for a time before continuing their discussion concerning how to solve the irreconcilability of the Law of Moses and the authority of Caesar from precisely the point where they had stopped now in the light of the road Jesus became bashful again and walked meekly beside his stepfather till he saw Zovee who was the same age as he was playing heads or tails with a copper coin outside the corner greengrocer's and then the boy recognized Jesus because they had once had a mutual friend from Galilee and he shouted to him and Jesus turned round again and looked at him but hesitated to bless him mentally as he would have liked because he knew that this boy was not yet ready to receive a gift infinitely greater than the limits of his gratitude so he confined himself to changing the copper coin into a gold one and in this way he caused an infinitesimal rise in inflation in the monetary system of the eastern Roman provinces but such an imperceptible shaking of the world order was something that Mary instinctively felt and of course she didn't know quite how to react but meanwhile Jesus realized that he was the cause of his mother's upset and he was suddenly overcome by the desire to immediately grant redemption on the spot to the entire world uniting everything namely angels people animals plants minerals and demons but at the last moment he also realized that it would be pointless or rather premature extremely premature and this was something that he remembered years later and he said to his disciples always remember that hesitation of mine and in order that it may not be forgotten please let it be symbolized by the slow pace of the Good Friday procession because that slackening of the pace is the emergency exit to spring and there is really no need for any haste he added since we are still talking about the childhood of things in other words about love and in particular about that love that the Greeks will one day call mourning.

Original title: "O Iisous 12etis sto nao." Published in Evyenios Aranitsis, *Istories pou aresan se merikous anthropous pou xero* [Stories Liked by Some People I Know], Athens: Nefeli, 1995, pp. 73-77.

Sotiris Dimitriou

The Plunderer

He shopped at the kiosk, but he was so discreet that although he'd been coming for over a year, as he told me after we had become involved, I only started to notice his presence much later. He tried not to be at all bothersome and he always had the exact change for his cigarettes. He didn't demand his turn and he always spoke in a low voice, with a kind of reverence. As was only natural, we began exchanging a "good morning" and a "hello," and he eventually started looking at me in the eyes.

I didn't know then what it was that both bothered and excited me about that gaze, though now, after everything that followed, I know. A deep well of eroticism hidden behind an embarrassed and, for that reason, convincing shyness.

One sunny morning, he asked me rather timidly whether he might give me a book of his poetry. In it he wrote a rather formal dedication "...with warm wishes" or some such thing and immediately left. Thumbing through it, I saw that above one poem, he had written in ink "for you."

I spent all night reading and reflecting on his poems. I liked them and at the same time they repelled me. I liked them because they contained pain, something that always fascinated me in art. But they were also sick, as was obvious from the loose, weird syntax. Exactly that same nervous inconstancy that there was in his facial features. They revealed a man who was unbalanced, but with an enormous zest for life, with what it took to be the man who, having himself been deeply hurt, could love and be loved by a woman like me, a woman with a story like mine. Here it is for you in a few words.

A foundling. Till five at the City Nursery, then, till fourteen, at Juvenile Home and, later, because of premature development, a cleaner in the municipal car park. But not for long, because my father, who hadn't lost track of my whereabouts, claimed me and took me away.

I don't have to tell you how men behaved towards me, even as an infant. For them, I was a little stray female animal with which they could do as they pleased, without answer to any law of their own or of society.

Later, using my savings, I became joint owner of a street kiosk. There, I continually read whatever magazine came my way. It was some sort of relief. But I was stigmatized, frightened, and there was a gloominess about my face that over the years became even darker.

In fact, as he told me when we'd got to know each other, he was above all attracted by my face that emitted a Byzantine sadness and surrender. He had his reasons.

The night that I read his poems, and particularly the one "for you," my life was turned on its head. I cried instinctively and filled with expectations.

He asked me out one evening and offered me a rose with all the thorns carefully removed from its stem.

That same night we slept together. For the first time in my life, I felt the tremendous sweetness of life, the enormous, revitalizing power of love, though this man didn't make any emotional promises, either in words or gestures. On the contrary, he literally plied me, though I didn't find it unpleasant, since he had an innate, natural hunger for love. I was sucked into his vortex, I who usually puked at such things.

I no longer lived other than for his embrace, yet in his way, gently, politely though absolutely, he continued to be averse to what I wanted: deep, heartfelt love. Something beyond the physical.

The only line that he held out, cleverly and deliberately, as I later discovered, was his interest in my past life. Cleverly, because he didn't encourage me to open myself to him, but simply spoke to me with anger and resentment at the cruelty and avariciousness of human nature. I considered that, in the absence of any inner spark for me, pity was at least something, and so I began with my stories. I trembled at the thought of our breaking up.

I began to tell him of the caregivers at the Nursery, of the wardens at the Juvenile Home, who squeezed my body against their organs, of the drivers in the car park, who pushed me into their cabs and groped me all over. I even went as far as to tell him of my father, something that my memory had almost erased. I told him of that night, when he came before daybreak and threw himself on me.

He listened silently, supposedly indifferent, and every so often he interrupted my stories with something completely unconnected or he stroked my hair saying "poor dear, poor dear." I hung onto that crumb of kindness and hoped, just as I hung onto something else that I'd noticed. My stories excited him, because afterwards he'd throw himself on me, like an animal, and made me do indescribable things for him. But it no longer bothered me. I trembled at the thought of breaking up and I began inventing stories even more shocking and my vocabulary became intentionally more provocative.

But in vain. He began to distance himself. My body ached and at night I grew alarmed. Once, he came round and, without saying anything, immediately put the condoms on the bedside table and told me to undress. I couldn't bear it and I burst into tears, uncontrollably. Then he stopped it.

"I have a love, a breath, a life and all this is governed by my work. I'm guided by creation. Can't you see? I'm sick."

And in order to corroborate his words, he confessed to me that whatever happens to him, whether good or bad, he passes it through the filter of his art, to turn it into a work. That in everything, everything he perceives, even himself, he is a stony yet sensitized observer. That very few people arouse in him anguished love that extinguishes his mania for observing, that paralyzes his hand. That even the things that happen between us at these moments, my desperation, my pain, he greedily swallows and passes through the filter. His accursed filter.

He was unable to do otherwise, he told me. He had many failings, both emotional and physical, many phobias and social insecurities, and in order to find some equilibrium he had to produce work. That his only reward, the only redemption for his art, was, by means of this, to conquer as many women's bodies as possible.

He left the neighborhood because my passion for him was much greater than my dignity and it put him in a difficult position. You'll understand if I tell you that, in full view of everyone, I fell down at his feet and told him that he didn't have to marry me as he'd promised, that I'd accept all his terms. He went crazy with anger and said that he'd never promised to marry me. He thought that I was lying to him.

For a long time, in a state of frenzy, I tried to subdue my body, the pores of which were all open wide to him. Slowly and tortuously, it was my fate you see, I even organized this pain of mine and I accustomed myself to a life that was now completely broken.

One day, I saw a book of his in a bookstore window. My first reaction was to take to my heels, to run, to disappear, but it was as if it drew me to it. Benumbed, I went inside and bought it, sat down on the steps in a doorway and began to read it. To encounter him in his words at least.

I quickly realized that his book was nothing other than the price I had paid for his love. The business with my father was valuable plunder for this man. He hadn't even gone to the trouble to alter insignificant things or reformulate my own words, from my accounts of what happened. It was as if as soon as we had broken up, he'd noted down word for word everything I'd said.

The only alteration I noticed was that he'd added elements of his own personality, obvious to me, to my father's filthy desires. The brute wanted a part in it too. An identical story, except that now it had the catastrophic power that only the printed word has.

I again experienced that rape, more real, more intense, than it had been in actuality. But my decision to kill him imprinted itself in my mind and heart, like a firebrand on an animal's hide, when I read with horror how he had the heroine, me, that is, actually wanting her father to come to her bed, long before he appeared, and how the waves-cries of her erotic passion aroused him.

And furthermore, she didn't rebuff him, but pretending to scratch and push him away, she greedily and insatiably pinned him against her.

I swear to you, believe me, believe me, that man is sick. I thought of it for just one fleeting moment, without wanting to, just one moment in my sleep, he had made it all up in his sick mind.

I had to kill him.

Over the next few days, calmly and soberly, I tried to find the most effective way of killing him. Of killing every pig reflected in his face. I joined a hunting club, where I was received with open arms. They found it quite original. I hunted for two or three months, and with every shot, I mentally pulverized his face.

One evening, I telephoned him to say that I'd read the book and that it had really aroused me; that it had filled me full of fantasies. He shouldn't have written that lie, but what could I say, it had turned me on. Would he like to come round to my place? Meanwhile, I'd got hold of some cartridges for hunting wild boar. He came round and the moment he walked through the door I shot him in the face. Nothing remained.

I would have turned the gun on myself, but I was overcome by a sweet langor that made my knees buckle. I began to feel a buzzing in my head, a tingling and warm rush in my organs, sweet bites and sensual pricking in my body. A strange delight laid claim to my desolate body. I wanted it. You do as you please.

Original title: "O leilatis." Published in Sotiris Dimitriou, *I vradiporia tou kalou* [Good's Slow Pace], Athens: Patakis, 2001, pp. 110-118.

Maro Douka

Carré Fix

Outside the university gates she saw various groups—the usual ones, with placards expressing support for the midwives; any more and they'd be setting up tents on the grass. Good luck to them in the midday sun! she reflected. And even if the midwives are on strike, what business do they have outside the university campus? She stopped at the first kiosk and phoned Pelopidas, her fiancé. She told him about the bridal dress that she'd ordered—a hand-woven one with fabulous birds embroidered on the breast. Pelopidas was overjoyed.

Clio continued on her way with unclear feelings; a fluttering inside her and a decisiveness in her walk, in the knowledge that she was a beautiful girl and that the cyclamen color of the dress's embroidery would match her own colors, and her hair, shiny and straight—since the first time she'd straightened it in the style of West Side Story—always provoked admiration and Pelopidas playfully called her his "Juanita."

On her way to the bus stop, she bought an ice-cream cone. And as she licked it, she decided to take a taxi—what a tiring day, all morning going from shop to shop. She closed her eyes. Her dream was a trip to the heart of Europe. And now they were going to spend their honeymoon amid the innocuous landscapes of Switzerland.

By rights, she thought, she ought to buy two or three other outfits for the trip. Imagine having dresses from indigo to eggshell blue and from almond-white to violet in every shade of color. Clio's mother thought her greedy. But what could she discern beyond the colors that exist? The rare color tones that Clio had discovered in the expensive boutiques were completely unknown to her mother. Because, as she's always done, she buys material and has it made up by seamstresses and persists in the sober combinations of gray and olive.

Clio had never imagined that getting married involved so much. Yesterday, two uncles had sent her the carpet for the living room as their contribution. Her mother had got it right: "Only the close relatives give expensive gifts. The others with their pots and pans are a headache." That afternoon she had to sort through some gifts, pack them up and perhaps late in the evening she would take them to their own place in Amerikis Square.

As she was opening the garden gate, she stumbled and momentarily the surprise welled up in her eyes. She pondered, though not deeply, on what can happen to a person completely out of the blue. But at that time of year their garden was a picture of joy with its blooming roses and the scent of orange blossoms.

She took a shower and then went to lie down a bit to rest her eyes. Her rested eyes opened with their innocent wonder. She had noticed it; all she had to do was to sleep for a while, then her eyes would open wide.

She was wrapped in clouds, Pelopidas held her in his arms, between them was a chubby little angel like cupid, whom she'd once seen depicted in a painting, but who was now their child in the dream. And she felt that they rose up, flying on the rug contributed by the uncles, in an apotheosis of *carré fix*. When suddenly, as if the carpet were a balloon deflating, she heard the air rushing out and was alarmed. She woke up with the feeling that she had fallen lightly and because she knew that in dreams you become a feather, though you're not a feather, she felt all over her body out of fear that it might be broken.

She got up and made herself a coffee. She looked at the cacti lined up on the kitchen windowsill, made a mental note not to forget to put a little water in the pots and, at the very same moment, something like spite or anger, but old accumulated anger, rose up in her. She heard her father coughing in the bathroom, then he came and stood before her with that look of his that immediately put a value on you—always less than your actual worth. And it wasn't that Clio had grown up on bon filet, but she had blossomed into a girl without even realizing it, whatever she wanted she had had and she finished high school without any trouble, from home to high school, from home to French lessons and vice-versa. Her father buttoned up his short trousers and listed all his complaints to her, that day, he said, he'd wasted all morning at the Land Registry Office and his daughter should realize that this was her fiancé's job and it wasn't for him to be chasing around, leaving his shop at the mercy of his employees, and he also asked her just what kind of upbringing that young man had had when he'd openly announced only yesterday that he wouldn't wear a tie in church. Clio listened to him without saying a word and thought of Pelopidas at his desk, poring over accounts. In the past, he used to always phone her around that time to remind her how much he loved her. And in the past Clio used to love the afternoons because she would be waiting for Pelopidas to phone.

Her mother was sewing lace strips onto pillows. A family friend would come to sew lace too. But Clio hated all that. So she shut herself up in her room to unwrap the gifts; she would poke fun at her bourgeois friends and their taste. She didn't like porcelain, she liked clay pottery and glass. Folk craft, that's what she liked. And antiques. She'd make a home that everyone would be envious of. With objets d'art, choice items. She imagined her home with paintings by famous artists and a bookcase made of Danish wood taking up a whole wall. But, for the time being, for the next five years at least, they would have to be patient. Furnishings of that kind were out of the question. Her father was not prepared to pay out more than seventy or eighty thousand drachmas and he said it outright: he didn't have the wherewithal, he wasn't a goldmine, he kept saying in a singsong voice, believing that he was being witty.

She went into the bathroom to put a comb in her hair to hold it up. She heard the sound of the hose in the garden, her father was watering the flowers. When he was in a bad mood, he openly expressed his dislike for Pelopidas. Because his only daughter should have married an industrialist—not some salary-earner without the prospects of even a civil servant. And as her father, he was the one who was responsible for planning his daughter's future. Though he never went without an answer from his wife, the daughter of a rich Athenian with a perpetual feeling that life had wronged her, she had so many talents, but she had found herself married to a provincial chosen for her by her father. And she said that she'd rather be struck down by a lightning bolt than stand in Clio's way. Never mind if Pelopidas was a poor employee, the feelings were there—and when these exist, everything is possible.

Her mother and her mother's friend welcomed him. It was Pelopidas, a pale, introverted young man. Clio kissed him and made him a coffee. Then they sat in the dining room all together. She had met him at a party and as soon as they had looked at each other, he told her later, he had felt something deep inside. They exchanged telephone numbers and from their first date Pelopidas began his pitiful story and Clio found herself in the position of the compassionate listener. Particularly his childhood, a depressing convalescence. Motherless, he came to Athens to study and he had to work at the same time; his father's savings didn't help, and, meanwhile, neither did his mother-in-law, so if there was anything for him to remember, it was only sadness, in the School of Economics and then as an accountant and whenever there happened to be some girl, a few meaningless affairs. And then Clio said: what was the difference even though she had always had whatever she wanted? It had always been second- and third-rate stuff. She had her father's long finger wagging at her tyrannically—he'd talk about things coming easily to her: and he'd once taken his belt off to her and beaten her black and blue, and once he hadn't bought her a bicycle; and all this because she had to be equal to Pelopidas in unhappiness and, through instinct, she had achieved a remarkable balance.

His legs crossed, Clio's father every so often pursed his lips, with his now-standard expression of the slaughtered lamb that in the end accepted its fate. Her mother gestured to her that it wasn't proper to show themselves up before Lela, her friend. Pelopidas changed the conversation, smiled rather stupidly, abashed, uncomfortable with all this. A little more and they'd be calling him a fortune-hunter. He'd never been able to stomach them, that class who with a few crumpled thousand-drachma bills—though the purchase of the two-bedroom apartment in Amerikis Square, Clio's dowry, was most welcome—thought that they ruled the roost. Clio's pulse raced, more than was bearable, Lela openly took the side of the young couple, good heavens! They shouldn't forget that they were young once.

Feeling annoyed, she went through the various details once they were alone. The problem was this: what was going to happen with the car. Would they give it to them or not. Given that her father had objected that the car belonged to the family and she had no right to take it. We're giving you this, we're not giving you that, we're buying you this, we're not buying you that. She came to regret having accepted even the least thing from them. But then she dug her heels in. She would get as much out of them as she could, since they had it, she'd take it from them. Isn't that what they were always saying? Whatever we have is for our daughter. Because when Clio and Pelopidas are fifty, what good will it be to them? It's now that they want it, while they are still young and can enjoy it. And continually in a state of upset throughout this whole period, they feel as though they've been erased as people. Clio gesticulated heatedly and Pelopidas added fat to the fire by wearily acquiescing.

They looked at their gifts, sorting them out. So far, three ice-cream sets and all roughly the same kind. But it's her mother who is to blame for not arranging with the relatives, so that they'd know what each one should bring. Most of them, a whole pile of objects, would have to be returned and they would choose something else, perhaps more useful or at least more presentable.

She went up to him nonchalantly, what about it? Did he want to make love? But Pelopidas had told her before that he felt uncomfortable doing it in her room. It simply wasn't on for them to make love in her room while listening to the others conversing in the next room. She tried to get round him, come on, don't be silly, how could he be afraid of her parents? Weren't they getting married in two weeks' time? Or, did he think her parents were from the backwoods and didn't know that she and Pelopidas had consummated their relationship! She tried to persuade him. He responded unenthusiastically, so much so that he annoyed her and she left him.

They agreed to go to the cinema, then they were too tired. So they started to chit-chat, this, that and the other about their friends. They talked about their trip to Switzerland, he would have preferred London, but he didn't go on about it, all he wanted was to be with her. He said that the next day they could go to his place. Never mind, Clio replied, better for them not to make love till their wedding night, to add a little spice to it. Pelopidas preferred to ignore her raised eyebrows full of innuendo. He knew her by now. Once they had agreed to get married, he felt at ease and kept the essence of it for himself: his peace—he was content.

The conversation turned to the question of kids again, how Clio loved them. But Pelopidas didn't love them. His view was that they should enjoy their lives just as they were. And he always had politics on his mind. His friends said: women and politics! Even from being students, when they hung around the low-class tavernas swinging their worry beads and analyzing burning issues. The first time he confided his dream of entering politics to Clio, she didn't have any objection. All she did was to make a slight shift to his dreams for the better. First he would have to create a steady home life. First he would have to find professional success. Didn't he see? Those who are successful in their professions are also successful in politics. Didn't he see? All the parties open their doors to you provided you are successful professionally. Of course he saw it. And among all this, what harm is there in a child? Two, three children? As always, there was a vagueness about Pelopidas' words, misgivings in his voice. Clio had no doubts that he was pursing his lips deliberately. Right from the beginning of their relationship, he had presented himself to her as being incurably unhappy, and so she philosophized on an existential level about their marriage. As for children, it was in her hands whether she got pregnant; she had so many examples, how, that is, it often happens that the best fathers turn out to be those who became fathers against their wishes!

How did it get to ten o'clock without them realizing it? They packed up a few gifts, but it was now too late to take them to Amerikis Square. They preferred to watch a bit of TV. They smoked, relaxing beside each other, her father yawned every so often and her mother was still there sewing the lace and narrating a story she'd heard from her mother, this too about final finishings—as those night-long shifts were called. Silence fell between all this—plop, you could hear it, when the excitement had died down in the detective story on the TV and when her mother happened to be threading the needle and her father had closed his mouth, then the room became dangerously quiet, Pelopidas remarked tiredly, an empty, irritating tiredness from within him.

At suppertime, they again got upset when her mother said offhandedly that the engagement was starting to tire her. They ate without speaking and with their eyes fixed on the floor, with ambiguous creaking of their chairs, with aversion all over their faces. And if Clio hadn't been Clio, she might even have burst into tears. But patiently casting her eyes over her parents' chubby faces, she nudged Pelopidas' foot under the table.

At the garden gate, as they said goodnight, so softly that Pelopidas frightened her, he rather formally announced to her that he had been patient for a year now, but that was enough, he'd put up with that atmosphere for long enough. He asked her to try to understand, he wouldn't come to her house again other than under special circumstances. That daily, ongoing situation every night had literally exhausted him, he preferred to eat out. No more, he said, kissing her. Then Clio watched him running to catch the last bus, without turning to look back even once. It seemed to her as if he were running to get away.

∽❦∾

She cleaned her face with cream, gently rubbed in the night lotion, brushed her teeth, sighed as if blowing to drive out any bad thoughts, and lay down. She was unable to get to sleep. How could she! She still had to take care of the confetti, the invitations, the thank-you cards to the relatives for their gifts. There was still the furniture that had to be taken care of, the curtains to hang, the light fittings to be bought. For two whole months, she thought, she had spent every day on the preparations for the wedding. And it was still as though she'd only just started.

Original title: "Carré Fix." Published in Maro Douka, *Carré Fix*, Athens: Kedros, 1976, pp. 155-166.

Michel Faïs

Halima, Desdemona, Bubu

1

"A python was snoring on his back. Two boa constrictors were kissing on his chest. On his legs, rattlesnakes were shaking their tails. Snakes everywhere. Tattoos all over his body. On his arms, a tangle of watersnakes. A viper's forked tongue on his every fingernail. Only low down on his belly did he have a tattoo of Christ; of Christ giving his blessing. That's why he went berserk whenever he was on top of a Muslim woman. His eyes rolled and his teeth gnashed. You could sharpen a knife on his skin. And appropriating the voice of the wolf gazing at the moon and of the bear eating honey, he'd ask his oriental delight: *Is Christ getting fucked?* And if the wretched woman underneath him didn't reply *He's fucking, master*, then, compared to what was in store for her, death was mere child's play."

"Is that Yanko Yanic?" Desdemona asked Halima. "That's the snake," replied Halima.

Halima had a way with words. She could serve up the most tedious tale in such a way that she'd have you aching with laughter or shaking with alarm. Just the opposite of Desdemona, that is. Of course, Halima had lived through all that. She had seen it through her slant eyes and heard it with her pointed ears. But even if she hadn't lived through it, you'd still have found yourself hanging on her every word.

Reporters had been here, asking questions. They went from one person to the next. The gravedigger, the workers, the relatives. They all shrugged their shoulders. Only one woman, a basket case who comes here to pass her time, went on television and started talking about ghosts. "And what about the excrement on the graves?" a bearded reporter asked her. "Oh, the excrement, it's the devil's," she replied.

Old-wives' tales. They should have asked Halima, Desdemona or me. We saw everything. But, you see, no one takes any notice of us.

The story is as follows. Halima's mistress would enter through an opening in the wire fence made by Ivan and his gang. During the first few days, some greedy pigs would follow on her heels. The idiots thought that she must have some pasta or sardines in her bundle. She had nothing of the sort. She'd put her bundle down beside the waterfount, wash her hands, tie a white kerchief round her head and wander along the paths between the graves. She'd keep mumbling something. Halima, who knows, told us that she was reciting verses from the *Koran*. Then she'd be overcome by grief. She'd weep and weep and weep. Halima's mistress would cry her eyes out till she turned red in the face. And she'd shout out Ali, Husein, Suleiman. More and more names. Nuredin, Ibrahim, Eminé. Different names, lots of names. Names of her kin killed by the Bosnian Serbs. Finally, she'd start spinning round and round like a top. Then Desdemona would break out in a giggle. Halima immediately put her in her place, explaining to her that her mistress wasn't playing, but meditating like the dervishes. And sure enough, as soon as she stopped spinning, she'd be pointing at a grave. She'd sit on it and defecate. She'd spread her shit over the marble as if it were paint. She even daubed her face with it. And like this, covered in shit, she'd again began her lament. Ugh! You felt sorry for her, of course, but you also felt disgusted.

This would take place three times a week. Till midday, Halima's mistress would wander through the city with outstretched hand. In the wealthy neighbourhoods. You'd find her outside banks, restaurants and cinemas. And she made a tidy sum each day. She carried a piece of card that read: "Am Serb. Husbend is killd. Children is killd. Very hungery. Thank Crist."

Lies, all lies. What husband, what children, what Christ? But, you see, in Kolonaki Square, Dexameni Square and Skoufa Street you can find plenty of victims. They're just lining up, as Desdemona says. It was at number thirteen, Neophytou Vamva Street that Desdemona lived before she took off. Six whole years in Kolonaki Square. She knows the rich like the back of her hand. She lived in the home of a filthy rich old maid. The only daughter of a ship owner. She'd had a Greek mother and an English father. Half and half. Just like Desdemona. A ginger, American wire-hair for a father, and a gloved rag doll with chocolaty spots for a mother.

Anyhow. With this and that, the relatives eventually complained about the spectacle presented by the last resting places of their kin. They lay in wait for Halima's mistress and arrested her. The reporters had a field day with her. One minute they were saying that she was possessed, the next that she was a Turkish spy. In desperation, Halima's mistress jumped out of the fifth-floor window of the police building and put an end to all that yap-yap-yap surrounding her person. The papers said later that it was divine justice.

Whether we like it or not, reality is reality. And reality reveals other things. It reveals that sometimes pain causes you to lose a screw. This is what happened to Halima's mistress. A young girl, only fifteen years old, and to have Yanko Yanic and his gang hold you down. And not once or twice, not even ten times. A hundred and ten times. Can you imagine? She reported it, complained to the United Nations. And the blue-helmeted soldiers took about as much notice of her as they would a worm under their boots. So that's how you are, is it, said Halima's mistress. She hung an imitation gold cross round her neck, put Halima in a basket and crossed over into Greece as Nicoletta Ostojevic.

"What was the Snake like?" I asked Halima one day. "Lame from the cradle, dirty as a pig and with a smile like Death on his ugly mug," she replied, stretching her front paws. "I can't fathom it out. Such hate for the Muslims...," muttered Desdemona. "There's nothing unfathomable about it. If you showed him a louse and if you told him that this louse had crawled on a Muslim's head, he'd take out his pistol and shoot it. Do you understand what I'm saying to you?" replied Halima. "What, wasn't there someone in authority to keep him in check?"

Desdemona went on, obviously confusing the London fog with that of Belgrade. Licking her whiskers, Halima said: "The Snake was one of Maximovic's sidekicks. But what do you know of Vojslav Maximovic? You've no doubt heard of Karadzic. Well, Maximovic is one of his henchmen. One day, Radovan said to him: '*Listen, Vojslav, I don't want to see another fez, or hear another oriental strain in Fotsa ever again.*' The other one wracked his brains. Who's the most ruthless soldier I have? he thinks. And he immediately sends for the Snake and says to him: '*If within forty days you make Fotsa ours, I'll make you a captain.*'"

"And how was the dirty work done?" asked an ant, continuing to drag a crumb to its hole. And seeing another thirty ants halting behind the one asking the question, Halima took a deep breath and began to relate how the Snake had had his photo taken with six red stars, three on each shoulder, behind the sign saying Sbrnja instead of Fotsa.

"There were five or six of them, girdled with cartridge belts. They were having difficulty walking as they kept tripping over their long beards. As soon as they saw the imam coming towards the Alatzas mosque, they grabbed him. They shaved him in double-quick time and stripped him of his clothes so he was just like he was when his mother gave birth to him. The poor wretch felt such shame. Then they doused him in paraffin and hung him upside down from the rafter where Rasif hung his copper pots. One of them, with a huge belly as though he'd eaten an army of rats, dipped the *Koran* in petrol and threw it at him. All he managed to say was *Allahu Akbar*, Allah is great. Whether great or small, the Snake and his gang laid mines around the mosque and disappeared. And those who put their faith before their common sense... boom, boom, boom, are walking around on crutches now."

"And after that, the inhabitants of Fotsa were no doubt terrified and surrendered the keys of the town to the Snake," said a real snake, who at that same moment went out like a light. But no one took it the wrong way. Not even Halima. No one was worried. Besides, it was a common secret that every morning the snake drained the oil lamps, and from all that slurp slurp, it was dead to the world in the afternoon.

And this is why the snake that reckoned the earth with its belly couldn't understand why the snake that reckoned the earth with a blade rounded up fifty women from Fotsa in the Palais. In the famous

Partizan basketball stadium, that is, and with little time to spare. It was the thirty-seventh day. But didn't he understand? That no matter how many mouths the Snake opened up in the Bosnian Serbs' bodies, they would never oblige him by calling Fotsa Sbrnja. For the only mouth that men can't endure is the one that whispers to them that their wife has been dishonored.

"You know how the victims of the Bengal tiger look to us?" as Desdemona would say when she wanted to tell us something horrible, to describe something too horrible to see. That's how the UN soldiers saw the women of Fotsa.

"This festival of disaster brought together the hare-brained wife of the butcher and the distressed wife of the dispenser, the stuttering daughter of the t-t-t-tavern-keeper and the watchmaker's cross-eyed twins, who left their handicaps behind them the moment they set foot on the wooden court. But the miller's vulgar wife and the gravedigger's touchy wife also heard the same foul language. While the undertaker's blind wife, the grocer's beautiful wife and three beautiful daughters and the good-for-nothing wife of the goldsmith spat with one mouth on their womanhood when they saw the soldiers making the sign of the cross before unfastening their belts. And finally, the cooper's shrewish wife, who had cast spells on the epileptic wife of the quilt maker and the jolly wife of the farrier, certain that they were the ones ruining her marriage, didn't have time to hear their forgiveness as the Snake drove a cornel twig through her from ear to ear. And so on and so forth."

As far as the clouds. When Halima reached that point, she'd always raise her eyes to the sky. Always, always. And she'd gaze at the clouds. At the changing colors. The shapes they assumed. She'd drift off. Was it to forget? Had she perhaps been friends with the cat of the cooper's poor wife? Who knows.

"Well, she's got quite an idea of herself to make out she knows all this, hasn't she?" a fat worm once whispered in the spider's ear, poking its head out of the cracks in a family grave. And the spider, who had set up home on the rotting photo of some smiling man, laughed, trembling like lace steeped in parathion. Halima pretended not to hear. With the eyes of an owl and the gait of a crab, she went back to her corner and the group dispersed.

In the graveyard, however, we all believed Halima. We all knew she had been a target in Fotsa. A gift from the mufti of Constantinople, she was the imam's greatest love, after Allah. He had given her the name of Mohammed's wet nurse. A snow white from Ankara, with eyes that didn't match, a whining voice and brush tail. They exchanged wedding rings; he, devoted as he was to God, she, now doctored. They lived as though they were married. He read her passages from the *Koran*. She had a prominent position on his lap during Ramadan and Bairam, and he fed her on the famous salted sardines of Savos. During the cold winter nights, she would curl up at his feet and purr softly when she saw him worn out at the mischief of the faithful.

Anyhow, when her protector was burned like a candle lit at both ends, all she did was hide in the loft. Peeping sometimes with her orange eye and sometimes with her blue one from behind the latticed window, she watched the activity in the street. Eventually her heart left the pink cushions at her paws and returned to its proper place. Then she put her mind to work.

"If I die, you must go to my sister's. You know where she lives." This is what the imam had once told her when he'd had a raging fever. Of course, she knew. Halima followed his advice as closely as she would her pee. The imam's sister lived close to the Turkish baths. She was a plump, kind-hearted woman who spent her whole life in the company of her geese, her corn and her adopted daughter, Aïshé. Aïshé was the name of Halima's mistress.

2

"Istori, good by. Memory, good by," as Desdemona would say. And as Shakespeare would say in *Macbeth*. For, in her company, we became Shakespeare cats.

The truth is that the two of them didn't get on very well at first. When the one scratched the other's tree, the other went and peed on the first one's path. The rivalry between them had to be seen to be believed. They'd wait to see when the other one would get up to stretch in order to go over and rub up against her corner. And for no particular reason. It was simply that Halima thought Desdemona snooty and Desdemona thought Halima soppy. Yet in the end, they sorted it out. They became inseparable.

Of course, Desdemona ended up in a crazy household. Her mistress was as ugly as sin and couldn't find a mirror in which to comb her hair. As soon as the mirrors saw her ugly snout, they leapt from the wall and fell on the floor, as if there'd been an earthquake or as if they'd suddenly got an itch. And the older she grew, the more she tormented her cats. Do you know what it means to be coddled to death? That's what I'm talking about. Anyone would think that her crooked nose and short legs were the fault of the twelve cats she had in her house. And all the cats owned by Desdemona's mistress were from the best families.

"There was Viola, an aged long-haired silver chinchilla; Ophelia, a dear little thing; Balineza with her caramel stripes; and Gertrude, a hypochondriac, a furless mau. There was Ioulietta, a sorrowful, ashen mau; Rosalinda, an ebony Bombay cat, who thought she was the reincarnation of Indira Gandhi; and Tamora, a mystic Russian with blue tints. Then, there was Beatrice, an American curly with turned-up ears, who meowed like Marilyn Monroe; Rosalinda, a mottled Japanese, who wrote haiku in the sand with her truncated tail; and Phoebe, a Turkish cat, who shook like a rabbi at the sight of water. But her favorite cats were Lady Macbeth, a snooty cameo tortoiseshell longhair, Margarita, a moonstruck spangled cat, and myself."

We'd heard this same spiel countless times. That was Desdemona... Whenever she got a bout of nostalgia, there was no stopping her, even if God himself were to come down from heaven. She sat you down to tell you of the good old days, now long gone. And she didn't spare any details. Not to mention the fact that she had a thing about pedigrees. She'd spent hours on end reading encyclopaedias about cats. Feline anatomy, biological cycles, types of fur, crossbreeds, pure breeds, she had it all at her fingertips.

Her mistress was the honorary chairperson of the "Cosy-care" Society; an animal-lovers' society that had its offices in the wealthy suburb of Ekali. There, a sharp customer had sold her a lot of baloney about being an animal lover himself and had gone through her money by the bucketful. He pretended to love stray mutts like Ivan and alley cats like myself.

Do you know what it's like to have to wear socks so you don't scratch the wooden floors? What it's like to be doctored? To be continually fed on health food? To be given a bath every three days? Horrible. To be given milk with tea in a porcelain cup. To be obliged to watch Shakespeare on video. And woe betide you if you happen to doze off at the moment that Lawrence Olivier is racing like a fool to the castle of Elsinore.

Desdemona told us that when they went out for a walk in Kolonaki Square, the sniggering that went on was something else. The freak with the twelve cats. Girls from Poland, the Philippines and Ethiopia held their leashes. Freshly bathed, coiffured, perfumed, prettified with bows and knitted jerkins. I shudder whenever I think about it. And leading them like a general at the head of his army was their mistress.

It was only natural that the cats should want to run away for dear life. Some burst open like melons plunging from the top floor. They fell on their backs in Neophytou Vamva Street and their nine lives all went up in smoke. That's how Desdemona came to us. One evening, her dotty mistress had taken her and Ophelia to visit the vet, who lived across from the cemetery. At one moment, Desdemona somehow found herself out on the balcony. She was spotted by that idiot Ivan, who acts like he's just stepped off the ark, and he set off chasing her. By accident, she ran into the cemetery. By accident she became our friend.

3

It's all very well for Halima and Desdemona. That's how they live. But who's going to come forward and talk about my life? Though, you see, I've got used to listening to others moaning. To wiping their asses. To comforting them. And don't think I was always as I am now with one eye and only half a tail. You should have seen me in the past. Dress, shoes, stockings. All white as snow and starched. Three or four years ago. There wasn't a patient who didn't want me attending him. Not to mention the young doctors. They used to jostle each other to get me on their shift.

And what hospitals I've worked in. Naval hospitals, state hospitals, private clinics. Major hospitals. I used to sit and stare at the peeling walls in the corridors and reflect on my life. It was the time I'd just arrived from Dolno Kotori.

Troubled years. If you came out with as much as *boo*, you paid for it through the nose. Back then ... the gendarme would come for you. From around here or a refugee? he'd ask. Greek, you'd reply. Grecomano, eh? Take that, and that and that. It was no joke. One wrong word and they beat you black and blue. And torture, too. A lot of it. They once kept my father without food for eleven days. Go on, what else? What more can I say? They put him next to a stove. One of those wood stoves, the big ones that they have in village cafés. For three days and nights they had him standing. The blood ran out of his body. His shoes split open. Go on, what else? What more can I say? They subjected him to bastinado. They wouldn't tell him what to say. When one got tired, another took his place. Then they heated some oil in a frying pan. They disfigured my father. When they let him go, they told him to say that he'd burned himself on the anvil. Supposedly done it on his own. Because my father made horseshoes.

We were subjected to interrogation every day. They'd submit false statements. So-and-so said that about you. They saw you doing such-and-such. They sent the men in droves to the island of Chios. Exiled them. They even threw one man from the boat into the open sea off Chios. The two of us were secretly in love. My first love. A builder. And my only love. His grandfather was Koziupov's righthand man. The famous architect. Most of the rich mansions in Florina are his work.

We'd find the best of them dead. I had my father's brother, a schoolteacher he was. They threw him down a well. Others, they forced to leave. What are you doing here? Get back to your own country. This is our country. This, eh? Right. They burned our churches. The priests put them up to it. They smashed our graves. Nothing was to be left standing. There was one man, an archaeologist. He was known as Kostas Bulgaroctonus, the Bulgar-slayer. He was the one who gave the word to begin. He went round erasing the Cyrillic inscriptions; he daubed our frescoes with whitewash. "You learned about Christ from us, now you're going to unlearn him," he yelled. We later heard that he had grown rich by selling our portable icons abroad. He uprooted whole iconostases.

Terrible. The gendarmes stuck their knives in the bagpipes at festivals so that we couldn't play our songs. We were scared. We shut the windows in order to be able to talk at ease. In our own language. A stultifying life, it was. And those who got involved with the partisans had other kinds of trouble. The Communists crucified them, the others hounded them. What were we to do? With all that was happening, most people took off for Australia. They left behind their fields, houses and graves. They left everything, left it all behind. The smarter ones brought down Albanian Vlachs from the hills and settled them in our villages. Whole families were decimated. And those who left for places behind the curtain regretted it. And those who boarded the boat for Australia also regretted it. And those who stayed here with their arms folded also regretted it.

That's how it was at first. Then someone fell in love with me. He worked in the Ministry of Justice. A coroner. He'd come to our parts on account of some murder. It was in Florina that he met me; he saw me. A photographer had put me in his window. That's how beautiful I was! He was quite old. He limped too. Only a little, but he limped. I didn't love him. He was old, like I said, well-educated, he'd take care of me. My folks gave me to him, so I'd escape the hardship. But I only ended up worse.

His mother was an old shrew. She had him wrapped round her finger. He was like a little robot. What she wanted was a maid not a daughter-in-law. And she watched every penny. She had me doing all the heavy work. It was less tiring back home in the village. On his mother's name day, I saw something I would never have believed. What was I thinking of when I went into her room. Tell me so I might understand myself. The old shrew was lying on the bed with her nightdress up above her belly. And he was sprawled on top of her. Sucking at her breast like a puppy. It turned my stomach. I began to tremble. I went out into the garden. I knelt beside the rosebushes. With my own hands, I dug a hole to crawl into.

Of course, I'd had my suspicions. No social life whatsoever. Office, home; home, office. Not one friend ever set foot in the house. Maybe a relative, though vary rarely. But there's no comparison between the one thing and the other. Is there?

The next evening, he booked train tickets to Thessaloniki. He took time off work. Was he scared of me telling on them? Did he see me in a new light? Anyhow, in Thessaloniki, he couldn't do enough for me. He bought me expensive clothes, we went to clubs, we danced. There, I felt like a woman. It was there he got me pregnant. Throughout the pregnancy, the old shrew behaved as though we weren't living in the same house. She walked past me as if she were walking past a chair. Not a word. So much the better, I thought. Leave me in peace. They even got a girl to do the housework.

To cut a long story short, I gave birth to a baby boy. We were going to call him Tassos. After the old shrew, Tasia. The baby looked just like Alexander. My little darling, just like my lasting sorrow. He was a quiet baby, strong; he squeezed me with his little hands. Who knows. Maybe because when I was pushing, I was thinking of his face. During the birth. His eyes, his laughter. Just like Alexander.

I had a straightforward and uncomplicated childbirth at the "Elena" maternity clinic. The doctor told me they'd keep him in an incubator for a few days as a precautionary measure. You go home and your husband can come on Monday to take the baby. It was Friday then. I thought, it's only three days, it'll soon pass. I was a bit surprised as the baby wasn't premature or anything. Anyhow, if it's for his own good, I thought. I went home. The old shrew had filled the place with roses. Yellow roses everywhere. In the bedroom, in the living-room, even in the lavatory. "Do you need anything?" she asked me with a smile. The baby's mellowed her, I thought.

On the Monday, my husband went. They told him they'd keep the baby a few days longer. No cause for concern. Come back on Wednesday. He went again on Wednesday. I got all dressed up to hold him in my arms. The telephone rang. "It's a blessing that your baby's dead," a voice said. The light disappeared from before my eyes. Tell me what mother would wish such a thing? I phoned back. Sin na yiaolo si rontil? So mi go kriete deteto. My pain was such that I was speaking in my own tongue. Do you understand? I'd forgotten my Greek and the doctor couldn't understand what I was saying. I want you to give me my baby back. Tell my husband not to think of coming home unless he brings the baby. As soon as the old shrew saw me in that state, she turned the volume up full on the radio and shut herself in her room.

Before long, my husband arrived. They'd wrapped my Alexander in some green surgical cloths. A tiny, little shroud. I began to unwrap him and the earth slid from under my feet. One hand, three legs and a body as thin as a toothpick. I fell to my knees. I bellowed with grief. I rolled around like a pig in pain. For fifteen days, I put nothing into my mouth. I swallowed sleeping pills by the handful. They ended up taking me to the hospital. They kept me there for a month. They gave me serum, did all sorts of things to me. My nerves were gone.

One doctor felt sorry for me. I told him of my ordeal. They sold your baby in America. Don't even think of trying to find it. Not even if you search till kingdom come. A Jew sells them to rich childless couples. It's a whole ring. He's taken lots of babies. This doctor got me a job helping in the hospital. He, too, opened his heart to me. He was Armenian. He'd lost all his family. The Turks had done it to him. He showed me a family photo. Forty people, phew! All up in smoke. He was the sole branch left.

Anyway, this Armenian had fallen in love with one of his cousins. Veanus. Talk about passion. She was all he thought about. He'd talk to you so much about her that you thought she'd walk in through the door. Every Tuesday, he'd get together with his friends and summon her up in his glass. He was faithful to her till the day he closed his eyes. And she worshipped him, too. She'd often write on the table *I'll love you for all eternity*. They're supposed to have even made love together. But they didn't make love in this lifetime. They didn't have the chance. So how could it have happened... in a glass? In his memory? A mystery. Anyway, some nights I'd hear moans and sighing from his bedroom. As if there were two people in there, not one.

And the doctor was no lunatic. He was a first-rate specialist. A dermatologist who'd studied in Paris. With a good clientele. His patients held him in the greatest respect. Anyhow. This Armenian read the weirdest books. About metempsychosis and reincarnation and previous lives.

He told me that his cousin wasn't his cousin, but his dead grandmother. And because he'd never known his mother—his grandmother had brought him up—that's why he'd become so attached to Veanus. Once, I recall, he'd told me that it's not only the lives of other people that are repeated inside us, but their deaths too. And that he'd seen his dead father dying again in his sleep. His father had died years before. And he believed it. Because when he'd got out of bed, he'd found a mole as big as a French bean under his neck. Identical to the one his father had. Before the Turk had cut his head off.

He told me a lot and I mean a lot. People often wake up in others' souls, he told me. That's why they separate. That's why love fades. One day you wake up and the person beside you is a stranger. What's happened? Have you got tired of him? Why weren't you tired of him from the start? Do you find him ugly? So, was he handsome before? Nothing of the sort. Your soul has taken a breath of air, a new breath of life.

But let me finish. The doctor had a cat in his house. Bubu. One Tuesday, Asadour summoned up Veanus in his glass. But Veanus didn't appear. They changed places with each other. Nothing. They turned over her favorite glass in which she drank her sherry. No response from her. Someone left-handed wrote the alphabet from the beginning. They began to get irritated. The doctor suddenly banged his fist on the table. The letters got muddled. At that moment, Bubu was sleeping on the chest of drawers. It was as if an electric current had passed through her. The animal leapt into the air. From that time on, she became strange. She didn't eat, didn't sleep, didn't play. Nothing. She sat shrivelled up in a corner. She would go over to Asadour and watch him. The way certain creatures look at us in our sleep. As if she were trying to tell him something.

This situation continued till Asadour died. Bubu watched him like a dog, like a mother, not at all like a cat. On the night he died, it was drizzling outside. It was October. I was sitting with the nurse who was attending him that night. The doctor let out a slight sigh. He sat up on the pillow. It was as if someone had entered the room; someone unknown to him. At the moment that his soul took flight, Bubu dug her nails into his pillow. First into the pillow, then into my thigh.

I passed out. And when I came round, I got the shock of my life. And I mean shock. I was in the graveyard. Yes, I who never went near funerals. There I was. I who read fortunes and ate from the rubbish and listened to cat stories. The one thing, of course, that didn't bother me. Horror stories, sad ones, funny ones, short ones, long ones, half-finished ones, half-begun ones. You know, hunger like this can never be satisfied. If you were to feed me all the stories in the world, my mouth would still not stop watering. Has anyone ever burst from too many stories? For me there's no sweeter death. Not in the whole world.

As to how this happened, don't ask me. I've no idea. All I know is that I lost consciousness as Eleni Gotsi and came to as Bubu. And how did I get from Kypseli to the Town Cemetery? Hope it never happens to you, as they say. You'll tell me that everything's possible in this world. Of course. Are you laughing? Don't laugh at all. Whoever wants to believe me can do so. Whoever doesn't believe me will have to swallow his pill. His time will come. And the pill will be a bitter one. Very bitter.

Original title: "Halima, Desdemona, Bubu." Published in Michel Faïs, *Ap' to idio potiri ke alles istories* [From the Same Glass and Other Stories], Athens: Kastaniotis, 1999, pp. 65-86.

Rhea Galanaki

An Almost-Blue Arm

In memory of Freda Liappa

I dreamt that it was night—and it was night. Close by I could hear the scattered bells of a flock. Hidden, the flock moved behind the nocturnal green of the osier and the oleander. I began walking, following in the direction of the sound. Above me the starry sky's labyrinth, below my feet touched its sculptured image: earth and smooth rocks, grass, undergrowth. And so many whisperings all their own. I stumbled, but I didn't stop to see whether my ankle had swollen, as the sound of the bells had wound itself like a rope around my waist and was gently pulling me. And I had surrendered myself to it.

I went down, down, till I reached the water's edge. It was the time when the water sleeps like a baby. The moon was bright and I saw it: huge, calm and pensive. Then, as though I were taking off a piece of clothing, the sound of the bells dropped from my waist and fell in a silent heap at my feet. I sat down to reflect on what I was doing, having been called all alone into the wilderness; me, a city woman.

At the thought of the city, it was as if a big stone were cast into the water. A hum and echoing arose from the quiet of the place. A whirlwind passed overhead. Alarmed, the water awoke and started to cry. I said to it: "Don't cry." And it was calmed.

I said "don't cry" and immediately you appeared. Again the long blond hair, white, almost blue skin, a black gaze. Except that instead of the plain, almost boyish clothes of our youth, long veils, pure-white, streamed around your figure's nuptials. You glided over the water, your sheen. You stood facing me. An unbeliever—and yet I said "Lord, how can an image possess such memory?" You smiled at me. You raised one arm and gave the signal. All the stars, so many tabors and fiddles suddenly began playing in the heavens, though these too were invisible behind the nocturne's sigh. Then you reached out your other arm towards me, inviting me to follow you.

I shrank back. How could I step on the water without my heavy body sinking? And what did I know of such things? Only what we all know more or less. That they enchant solitary men, that men go with them and afterwards suffer, if they are fortunate enough to return to an "afterwards." But what was a woman doing amid all this?

I saw your face clouding with sorrow because I was afraid of you. The music changed slightly too, as if the drums became louder, as if the fiddles needed tuning. What could I do? I got up to follow you. You laughed a triumphant laugh. You took me by the hand, just as when we were students together, during the time of the youth movements, of our endless Athenian discussions and strolls before and after your imprisonment, the time of our first parties and also of our quarrels, of the banned demonstrations, of young loves, of books and excursions. That unhappy time when you'd fallen ill, though I no longer saw you very often, I no longer lived in Athens. Your hand was neither cold nor warm, as though it hadn't even touched me. I sighed. You turned and said to me: "Don't be silly, it's time for you to stop believing—was it 'believing' you said, or 'fearing'?— all those fairy-tales. They exist, but not in that way."

So I didn't attach any importance to the fact that we were both gliding over the calm water and that we immediately arrived at the other shore. Still holding hands, we began walking over the carpet of a meadow strewn with delicate flowers. For a moment, it seemed to me that you were limping; stealing a look, I saw that one of your blue-white slippers resembled a goat's hoof, but I didn't attach any importance even to this detail. You spoke and maintained using—as always—the most logical arguments that a person can live again only what they've already lived, dream only what they've already dreamed.

And even so, you said, nothing ever returns exactly the same. Which is why what we live again are the variations on past events in our lives. Variations sometimes so self-sufficient that they enable you, though very rarely, to forget what actually happened—or even replace this with a more or less arbitrary interpretation. There's an immaterial world moving around us, that has always "burdened" us, without appearing to burden us...

You went on talking to me in the same way. I believed you, because I wanted to believe you—as always—though, I have to admit, I had never imagined the words of such encounters in this way. At one moment, you stopped walking and speaking. You listened to something that I couldn't hear. You turned again towards me. Softly, you told me that we still have a little while, even though time never concedes anything to us. Then you screamed at the tabors and fiddles to play louder. Louder, much louder. To drown that damnable crowing of the cock. "Come, whatever we have time for," you said, heaving a sigh.

Just as a director hits the white screen with his cane in order to demonstrate—after all you were a director too—,so you stretched out an almost-blue arm to the far reaches of the horizon. I just had time to see golden tables with my old friends tasting invisible bread, drinking ethereal wine, singing the last songs sung in our land. To see fairies dancing and pulling the kerchiefs from their faces, revealing the faces of dear girlfriends, and the boys around them trying to grab hold of the kerchief of their love. To see, in the years passing without any other support, the contribution of a word, an image, a sound, so that the next day might dawn as a normal day. To see the harm and the benefit of that youthful imprisonment on people, who from that time never entrusted their lives to anyone, apart from those they had met during those years—and though each of us has followed our own path, this means nothing. To see you, my dear friend, bidding farewell to the light, while the rest of us, phantoms of an old and actual court-martial, carried you on our shoulders for your last walk on earth.

I awoke sobbing. Since then my left foot has turned into a goat's hoof. Naturally, I conceal it. Besides, who's interested in all this today...

Original title: "Ena schedon galazio heri." Published in Rhea Galanaki, *Ena schedon galazio heri* [An Almost-Blue Arm], Athens: Kastaniotis, 2004, pp. 41-45.

E. H. Gonatas

The Preparation

> I see scales even though blind.
> And I blinded myself so as not to see scales.
>
> Antonio Porchia

The door was half-open; I pushed it and entered, closing it quietly behind me.

I found him, just as all the other times, in his office, sitting on a high stool with his body bent over the table. His legs hung lifeless, like wood, beneath the wide nightshirt he was wearing.

"How are you, Agelaos?" I asked, going over to him. "Am I disturbing you?"

He had his head resting on the pan of an old pair of scales with springs; he was supporting himself on the table with his chest and left hand, and with his right he was fumbling with the weights lying beside him. He chose one, turned it in his fingers, and dropped it onto the second pan, while his eyes, behind his wire spectacles, almost popped out of their sockets, as he strained to see the arrows—two doves' heads, made of lead and painted silver, which began moving their beaks up and down.

"Never mind the civilities. You know I've been waiting for you. That's why I'd left the door open," he replied through his teeth, without turning round.

"Thanks; but don't you think that your friendly gesture was perhaps a little rash?" I commented, at the same time stooping to pick up various sheets of paper scattered all over the floor and covered in illegible notes and the hieroglyphics of his mathematical calculations. "Just imagine if, instead of me, some undesirable visitor appeared at the door!" I added, sitting down beside him after having placed the papers on the table.

He very slowly lifted his head from the pan and said:

"No, Procopis, you know very well that your friend Agelaos no longer practices the profession; he assigned the care of his clients to reliable colleagues a long time ago and no other friend or acquaintance—apart from you—knows where he now resides."

"But there's always the possibility of an unforeseen intrusion by a neighbor, a tradesman, someone who has got the wrong address and heaven knows who else," I insisted.

"Such a thing is highly unlikely, provided—it goes without saying—that you make sure you're punctual, as you always were—I have to admit—at first. But I've noticed, to my regret, that recently you've been coming later and later. Should I take this lack of punctuality as a sign of reluctance? As a hidden wish to end our collaboration; something that perhaps you prefer not to tell me straight out? Be honest with me, are you trying to get me to release you from your promise?"

"What do you mean? Are you daring to accuse me of defection?"

"Nevertheless, you're a whole hour late again today!" he grumbled, glancing at the clock on the table, the hands of which showed that it was five past seven.

This clock was a sharp contrast to the room's ill-matching furniture and tasteless decoration. Its black metal case (the back of which was engraved in calligraphic letters with the dedication: "The lecturers of the Rois Medical School to their Director, Doctor A. Avvakis, 23 April 1907") was, taken as a whole, an admirably positioned, microscopic monument. Its broad, hollow base, which was elaborately decorated with embossed leaves and fruit, supported a statuette of a naked girl nonchalantly sitting on a lioness' back.

"Allow me to say," I protested, taking my watch from my pocket and letting it hang from its chain, with the lid open, in front of his eyes, "that you are being unfair to me, because the time is—as you can see for yourself from this precision mechanism that I check every morning without fail like a punctilious employee at the Observatory—just six fifteen. Your clock may be a work of art, but, and I've told you before, it ceased a long time ago to perform its function, to show the correct time. I admit, however, that I am a quarter of an hour late because, given that today is a feast day, I had difficulty in finding a cab."

"What feast day might that be?" he snorted irritably.

"Anyone else in my position would be angry at your indifference. He'd at least expect you to wish him "Happy name day," and not take him to task as you did with me."

"So it's Saint Procopius' Day, is it? I'm sorry, my friend, I didn't remember. Many happy returns! I wish you health and happiness! And I mean it from the bottom of my heart. I'm not just saying it because I need you. But why didn't you mention it to me yesterday? I would never have let you come today if I'd known!"

"Even if you'd forbidden me, I would still have come."

"Don't take offense if I behaved badly before. I'm extremely tired…and ill-tempered…" he said, listlessly bending over the scales again. "Pull your chair up closer, come and give me a hand. See, there's a weight too many this time. That small one there has to go, I think."

"Don't worry, leave it to me. But you've got your whole neck in the pan. How have you managed to get like that again? Straighten yourself up first."

"I told you, I'm exhausted; I have difficulty concentrating. At first, for as long as I'm rested and in good spirits, the work goes smoothly and I take account of every detail; but after three or four hours, I am unable to control myself. My endurance wanes, I become careless and irritable. As a consequence, I make mistakes, which only increase my desperation, till in the end I can't even distinguish the weights… Am I all right now?" he asked, removing his neck from the pan, as I'd told him.

"Let me see; no, a little more yet. Don't tense yourself; that's it; now you're okay. But tell me, isn't that why you have the mirror? Don't you use it any more? I thought it helped you."

"Of course, it helped me. Thanks to it I was able to see everything more easily, without torturing myself as I am now. It was a wonderful idea of yours for us to hang it there."

"So why did you take it down?" I asked, looking over at the bare wall. "You remind me of someone who, atop an iron ladder on a pitch-black night, asked to be given a light; but the moment he was handed a lighted candle, he began to descend...with his eyes closed. You're the same. Why don't you use the mirror? I don't understand you. It's a bit odd, isn't it?"

"I was afraid you would be quick to criticize me," he shouted, jumping up from his stool.

The emptied pan shot into the air, while the other with the weights banged on the table.

"My joints are creaking; can you hear them?" he groaned. "And my eyes have become blurred through watching the arrows for so many hours upside down."

He walked around the room and then collapsed into an armchair.

"It's impossible for me to continue. While I rest, why don't you tell me that story of yours?"

"What story?"

"The one you began, with the man up the ladder."

"Ah, yes...Well then...

I was with a large group of people and we were returning that night from a party. The man, as I told you, actually did appear to be in a difficult spot. 'For God's sake,' he cried, 'isn't there a man among you to give me some light? I can't see my own nose. I'll fall and break my neck.'

But let me think; where exactly was he standing when we found him? On top of the ladder, high up near the roof, or on the bottom rungs down by the yard? No, he was standing in the middle. His face wasn't very clear; only his white cape stood out in the dark.

Suddenly, one of the group, who was always trying to be clever, came out with this silly question: 'Do you want to come down or go up?' Amid all his shouting, the man appeared not to hear and continued to yell: 'Get me a light!'

The question had a totally unexpected effect on everyone. Imagine, not only did it not even occur to us to frown upon him, we actually found his question exceedingly logical, and given that our curiosity had begun to grow, we tried to guess what the man wanted to do: to get down or go up? And as we were all slightly tipsy, we began making wagers. I, along with two or three others, wagered that he wanted to go up; all the others that he wanted to get down. We had withdrawn to one side and were speaking softly so that we wouldn't be heard. The man—who had stopped his shouting as we had approached and, relieved, was waiting for us to help—now started screaming in anguish, thinking that we were about to leave and abandon him.

When we returned to the yard and gave him the candle that one of us had run to fetch, he grabbed it and, without saying a word, waved it to and fro a couple of times in front of him to make sure that its light was steady; then, in its strong flame, to our amazement we watched him shut his eyes, toss his head back, and, holding the candle in his outstretched arm, begin to come down. We hadn't expected him to shut his eyes, but not for a moment did we consider that for this reason the wagers would have to be cancelled."

"It wasn't a serious enough reason," Agelaos admitted. "And it's to your credit that you who had a vested interest didn't suggest it, given that from the very first moment it appeared that fortune was not on your side."

"None of us said as much as a word," I went on, pleased with the praise I'd received, "and we waited for the man, who was still coming down with his eyes closed, to set foot on the last rung so that we might announce the winners. (We had agreed to prohibit even the slightest display that might influence his decision as to the direction he would take.) Whereupon, and though there were but two rungs left before he would reach the ground, he stopped, and in the same way that he had come down, namely with his eyes closed, he went back up again; but as soon as he was on the penultimate rung before the top, he halted, turned, and began coming down again. And this coming and going, up and down (which we watched transfixed, bound not only by our initial curiosity—the outcome had by then ceased to concern us—but by an unfamiliar magnetic force, which emanated from the spasmodic movements of the man on the ladder and mesmerized us), went on for a long time, and perhaps it would have gone on even longer if a gust of wind hadn't blown out the candle. Sensing the darkness surrounding him again, the man again began crying out. It was then that we emerged from our torpor, which was replaced by an indescribable feeling of panic—his flapping white cape seemed to us like a shroud—and we took to our heels. We had gone some distance, but his cries still hounded us. Right up until the time we parted, we never exchanged a word, though we were tormented by numerous thoughts. Only the smart ass in the group said, as he was bidding us farewell: 'I've never in my life come across such a hesitant, irresolute man. Why don't you let me go and set fire to his beard? It's probably the only way to get him to hurry up and make a decision'."

"An amazing story...And what happened in the end?"

"I wish I knew. No one went back to see...Now, may I learn what happened to the mirror?"

"I didn't dare tell you. It was broken today by the young girl who tidies up. You can't imagine how upset I was. It was so precious to me!"

"If you said so useful, I'd agree. But don't worry. We'll replace it first thing tomorrow. I have another one in the storeroom."

"How can I ever thank you?"

"There's no need, and till tomorrow—who knows—we may not even need it!" I said encouragingly, giving him a meaningful wink.

"Do you really believe that or are you just saying it? Anyway, I'll repay you; yes, I promise you, I'll repay you for everything you do for me whenever the need arises."

"Don't even mention it!" I cried and jumped up, as I grasped his meaning, namely that sooner or later—I had to prepare myself—it would be my turn to try. "Don't give it a thought; the need won't arise."

"You misunderstood; I meant *if* the need arises," he said, guessing the cause of my alarm and correcting himself.

"Enough of this dilly-dallying; time for work."

I helped him to get up, to go over to the table and to once again place his head in the right way on the scales.

"Careful! I'm about to remove the weight. Let's see if we manage it at the first attempt. Don't talk... The sound of the voice causes vibrations that are transferred to the pan, adding weight."

"Only the sound of the voice?" he muttered as though babbling to himself.

Using the nippers, I carefully removed the extra weight, and the arrows on the scales, after wavering a moment, found their equilibrium.

"Your doves are kissing!" I shouted in joy, looking at the lead heads of the birds, whose beaks were touching.

He took a deep breath and smiled.

"Now be so kind as to count the weights."

"Three okas and two hundred and fifty-five drams exactly!" I announced.

The smile immediately disappeared from his face.

"I can't take anymore," he said, noting down the result on a piece of paper. "I've tried so many times since this morning and it never comes out the same."

"Perhaps you don't subtract the weight of the spectacles?"

"No, I did. It's always the first thing I do. The error is elsewhere. I'm never going to find it."

"Don't be disappointed. Your failed attempts most likely contain the seed of future success. And don't forget that whoever has never known failure cannot possibly be a great man."

"But I'm not a great man. And my ambitions are extremely limited…"

The sound of chatter was heard through the open windows.

We went out onto the wooden balcony that extended the full length of the house. In the dirt yard, two women were ironing some huge sheets and chattering. The heftier one lifted her head, admired the tufted branches of the trees touching the railings, saw us and said with a deep sigh:

"Down here we have the roots and up there you have the garden."

At that same moment, an unnaturally large, ripe, yellow pear fell from the branch and landed in the basket with the clothes to be ironed.

"Thank you," she shouted and stooped to take hold of it. "Don't you eat the giant pears? Don't you like them? They're extremely tasty. Down here on the low branches that don't get any sun, there are only small ones, no bigger than that, and they're not at all juicy."

She smelled the pear with delight and then turned it in her hands.

"It's exceptionally heavy. I've never held such a big one. It must weigh half an oka. Here, take it, well, what do you think?" she said, handing it to the other woman.

"Did you hear Procopis? Did you follow that? Did you see everything? What do you make of it?" asked Agelaos, and his now-wan face was stricken with grief.

I made no reply.

He looked into my eyes, which reflected his own terrible anxiety, and whispered:

"On second thoughts, don't tell me."

"No, I'll tell you: You are a brave man!"

Original title: *I proetoimasia*. Published in E. H. Gonatas, *I proetoimasia*, Athens: Stigmi, 1991.

Tassos Goudelis

Afternoon with Alcoholic View

After a certain point, my shell no longer protects me. At first, my insides begin to throb, as if wanting to test the limits of my forehead or chest. My eyes see themselves looking. With a swinging soft sigh my second presence comes out, tentatively at first, and goes back in: as if this wasn't the stop it wanted and it were rushing to get back inside before the doors of the train closed behind it. In its old place, it no longer feels secure of course, but it keeps a hold of its impatience in the listless compartment. Through the windows it watches the landscape reeling and temporarily falls silent, like the considerate fellow passenger opposite us who refrains from even leafing through his newspaper so as not to disturb our torpor. Nevertheless, this calm is only temporary, as my second presence and I both know, for even from now the very fingers that stretch out so we might see whether they're shaking before our darting eyes ask to learn their names.

It's not that my second presence has given up. That's out of the question. On the contrary, we've only just begun. I've been ready for some time, I slept early yesterday, with my mother's rough blanket tight under my chin, and today my friend Eric visited in our inner yard's tiles. I'll never let him leave now that imperceptibly I see him at our sweaty game, as if he doesn't exist when he runs off to get the ball. I'm afraid that he left me before coming close, again kicking the headache's round leather with the football of a days'-old concussion. I'll get through it with a stiff upper lip, so as not to let on to Eric, who sometimes becomes a blur and sometimes crystal clear, despite all the tastes of the drink that I'm analyzing in my mouth as though it were my main concern—I know how to do two things simultaneously, perhaps even more. I've already realized that I've surreptitiously emerged from myself, but not only as far as the next chair in the bar where I am right now, sitting so naturally as to be staring at myself in silence. My second presence got up on the pretext of going somewhere roundabout: however, it doesn't miss the opportunity to watch me from close up, only if things were different would it do that. Here you take a risk as you well know in order to get to where you want: as if hypnotized, prepared to have revealed to you what it is you're afraid of. You manage it without help, without any intense focusing on the quack hypnotist's flame; you just listen to your own voices till you're relaxed. Which is an external relaxation, because there's a gap in the wooden floor and voices can be heard. Through the cracks I can see people downstairs; it smells of wet grass piled up on the farm where we were lodged just outside Chalkis in 1960. The villagers didn't know how to swim, and so behind my father's armchair beside the seaside pine tree in the photograph you see the waves unwanted; only the restaurants on the beach consoled them by serving salty drinks like mine, which I'm now smelling as I watch the sea urchin at the bottom of it.

Before me on the plates are exquisite paleontological finds with colors that I don't dare to touch. In the bar's window the outer and inner scenes mix irreverently and together walk in an absurd direction, even more worried than I am, who can, if I want, right now recall with the precision of a salivary gland the taste of the wall with the nourishing whitewash of my childhood appetite. I'm able not only to list in turn the names of the stops made by the Peloponnese railcar, but also to pick from my ear the most passionate whisper of promises and leave its dust in the atmosphere of the room. I also know how many times my handkerchief is folded and in which pocket, how many lemons I have in the fridge, on what day Pasternak died, the chemical formula for *chloi alumenti*, if the stranger on my left has a sister, how many white corpuscles I had three years ago and if the office telephone is ringing at this moment. Despite my sobriety, of which I alone am aware, I'll admit my confusion when I have to listen to the defense plea in my voice, which is virtually unrecognizable, as if it were coming reworked from a recording. I don't know who confesses to nonexistent things, or why this absolutely has to be done by my invisible table companion who didn't sit beside me feeling melancholic merely in order to be poisoned. Unless he believes that this is how one is saved by means of the asphyxia of closed rooms or is abandoned beneath the ruins of marvelous landslides on the summer gradient. Someone allows the clarity to sweep him out to sea with feeling; he doesn't have to suffer and surrender to exhaustion in order to die, as did the suicide swimmer with the incurable illness, desperately seeking the horizon in the island's deep waters.

You may think for some time that nothing escapes through your permanent window and then, one morning, slightly changing the angle of your body—as though you hadn't already tried every visual perspective—you notice the awful truth. So, I'm sitting in roughly the same spot in the bar, usually facing the entrance, where actually anything might happen, even the unborn might come through without surprising anyone. That well-known snapshot on the wall with the obscure drinker changes, suddenly something that constantly transforms itself comes to the surface, your fingerprints on the glass are enlarged on the screen as if being examined by the forces of law, hot on your trail at last.

My second presence comes and goes, changed now to the point of confusion. I'm disconcerted by that haste, and the worst thing is that I can't reach any understanding with it. So I lower my head and monitor a point on the table in case the wood changes shape. In this way the hypothermia of abandonment that I'm seeking slowly comes into the waiting. As though the last tenant of my old house had returned in the evening, just before the late bus passes outside in the street, and I'm ready for the slack goings-on. Now I can hear everything that concerns me, but even the neighbors' walls happen to be silent. It's not that they are doing me any favor and allowing me to think. Others with me felt equally relaxed, determined, so it seems, to also surrender after so much impressionism in that twilight that resembles today's. But till I too arrive at last at the sympathy that is so close to me and call for help, I must check the garden one more time with the flashlight. Lately I've heard huge wings there, evidently looking for shelter rather than announcing something to me.

Original title: "Apoyevma me alkooliki thea." Published in Tassos Goudelis, *I yinaika pou mila* [The Woman Who Speaks], Athens: Kedros, 2002, pp. 41-46.

Vassilis Gouroyannis

The Cock's Crowing

I was serving in Popovo in the district of Paramythia. We were informed that a girl in the village of Zaravoutsi had eloped and we had to go there in the middle of the night. The chief sent me and another colleague, Costas Sabanis from Margariti. Just before we "stumbled" into the Satyr's pit, we heard music being played on a fiddle. We stopped to ascertain just what the sound was and where it was coming from. We ascertained that it was coming from the gully. Then I drew my revolver and fired twice in the air. The music stopped for a moment and then started again. My colleague grew angry. He, too, drew his revolver and fired twice in the direction of the gully. Once more the fiddle stopped and then started again. After that we decided, nevertheless, to wait and see what would happen. It was a pleasant tune and we liked listening to it, despite our fear. I don't know how long this went on, but as soon as the cocks in Loziana started crowing, the music stopped for good. When we reported the incident to the chief, he told us that there must have been a wedding or some other celebration taking place a long way off and that the sound must have been channeled through the earth, which is a good conductor, before emerging in the gully.

IOANNIS MANTZIOS, RETIRED GENDARME,
The Village of Grannitsa near Ioannina

Despite the ostensibly scientific explanations, there is no doubt that the two gendarmes overheard the performance of a paranormal being. It was only to be expected that this would not be frightened by the gunshots or by other methods of conventional force.

What remains to be explained in this story, however, is why the performance stopped at the sound of the cocks crowing. Besides, it's common knowledge that paranormal beings are unsettled by the sound of cocks crowing. Cocks signify the dawn and the coming of the light. Though it's a mistake to think that paranormal beings are afraid of the light lest they be discovered. On the contrary! They are afraid that the light, as it spreads, will "oblige" them to discover the world: the world that invariably alters and distorts familiar forms and landscapes. A similar reaction occurs during a disinterment, when all those who love shut their eyes so as not to destroy forever the image of a previous form. As it was depicted, so it remains depicted. It will not allow any alteration of the forms. The world, for its part, has its own mirrors. These constitute the embrasures through which time fires at us with complete accuracy, given that we bring our faces right up to the barrel. These mirrors are known to the paranormal beings. That's why they reverse them and see themselves only in their dark, other side. If they gaze on creation in the light, they suffer the same shock as the butterfly trapped in a locked-up summer cottage. It rests against the windowpane and sees...And sees the flowers disappearing, the cool trees growing bare. Whereas nature fashioned it to experience only one season! These inconceivable sights destroy the insect's biological make-up and it endeavors—though without having the necessary weight—to smash the glass, to give itself up to the wind that will analyze it into radiance and wings.

Original title: "To lalima tou peteinou." Published in Vassilis Gouroyannis, *Diiyiseis parafysikon fenomenon* [Tales of Paranormal Phenomena], Athens: Kastaniotis, 1990, pp. 65-67.

Christos Homenidis

Not All Fingers Are Equal

When, at thirty-five, I became creativity department manager at Balzac International, I didn't stop to gloat over the doubling of my salary or over the big office I was given with modern, arty furniture and with a panoramic view of Athens. What filled me with delight was the fact that I could at last select the people I wanted to work with. I'd form my own team, hiring a few new people, a state within a state, which would not only rejuvenate the company—my ultimate goal—but also the advertising market in general. As soon as I took over, the better newspapers and magazines carried ads to lure the kind of young person I was interested in. And from the very next day, I began receiving CVs and interviewing candidates.

Within a week I'd seen more than a hundred and I was sick and tired of the superhuman efforts most of them made to try to impress me, displaying what was only to be expected: education, wit, industry, talent. I've no doubt that quite a number had all these things in abundant quantity. But not one of them had that "something" that I was after and that I wasn't really able to describe even myself. "You're looking for people you can work with, not fall in love with!" was the advice given to me by Balzac's vice-president, an old hand in the advertising business. "Go on, weigh up the pros and cons of each one and make a clear-minded decision."

Half an hour later, my secretary brought me a sheet of paper with just nine words, written by hand: "I am your alpha and omega. Take a risk!" The signature, in bright red felt-tip, was illegible. "What else are we going to have to read!" I chuckled. "What else are you going to have to see!" said the secretary almost threateningly. "She's parked herself on the couch in the waiting room and is carrying on as though it were her own home! She's varnishing her nails—before long she'll be taking off her shoes for a pedicure!" "All right, show her in."

At first sight, the only thing remarkable about her was her tender age. She was a tall, thin girl, with hair tied back and eyes wide open, that nevertheless gave you the impression that they were turned inwards rather than outwards on the wild world. She didn't look more than sixteen. "Xenia Dogani," she said holding out her hand to me, after first blowing on it to dry the varnish. "Have you finished school?" "Just." "Okay, tell me about yourself." "I have a flair for design, not for words!" she informed me. "So be it. Show me some of your work, then." She was carrying a sailor's sack that was bulging and looked ready to burst at the seams. She leaned over and began feeling inside it. I prepared myself to have to suffer hundreds of sketches and scribbles done by the girl from her years at primary school down to the present day. Instead of that, she pulled out a brand new sketchpad and a pack of colored crayons.

"Tell me what product you've been commissioned to promote and I'll do the art work for you in a jiff." "By the time I've smoked my cigar?" I said, giving her a sideways look. "Perhaps even sooner." It didn't seem to even occur to her that perhaps I was being sarcastic and—strangely enough—I found that charming. "The campaign that we're working on at the moment has to do with *wonderbra*. Bras that work miracles!" I announced to her, resisting the temptation to stare at her breasts. "Fine!" she said and immediately set to sketching with a will. I noticed that she began from the bottom right-hand corner of the white sheet and that she used only two or three colors.

After about a quarter of an hour, she put the crayon down, admired her work for a moment, then held it out to me. All I could see was a composition consisting of green and blue spots, without rhyme or reason. "What's it supposed to represent?" I asked her. "Is the aim to represent something or to increase sales? I guarantee that as soon as women see it, they'll rush to the underwear departments! Go on, test it on your female colleagues!" I wasn't, of course, going to follow the advice of any Xenia Dogani, especially one who spoke with such impertinence. "Our tests are quite adequate," I said to her, in a paternal tone. "Besides, you're too young to go into the production side. Go and study design—or whatever else you like—and come back in five years and we'll talk again." "What, aren't you going to hire me?" she said, raising her voice even more, with her astonishment appearing to be even greater than her displeasure. "No." "I feel sorry for you," she retorted dryly and disappeared from my office without another word.

That same evening, I had parked myself on the sofa and was watching a prewar horror film on the television. Milena had both an evening and a late-night performance at the theater, and had arranged to go out afterwards with some other two-bit avant-garde actors and wouldn't be back much before daybreak. I had a meeting at nine in the morning with a major client (a yogurt producer)—so I should have gone straight to bed—but my empty house seemed so peaceful that it would have been a shame to deprive myself of it. The peace was shattered at twelve-twenty by the hellish sound of the front doorbell ringing. I went and opened the door and found myself face to face with Xenia Dogani. She was still wearing the same clothes and carrying the familiar sailor's sack. "I've come up with some new ideas and came to show them to you. I think I deserve a second chance..." she said, almost imploringly.

I've never turned away a visitor in my life, not even a peddler. I invited her in, gave her a tequila and then took hold of the sketchpad from her hands. "I tried to be more explicit..." she explained before I even opened it. Just so: she'd filled it with hundreds of representations of the sexual act in its most likely and unlikely variations. The only thing that remained unchanged, from one page to the next, was the faces of the protagonists: hers and mine! In one of our later acts, I was presented standing on the ramparts of a crumbling castle with her in a sailboat cutting through the waves. We were linked by my superhuman penis, hanging from the entire length of which were Chinese lanterns, freshly laundered bras, even bats. And yet it wasn't intended as a cartoon.

I lifted my head and saw her waiting for my reaction, while sucking at a hollow piece of ice between her lips. "You know that life imitates art?" I snarled. "If it dares..." she said provocatively and sat up on the sofa.

When I again lifted my head, the time was three-thirty and there was the danger that Milena would show her face at any moment. "Time for you to be going home," I said to Xenia, caressing her tenderly. "Impossible!" she said, cutting me short. "This morning, I butchered my parents, my grandma and her sister. How am I going to get any sleep with so many corpses in the other room?" "Go to a hotel." "I'm still under-age. They ask for your identity card at the desk." "Didn't you tell me that you'd finished school?" "I gained a year. I'll be eighteen in February." "But my wife is going to be back soon!" "Either you'll put me up for the night or I'll sleep in the park across the road, in the freezing cold. It's up to you!" she concluded, quite calmly.

With all this chit-chat, I unconsciously came to accept her irrational line of thought. I made her gather up all her things and led her to the basement, that I'd christened "my private and inviolate space", so that even when married I might maintain a semblance of autonomy, an adolescent whim that Milena respected. I gave her an old sleeping bag of mine and a jug for her to use as a chamber pot. She took them with a smile of gratitude. I told her not to make any sound and switched off the lights and closed the door behind me. Four hours later (after I'd started to doubt her existence in my life), I unlocked the door and found her in exactly the same position, except that her left nipple was sticking out through her half-open shirt. "Get up and get dressed, let's be going!" I ordered her. "Lie on top of me a bit!" she said, stretching herself coquettishly.

I dropped her off outside a café on my way to Balzac's. At half-past midnight, she was again standing on my doorstep. Milena was away, making a film this time.

To cut a long story short, I secretly put Xenia up in my home for two whole weeks. From the second morning, I stopped waking her up and sending her away—I simply took a flask of coffee down to her and anything edible I could filch from the fridge without Milena noticing. She dutifully respected the rule of silence. She spent entire twelve-hour and even sixteen-hour periods without so much as a word. I'd visit her as regularly as I could and, after we'd made love, she'd show me her latest work. She sketched feverishly, usually whatever happened to be before her. And I have to admit that while I immediately recognized the furniture, books and surfing equipment, her sketches revealed new dimensions to me, unfamiliar nuances of a familiar world. Is this what we mean, I wonder, when we talk of "talent"?

Xenia seemed overjoyed by that state of voluntary incarceration—twenty square meters, it seemed, were ample to enable her to spend the rest of her life there. The only thing that caused her concern was the fate of her butchered family. "I have to go and bury them in the garden!" she anxiously repeated every day. "Are you afraid that the police won't find them?" "No, but it's an age-old moral law. Didn't Antigone do the same thing for her brother?" "But she hadn't murdered him beforehand!" "So I'm under an even greater obligation!"

Though seemingly rational, the discussions about the murder didn't lead to any meaningful conclusion. Xenia described her supposed victims as absolute wretches who sank more and more into the mire of daily life and subconsciously were looking for a way out. "So you'll understand," she said to me, "my dad was a corrupt cop. With the money he took from bribes, he built a villa and sent my mum and grandma on exotic trips so he could spend his time with whores. They knew all this and accepted it!" "And you punished them for it!" "No, I saved them from it!"

I could—so I thought—determine precisely the dividing line between truth and falsehood. Xenia had indeed grown sick of her folks and one fine morning had simply run away from home. I, on the other hand, was not worried so much about being found out and nabbed for kidnapping a minor. What frightened me was that, day by day, I fancied her more and more. It was as if I were beginning to fall in love with her. A powerful time-bomb was ticking away at the very foundations of my marriage! If it were to go off, we'd all go up in smoke. By the end of the first week, I'd decided to get rid of Xenia...

I am a cowardly and resourceful fellow, like—so I believe—every true Greek, apart from the heroes of the Revolution and the Resistance. Telling her directly to get lost was out of the question. I wouldn't have put it past her to dig her heels in, or even reveal herself to Milena and fight it out with her as her equal. Consequently, I had to get her out of my home using some ruse or other.

"Let's go!" I said to her one evening, when my wife was away again, visiting her mother in Thessaloniki. "Let's go and bury the members of your family!" I shoved her into the car, threw a couple of shovels into the trunk at her insistence in order to dig the graves and, following her directions, I eventually found myself outside a nouveau-riche bungalow in Ano Glyfada. There was a light coming through the windows and I thought I could hear the sound of voices. "This is where I spent all my fucking adolescence!" said Xenia, as though about to spit on the ground. From a huge bunch of keys, she selected the one for the gate and the front door. "Dogani Residence" said a polished plaque attached to the garden wall. "Where's the stupid girl taking me, to introduce me to her policeman-father?" I thought as we crossed the garden. I let her get two or three steps ahead, made a sudden about-turn and started running towards my car. I leapt inside, switched on the engine and disappeared at top speed.

On the way home, I ran over a dog. Before I splattered it, I saw its eyes for a split second. There was no fear in them, only scorn. As soon as I entered my living room, I rushed to pick up the phone. "You deserve your mediocre life, you fool," Xenia said and hung up.

By the time three years had passed, I'd erased all these events from my memory. My darling little son is already crawling, my work at Balzac is going great (particularly now that I've given up on my unrealistic ambitions) and Milena has found her mild antidote in the figure of a young female scriptwriter. Perhaps I'd never have given any thought again to Xenia Dogani if I hadn't bumped into her the other day at a dinner given in honor of Yannis Pardalis, the only contemporary Greek painter who has distinguished himself—and rightly so in my opinion—abroad. Xenia was with him and he was gazing into her eyes, clearly in love. Fortunately for me, we were sitting virtually opposite and so I was able to watch him, while he ate, with curiosity and admiration. However, it seems that I wasn't discreet enough. Just before the dessert came, he held out his hand towards me demonstratively. His middle finger was missing. "You're wondering where I lost it? Where else? Digging!" Xenia burst out laughing and avoided looking at me for the rest of the evening.

Original title: "Ola ta dahtyla isa den einai." Published in Christos Homenidis, *Defteri Zoi* [Second Life], Athens: Hestia, 2000, pp. 193-204.

NIKOS HOULIARAS

The Body

His body was everything that Victor Tzialas had in the world. He had his body, and young Nettas. It was something he never forgot.

Looking down, he walked with short sharp steps and drew the white line behind him. He let the lime run from the sprinkler onto the ground as he thought of that. His body.

For a couple of years now he hadn't needed to puff himself out at all. His biceps had grown to such a size that he had difficulty in finding T-shirts to fit him. "What are we going to do to keep you in check, Victor…" they said to him down in the marketplace, in the shops where he went to buy clothes. "You're the size of a double wardrobe!" they'd say to him, supposedly out of admiration. They looked at him with those slant eyes that businessmen have, with a fox's cunning they looked at him, but Victor Tzialas saw fear there too.

That's what he wanted. He wanted them to fear him. In any case, this was the only thing he'd managed to achieve in his life.

Women didn't want him. What did Victor have that they might crave? His good looks, his money? There were plenty of punks around who had both.

That's why he turned his back on all this from an early age. From a very early age, he turned his back on it. He put all his efforts into the horizontal bar and weights. He had to become strong. Since he couldn't become good-looking, at least he'd become strong. The strongest. He'd have to become a Samson if others were going to notice him and admire him.

He realized this from an early age. He'd realized it from as long ago as the children's home. In this world, if it's not in your make-up to have them like you, at least you should have them fear you.

He wasn't one to make money. And he didn't have a head for letters and the like. Nor for business. He couldn't be bothered with all this. Besides, he was in a hurry. There was something inside him that drove him towards people. Victor Tzialas wanted people and wanted them badly. But you had to be someone for people to want you. You had to be something, anyway.

Which is why Victor had no other choice. He had no one to speak of to support him. His mother—anyway the woman who took him out of the children's home and brought him up as her own—was a wreck. She'd turned into a nag. She did nothing but swear at him. She got worked up at the slightest thing. She made a laughing-stock of him. After all he'd gone through for so many years to at least make them fear him, now she was making a laughing-stock of him in front of everyone. She even beat him. She beat him in front of others and cursed him because, she said, he couldn't hold down any job. She even went and wrecked the horizontal bar that he'd rigged up next to the wash-house.

She had no idea what he'd been through in order for him to become what he was. For Victor to become "the body." For all to see him and tremble. For them all to fear him and to want to be like him. She'd no idea that he also had to quash that filthy story that had been put around some time back in the neighborhood that when he was small, they'd taken him behind the Kourabas hospital and given it to him in the ass. His mother had no inkling of all this. She'd spent her whole life working in others' houses and she wanted her son to make something of himself in the world. To get a job and have the respect of others. To have security. In some kind of job.

This is what Victor was thinking about as he went. He walked with short, sharp steps, drawing the white line behind and to the right of him.

He let the lime run from the sprinkler, and thought about his body. About his body, and about young Nettas who was beside him.

He had him with him and they were marking out the lines on the football pitch. He went in front and the youngster ran beside him with bucket in hand. He was holding the bucket but his eyes were fixed on Victor. He stared at his shoulders and the biceps bulging beneath the T-shirt.

Victor had completely won over the youngster, who was devoted to him. Sometimes, he felt like reaching out his hand and stroking his hair, but he didn't do so. He realized that he shouldn't. He had to be tough. To say little. To say virtually nothing to him.

He had the youngster beside him and said virtually nothing to him, because he realized that this was how the youngster wanted him to be. That's what Victor was. The body and the idol. He had to be careful. To keep him at arm's length, but be sure not to lose him, because the youngster had got a whole group together. He had drawn other kids to his side. He needed the youngster, because there was another body, Markos Bakros from Siarava, who had his own followers. There was a whole crowd of kids in the neighborhood, who followed on his heels. Bakros was younger and better-looking, and Victor Tzialas was afraid, very afraid, of this. So he had to be careful. To take good care of young Nettas, but not to show it.

That's why he walked in front. He walked and drew the white line behind him without saying a word. Every so often, though, he turned and looked at him, supposedly indifferently. He shot him a quick glance out of the corner of his eye.

A breeze had got up and it was starting to blow; it had taken hold of his hair and was flinging it back. But the youngster was still there! His eyes were on Victor. He had them fixed on Victor's back and was staring at his biceps. He watched them changing shape as Victor turned. There, at the corner flag.

The earth was soft from the rain that had fallen just previously and, before long, Victor Tzialas would be finished with the lines.

The work thoroughly bored him but what could he do? He didn't know how to do any other. Besides, he had all the equipment at the football ground. Everything he needed, that is. Two horizontal bars behind the goalposts, and weights. He also had some springboards. He'd found them discarded in the changing rooms.

In the past, he'd told the sport's director that they ought to get more equipment. So the kids can come and work out, he'd said. Vaulting-horses and such like. He could train them. He wasn't asking for any extra money for this job. They could pay him simply as a watchman. He'd train them for free. He didn't want anything extra. On the contrary, he reflected that this would give him some standing. He'd have lots of people around him, and Victor wanted people.

The director told him, however, that they had no funds for things like that and so he forgot the idea. Becoming a teacher wasn't for Victor. He remained a simple watchman, but he exercised.

If the truth be told, he did nothing else. He exercised all day long. He had to keep himself in form. Take care of his body. Take care of it well, because it was through his that he had won over young Nettas. And the youngster had a whole gang behind him. This meant a great deal. A very great deal, in fact.

You see, he didn't have anything else. He didn't have any girlfriends anyway. That was out of the way. He'd buried that deep down. Love and all that nonsense. Every so often, he'd visit Vassilo, toss a fifty bill in her lap, give her a quick one, and relieve himself. No. Victor Tzialas had no girlfriends, nor did he even think about them any more. All he had was his body and young Nettas. These were the two things he had to think about, which is why he pretended not to see anything when the youngster sneaked the nippers from Siarava into the ground.

He knew that he sneaked them in to see him. To see that there was only one body and that was Victor, and that Bakros wasn't in the same league with him. Because those kids were from Bakros' gang and they'd come from Siarava for that very reason. To get a look at him from up close.

~&~

It was quiet in the stadium at that time. Not a sound could be heard. The breeze swept the papers and plastic through the stands, while lined up below were Bakros' kids who watched with their hands in their pockets. They were watching Victor Tzialas, who was drawing the lines on the pitch for Sunday's match.

It must have been around four in the afternoon and Victor Tzialas was in a hurry to get finished with the lines. He wanted to be done with work and to go down to the dock and sit on the jetty. He liked sitting there on the steps and gazing at the sea. Watching the people fishing with their lines, quietly, without speaking. Simply waiting for the fish, and continually looking at the water as though it were forever.

Victor liked that. He liked it a lot because it helped him relax. He relaxed deep down and forgot everything.

Of all the places he knew, this is the one he considered the best. There, on the side where the workshops and sawmills were. In the distance he could hear the monotonous drone and the irons beating every so often in the workshops, and he felt as if he were young. Very young, inside a house, listening to the pans, and that relaxed him. Greatly relaxed him. To the point that he felt sleepy. He was overcome by sleepiness and he liked it. He felt secure and let himself go. He let himself go and unwound. He unwound and thought about nothing. Victor Tzialas even forgot about his body.

This is why he wanted to be done quickly. To finish with the lines and go down to the dock.

Since the team didn't have training that afternoon, he was free to leave early. He'd finish with the lines and leave. He'd do a couple of pull-ups on the horizontal bar to stretch a bit and then leave.

He still had one of the penalty boxes to do, the goal area and the penalty spot. The weather was mild. Just right.

He turned and looked for a moment at young Nettas who had abandoned the bucket and was signaling to Bakros' kids.

"Hey, the bucket!" he shouted, "bring the bucket so we can get finished."

The youngster went over to him carrying the bucket with the lime. Victor went to take the bucket of lime to fill the sprinkler, but the youngster pulled it away from him.

"Let me, let me!" he said, and hurriedly emptied the lime into the sprinkler as if doing something extremely important.

Victor took the sprinkler and began drawing the lines around the penalty area. He reached the corner and turned. Then he did the goal area. He went to do the penalty spot. But the youngster stopped him. "Victor..." he said, "can I do it?"

"Go on, then. Do it." Victor said, "but carefully, don't splatter it, okay!"

The youngster took hold of the sprinkler. He shot a quick glance in the direction of the stand to see whether they were looking at him, and then, with a quick movement, made the white mark that signaled the penalty spot.

Then he raised his head and looked at Victor as if waiting for something.

"Fine. That's okay," said Victor and headed towards the changing rooms.

The youngster quickly gathered up the equipment and ran after him. With small, quick steps he hurried to catch up with him.

On the opposite side, all Bakros' kids ran too. They went just beyond the wooden dugout and watched. They watched Victor Tzialas and young Nettas, who went into the changing rooms for a while and then came out again. They came out and went towards the tap. With a sudden movement, Victor took off his T-shirt. He took it off and revealed his biceps. The bulging muscles and the taut nerves. His whole body glistened from the sweat.

He put his hands under the tap and rubbed them. He rubbed them with the soap and his muscles rippled.

Young Nettas stood beside him. He was holding a towel and watching him.

A little way off, all of Bakros' kids were lined up, examining him. They examined each and every contour made by the muscles and biceps on Victor Tzialas' body. They stared at them and assessed him with their eyes. And Victor was aware of this. He could feel their eyes fixed on his back. And he took a deep breath. He took a deep breath and held it. He held it and puffed himself out. He even took care to make his movements tighter. Tighter and quicker. They were looking at him! They were there and they were looking at him!

This pleased him a great deal, yet it also bothered him somewhat. It bothered him a lot, because he had to keep himself continually tight. But what could he do? Whatever you do, you have to do it well. You mustn't relax for a moment, because it doesn't take much for you to lose everything. It takes hard work to remain on top. Hard work and sweat is what it takes. And Victor never forgot this. Life is extremely competitive. You have always to be up to your position, or you come toppling down. Life does you no favors. It does no favors to anyone. Just like others have their learning or businesses and are always there, dogs, hanging on by the skin of their teeth, so Victor has his body. This is what he had to fight with. This was his strength, and his standing. This was all he had.

～❧～

However, he also had young Nettas, who was beside him with towel in hand.

He turned and looked at him. The soap ran into his eyes and made them smart. He saw him as if through a misty window standing there beside him and waiting. Further off, he saw Bakros' kids staring at him, and the whole empty stadium, as far as the yellow wall with the acacias.

He splashed some water into his face, washed himself, then turned his head slightly and called out.

"The towel," he said.

Young Nettas immediately handed him the towel and Victor wiped himself. He came out with a couple of "ahs," stretched a little, then trotted over to the horizontal bar. He took hold of the bar and began the pull-ups. He did about ten of them. He also did three turns. He jumped down, put on his T-shirt and went to the changing rooms. He locked them up and made for the exit.

The sky had cleared up again and there was a light breeze. The few clouds drifted away towards Drisko, and it was five o'clock.

Bakros' kids ran out all together into the street and waited. Victor came out too with young Nettas.

Victor shut the gate, went and said something to the kiosk vendor outside, and then set off down the street. The kids followed on his heels and all together they went down the street that led to the shore.

~❦~

They passed through the marketplace. Past the shoe shops and the other stores. Victor and Nettas in front and Bakros' kids a few steps behind.

Victor walked without saying a word, but he could sense the kids behind him. He could hear them as they kept muttering among themselves. Words and whispers. Sometimes about Bakros and sometimes about him. A couple of times out of the corner of his eye he caught sight of the youngster, who halted and made as if to lunge at them, but he said nothing. He pretended not to notice. He had to be up to his position. Say nothing. Yet he was also overcome by a sense of bitterness. It weighed heavily on him and somewhere deep down he felt as if he wanted to get away from all this! To get far away, where no one would know him and where he could find a little peace, because he couldn't deal with this burden anymore. It was as if he were dragging an iron ball behind him. And that ball was Bakros' kids, and even more so, young Nettas, who was on his side.

Victor was well aware of this but what could he do? In this world, you can't keep yourself on the wave's crest without some effort. Whatever he has to do, he has to do it well and drag his burden along. To drag it without saying a word. This is why he was in a hurry to get down to the dock. To go and sit on the steps. To relax for a while. There, at least, they'd leave him alone. They'd find others to play with and would leave him alone.

He thought of this and quickened his pace. He dodged into the Aghios Nikolaos arcade where Davartzikis' café and the distilleries were. It was cool inside the arcade and coming from the café he could hear the sound of Kazantzidis singing "At the table where I'm drinking..."

Sitting in their chairs in front of the shops were the market traders, who stared at him. It was him they were staring at. At Victor Tzialas, who was striding down the street.

A little way off, someone was hosing down the street. "Hi there, Victor!" he called, lowering the hose.

Victor said nothing. He simply raised his right hand as though in greeting. Not a word. He simply raised his right hand. Just enough as was necessary. At the right angle. So the muscle would bulge at the right spot.

He had studied all this. It was his job and he had to do it well. He knew which was the right position. What angle would give him the best result.

So, he raised his arm and lowered it again quickly. Quickly and ostensibly indifferently. He held his breath inside and puffed himself out, till he emerged from the arcade. Then he chose the left side of the road, where there were trees, passed by the workshops that were a little further on, and arrived at the waterfront.

☙

The dock was very quiet. The waterfront restaurants were empty because it was still early, and anyway the summer was nearly over. Occasionally, someone passed beneath the big trees, while the waiters got the tables ready for the evening.

There were two or three others on the jetty sitting quietly and fishing, and Victor headed in their direction.

He went and sat on the steps and for a while gazed at the mountain opposite. A shadow shimmered on the water before him and the man sitting beside him who was fishing turned and looked at him.

"Good to see you, Victor," he said.

"Are they biting, Thanassis?" said Victor Tzialas, without even looking at him. It was all he said. He simply turned to look at the circles on the water made by the fishing line.

Victor collected his thoughts inside these tiny circles and gradually began to unwind.

From beyond the vegetable gardens came the sound of the monotonous whirr from the sawmills and this calmed him even more.

He unwound. He unwound deep down and gradually let the air out that he kept inside in order to puff himself out. Victor Tzialas let it out and stopped thinking about his body.

⁂

A little way off, Bakros' kids had got young Nettas on his own and were saying something to him. They'd put him in the middle and kept pointing at Victor, who was sitting with his back to them and was staring vacantly at the water.

They were coming out with sharp words, saying nasty things to him. They were goading him.

The youngster appeared flushed and once or twice almost came to grips with them. But there were a lot of them and he didn't dare. Nevertheless, he was very agitated and kept moving further and further back as though they were shoving him. Then, it was as if he suddenly thought of something and he stopped. A light suddenly flashed across his face. He said something to them and then he quickly turned and ran towards the workshops.

The kids immediately ran after him. They went all together and stood in front of the workshop.

Young Nettas glared at them for a moment and then rushed inside. He quickly came out again holding a sledgehammer. He once again gave them a meaningful look, then brushed them aside and ran towards the steps.

Bakros' kids ran after him. Two lads came out of the workshop and stared at them.

It was quiet on the dock, and the sun was going down over the vegetable gardens.

Young Nettas went and stood a couple of paces away from the steps. The kids stood there too. One even took out a cigarette and lit it.

A little way off, with his back turned to them, Victor was sitting quietly, gazing at the water.

There wasn't a sound to be heard. Everything was quiet and listless. Only young Nettas was in a state of agitation. A state of great agitation, but also of greatness.

For a moment, he turned his head and looked at Bakros' kids. He looked at them, and then, suddenly raising the sledgehammer with both hands, he cried at the top of his voice.

"Victooor!" he shrieked like a lamb being slaughtered and ran. Gathering speed, he ran and bam! He brought the iron sledgehammer down with all his might on Victor Tzialas' head.

⚜

For Victor, everything happened quickly. And suddenly. He passed from one side to the other like lightning. A black flash brought him back. Brought him back again into his body.

Victor Tzialas had let go. Let go like a lump of dough, and he spread into a thousand and one little things. Into pleasant little reveries. As though he were lying on soft mattresses. In a room. With aunts around him and relatives. Going about their jobs. Going to and fro without paying him any attention. Letting him laze beneath the covers, but knowing that eventually they would call him and say to him: "Victor, come on child…Quickly, wake up so we can eat."

Then again they might say to him—why not—they might say to him "Your cousins have come. They're asking for you. Come on Victor… Come on dear, wake up, they're waiting for you…"

Anyhow, Victor Tzialas was lost in pleasant little things of this sort and he felt content. With his head sunk into the pillow and with a cat purring beside him.

And while he was like this, still and loose like dough, suddenly, thwack!… the cat, he winced and shuddered as if an electric current had passed through him!

Then all at once everyone vanished from the house and Victor was alone.

The cat let out a shrieking cry. A black cry like a shudder and it rose in the air. "Victooor!" was what the cry seemed to be, and it echoed wildly in the empty room. The cat let out the cry and thwack! It leapt and smashed into the back of his neck! It smashed and, a bundle of teeth and nails, lodged in the back of Victor Tzialas' neck!

He then quickly gathered up the dough. He turned into a ball and felt a burning in his head. A black numbness suddenly gripped him, and Victor jumped. He jumped inside his own body! He suddenly found his huge body again and, like this, the years that he'd spent on it raced though his mind like a bolt of lightning. The years that he'd spent exercising that body.

All at once, Victor Tzialas remembered that he was again in possession of his strong body. The sudden flash, that black thing, brought him back again. It told him that he had to defend his life, as he sensed that someone was making an attempt on it. That someone was behind him and was toppling him. And so he leapt up. Leapt like a spring. He turned suddenly to see who it was, and he saw Nettas!

He saw his own Nettas standing a little way off, holding a sledge-hammer and staring at him. Staring at him in wonder and amazement.

The sledge-hammer was dripping with blood, but Victor Tzialas didn't understand. He had no time to understand because he felt a weight in his head. Something like thick mud kept rising from his nose towards his eyes, and everything around him began to blur.

And, like this, he saw everything blurred. Bakros' kids, the crowd that had gathered outside the workshops, and the whole place round about, houses and trees, gradually growing dark and vanishing.

There wasn't a sound in the street. It was a though everything had frozen. No one was speaking. They were all standing in line. They were all standing without talking as though they'd gathered to watch a show. As though they were waiting for Victor to do something.

And Victor Tzialas didn't understand. He didn't know who to lunge at. What he needed his strong body for at that moment.

Then there was that mud that smelled of iron. That kept rising behind his eyes and numbing him. There was also the crowd of people who were waiting to see what he would do.

Which is why, given that he didn't know what else he ought to do, he at least tried to smile. To show the crowd looking at him that he had no need of such things. Big deal! What was a blow over the head to Victor Tzialas. He was strong. A veritable Samson! For years, that's how they'd known him, he wasn't going to spoil it now at the end!

So he looked at young Nettas and tried to smile. To shake his head a little as if to say, "So what!"

Victor prepared this slight smile. He brought it up from inside with difficulty. He brought it to the surface. He got it to the edge of his mouth and tried to smile.

But what he brought up drained him. The effort, it seems, was too much for him, and inside him everything began to creak. He heard a voice. A monotonous child's voice that kept saying the same thing over and over again: and here comes the chopper to chop off your head . . . It was like a pulse that faded as it went on, and then he felt his insides cracking. Becoming fragments.

Victor went on trying a little longer. He held on with his teeth to these fragments and fashioned the slight smile that he needed.

He smiled and then Victor Tzialas let himself go completely. He let himself go and was taken by the darkness.

Original title: "To soma." Published in Nikos Houliaras, *To Bakakok* [Bakakok], Athens: Kedros, 1981, pp. 130-147.

Yannis Kaisaridis

The Old Man and the Tree

His stout son emptied the last kettle of that year's raki. All night his rough hands had been wrinkled from the steam. He'd had his face hanging over the vapors and the hydrometers, his throat had closed and the morning dew now cut the legs from under him. And all this had been going on now every night for three months; Christmas was approaching, the weather this year was upside-down and had disoriented the raki, the trees and the people too.

For another night, Michalakis had slept on the floor a little ways off, between the kiln and the cistern. His legs stretched out towards the open door, his black, greasy hair turning sometimes towards the fire, so he got singed, sometimes towards the cistern, so that he almost drowned in the vat with the fresh alcohol, truly drunk. Light in build, but he did his job, the fire was never without wood and the raki arrived from the barrels on time. It wasn't till around morning that he fell asleep.

"Michalakis, that's it for this year," shouted his son, the stout one, to the boy.

He shook him, and he leapt up and his eye went straight to the fire.

"Shall I throw on more wood?" said the boy.

"No, there's enough."
Michalakis went out into the yard.

Father and son sat side by side on the bench, leaning against the wall. He slapped him on the knee.
"So, father, that's it for this year. We've done well…"

They remained and watched the fire burning out. A long time.

The next morning, the three of them began loading the cart for the fields.
The son set off, the black smoke shot out from behind and filled the fresh air, Michalakis almost fell over but steadied himself, smiled and looked towards the road.
"What do you think of him?" the stout son asked the father, and they both burst out laughing.
The village was on a rise with the valley beneath.
Drunken clouds were drifting high up in the sky. They were bidding farewell to that endless autumn. They moved off, wet and nonchalant, smelling of must. The tractor rolled down the slope, overtaking them. They weren't talking now, the morning air took the place of the soot and intoxication in their chests, making them dizzy in its own way. The stout son leaned further forward over the wheel and opened his eyes wide for the first time in three whole months, his pupils burst open in the light.

The journey seemed endless to the old man.

When still young he could make out the fields. At the edge of the village, on the rise, he climbed and played with the light and the colors. Mist in the valley and there was the road, barely discernible, but he knows the place and its habits, knows where the rain walks, what's hidden behind, where the cloud sits and even how long, how long the mist lasts in these parts. With his eye he fixes on the valley's greenery at the correct spot, there, yes, the two poplars they have in front of the fields, the crops and behind, an enormous shadow, the mulberry tree.

Now trees instead of crops, peach trees, and when autumn decrees, the leaves dying in mauve and brown, he even discerns the turn of the wind among his trees, high up from the same position where he looked as a child, and behind, in the distance, the enormous shadow, the mulberry, hiding the sun.

With the engine barely running on this last downhill slope, a steep one.

He now clarified in his mind the entire course of the autumnal disguise of the landscape of his life, which hounded him everywhere, a notable restraint when it came to people and a silence enfolding him every time he should be joyful, a large shadow, a mist in the fields. He stubbornly rejected all joys, drove them away when they came on their own. He wanted it to be seen from above and only by himself—poplars and, yes, like his crops or his trees—that he really suffered deeply. A drunken cloud, he didn't know why.

That cherry tree doesn't seem to want to discard its leaves this year. Behind that broken border fence. Temptation. The ditch once passed by here, the water from the village spring ran down, now they keep this up above too, the remaining animals are confused and on returning plunge their snout in there, the soil around retaining an old dampness, water below and greenery caressing it with its roots. The smell of earth when it's refreshed by wind and water.

Life is like water, he thought, like the leaves, how many trees he'd planted and what fruit he'd had, and what remains in the end, wickedness and loneliness, there, the neighbor's already come down and is gathering his twigs, the earth is dry this year and has fooled everything, sometimes his son's driving makes him dizzy, he's told him about it...a thousand times, nothing...they haven't quarreled for years, but neither has he listened to him, a good soul and full of jokes, he learned how to rib people, wisecracks, the old man doesn't like any of this, who did he take after? There he goes again in the potholes, laughing away, the trees appear hungry, branches with half-dead leaves on their nodes, children from Africa on the television, fingers, hands, feet, body, all given by God and all taken back, a knife in man's heart, not that he asked for much, he'll have little to give up when the time comes, he's cold, old age, old age, and when at night I think of this soil that has surrounded me since I was a child, one evening he left and returned in the morning, and the soil smelled, smelled, and it's different in the darkness, the branches bend closer to the ground, and I remember that I heard voices and the trunks creaked just like cucumbers growing at night—if you've ever heard them, you'll understand—that's when I was happier than... no, and when the child was born and my poor old missus said to me, "You didn't want it, you didn't want it, that's what I've understood all this time, and you never said anything, you keep everything to yourself...," those are the evenings I remember.

The water reached right down here. Outside the fields.

Michalakis was the first to leap down from the tractor, an apprenticed lad, so he might learn something. He disappeared behind the cart and began unloading spades and picks and axes. His son slid down over the wheel.
"What do you think of him?" he said, dusting down his pants.

He didn't want this job at all. He cursed the hour that he'd said yes. Yet he couldn't not be there. Given that it was going to happen, he had to be present too.
He didn't sleep all night.

Dry and bare like that, without its leaves, it frightened him more than ever.
In the past, his every thought in the fields, his every movement, had to be approved by its branches, had to be given permission by its trunk; the crop depended on it, whether it would allow the sun through so the flowers might bloom on the branches of the peach trees, whether the breeze would scatter the pollen, and who kept the rain away from this side of the field?
As time passed, they grew apart from each other, tree from man, the old man stayed away from the fields and the son never respected it, never considered its opinion or its strength, even though it was the

envy of all in the valley; the huge shadow, the singular protector, the mulberry tree.

And the tree—with open arms felt loneliness: fierce winds ravaged the crops in recent years, the fruit fell from the trees, it gathered in its branches and waited for him not brought by the north wind's black clouds in the mountain rain, not even the heart of a frightened beast tied up in the hail and not even the drought of the recent years of the valley's silence, though yes, this it was that makes the train lines spark delay fifty meters behind his back when the regular services pass with the rails' dirty oil for years licking the snakes, deathly fertilizer for the trees. Till recent times it kept a hollow open in its trunk for the birds that had still remained and it awaited the day and the moment.

The drunken clouds were getting closer.

Getting closer too was Christmas and everyone in the village was preparing the wood for the big fire: on the evening before Christmas Eve, at midnight, they light the cedars, drink and sing. He'd ceased going up to the mountain, two pieces from the mulberry and that was all for this year, the rest for the raki, in the kiln, next autumn.

But how do you bring that giant to its knees?

His son spat on his hands and, together with the boy, picked up the pickaxes and the spades. They stood around the tree and began examining it. There was no question of them cutting through its trunk. They would slowly dig up its roots and then chop them accordingly so that it would fall on its own into the fallow field opposite.

They began digging the pit.

The old man at a distance.

He hung his life somewhere in one of the tree's shadows one afternoon when it was blowing, a tiny breeze lost among its leaves. He hung his life caught in its tangled branches and a few marks from its fruits on his face, like a blotch or a wound. His hands picked up the harshness of the trunk, of life that is, and they appear as one, smooth material, dark like solitude's all-night vigil. How often he dyed his clothes in its soil, both of them a variation on the same bit of life, on the same enemy.

Now his thoughts were tingling, they clouded in the light of the sun. His step took him to the edge of the field, opposite the tree, and he stared at it. He knelt down. The morning dew caressed his legs. From that place there he could see all the trunks of the trees arrayed, an endless line painted with asbestos—for the seasonal microbes—,and in the distance the border of his lonely life, the tree...

With the very first blows, birds flew out of the hollow of its last season. They scattered in its highest branches and waited for its reaction.

The pit was getting bigger by the hour.

"...and the field is changing now, and I won't come again, what's to keep me here now? Just a few years remaining and these alone."

He went over to them. Michalakis was chopping as though possessed, excess was a mark of these people, his son, sullen and sweating, raised his eyes and said, "What do you think of him?" and burst into laughter, the boy didn't speak, the roots had sprung up into the light, huge and red and white where the blade cut through them, milk the thread of life, and now they gazed at them and they spread all around them, the tree unmoving.

"...the old rogue can take it, it will put them through it, it's well entrenched in the soil...they're still digging, it's not easy to wait, I'm fed up...is it starting to lean or is it my imagination? The pit's got bigger...that's how I found it—that's how I ought to leave it...I didn't want to go against him, leave him, let him do as he wants and good luck to him...what, aren't they going to stop for a while..."

"Come on, take a break," he shouted over their heads, angry, now the roots had stuck in this throat, he cursed that choking with its smell of soil...

"...I can't bear for others to do it while I stand by watching...I don't want it, I want the tree, stop chopping, damn it..."

"Bring the water over so we can have a drink," his son said. "At last, the old rogue is starting to give."

All this, just before he himself jumped in and grabbed the pick axes from their hands.

He looked him in the eye and took a couple of steps back before going off for the water. The dark shadow split in two when he heard the birds flying at the very last moment as the great arm of its last season broke and he thought. 'They'll be...' he just managed to see the ditch on the border bringing down water, his life and his lungs being filled by a dampness just before in the corner of his eye a drunken cloud blotted out the last light of the sun.

Original title: "O yeros kai to dendro." Published in Yannis Kaisaridis, *Chroniko mias premieras* [Chronicle of a Premiere], Athens: Exandas, 1992, pp. 77-87.

DIMITRIS KALOKYRIS

Militsa or Mid-August Reverie

I have a well-known passion for libraries. In fact, even as a child, I always wanted, if I couldn't be a hunter, to become a librarian.

I've visited countless libraries: from the scantiest—a single book, albeit a thick one: *The Black Brigand Chief*—belonging to my grandpa, to the Grottaferrata in Italy, with its superb manuscript of the *Digenis Akritas* epic, its atlases, the maps of Ptolemy etc., and the national library in Buenos Aires, a building that was originally intended as a casino, but that ended up as the entrance to the library of countless books: the library of Babel, where piously guarded is the book of Sand.

One summer, in the mid-sixties and in the spirit of a rock internationalism diffuse in that period, I took part in a gathering of young people from West European countries. Our base was the Dalmatian coast, an area near Split, and from there we made various sorties to offer support to the unfortunate, while in the evenings, around fires, we solved the problems of starvation in the African continent, sorted out everything to do with the war in Vietnam and strummed guitars to folk songs and Dylan ballads, dreaming of poolrooms.

The program, however, provided for a period of practical aid. And so, with three others (two Dutch guys and an almost invisible Danish girl who night and day ate pale, shiny cornflakes that reminded me of fish scales), in return for basic food and even more basic accommodation, I lodged for two weeks in an Orthodox Serbian monastery, not of course with any inclinations towards the monastic life, but with the intention of getting away from the commonplace. Our task was to help in harvesting the vegetable crop from the monastery fields. I tried to limit my own particular task to the alphabetical and subject classification of the Greek books in the monastery library (for the most part psalters and similar) given that the other three were Protestants and, in addition, no one else knew Greek.

The term library is used here in a collective and metaphorical sense. In the huge room there were, indeed, around one thousand pre-war ecclesiastical works mainly in Cyrillic, the majority with red initial letters and red subheadings, a few in Latin and Arabic, an illuminated 14th-century gospel, the size of a daily newspaper and bound in leather, and some manuscripts of an instructional nature. The Greek ones were about a hundred in number, generally clothbound, the works of ancient historians published in Leipzig, a "Pilot" and two psalters. The one exception was a decayed parchment scroll, an undated manuscript containing the first four books of the *Iliad* in large-lettered script.

I occupied myself with the dusting and basic care of the books in the manner of a seasoned antiquary investigating the inner recesses of the great pyramid and I methodically wasted time by inventing librarianship problems so as to avoid any possibility of my having to work in the fields. As soon as anyone appeared at the door, I knitted my brows and began reading aloud passages from whatever book happened to be before me, with the result that the visitor, after feeling entranced for a while by the magic of the language and the rhythmic brilliance of the recitation, would turn on his heels in bemusement.

The books were stacked higgledy-piggledy in front of the east wall, which, by inference, had less damp. The rest of the room was filled mainly with old furniture, enamel kitchenware, chipped or broken glassware, vestments that had become breeding grounds for moths, old flags and a chest with low-denomination coins from various periods in the recent history of the Serbian monetary system. Strangely, all the monks, six in number, answered to the name of Chrysaor or, perhaps, because that's how I called them collectively, they thought that it was a Greek term of address, like "brother," "father," etc. and gladly responded. It goes without saying that we communicated usually by means of gestures or grunts, interspersed with a few words of Serbo-Croatian and Greek respectively here and there. For no particular reason, we had all, Europeans and Balkans alike, taken to calling the library using the Turkish word *kitabhane*.

Here too, our evenings were rounded off with marches, spirituals and raki from the cellar, while that of the monks by hymns and similar spirits.

One morning I was awoken by the sound of bells. Ten years later, I was destined once again to be awoken by the sound of bells in a hotel in Nicosia, where we had checked in the previous evening, having come to the island for the first time. I ran to the window and across the way saw a red flag with a crescent flapping in the breeze, while women clad in black were crowding in the street. I assumed it was an outbreak of fighting; I grabbed my bag and ran down four flights of stairs. In the hotel reception, however, total calm prevailed; various people were drinking their coffee unperturbed, others were reading their newspapers, and so I changed tactics, asking a clerk almost indifferently what exactly was happening. It was the anniversary of the July invasion and the protest march with photographs, banners and the pealing of bells organized by the relatives of those missing had just begun. The flag in the distance was from a guard post as we were close to the "green" line. At the same moment I was approached by a rather grave middle-aged man, who showed me his identification, a police badge, checked my name and time of arrival by boat from Piraeus by way of Rhodes, and just as, sweating profusely, I was ready to confess to all the literary crimes I was expecting him to pin on me, arresting me quietly and handcuffing my hands behind my back, he welcomed me with a handshake on behalf of the Tourist Police and politely wished me a pleasant stay. It seems it was a local custom. I was so relieved that I almost hated him.

So, one morning I was awoken by the sound of bells. The monastery was in turmoil. It was the eve of the Feast of the Assumption and festivities had been planned, while around midday they were expecting the local bishop. Some stalls had been set up with plastic toys and souvenirs, little cardboard icons and candles, light refreshments and some pitiful bobbin-like swings for retrogressive boat races for infants.

The festivities were poor, the faithful few, mainly women. Even His Reverence arrived on a scooter. He was quite young, despite his bulk, and his cassock flapped over the wheels gathering the dust. We were introduced with smiles and cordial addresses in languages incomprehensible to all of us. He also presented us to some of his relatives who had arrived earlier by lorry. Among them was his cousin, about my age, his mother, a farmwife with a colorful headscarf because of the occasion, and some little children of unspecified kinship sporting new haircuts.

Towards evening, and while more people from the surrounding villages had arrived on animals, bikes and trucks, fires had been lit, music could be heard from the yard and hymns from the church, and we all seemed to be playing in a neorealistic Italian film, I took my camera, an old East German Voigtlander, and went up to the bell tower to photograph the sunset and the festive all-night vigil.

The bell tower was wide and not much higher than the surrounding trees, yet despite this, a surprise was waiting for me at the top. Standing in the dark in one corner, over by the west pillar, was the bishop's cousin with her elbows on the parapet and her hands holding her face as she gazed at the festivities.

We soon struck up a conversation in our basic school English, though more through laughter, gestures and exclamations, like deafmutes during a fire alarm. We communicated chiefly through the names of bands and the titles of rock songs, even humming their tunes when it was necessary or feasible. We enlisted whatever we could in order to kindle the discussion and every so often we'd break out in peals of laughter. Everything seemed to us so funny, so bright, and we found a thousand pretexts to get closer to each other and let our hands touch exploratively.

And suddenly we found ourselves cut off from the festivities. As though the sound had been shut out on all sides. As though the night had been shut out on all sides. All we could see were our own shadows. I was thankful for the lightness of her clothes because of the summer. And just as an unusual excitement had spread all around and we saw the moon rising from the depths of our touching, our feet got caught up in a rope, we tripped and the bell rang. The sound was immense, deafening and dissonant, as though a shell had exploded, as though a gigantic ship were sailing off between us.

It was at that moment that I understood for the first time the meaning of the poet's imagery:

O ocean liner, you sing and ply...

She remained crouched among the ropes. An unwilling bell-ringer, I leapt like a prospective Quasimodo towards the parapet in order to look down below. All the people in the yard, the vendors, the clerics who were mixed in with the congregation, were standing motionless and staring at the bell tower as if waiting for the next move. As if waiting for an explanation for the alarm. As if waiting for an emotional outburst, a powder keg to explode, a minor doomsday, a miracle!

I noticed a hen crossing the yard and shining. And, as if by a miracle, I lifted the camera, raised my arm as if forewarning of a storm, activated the flash and supposedly took a commemorative snapshot.

There followed cheering and hilarity, a tumult of tetravalent consonants, uproar and applause. And so I went back down to the yard triumphantly. Of course, no one recognized me from close up with the lights. And when I thought, at last, to look around me, I couldn't see her anywhere either. Nor did I dare go up again and search more thoroughly. She, too, must have come down and quietly mixed in with the crowd. She was called Militsa; what that means, I've no idea.

Original title: "Militsa i remvasmos dekapendavgoustou." Published in Dimitris Kalokyris, *To mouseio ton arithmon* [The Numbers Museum], Athens: Agra, 2001, pp. 103-109.

IOANNA KARYSTIANI

Mrs. Cataki

F*inally, we offer our heartfelt thanks to the indefatigable Mrs Cataki, who, for thirty years now, has contributed through her baking skills to the success of the association's New Year soiree.*

I am a very boring person.
Unfortunately.
My surname, Cataki, is something I hear only in January, my month, and at least four or five times.
Five times.
This January in particular is one I like to recall in its every detail.
Unusual events had gone before.

The whole of the Governing Board and I, personally, as chairwoman of the town's High-School Association of Parents and Guardians, sincerely thank Mrs. Cataki for her kindness in providing us with three New Year cakes.

And yet it was raining seaweed.
Magdoula and I were waiting behind the drawing-room window, with everything ready so that we could dash over to the school's Christmas celebration.

Seventh of December.

All this happens rather early here, because those of us left go to Athens at Christmas, too.

Only cats are out on the streets.

Cats...

Forget the celebration.

Chaos.

Uproar.

Enormous waves.

They say it's the worst weather to hit us since '39.

Gale force twelve on the Beaufort scale.

The church's sundial took off.

The port was wrecked.

The pier was smashed.

The water surged forward, mountain after mountain of it, and it wrought destruction.

Foam burst into the sky.

Trees and empty cement bags flew through the air.

What we experienced was a Second Coming.

Houses sank in the face of the sea.

Lelis'...

Fishing boats and skiffs broke, crack-crack, as though made of bone.

It was two days before the gale abated.

And five hundred meters from the shore, the place was scattered with blue and red timbers.

Red timbers...

Shoes sank in beds of seaweed stuck on street corners and sidewalks.

During the storm, you saw people on rooftops, at windows, in bell towers taking photographs like mad.

The gale-force winds.

Kodak's pot-bellied employee did a roaring trade.

Suspect.

Very suspect.

December's harsh winter pushed all the planned celebrations into January. After the tenth. With the return to the island and to our own ways.

Our own ways...

So the orders came all together this January that stands out more than any other in my life, given that this year I completed my thirtieth year...

January and praise the Lord.
Fifth day of the month in Rafina.
The "Heptanese," a multistory hotel, ablaze with light.
All around, darkness and desolation.
Cafés and agencies all closed.
Scattered on the quayside, five or six people all in all, wrapped in their darkness.
Not yet half-past six.
Daybreak on Saturday.
January, my January, we've said that, at the beginning.
Winter at its worst.
Quiet as the grave in the ship's forward lounge.
Empty chairs.
Some sleepy seamen.
The piano tuner, where are you headed, the cakes is it, he said, poking fun at me, and disappeared in his own yawn.
Themos, the bookie's brother-in-law, was dozing.
Devil.
Though he finds plenty and does his business.
Nana, who's never given any cause for comment, is the only one not to be wise to it.
Silly goose she is.
Nondas next to the bar.
No longer the strapping fellow he was.
Finished.
In a crimson sweater and silk scarf, he's telling two aging blondes, unknown to me, about his cruise in the Norwegian fjords.
He was tired of telling them and they of listening to him.
The crimson sweater was wasted.
It did nothing to hide the pallor of the eyes, Nondas, you fool. You caught me looking at you, but immediately turned your ugly face

away, because you couldn't remember, and when did you ever remember, what my name is.

Not even my surname, no...

The time passed and the waiter standing behind the till was getting cold.

Newly hired.

Lily-white cheeks, smooth hands.

Up front on deck all the orange and blue plastic chairs were wet from the ceaseless drizzle.

My raincoat flapped.

Dry and rocky, Evia was getting close and it's bitterly cold. For God's sake, get the plastic cover out, said Takis, his first and last words to me throughout the trip.

Cousin.

Ensconced in his arms he had his big fat dog, a brown-haired bitch with swollen eyes.

Koko got seasick down below.

Every year, Takis—not to call him a twerp—takes a week's leave from work and goes with Koko to her island, to breed there where she's accustomed.

Out in the fields.

In the enclosure with the kumquats.

Kumquats.

Of all the family, I'm the one who gets burdened.

The others with parents or in-laws who have slowed down, small kids, karate, colleges, newborn goats.

January.

Besides, I'm unable to say no, what no, not even yes, it's so rare for them to ask me anything.

They simply announce everything to me.

Now, I too avoid saying too much.

They all regard me as a very boring person.

And they're right.

I spend Christmas each year in Drossopoulou Street. At Flora's.
Flora gets the benefit of having me; she hands me over the kids.
Devils.
She and George go out every evening, because he's a PASOK* party cadre.
Entertainment, bouzouki clubs, cards.
And I get the benefit of Athens. I have a Pap test and get my eyes checked as they're now in a pretty bad state.
And Takis, in his turn, gets the benefit of having me.
Company for him on the boat while he's taking his pet to the island, which through the thick clouds gradually appeared, gray and soft, like fur.
In no time at all, the boat unloaded, loaded, left.
Vanished.

Crowds of holidaymakers in summer.
Car horns, fights for the parking spaces.
The restaurants all lit up and playing cassettes with Parios songs. "Better to Be Alone" and you can't move an inch.
There's life. Movement. Money.
I don't like swimming or the hubbub, I'm also ashamed of all my extra kilos lower down...
And I don't own a car to be able to go a bit further out.
Sprats in the frying pan, Magdoula and I on the kitchen porch and waiting.
I've said it again and again, my month is January.
January and praise the Lord.

And as every year, we must not forget, we the conductor and members of the town choir, to offer our heartfelt thanks to Mrs. Cataki, who provided the delicious New Year cake, made with her very own hands.

Clumsily nailed to the north-facing balcony doors of the hotel's dining-room were strips of plywood to strengthen the panes of glass.
An awful sight.

---

* Panelliniko Sosialistiko Kinima. Greek Socialist Party

A forgotten rubber plant in a pot, its leaves yellowed and dusty, unwatered since the close of the summer season at the end of September.

When the tourist complexes rush to close, the restaurants stack the chairs under a shelter and the island shrinks, shrinks and once again becomes a drop in the ocean.

A drop in the ocean.

At the piano in his best suit, rotund and shy, is the assistant manager of the Electricity Board.

Not more than forty-eight, fifty.

Till now, he's never given any cause for comment.

On broad, white lining—not to call it a rag—Vasso had, rather poorly in my opinion, written A Happy and Prosperous New Year.

Beneath the rag was the teller from the Agrarian Bank, grumpy because of an ulcer, in my view.

The pediatrician with a new earring.

The paint-shop owner, another colorless character.

The shop owners from the main commercial thoroughfare, divided into two lines on the rostrum, according to their voices.

Their voices...

Smart at any rate.
With wide, grenadine-colored ties.
All of them.
Men and women.
The Christmas songs, German I think and various other foreign ones, the same year in year out. They sounded jaded now, twenty days and more after the festive season.
Jaded...
Up on the platform, the town's best singing voices bowed.
Below, the worst singing voices applauded.

This also happened at the cutting of the New Year cake at the Old People's Home, the shortest ceremony, and at the cutting of the New Year cake at the Seamen's Home.

Seamen's Home...

I don't mind baking for them, too, for free; it's a common secret that my husband is living with a second wife in Chile.
In Valparaiso.

Finally, let us offer our customary thanks to Mrs. Cataki, who, for precisely three decades now, has set her seal on our island's celebrations with her unique homemade New Year cakes.

My moment.
They all applauded me as I rushed from the adjacent room where I had been waiting for the signal.
Nimble, despite the extra kilos round my bottom, the gray two-piece, Ermou Street, garnished with a little velvet round the collar, a brooch on the lapel, a new haircut, and with Magdoula behind me.
The enormous cake on the wooden platter.
Sprinkled with confectioners' sugar.
Confectioners' sugar.
Thirty years, now that's a tried and tested recipe.
Nana, wife of that driveling Themos, and Diamanda obliged me, as always, by putting the pieces into paper napkins and handing them out to the official guests first.
Partly due to my nervousness, partly due to the chill draft from the door that kept opening and closing with all the kids and latecomers, I got covered once again by the white cloud. The confectioners' sugar fell like snow on my clothes. My glasses misted over. I could hardly see.
My eyes smarted. I hastily wiped the lenses with a paper napkin.
I looked all around.
They were all holding the little paper napkin, a pretty, yellow one with a sprig of fir and a red bow.
Red bow. Fokionos Negri Street.
The familiar one hundred and fifty people present.
With no absences.
The manager of the National Bank.
And of the Ionian Bank, too, with Nitsa and the sister-in-law.
The Port Authorities.
The teaching staff.

The abbot from St. Nicholas' together with his Belgian painter.

In an English coat, lovely thing, was Irene, somewhat loony, her defect barely hidden.

Fotis with his daughter, a prime pupil, just like I was.

Michalis and Peppy.

Nondas with the aging blondes he had with him at the "Heptanese."

The verger and all his family.

Takis, who was trying to find homes for Koko's puppies.

The twerp with the expensive cologne.

Leonis the sandwich vendor, ready to sacrifice himself for PASOK.

And the ever-present Mayor, who greeted me with a handshake, and said word for word, you've no luck at all, my dear woman, not to find the florin this year after a whole thirty years.

It fell to the priest's wife yet again.

Just like last year at the Seamen's Home and the Philharmonic's party.

Betty's bursting with luck, they all say.

And bursting out of her dress, in my view.

I received the usual questions about the baking powder.

I gave the usual answers.

Throughout January, the directors' wives shook my hand and presented me with gifts for my having completed thirty years.

A basket with various products from the Body Shop.

Athenian pralines.

An extravagant brooch.

Six good pairs of support stockings.

I always have need of them.

Magdoula ruins them.

And the piano, the assistant manager of the Electricity Board was playing blue eyes of summer, like two drops of the Aegean.

Beside him, the public notary was singing the wrong words.

Round about them, the others were holding their pieces of cake in one hand and in the other a pack of photographs, which kept changing hands in the near-freezing hall.

The gale-force winds.
The sea's fury.
Foam swallowing the sports ground.
Half a skiff perched on Anastassoula's pergola.
A mountain of broken timbers that the sea hid in a hollow in the rocks, next to Niki's pizza parlor.
Nondas' fishing boat, a nutshell turned on its side on the water's swell.
Heaps of seaweed by the rented rooms, Frau Lily and the Archipelago.
A giant eucalyptus lying on the pebbles, in front of the Association of Farmers' Cooperatives.
A dog, the gas station owner's I think, drowned with its chain wrapped round a marble column.
A marble column...

My month also has a lot of name-day celebrations.
John, Anthony, Athanassios, enough to elect a deputy, as they say.
The disastrous storm in December had put all the soirees back and so we had a succession of them.
Eleventh of January the boy-scout movement.
Fourteenth of January, parents and guardians.
Sixteenth, the Old People's Home.
Twentieth, the Seamen's Home.
Twenty-first, the Yacht Club.
Twenty-seventh, Kleanthes' newspaper.
He, himself—not to call him a gentleman—wrote and printed on the front page, in the top right-hand corner.
Mrs. Cataki, for thirty years the indisputable queen of the New Year cake.
And very flattering words below.
With tasteful humor.
I know about that.
The coin, an old silver dollar, was won by Mimi.
The very soul of the New Democracy party.
Fanaticism beyond all belief.

Everyone, however, had had their fill of pastry.

I saw my various paper napkins, tasteful they were, from various expensive stationery shops and department stores in Athens, left on the ledges, on the platform of the choir that had just ended its performance with the same program, in the pot of the lonely rubber plant.

The rubber plant...

Thrown down together with photographs of the gale-force winds.

The slices of cake in fragments.

Some had crushed them looking for the coin.

Some had taken just a bite.

The kids had simply licked off the caster sugar.

The familiar one hundred and fifty became a hundred, seventy, fifty.

There were just the last ones left.

I sat to one side.

At the piano, the assistant manager of the Electricity Board was playing Ah, Annoula of the Snows.

They had pulled up their chairs next to him and were singing along: the public notary who again had all the wrong words, the priest's wife and the bald-headed doctor from the Health Clinic.

Vekrellis, if I remember right.

From Mytilene.

Up to now, he's given no cause for comment.

> *Ah, Annoula of the snows*
> *I'll no longer be with you*
> *on the ninth of December*
> *when, Anna, it's your name day.*

Marios Tokas, whose songs I listen to, has never given cause for comment; he writes wonderful songs.

I sat back a little in the chair and took up the verses myself under my breath.

I knew them but I've no singing voice.

Half an hour later the north wind had abated.

Mrs. Cataki, it goes without saying that we've booked you from now for next January, the public notary shouted to me as he was putting on his scarf.

The priest's wife shut the piano and put on her gloves. Her husband was waiting impatiently in the reception.

I gathered up the baking tray and dusted off the sugar.

In my pocket, I felt the gift from the newspaper, a heavy metal horseshoe, a lucky charm for the New Year, and I went outside.

Outside...

His collar turned up, the assistant manager from the Electricity Board was hurriedly going down to the lot where he always parked his car.

He didn't offer to go two minutes out of his way to drop me off.

January the year before last, always January, January and praise the Lord, not to say the same things all the time, after the boy-scout soiree, the hall had emptied of kids, officials, parents.

The group around the piano was in full swing.

What a shame we parted, what a shame,
What a crime it was that we committed...

Outside it was drizzling continuously.

He closed the lid and got up, the last one. I waited discreetly sitting on the edge of the rostrum with the baking dish on my lap and the public notary's grenadine-colored tie folded on top.

He always loosens it when he starts singing; he puts it down anywhere.

Beside me is Magda.

Magda...

I'm very sorry, Mrs. Cataki, that I can't take you home, but I can't have cats in the car.

I'm very sorry, Mrs. Cataki, that I can't take you home, but I can't have cats in the car...

Original title: "I kiria Kataki." Published in Ioanna Karystiani, *I Kiria Kataki* [Mrs. Cataki], Athens: Kastaniotis, 1995, pp. 125-141.

Menis Koumandareas

Seraphim

He's called Seraphim. Short and rather chubby; his face along the same lines, round and sort of smiling, with brown eyes that allow a light to pass through. Given that his name happens to recall Holy Scripture, my mind goes to those little angels, the bare and chubby ones, with rolls of fat round their bellies, fleshy arms, unkempt curly hair and, of course, wings attached to their backs. Whenever I try to reconstruct Seraphim, this is how I imagine him, bare and rosy, and flying through the sky of my school years, and placed as if by mistake in the cubicle where I left him, in a railway uniform, collecting tickets.

He couldn't have been more than twenty-two when I first met him at the house of the director's wife; an agreeable youth with a broad forehead and fleshy lips, brown and friendly eyes, a shade plumper and possibly shorter than what youth reserves for its elect. He must have weighed at least a hundred and seventy pounds and he was no taller than five feet four. And being in the army at the time, he almost disappeared inside his baggy uniform. He was like an angel disguised as a Legionnaire mercenary. Nevertheless, even in his khaki tunic, at a time—forty-five or forty-six it was—when young lads did everything possible to get an exemption from their military service, he managed to survive.

The truth is that fortune must have smiled on him. A village boy from somewhere near Karditsa, without any pull or connections, he managed, instead of finding himself in the line of operations, to land himself a soft job in Goudi as a seconded driver. Shirking and *mañana*. He drove one of those enormous James trucks that carried soldiers like sheep to the slaughter, and with him completely nonchalant, always a fag and a smile on his lips, taking them and bringing them from the barracks to the firing range that was somewhere near Dionyssos, the place where they train marines today. Before long, those soldiers were sent to the Skra outpost—just as later they would be sent to Grammos and Vitsi—and to other key spots where the pot was boiling, ready at any moment to blow its lid. But he, Seraphim, was forever mounted on his James, with his rifle at his feet—an Enfield 32—charged with making the same journey, and always optimistic. Optimistic that he would never find himself in the firing line. Those monotonous and somewhat stifling journeys must, I think, have played a role in his later development, and I don't deny that his subsequent appointment as a railway employee was not simply coincidental.

At the time I am talking about, I used to frequent the house of some neighbors with whom my parents were on friendly terms. It was an impressive house; its master was the retired director of a Ministry, and his wife a lady of the old school who wore mauve hats and dresses made at Tsouchlos' and Etam's, two renowned fashion houses of the time. They had a daughter, Ismene, who during the Nazi Occupation had a fling with some Fritz from the Occupation Forces, whereas later following the liberation, she hooked up, officially now, with a Johnny, a New Zealander, ruddy-faced and ever carefree, a complete contrast to the hefty German, who always looked pensive. It was through him that I first learned of Beethoven's *Appassionata*, played by Ismene on a rickety piano. But what chiefly remains from that period is the music from the "Twilight of the Gods." Whenever I hear it broadcast on the radio from the various European festivals, it is always accompanied in my imagination by the step of the German sentry, with his helmet and jackboots, outside the command post that they'd set up in the same street as our house.

Much later, after having first rent the skies with the heavy Junkers transport aircraft, and having also meanwhile tasted the lightness of the spitfires, Ismene eventually made a safe landing. She married a Greek businessman, and is still alive, a wife and mother, with her record only slightly soiled with the memories of her wartime feats. It was in this same house, belonging to the director, that Matina worked as a maid.

Matina was from Olympia, Olybia as she used to call it. Twenty-three years old, plump, rosy-cheeked and ox-eyed, she suffered from overwork. She would wake up at daybreak in the tiny room they had given her, and that she called a hencoop, in order to be able to get through all the household chores—washing, cleaning, shopping, cooking and whatever else happened to pass through the mind of the director's wife. The only thing that came ready was the ice, brought by Michalis, always in his woolen undershirt—whether winter or summer—in his wooden cart, which he manhandled with a lot of noise in the back streets around Kyriakou Square.

I can still see poor old Michalis, in the same dark undershirt or one similar, and a jacket flung over his shoulders, without his cart, which became redundant with the coming of electric fridges, in the same way that he became redundant. Obliged by fate to retire, he now wanders, wracked by arthritis, through the streets of the same square that today is called Victoria Square.

It was this same Michael that Matina had eyes for. Strong and healthy the both of them, well-matched in everything, we all hoped that they would be united as soon as possible, "that those two people might settle down together," as the director's wife said with a lump in her throat. But Michalis remained cold, a real pillar of ice. And so Matina, who from morning to night shook her duster in the two-story neoclassical house in Ioulianou Street, had to be content with her sleepy eyes and her posing, rather like a roughly hewn Caryatid in her very own ancient Greek temple.

Whenever she wasn't dusting or cooking, Matina was always quarreling with her mistress. Their shouting, I remember, could often be heard as far as our house, which was on a parallel street, at that time without any intervening apartment buildings, together with the songs of Nassos Patetsos, Gounaris and the other idols of the period.

When the concert died down, Matina would shut herself in her hencoop to read "Treasure" or "Bouquet," the same magazines, that is, that her mistress read—and this is where all comparison between the two women stops.

One of those afternoons when I had popped round to the house of the director's wife on some errand or other for my mother—in reality to get away from my schoolwork—I found Matina sighing and with her eyes red.

"What's wrong, Matina? What's happened?"

I was sorry for girls like her and felt for them. I was sorry for their youth and their healthy villages, from where they had set out, unsuspecting, in order to conquer Athens. These girls, after having first been promoted from servants to maids, have today been renamed home help and have their own union. It's now rare to find them living in; they come late and leave early, with their National Insurance booklet in their pockets, and they refuse to work on Saturdays. I have to admit I no longer feel so sorry for them.

"So, what's wrong, are you going to tell me?" I asked her, looking through the half-open door in case the director's wife appeared. "You're always hanging around the maids," she'd said to me once, "you ought to know that your place is elsewhere!"

Matina sighed, lowered her head to one side, just as she'd seen the movie stars do, and remained silent.

"Don't you trust me? Pity, and I thought we were friends..." I said, glancing continually at the half-open door.

"What can I say..." Matina began, coquettishly twisting a lock of hair next to her ear.

With much ado, asking one way and then another, I managed to get it out of her. The reason was not, as I'd thought, her mistress or Michalis, but another star that had just risen on the horizon.

It was Seraphim.

She introduced him to me one day in her kitchen, while she was ironing and he, sitting on a stool with his army beret lying on the marble top, was smoking and drinking his coffee prepared by her very own hands. At first glance, I immediately took to him.

From that time on it became the routine; Matina ironing, him drinking his coffee and me coming and going, stealing time from the living room in favor of the kitchen. We'd start chatting. He'd ask me about school—to which he had never gone—and I'd ask him about the army to which I would inevitably go one day. With curiosity, together with a little worry, I'd try to pump him, how, I wondered, did the military see things, and whether the operations were coming to an end.

"Who's going to win, Seraphim?" I asked, provoking him, as though it were a football match, "Papagos or the other one with the beard?" Because I wasn't at all sure, and I was fed up of hearing my father talking about guerrillas and the Armed Forces Station broadcasting military marches. "Well, Seraphim, what do you have to say about it all? What's your opinion?"

"Oh, it's all the same," Seraphim said, raising his arms in the air, "I don't get involved—all that's for the bigwigs, and we," he added, with a sideways look at Matina, "are small fry and poor." And he went on smoking his cigarette and drinking his coffee.

His face, I noticed, clouded over slightly, but it didn't last long. He was soon full again of the good cheer that usually characterized him. Lucky man! He belonged to those few who have something inside them that communicates directly with what is to be found in nature. This makes them continually carefree and content, and if they ever become melancholic, the shift takes place completely naturally, something that in others, who are less privileged, requires work and technique. Whereas, I reflect, he was totally innocent.

"Ah, so that's it, is it," I persisted, "Papagos then…"

"Ooh, come on now, enough of all that," interrupted Matina, who never took her eyes off Seraphim and had scorched three pairs of Ismene's panties, "this week, they're showing 'A Girl and Three Sailors,' what about it Seraphim, shall we go?"

How had they met, I wonder? It was a period full of question marks concerning everything and everyone. "At the home of one of my cousins," said Matina demurely. "At the movies," said Seraphim, with a cheeky smile, like a little boy.

They had met in Omonoia Square, I think.

What was Matina doing in Omonoia? That was yet another mystery. I suspect it was on her way when going and returning from her cousin's who lived in the Thisseion district. But to go and return, she took the electric train. So why would she be in Omonoia? Anyway,

Omonoia suited Seraphim because it was there that the soldiers used to hang out, in front of the "Cronus" cinema, which, following the liberation, used to show all the latest cowboy films—and the enormous canvas advertisements outside the cinema were a sight for sore eyes, with their galloping horses and their tall cowboys waving lassos and chasing Indians.

It was at this cinema, after the Occupation, that, overcome with emotion, I'd seen my first American movie: "May Dawn Never Come," with Olivia de Havilland in the role of a highly sensitive woman who, towards the end of the movie, is involved in a car accident—something hitherto unknown—and Charles Boyer, a newcomer to Hollywood, goes to visit her in hospital, saying to her in a heavy French accent, "I love you darling." In somewhat similar fashion, though more à la greque, Seraphim must have said to Matina outside the "Cronus": "You really turn me on, baby!"

Seraphim's visits to the house of the director's wife began taking on a more official character—when, of course, Matina had assured herself that the young lad was coming with honorable intentions. His entries and exits were by way of the kitchen door. At that time, there were still servant's staircases, servant's rooms, and at least from what we heard, there were even servant's elevators in the rich neighborhoods like Kolonaki. But in any case, Matina was in seventh heaven. Seraphim may not have had the shoulders or the manly build of Michalis or his restless eyes that sparkled as he cried, "ice…ice for sale…" Perhaps, even for Matina's tastes, he was a bit too chubby and moon-faced. I imagine that Seraphim, too, for his part, must have had his reservations. As I quickly discovered, our soldier lad looked with boundless admiration at Miss Ismene, who, of course, seemed tall and slender and who also bought her dresses at Tsouchlos', and while drinking his coffee with his beret always lying on the marble kitchen top, he watched her out of the corner of his eye, greedily licking the edges of his lips with his tongue. People are never satisfied with their match, I reflect, but are always drawn to what is less of a match for them. However, it seems he willingly put aside his reservations, because, whatever the case, Matina had a little house for her dowry in distant Olybia and this more than managed to conceal her fat legs and soften her ox-eyed expression.

Anyhow, the soldier's visits to the house had become official and Matina sheepishly introduced him to her mistress as her "fiancé"—an expression that brought a slight grimace to the face of the director's wife—treated him to strawberry preserve and at midday, whenever he happened to finish his duties early, she had lamb fricassee or chicken Milanese waiting for him. I don't know what they both did during the week, but on Sundays, which was Matina's day off, they disappeared together, and when Seraphim happened to be on duty on Sunday, Matina, thoroughly inconsolable, would go to her cousin's, who hardly set eyes on her any more, and without stopping off at the "Cronus" to look, like the other girls from the provinces, at the photos of Gary Cooper.

I think they spent their Sundays in hotels. At that time, these hotels were still called "family hotels" though they were exactly the opposite of what their name suggested. It was the riff-raff who visited those "vile places," as they were referred to by the director's wife, who had a tendency to preach to Matina and do all she could to keep her from worldly temptation. In her little sermons, which were usually given in the intervals between their quarrels, the good woman's voice had a genuine note of emotion, given that she never passed over the doorstep of any hotel, nor did she ever see her image in the mirror in unbecoming positions, but always with a clear conscience and a gentle sigh, she enjoyed the tranquility and dignity of the family.

The comings and goings to the "family hotels" did nothing, however, to further the relationship between Matina and Seraphim. Despite all the girl's pleading with him "not to go with other women," "to write to her family and meet her folks," Seraphim remained adamant. "Leave it for now," he'd say to her, "it's not the right time—you can see for yourself how the situation is…" and he'd go on smoking furiously, sitting cross-legged in the kitchen. No more than two or three months had passed since his star had risen in the impressive house in Ioulianou Street when the soldier's visits began to get fewer and the delicious ragout went into the trash can—cold and spoiled.

I don't know what had come over the man. In my eyes, he seemed the most faithful and most grateful of men. Apart from his polite greetings for the director and his wife, he always expressed the warmest sentiments for my parents. For me, in particular, he nurtured a feeling of protective friendship, which was due to our age difference combined with respect stemming from the social gap between us. In fact, I imagine that, had the situation allowed it, Seraphim and I would have got on well together. Something that, later, remained a repressed desire of mine with others—"common folk," as my grandmother would call them. For the social boundaries were at that time still clearly drawn, even though polite society may have been moved by the friendship between Pit and the convict in Dickens' "Great Expectations," a movie that was being shown at all the main cinemas at the time and that was a resounding success. But movies are one thing and reality another.

And that's how it was with Seraphim.

For my father especially, who, as we shall see, became his benefactor, our soldier lad had the most selfless feelings. Whenever he would offer him a handout, he refused to accept it on the grounds that being a soldier and serving the country that fed and clothed him for free, it would be shameful on his part to accept money from others. "Heaven help us, sir, there's no need at all! Don't even think about it..." and he blushed like a little boy.

And this was also the reason why he refused to go and sleep at the home of his relatives, some cousins of his father's who had settled in Athens. Because, above all, what distinguished him was his sense of pride. So he was more than satisfied with the chicken and with the few crumpled notes that Matina managed to slip into his pockets or inside his beret, whenever he placed it on the marble kitchen top.

I still remember that hat. Floppy and greasy, supposedly from English cloth as the government and the allies would have liked to make believe, but in fact Greek felt from the flea market in Monastiraki. Lying on the marble top, it seems to me that it was in fact his halo.

Matina soon began appearing again with eyes red from crying. The director's wife came and told us everything chapter and verse. "Why are you crying, child?" "It's nothing, ma'am," answered Matina with a certain affectation. "It must be something!" Whereupon, together with the ducts in her eyes, Matina also decided to open her heart. To put it plainly, Seraphim was cheating on her.

"But that's impossible, who with?" she asked her in amazement.

"With her," she said pointing with her thick finger from Olybia at the house opposite. "Do you mean that he's found someone else? But how could he do such a thing!" "I told you, it's her," and she used the handle of the fluffy duster to point across the way.

As the director's wife was quick to realize, she meant Anthoula, a blond, saucy female that worked as a maid in the house across the way.

"Impossible," she said in order to shake her out of it, "she's short and scrubby, it's unthinkable that Seraphim would like that ninny!" But, of course, compared to Matina, Anthoula looked like a top model. And Matina shook her head with that wisdom that women have from the cradle: "I know what I'm saying, and if it's not with her, then it's with someone else!"

When the two families appointed me to ask Seraphim in a roundabout way and with tact, that forthright young man answered me: "Just between us, something was about to get going, but Anthoula is stuck-up and her mind is elsewhere." Who knows, I thought, perhaps she's managed to get round the usually unyielding Michalis. I tried to make Seraphim aware of his responsibilities to the girl, and without being too upset about it, he assured me that there was nothing amiss, that everything was over with Anthoula. "All right, but what about Matina?" I asked, looking him straight in the eyes—just as my mother did whenever she wanted to get the truth out of me—in an attempt to awaken the manliness in him, together with his feelings, the things that were slumbering deep inside his guileless soul. "Eh, Matina..." he replied, and leaned over to drink the coffee that she herself had prepared for him.

Meanwhile, apart from Matina's heartache, we also began to worry about Seraphim. As he told us, he was soon to be discharged and he was out on a limb. "How will I be able to take care of the girl, sir," he said to my father, "without any job waiting for me!" And my father remained pensive. It seems he'd spoken with the director, who had insisted that the relationship between Matina and Seraphim be preserved "at all costs."

"Heaven help us if she takes it into her head to leave!" exclaimed the director's wife, raising her hands to the heavens.

As I realized, it wasn't so much the fate of the girl that concerned them as that they wanted to keep that "treasure" in their home, so she wouldn't leave and take up with some bum or other. Because what other girl would put up with the shouting of the director's wife, what other girl would be so patient with Ismene, who flung her bra to the East and her panties to the West? The girl's untidiness, as her own mother once admitted, knew no bounds. In any case, I don't know why exactly, perhaps out of friendship for the director, perhaps out of pity for the girl, and without doubt out of fondness for Seraphim, who had won the affection of all of us, my father decided to find him a job.

This was a crucial turn in the life of the soldier, who until then had been doing the journey between Goudi and Dionyssos roughly two or three times a day. His only outlet would have been to return to Karditsa and settle there for the rest of his life after having seen and savored the marvels of Athens. Instead of that, he preferred a job as a ticket collector on the electric railway.

Up until then, the train had started out from Piraeus and ended at Omonoia. At that time, the route had just been extended towards the northern suburbs; the first station being Victoria Square, which, although constructed and ready for some time, had only just then begun to operate. Through his pull and connections, my father was able to come into contact with some officials at the Railway Company, and so, immediately after being discharged, which was in May I recall, at the height of a glorious spring that caused Matina even more heartache, Seraphim was appointed to his new job.

We celebrated his discharge and appointment at the director's house, opening a bottle of vintage Cambas red, and the small celebration painted Matina's blighted kitchen in rosy hues. That night, Matina even got tipsy and embraced Seraphim in front of everyone, and the soldier himself, now dressed in civvies that were slightly too tight for him, given that in the meantime the army had fed and fattened him up, danced a folk dance, knocking over a chair and breaking a plate for luck. We wished him "all the best" in his new job and secretly, of course, we also hoped he would soon "settle down." After the party, however, Matina's eyes were sorrowful. Seraphim's were innocent and joyful like a child's.

And so, from one moment to the next, Seraphim went from the khaki uniform of a soldier to the equally dull and undistinctive uniform of the railway employee. Once again a Legionnaire mercenary.

Yet the short time that he was in civvies was sufficient to dispel any delusion that he might have been under in the army. Did he take up with other women? Did he have a change of heart? Did he change his mind? Did he get scared? No one ever found out. Nor ever will.

From the very first day that he undertook his new duties, he disappeared and we never saw hide or hair of him. Sometimes he phoned to say he was "on duty," and sometimes he sent one of his colleagues—a long-faced and sickly looking guy—to tell us that he had "business to attend to." Matina remained in her kitchen washing and ironing; the quarrels with the director's wife began again, their shouting could be heard as far as Kyriakou Square, and the director took himself off to the café to play cards.

As for Ismene, who meanwhile had broken off with Johnny and didn't know what to do with herself, she brazenly announced to her mother: "Either she goes or I go—make up your mind." At that time, Ismene was without charm and without men, completely engrossed in her piano, which she played at the most unsuitable times and with the most off-key notes. "Get lost!" she snapped at her whenever Matina happened to be before her. And she'd adopt the air of a great tragedienne. And, for her part, Matina would give her the rough side of her tongue. In the rush of work, when she was in the thick of cleaning the house, she'd fling all the doors wide open and yell in her mistress' face, "Either you sort your daughter out or I'm packing up and leaving!"

It was a strange thing, I reflect, instead of the double disappointment in love uniting the two women, it in fact opened a rift between them. Because, of course, I couldn't possibly imagine that a director's daughter could be in any way the same as a servant girl from Olympia!

There passed a week of détente. No piano. No Seraphim. A worrying calm emanated from both houses. As though everyone was waiting for something to happen at any moment. I went back and forth with my schoolbooks under my arm and my heart in my mouth. Where would it all end?

Eventually, it must have been less than two weeks after Seraphim's disappearance, Matina, amid sobs and lamentations— which again could be heard as far as Kyriakou Square—asked for her wages and a reference letter. Amid sobs and entreaties, the director's wife tried to dissuade her. "Say something to her!" she said, elbowing me, "she listens to you!" But I, too, had lost all my influence. Seraphim was gone. Everything was gone.

They cheated her, I think, with her wages. They calculated days when she'd been sick and others when she'd been away at that infamous cousin of hers, and the girl found herself with only half the money due to her. No insurance, no nonsense at that time. Though they gave her a reference letter, and it was—because I happened to read it personally—an exceptionally glowing one; it mentioned the girl's good character, her skills, her industriousness and, above all, her ethos, which is what Seraphim had found so endearing.

It was a long time before I saw Seraphim again.

After everyone, in both houses, had vilified him and characterized him in the most defamatory terms—all except my father, that is, who, perhaps because he'd found him the job, always took his side—I was coming out of the station in Kyriakou Square one afternoon when I heard someone calling to me from the collector's cubicle. I stopped in surprise.

It was Seraphim.

Full of emotion, almost with tears in his eyes, he didn't want to let me go and kept asking about my mother, particularly about my father and, somewhat more discreetly, about the director and his wife. Not a word about Matina. Did he know, I wonder, that she'd left, did he know anything about the fate of that girl who we never saw again? I've no idea. In this matter, the ever-smiling Seraphim proved to be a veritable sphinx. I thought I saw a shadow passing across his face when I suggested he drop in on the director's wife. "All you have to do is knock on the door," I told him, "why don't you call, you never know…" For, it seems, the good lady still had her hopes pinned on some clandestine affair that supposedly still existed between Seraphim and Matina. The dreams of ladies at that time…

"Better, not," Seraphim said, "we can do without any more complications—who knows, maybe in time…" His face had clouded over again. And just as easily as he passed from one mood to another—as he'd passed from Matina to Anthi and then only God knows to who else—he said to me again: "Say hello to your father from me. Give him my regards, and tell him that I haven't forgotten him."

And for years, on Saint Anthony's Day, every year without fail, my father always had a gift left for him in the entrance to our apartment building, entrusted to Anestis, our janitor. Sometimes it was a cake, sometimes a bunch of flowers, sometimes a pullet from his pretty village—which he'd left for the mold of the underground—always with a note, a dog-eared card, on which he'd written with his poor spelling: with infinately good wishes, your divoted Seraphim.

Since then, journeys using the electric train have become more common, more carriages have been added and it is able to carry more people. I travel as a stranger among strangers, while outside the city unfolds, a stranger too, with its sleepy lights. But I, at least, am convinced that at the end of the journey or at some station along the way, a voice from a cubicle will stop me, calling me by my name.

A fraction fatter as the years pass, and rounder in the face, his hair thinning, and with a tired look; but with the eyes unchanged, light brown and ever-smiling, like an angel grown old nodding to me from within the cloud where he's parked himself in his retirement. A little more and from beneath his braid, tiny wings just so big will begin to sprout.

"Seraphim, it's you!"

"Me, me!" as though not fully believing it himself, with his hands straightening the lapels on his uniform, that was earned "at such sacrifice."

Might he have got married in the meantime, I wondered. I looked at his thick fingers—no trace of any ring. I gazed at the smiling face and tried to sound him out: "Who do you think is going to win, Seraphim; Papagos or the other one with the beard?" No reply. Veritable sphinx. Did he feel remorse, I wondered, for the price that others had had to pay, so that he might get his chance in the world? No, no sign of that—not even a trace. Lucky man! We exchanged a few words, recalled the past a little, laughed, felt sad more than anything, and then with that characteristic phrase of his, "regards to your father," we parted again.

It was years before I saw him again. As if his absence was deliberate, for some reason that I, at least, couldn't possibly imagine. At any rate, when I did see him again, he was no longer alone.

Original title: "Seraphim." Published in Menis Koumandareas, *Serapheim kai Herouveim* [Seraphim and Cherubim], Athens: Kedros, 1981, pp. 11-30.

Achilleas Kyriakidis

Nebraska

FOR IOANNA

TUESDAY, 4 JUNE

He removed his leg and placed it on the sidewalk. I was sitting in the café opposite. Then I saw him take out a small dish and place that beside him too. The merchandise and the cash register. All the time I was there, I saw no one giving him any attention, let alone money. He seemed resigned. He must have been between forty and forty-five. He was holding up a piece of card to the passersby, who didn't even look at it. Written on the card must have been something like I AM A CHRISTIAN SERB. I couldn't make it out exactly. And besides, my mind was elsewhere. My coffee was too strong to drink. I kept adding more and more sugar until it was too sweet to drink. I must

We'd agreed to meet at seven, in that café (is it still there?) opposite the church, in the small paved precinct. I shuddered at having to go down that narrow street with its fathomless potholes and with the cars parked on the cracked sidewalk. I left the car in the first parking lot I found and decided to walk. The weather was good and it was still daylight. I was wearing that checked shirt with the sleeves rolled up to the elbows. Images of her were going round in my mind: she gets there early, earlier, chooses a table in the sunlight, sits down, hesitates before ordering anything; she doesn't like coffee, doesn't know how to drink it. If the place has got music, it'll bother her, she have appeared upset. A man at the next table looked at me. And another one. Not suggestively. No. Just looking. Then one of them leaned forward and scribbled something in a notebook. A student. Somewhat old for a student. A writer. I looked at my watch. He was five minutes late. My heart was pounding. You're a fool, I thought to myself. You've known him for twenty-three years. Twenty-three! Wasn't he always late? He'll be here.

That first time, we both felt awkward. He spoiled it with his "I'm here!" Meaning what? We'd agreed that he would sit across from me. And look at me. Like the other man who was scribbling in his notepad. So I'd find myself in a difficult position and have to lower my eyes. Then he would buy me a coffee or something. From a distance. Or I'd ask him if he wanted to join me. But not "I'm here!" I was taken aback and said to him: "You're late." He ordered an expresso and for two minutes we said nothing. It was as if he were avoiding my eyes. Then he noticed my coffee. I understood and told him that, since we'd agreed to change everything, what better than to begin with our habits. He drank his own coffee in one gulp and got up. We paid on the way

doesn't want it: "I prefer to think a cappella." I turned and saw the paved precinct, the church, and a bomb-victim sitting under the steps begging. I looked at my watch: I was five minutes' late. I took a deep breath to gather strength and walked on determinedly. She was sitting with her back toward the door. I touched her gently on the shoulder. "I'm here." I couldn't play it out as we'd agreed. It was as if I'd come down with anchylosis, as if I were striving, in a script built around a lie, to prove my sincerity, to separate acting from playacting, to show my sound éducation sentimentale. I had to ask her before sitting at her table, to fabricate excuses, compliments and courtesies, to show my surprise when she told me her age and that she had two children, one of which was actually about to graduate from university. Instead of this, I preferred to show surprise on seeing her half-empty cup of coffee. As always, she had the answer ready; something about habits that we'd sworn to change. I said to her: "Shall we leave?" and I got up. I don't remember ordering anything. Nothing would go down—the lump in my throat had installed itself there since the morning. Outside in the street, I was about to take her arm, but held out. As we left, the Christian Serb was screwing his leg back on. It was getting dark. No more than two blocks away the neighborhood become disreputable.

Thursday, 20 June

I prefer to forget that disaster on the first day. Today, things went better. The guy in reception didn't give me that look. Perhaps he remembered me. Perhaps I don't remember well and it was someone else. We took the elevator and came out facing number 112. The previous time it was on the second floor. Same decorations, same light. Pink and green and dim. A smell of surrendered flesh. On the wall, a naked couple in a vulgar position. Rococo frame. In the other room I hadn't noticed any picture. Perhaps there wasn't one. Definitely there wasn't. I would have remembered. Just as I remembered the small television. In reception, together with the key, they give you the remote control. The first time we didn't turn it on. The first time we didn't do anything.

I sit on the bed trying not to look at him, but I can feel his presence beside and behind me. "Aren't you going to get undressed?" he asked me in a different voice. I get up. I take off my raincoat and myself back. I simply touched her slightly when, two streets further on, I saw the hotel sign lighting up.

This time she was standing in the street, waiting for me. It was hot, but she was wearing what we'd agreed: a short skirt and T-shirt under a lightweight raincoat tied loosely round the waist. I went up to her and said: "Lila?" She stifled a giggle before answering yes. "I'm Stathis." I took her arm and we went across the street. One of the letters on the illuminated hotel sign was flickering. "The B has burnt out," I said to the receptionist, vaguely pointing outside, just to break the ice. He didn't understand what I'd said and looked at me in the way someone looks when they haven't understood what you said. He handed me the key and the TV control. "112. On the first floor." We took the stairs.

The first time, we hadn't done anything—a complete disaster, ruined by our uneasiness. We stood in the middle of the room listening to the whir of the elevator and the humming of the air-conditioner. When I suggested we leave and do it again after a few days, she said we should wait a little, so as not to shoes. Still without looking at him. I don't know what he's doing, he's behind me. I sit back down on the bed and turn to look at him. He's standing there naked. Not completely naked. He's wearing a pair of those briefs that I bought him for Christmas, the white ones with patterns. He's acquired a paunch—he doesn't exercise.

He comes close and stands before me. He takes me gently by the neck and pulls me to him. My lips touch his flesh. He still smells of Yannis. Then he kneels on the carpet. I raise my eyes and meet his gaze. His hands reach up to my breasts, fondling them through the T-shirt. I help him to take it off. He leans forward and kisses my nipples. I fall backwards. Now his hand slides under my skirt. He's going to get a surprise.

give cause for gossip. The room today didn't have air-conditioning. I quickly took off all my clothes, apart from my briefs. She didn't look at me, but I wanted her to see me; to see that I was wearing the gift she'd given me. My body was getting flabby—it didn't suit me.

I recall that she was sitting on the bed, I knelt down before her and undressed her. I was careful not to let her name escape me, and I kept repeating Lila, again and again, four or five times, as if there was no other way for me to consolidate that false name, to familiarize myself with it, at the same time that a sense of forgotten trepidation grew inside me once again like a stalactite; at the same time that my hands traced the familiar and unfamiliar geometries of her body; at the same time that with a sweetly adolescent flutter I discovered that she wasn't wearing anything under her skirt.

Monday, 1 July

It's raining. And today when it's raining, I'm not wearing my raincoat. I go straight to the hotel and ask for room 112. I wait for them to clean it. A couple comes down the stairs arm-in-arm. The couple that had used 112. The girl was radiant. The boy looked like our son. Has he ever been here, I wonder? The

It was a Monday and raining. "The nuclear tests are to blame," the waiter said to me. "They've upset the balance in the atmosphere." An ecologist. I felt like telling him that, at this stage in my life, I too was carrying out ecological tests. I arrived early and decided to have my usual expresso, to recharge my door to the room is open. On entering, I bump into the maid who takes one last look round the bathroom and goes out holding a bundle of dirty sheets. She's foreign. She gives me a passing glance. One that's humble, but also inquisitive. I don't know what she's thinking. I don't know in what language she's thinking or in what language she's judging me. I shut the door behind me with a feeling of fragile superiority. I get undressed and lie down on the bed.

The only light I've left on is the wall light over my side of the bed. And the bathroom light, that pours through under the door. As he comes in, his eyes are sparkling. There's nothing smiling about him. He wants me to be afraid of him. I want to be afraid of him. Stark naked, he comes and stands over me. Like the other time. Not like the other time: he grabs me by the scruff of the neck, lifts my head and presses it to his belly. And lower. My lips slide over his skin, catch in his pubic hair. My tongue smoothes the roughness; finds his masculinity swelling. He chokes me. And he says things to me. Then the stranger takes me forcefully, almost vulgarly. I don't say a word. He dresses and leaves. Vulgarly.

batteries. The coffee slid down my throat with its familiar bitter taste. "Mithridatism," I'd once told her. "Not even a poisoned apple can affect me." I walked the two blocks at a brisk pace and arrived at the hotel out of breath. "The lady is waiting for you in 112." In order to give myself time to get my breath back, I called the elevator and waited for it to come down from the third floor. Who knows who had just taken it up to the heavens. Some trashy music undermined the already crumbling aesthetics of the place. The door to the room was half-open.

Her eyes shone in the dimness. I threw off my clothes in almost threatening haste and let them fall to the floor. As I went over to her, she pulled the sheet up to her neck—Savina in the face of Evil. I was excited by that splendidly vain gesture of defense; the useless linen cloth that unfolded in all its whiteness. The familiarity fragmented into grains of fear and only fractions of a vague trust still survived behind the protection of the role. I subjugated her as I'd reckoned: depriving her of her last inhibition, of her last hidden desire that she thought was buried deep and impregnable. Then I made her mine as though I'd never had her.

Tuesday, 9 July

Our appointment is in the hotel reception. I arrive second. It's the first time I've ever arrived second. I stand for a while on the sidewalk opposite and try to guess which of all the windows with the closed shutters belongs to room 112. The B from the sign has given up its neon ghost. I point it out to the receptionist and remind him that we'd told him about it. Just like that: "We told you about it." *We* told you. He assured me that he would take care of it. When I asked him for the key, he said to me: "The gentleman" and pointed to him sitting on the couch, amid the Formica and the plastic flowers.

I ask him why he didn't go up; he asks me why I'm late. I tell him I had some problems at home, I couldn't get away, my husband. He tells me not to let it happen again, gets up and goes towards the stairs. "Come up in five minutes." He's gone up four or five stairs when he suddenly turns round and shouts: "Did you hear? In five minutes!" The receptionist pretends to be looking at his papers, what papers indeed. A disagreeable melody reaches my ears and deadens my nervous system. Within three or four minutes, my entire body is an anaesthetized tooth that doesn't

I arrived first at the hotel and started up a conversation with the receptionist. He told me that business was good and they were thinking of refurbishing the place, of installing air-conditioning in all the rooms. "I don't wish to be indiscreet, but isn't 112...I mean...doesn't the heat bother you? Isn't it too hot?" It was too hot. On the previous occasion, the sweat had been running down my face and I'd felt her hands sliding over my backside, like a wrestler trying to get a hold. "We like it," I told him. Then I asked him for the key, but I didn't go up. I collapsed onto the first of the mustard-colored couches and sat staring at the door.

Something came over me when I saw her talking to the young receptionist. For the first time a belated alarm sounded within me, a siren that had been dormant for decades, a warning signal for loss and alienation; the same alienation on account of which we both got involved in this farce, on account of which we changed identities, like snakes before summer, in order to clothe ourselves in the garb of refound love. And when she told me about her husband, I got up and went up know what kind of pincers to expect.

The room is pitch-dark. I leave the door open for a while to exploit the light from the corridor. I hear the sound of his dark voice: "Close the door!" I begin to discern outlines, shapes. The bed. I go towards it till my knee is touching against it. The finish line. Without any photo finish. I've passed the baton long before. I hear the sound of bare feet. Now his breathing. Now: "I don't know who you are, but this wants you." I try to stretch my arm behind me to feel, but he pushes it away violently. His arms close around me, grab hold of my breasts. Then one of his hands goes up to my mouth, forces it open. Like burglars, first one, then a second finger enters. I suck on them. Now all my senses savor his fervor. He slides his other hand beneath my skirt, finds the smooth triangular satin and trembles, pulls it down with small, knowing movements, till it falls lifeless at my feet. He pushes me onto the bed with his knees and gasps. His adolescent impatience. The pain of his impatience. And he's almost ready to come: "Does your husband know what a whore you are?"

to the room alone, while my head was spinning with the shades of fever, anticipation and retaliation.

I went into the room and turned on the television. On one of the hotel channels there were two men and one woman; on the other, two women and one man. Before turning it off, it occurred to me, two-bit intellectual that I am, that the difference between eroticism and pornography is that pretense of pleasure and pain. I got undressed and turned off all the lights. I felt an excitement I'd never felt before and surrendered to it. I wanted her like crazy. I wanted Lila like crazy; that unknown woman with an unknown husband, who made love in cheap hotels on cheap pretexts. I had to quell the arrogance of her independence, to turn her surrender into submission. Upright and erect, I saw her standing in the lighted opening of the doorway, on the border between the sensuous blackness and her colorless irresolution. I had to make love to her, showing disdain for her body, belittling her by not letting her see the face of the man who was debauching her white flag, who was penetrating her dry resistance, who talked dirty in hoarse whispers and, at the end, screamed: "Does your husband know what a whore you are?"

Thursday, 11 July

I'm at home and I'm getting ready to go out. My husband's in the bathroom. I wonder whether I ought to leave now while he's in there. I can't stand him asking me, I don't know what to say to him. I can hear him taking a bath, hear the water running, the water splashing out of the bathtub, the water that I'll have to bend down to wipe up when I get back. The kids are out. He comes out of the bathroom with the towel wrapped round his waist. His skin is pale; a few drops of water are still clinging to the hairs on his chest. I stop looking at him. I don't want him to understand that before I was looking at him and now I've stopped looking at him. My nervousness written all over my body in the bedroom mirror. His gaze is refracted into tiny threatening looks. I pretend to be fixing my hair. His reflection grows. He comes over and kisses me on the ear. He suddenly pulls back: "Have you changed perfume?" I make no reply, I get up to go. He holds me by the wrist. "Where are you going?" And then, louder: "Where are you going?"

She had turned on both reading lights. She was sitting on a corner of the bed, fully dressed and crying. I was holding a plain plastic bag, which I threw on the bed to reveal the black lace of a pair of vulgarly red panties. I went over to her, took her by the chin and lifted her head. "Did he hit you?" Beneath her tears, on her right cheek, was a wet scratch, the mark of an avenging ring, a crevice from which drama would sprout like a blade of wild grass, an underlining in red of a grammatical infelicity in Marina's schoolgirl composition "How I intend to save my life from life," a violent continuing solution for the skin, a continuing solution for a relationship that took the opportunity to escape whenever the kids opened the door to go out, that floundered in long mirrors no longer able to prettify anything, that had now begun to evaporate with the speed of a volatile perfume.

Friday, 12 July—morning

We're meeting at the café. I'm wearing my dark glasses. Because

I fell in love with her quietly, kissing her on the mouth, out of which of the sun, because of the bruise under my eye and because I haven't slept all night. I don't know, I told him over the phone, I have to see you. In the morning? In the morning. As I turn the corner, I see him arriving, almost running. "Why here?" he asks me, out of breath. I make no reply and sit at the first table that has an umbrella. An advertisement happily affords me its shelter. He sits down beside me and orders coffee for both of us. He takes hold of my hand and caresses it, and I notice his: nice fingers, long, the chewed nail on his little finger, the mark of the wedding ring on the one next to it. I tell him I simply wanted to; to see him, see him in the light of a late-summer morning before that momentary whirl of love. He says to me that nothing, never, no one else, nowhere. I say to him that everything, always, endlessly, everywhere.

came words both big and small, irregular breaths, in the glaring light of the unexpected tenderness, as through the open window poured the noise of the heat and the dust of a former life, frayed at the elbows. I fell in love with her with the humility of the victor and the courtesy of the vanquished, caressing her ear with unpronounced happiness, dowsing with my tongue its erogenous deposits. I fell in love with her patiently, and when, in the end, Lila uttered the verb, I too allowed the spasm to elevate me to that precipitous eternal moment. I turned over on my back, pulling her with me, while my passion abated amid the liquids. I held her in my arms for a long time, till I heard her break into sobs.

Friday, 12 July—evening

"You have new messages in your voice box. First new message: 'It's me. Your phone is off, but it's better that way. I can't take any more. That's what I wanted to tell you this morning, that's why I asked to meet, but I couldn't. I can't take any more, I can't take any more of him. Last night at home all hell broke loose, he tried to hit me again. This morning he followed me. I could almost hear him. He must have seen you arriving out of breath. He must have stood on the corner and watched us having coffee. Listen to me. I can't go on. We have to kill him'."

SATURDAY, 13 JULY

I'm standing across the road again and looking at it. I'm wearing that T-shirt and the lightweight raincoat tied loosely at the waist. Two Pakistanis pass by. They stop and naturally assume. I don't pay any attention to them. I'm looking opposite at the building with all its shutters closed, the building with all its sighing, with its neon packaging of love. A worker hanging from the third-floor balcony is changing the burnt-out B in the sign. I start to leave, then turn round again to look, Lot's wife without Lot: the hotel is renamed in the evening twilight. Now everyone will stop calling it NE RASKA.

Original title: "Nebraska." Published in Achilleas Kyriakidis, *Tehnites anapnoes* [Artificial Breathing], Athens: Polis, 2003, pp. 71-87.

Pavlos Matesis

Murder's Singular Taste

He stared at the fresh corpse exposed on the night-time sidewalk. He stared at it and it stared at him too. There's no point in you staring, he shouted. A sixty-year-old man, he shouted, and at last I've managed to commit a murder. Now that I'm a pensioner.

He put the revolver in his pocket. Thankfully, I got him with the first shot, he thought. He was forced to economize, the bullets weren't cheap, all he had to live on was his pension; a man without means, he had no room for any excesses. His money only just sufficed to allow him to eat frugally.

It was his first murder. At the age of sixty. Hitherto, the only pleasure his social circumstances had allowed him was eating; he had no money to spare for ideologies or mass demonstrations or memories, it was barely enough for his meager diet.

While still young, an endemic hunger, a greed for tastes had visited itself upon him; it lay heavily on him. All he dreamt about was tastes. He had no time for social mobility, nostalgia, ideological development or cultivation. Particularly during the last three years when he'd been economizing and had subjected himself to extreme hunger until he'd saved enough money to buy a revolver. Very occasionally, when he was afraid that he might rebel, he would buy foods with singular tastes like chocolate, eggs and peaches. He memorized their tastes, to have something to call his own.

And tonight, as soon as he had committed his first murder, the hunger ceased. He'd been given a reprieve, he thought. Afterwards he realized that it had left him for good. But another thunderous taste rose up and lay heavily on his tongue and eyes as he stared aimlessly at the limp corpse. A taste with colors. The young lad had started writing a slogan on the opposite wall. With a paintbrush. He had secretly watched him. The lad hadn't realized. And as soon as he had seen that the lad had made a third spelling mistake, he had pointed his gun and killed him with the first shot. Music was pouring out of the nightclub close by and the shot went to waste, no one heard it. Not even the sound of the body falling clumsily. The lifeless body, that is.

It looks like I'll be giving up food, he thought on the third day following the murder, as he engaged in blank target practice in his room. It had been three days since he'd had any desire for food. The taste that had stayed with him from the moment of the murder wouldn't leave him. That is to say, numerous tastes had pervaded him. Cheery, they had risen from the sidewalk with the dead body and, as if obeying him, were colored tastes in God's shades. That's my miracle, he cried.

Because initially he had hoped to perform a miracle. To no avail. He had tried to stop a passing bus with his gaze, but it had continued on its way and crashed into the kiosk opposite. He remained dissatisfied and, what's more, he was hungry; two days without a penny and his pension wasn't due for three days.

And that's how he came to decide on the revolver.

It was the third night following his first murder and he set off to go to the victim's spot, satiated, without having or wanting anything to eat. With a certain arrogance. The unfinished writing with the three spelling mistakes was still there on the wall; the music from the neighboring nightclub had gone, but the corpse was lying there obediently, an insignificant object. A young lad who made spelling mistakes on public walls. He felt angry and immediately went to the nearest police station, you've left a corpse in the street where I live, he said to the Duty Sergeant, it's stopping me from getting around, I demand that it be removed forthwith. Of course, you're quite right, I apologize to you on behalf of the Police Force and I thank you for your cooperation, the policeman said very politely. You in the Police Force have your work to perform, he said to the Sergeant, you're the ones who guard the Citizens, it's unacceptable that corpses and murders should hinder you in your work. Have it removed from your streets.

No one would ever have suspected that a socially insignificant and elderly man with a rather dirty collar could own a revolver and so no one bothered him and so he committed the second and third murders immediately afterwards. The third was a young woman who used heavy makeup, dressed lavishly and went out begging at night.

The demanding and voluminous taste now established itself permanently in his eyes and on his tongue, spreading through the whole of his stomatic cavity; he was no longer hungry, he no longer allowed himself to eat. And his saving on food enabled him to buy bullets, now he could shoot comfortably, up to two bullets for every victim. He began buying imported bullets. In fact he also decided to close the victim's eyes, for reasons of economy: why should they stay open given that they no longer functioned?

And from all the shades of taste he took in, he began to get fat. Initially, he was very slim. Now he was storing up the tastes. For a rainy day, he thought. Saving them. Some of them he hid in his pocket, others he arranged in his fridge. Sometimes, he'd take them out and rub them on the lapels of his coat in order to use them as cologne during his walks.

After the fourth murder, there was a full moon every night.

He went on night walks, moonlight patrols, and watched to see who was hindering the harmony of the Universe. And in this way he assisted the police in their work. He knew that the Universe was from its inception unfinished and that those who misspelled hindered its consummation.

For one night as he was looking up above, he understood everything: the Universe is a single Living Organism. A Body. But the Body's limbs don't know this, they think that they are self-sufficient and act independently. And man is a parasitical micro-organism, accidentally attached to this Lovely Body, but he knows nothing, he has understood nothing about this Universe which is a single Body. This was a secret that had been kept hidden from the parasites. In any case, man didn't know that he was a parasite, or even where he lived or that he was alive. Nor that he was being accommodated without having been granted accommodation permission. So, the parasite Man illicitly devours food from the Universe's body, lives and commits nighttime spelling mistakes and, disguised, begs in the moonlight.

The pensioner decided that the parasite should not be allowed misspellings. And he bought the revolver. He bought it with bloody savings, he yelled at the ninth carcass. He didn't even turn to examine the face, sex or age of the victim on the ground. Not even if it had blonde hair. He didn't even concern himself with closing its eyes. He hadn't eaten since he had shot the unfinished slogan with the three spelling mistakes; he no longer needed to eat, he had grown fat, with so many tastes laying siege to him, they'd become quite irritating now. He chose whichever one he wanted, pinned it to his lapel as a carnation, to have a taste for company. The others he kept in the freezer in reserve. And those that he kept in his pockets he gave to no one, not to beggars, not to anyone.

He recalled his first victim lying on the sidewalk, unknown. No one claimed him or desired his presence; it seemed that his absence carried the same weight as his life.

He roamed at night, patrolled, and guarded the Universe, he pampered it. On his own, he had guessed the rejection process. The Universe had got wind of the presence of the micro-organism called the parasite Man, it had caught him red-handed. And this is why the Universe had set in motion the rejection process, in order to get rid of the parasite Man.

He stood aside; a truck was passing with two open trailers. It was carrying a long coffin, some seventeen meters long, the road was narrow and the driver was having difficulty. He left his revolver next to the coffin and took off for the fields.

In the morning he encountered the countryside, it was green. Beside him was a snail, buried inside its shell, only its face was out in the world. It was raining. Pity that I no longer have my revolver, shouted the pensioner, now where am I going to find shelter?

He took off his overcoat and began creeping, headfirst, into the snail's shell. It was bewildered and resisted the intruder. But he shouted, I'm cold, I'm cold, and kept going, headfirst, so that in the end the owner continually gave way and the intruder was able to fit completely inside the snail's shell, only his shoes remained outside.

He tried to turn over, but there wasn't enough room, he was fat now. And so he gradually got used to looking at the world outside through the toes of his shoes, with his face glued against the flesh of the original owner, and he never managed to turn round and see the other's face. All he could hear was his breathing.

And the only taste left to him was the taste of the flesh that closed his lips and blocked his vision. And he lived all his life inside there. He got used to it. The original owner got used to it too. Though he always dreamt of running away, in the end he lived at the back of his abode, a captive and would-be escapee.

Original title: "Foni spanion yevseon" (1992). Published in Pavlos Matesis, *Ili dasous* [Wood from the Forest], Athens: Kastaniotis, 2000, pp. 79-86.

Amanda Michalopoulou

Lermontov

I would have recognized her anywhere. She still resembled a schoolgirl who had been hastily dressed by her mother: jeans with colored pleats, a mauve knitted dress over the top and over that an off-white three-quarter-length leather coat with stitched seams. She was also wearing a fisherman's hat. One of those with the wide brims. Ill-matching clothes, but which seemed to match because she was wearing them, as in the past, with ease and confidence. Her hair was unkempt and I felt embarrassed for having started straightening mine with the hairdryer. I raised my eyes, pretending to be looking intently at a gutter on a building in Solonos Street. But she had seen me. Nothing escaped her.

"For heaven's sake Irene! What are you doing here?" she said, as though we had bumped into each other in some distant corner of the planet. She grasped my elbow. I remembered her need for physical contact, the way she held onto shoulders and arms.

"I live here, just up the road. What about you?"

"I came to see my mother. These last few years I've been living in New York."

She didn't say "my parents." I confined myself to nodding my head sadly. It's often the case with old school friends. One of the parents is either in hospital or has died.

"So it's like that, is it?" I said. "A tree grows in Brooklyn!"

"Exactly. Isn't it funny? I live in Brooklyn!"

I said it on purpose to see whether she remembered the incident with the bookcase, but Katerina just laughed nonchalantly and added: "On East River's Other Bunk." We laughed uncontrollably, just like then, at the bad Greek translation of the book.

"Is Francie Nolan still sitting under her tree?" I asked.

"Yes, and she's chewing mints. The tree, the house and the wooden fence really do exist. They point them out to the tourists on the double-decker buses as an attraction." She smiled from ear to ear, in American style, like people who travel a lot and feel incurably homesick for everything. Something in her smile told me that for her the past was taken for granted, inevitable. Two old school friends were meeting in Solonos Street, on a weekday afternoon, to the accompaniment of car horns. Twenty years had passed and they remembered whatever suited them. The fact that they once went to school, carried satchels, wore uniforms is depressing in itself. Perhaps it overshadows the disappointments that girls get from each other when they are teenagers.

The thought flashed through my mind that perhaps I hadn't disappointed her too much. She may have not expected anything of our friendship or have placed things in their true perspective from the beginning. For me she remained the heroine in both dreams and nightmares. Whenever I felt shame or jealousy or a sense of responsibility, her image flickered in my mind: a girl in colorful clothes, red satchels, curly hair. The image of a sprite. In the school photographs she looks like a fairy. Whatever fascinated me about her dissolved through the intervention of the photographic pixel. What was it exactly that I was jealous of? And what was I so afraid of? I wonder at myself as to why I tirelessly attach intentions to people.

"And what do you do in Brooklyn?"

"Well, I live. I went there for a trip and stayed. I can't even tell you how it happened. I married a musician. I have a small health food store. What about you?"

"I work for a newspaper. I write book reviews."

"Book reviews?" She broke into a chuckle. "Only to be expected. What with that bookcase…"

"What do you mean?" I asked with some difficulty. I'd lost my tongue.

"You always had your books so meticulously placed. Order always brings perversion."

"Perversion?"

"Come on, I'm just teasing you. You had a craze for books. It was natural that it would lead somewhere."

So she had understood nothing. Was she less intelligent than I thought? Or was it simply that she trusted people more than I did? That must have been it: trust. She opened the door of her house and stood aside to let me pass. With dignity and politeness and giving. Come in. Shall we pinch some of my father's cigars? Have you read Mayakovsky? Oh, ask your mom to let you sleep over tonight! She was fifteen and she was opening up her house and offering it whole to one of her school friends. And her school friend went in, lit a cigar and walked mesmerized towards the bookcase. She blew the smoke onto the creased spines of books on history, sociology and poetry and slept sweetly beneath a hand-knitted blanket. Hanging on the wall was a poster of a naked boy peeing into a corona and two dark lithographs. The one depicted conflicts: profiles of warriors with long-barreled rifles. The other depicted women who seemed to be suffering. Concealed beneath their headscarves were hard, rectangular faces. The house smelled of coffee and cigarettes, even in the bathroom. Katerina's parents smoked, drank and read all day. They had a study in the house and concerned themselves with topics that, at that time, were of interest only to certain professors and radio announcers: how the educational system might be changed, whether there would be any protest rallies, how far the government was to blame. They always looked extremely busy. They shuffled papers around, phoned friends with similar interests, bought poetry by Ritsos and Brecht.

We didn't have books like that, we didn't have a house like that. Our living room was dominated by a rosewood bookcase. Reddish watermarks spread in concentric circles on the shelves, giving the impression that some forgotten crime had been committed there. A crime was indeed committed there, but it hadn't been forgotten. At least not by me.

Our bookcase served as a wall unit. It began from the ceiling and ended in a small movable table that creaked on its two metal rails. On Saturdays, the day the house was cleaned, my mother would push the table into the body of the unit. Order and absence went together in our house. We had to hide whatever stood out. During the rest of the week, the table remained opened out. We covered it with keys, newspapers, even jackets. Resentfully, my mother tidied them all away. She stared sadly at the table, as though she blamed it for being there and providing an excuse for our untidiness. In place of legs, this sliding desk was supported on two large cupboards in which we locked our books. The keys to the cupboards were huge, monastery-like. They would have been better suited to locking something else. But our parents insisted on our locking the books up so that they wouldn't get dusty.

They both worked in a pharmaceutical firm and had bought the *Domi* Encyclopedia with their Christmas bonus. They referred to the encyclopedia as though it were the quintessence of human knowledge. "Look it up in the *Domi*," they would say whenever my younger brother asked why the radiator was divided into segments or the elder one asked how birds are stuffed. My father would caress the twelve leather volumes with their gold edges, but he never opened them. It was sufficient that it added to our meager collection of books: two illustrated cookery books, the *Holy Bible*, the *Family Doctor*, *Conventional Lies*, Alphonse Daudet's *La Belle-Nivernaise*, *Mankind's Greats*, Grace Metalious's *Peyton Place*, *My Child Is Problematic* from the Parents' School of Paris, two or three *Polyannas* for me, *Huckleberry Finn* for Yorgos and Manos, and if I'm forgetting something it's because I can't bear to remember. Our bookcase made me feel ashamed and at an age when, in any case, you're ashamed of almost everything.

On the highest shelf my parents had placed three stuffed birds. Because of the height, for years my brothers and I saw only their bellies and the underside of their beaks. As for the other two shelves, these looked despairingly empty in spite of the fact that they were full of tiny objects: silver-plated bowls with chocolates in the shape of daisies, amber worry beads, a porcelain shepherdess with her goose, a lamp, an icon depicting Saint George plunging the tip of his lance into a faded yellowy-green dragon. I had instinctively realized that my parents were conservative in their tastes. They neither drank coffee nor smoked. They bought a newspaper that Katerina's parents scoffed at and they always left it open at the page with the TV programs. They had mats for the wooden floors and always wore slippers.

At my friend's home, everything took its course without any program, without any precaution. The books were taken from and put back on the shelves without ever being dusted and the tables were constantly full of various objects, magazines and cigarette ash. I was envious of the family's spontaneity and their lack of delusion when it came to matters of use and wear: the books were there to be read, the sofa to get dirty. I dreamt that I too lived in their house and that I read Steinbeck's *In Dubious Battle* or *Cannery Row* with my boots on the sofa.

For Katerina and me it was the first—and last as it turned out—year of our friendship. She had come at the start of the sixth grade, from another school and another neighborhood. She sat quite unaffectedly at the desk that I had chosen for myself. I was impressed by her outrageous clothes and the fact that she had grasped my elbow when earlier she had said to me as though confessing: "My name is Katerina Vrettou. I'm new here." That same afternoon she invited me round to her house to eat beefsteak and French fries. She was an only child. She explained that her parents hadn't had time to have another child because they needed all their time to reflect on what was happening in the world. I accepted that explanation. It was in keeping with their bookcase. It didn't shine like ours but was packed with books that invited you to browse through them. Even from that time, I had an inexplicable craze for books. I would often lose the thread of the conversation with Katerina; while she chatted, I opened the books and, at random, read verses which didn't seem like verses: "pipes, iron poles, iron rods / cylindrical deaths, cylindrical triumphs, cylindrical arteries / in here the blood of cities will flow" or paragraphs from Herman Hesse's *Knulp*: "You're free to rake up people's foolishness, to pity them or mock them, but you have to let them follow their own path." There was a magic seed in the room. All the books motivated you to put others before yourself. Katerina's parents didn't put anyone above themselves and hardly said hello to you. But they had more serious things to do. It would take them a long time to implement all the ideas in the books and to give guidance all those who use mats for wooden floors and stuff birds. I was ready for the change. I knew that whatever volume I opened, I would be transfixed, lose myself, cease to feel self-sufficient.

On the contrary, Katerina seemed self-sufficient without the books. Even with all those volumes at her disposal, she read the same novel over and over again. *A Tree Grows in Brooklyn.* In 1912, the heroine of the story, the young Francie Nolan, was roughly the same age as we were. She would spread a rug on the servant's staircase and read a novel from the lending library while sucking on mint candies. Katerina identified with Francie. It was inconceivable to me given the bookcase and the basic comfort that her home provided.

"When we read the book, we thought of Francie's mother as being old..." said Katerina, interrupting my thoughts.

Now she'll come out with it I thought. She has been waiting all these years to flatten me. But she didn't speak. She continued to look at me, smilingly, nostalgically.

"Not as old..." I said.

"Well, anyway, as a full-grown woman. A thirty-year-old. Now we're the same age as her."

"But we don't have any daughters."

"I do."

"Really?"

"She's three. I called her Francie."

I imagined the little girl, pink Plasticine molded in keeping with Katerina's fantasies. A creature growing in Brooklyn by the name of Francie and with a vague parental expectation: to struggle, to stand out, to suck mint candies. As for me, no one had imposed anything on me other than the mania for tidiness. If I were a little more fanciful, perhaps I would have become a writer. But already at fifteen, I was able to compare two bookcases and draw disheartening conclusions about the one of them. My critical acumen had caused me to suffer. I made various excuses so that Katerina wouldn't come to my home. I told her that my parents worked in the living room in the evenings and that my brothers and I sleepwalked. "It's not very pleasant," I added. I was being sincere. Our home wasn't at all pleasant.

Katerina grew stubborn and insisted on visiting us. I refused, gradually fashioning, during the course of the year, a tale that would hold up. My parents were lawyers, I told her, and they brought their legal work home. In these fantasies, my mother wore a two-piece costume, not dressing gowns with large blue cyclamen. My father wore reading glasses and smoked a pipe. They drank dozens of cups of coffee that helped them to stay up all night with their books. The stains from the cups remained indelible on the table because people who think a lot don't have time to clean up, as I believed then.

Katerina would grasp my arm. "I'm coming," she threatened. "If you don't invite me, I'll come uninvited and you're hardly going to turn me away." It was the most terrifying nightmare. One evening for the doorbell to ring suddenly, for my mother to open the door with her tired smile and in her dressing gown and to say: "Oh, so you're Irene's friend? Come inside. But wipe your feet well. Are you going to do your homework together? That's nice. We have the *Domi* Encyclopedia." All I had to do was to think of that scene for my eyes to fill with tears. Yorgos, my elder brother, found me like that one day sitting at the bookcase table with my face buried in my hands. He got a fright—I wasn't a girl to cry at the drop of a hat—and he promised to help me. Late that same evening he found a solution. He proposed that I invite Katerina on Saint Nicholas' Day as my parents would pay their customary visit to an uncle who had his name day.

"We'll make covers for the books," he said. "We'll change them all."

We bought some soft beige wrapping paper and spent the whole weekend shut up in my brothers' room. The plan was to fashion an impressive collection of books by wrapping the covers of *Domi* and the other volumes in plain, uniform paper and writing other titles on them. Manos, who was good at cutting paper, measured the dimensions of the books and cut the paper accordingly. Yorgos and I carefully wrote on the spines as many of the titles from the Vrettos's bookcase as I could remember. *Michael Strogoff, History of the Russian Revolution*, Marios Hakkas's *The Commune*, Vassilikos's *At Night in Security Headquarters*, Maro Douka's *Where Can the Wings Be?* And naturally I didn't forget *A Tree Grows in Brooklyn*. We had run out of small-size book covers and so I wrote the title on the spine of a cover for one of the volumes of *Domi*.

When our parents left, we dashed into the living room and feverishly began moving objects around. We locked the stuffed birds, the lamp and the shepherdess in the cupboards. We left the worry-beads because we considered them to be above social class from a decorative point of view. We arranged the books side by side. We threw a blue sheet over the sofa with its arty gold and red fabric. We got rid of the silver statuettes of the Nereides from the marble living room table. In their place we put a woman's pipe and a box with carved designs that someone had brought us from Romania. It gave off a heady smell of patchouli. We had tried so hard that when the bell eventually rang, I thought Katerina would reward us with a compliment. But she didn't look around her. She went over and collapsed onto the sofa.

"Do you want to see our bookcase?" I asked her, trembling slightly.

"All right."

She stood beside me while I explained to her that my father had a craze for fashioning the covers of his books himself so as to protect them.

"From what?" she asked.

Not from the dust. That was the wrong answer.

"From wear and tear," I said.

"You have *A Tree Grows in Brooklyn*?" she exclaimed and reached out her arm. I stood between her and the bookcase. "You're not allowed to touch it. My father sometimes leaves signs so he knows whether we've touched his books. Hairs, that kind of thing. We have to ask his permission."

She obeyed.

"Why is the book so big? Like an encyclopedia..."

I was ready for that question.

"It's an old, rare edition, with illustrations."

"What illustrations?"

"It has pictures of Francie, of Neeley, of all of them."

"Does it have the Tynmore girls? And Corporal Rhynor. And Ben?"

"All of them."

"Oh please, Irene. I have to see it!"

"Out of the question."

Then her eyes narrowed. "Why does it say Lermontov on the cover?" she asked. "The name of the author was Betty Smith."

I had got a bit confused in my first readings. All those Russians, Germans and Americans. Men and women with names difficult to pronounce side by side on the shelves. Periods and theories and histories. All mixed up.

"Lermontov," I repeated slowly, "Lermontov. But that was Betty Smith's penname. Yes, it wasn't easy for women to use their own names then. They were oppressed. It was only later that the truth was learned. Lermontov was…a woman." From the suddenness of the lie I felt my mouth becoming dry.

"Are you being serious? And why did she use a Russian penname?"

"Can't you see how concerned she is about the poor? Betty Smith was a communist."

Katerina shook her head in amazement and the matter ended there. From that time, I was never able to look her in the eye again. Every time she said to me: "I want to talk to you," and grasped my arm, I thought she was going to tell me about the real Lermontov whom she had at last discovered on the shelves of their bookcase. I would make the excuse that I was in a hurry and I began to systematically avoid her. Our friendship that had seemed urgent and inevitable began to flag. Distance didn't solve the problem or reduce the shame. Whenever we happened to meet on the staircase or in the bathrooms at school, I always thought she would mockingly cry out "Lermontov, Lermontov!" Every time that the music teacher asked her to the front of the class for the solfeggio exercises, I thought that she was singing the syllables in a different way. Ler instead of la. Mo instead of mi. Tov instead of te.

"So you called your daughter Francie." I sighed without wanting to because of the rush of memories. "You never forgot that book…"

"Actually, I had forgotten it," said Katerina. "But my husband is Scottish and of Russian extraction, can you imagine? When we first met, I recalled the business of Betty Smith's male penname, that Russian name. It's a small world, no matter what anyone says. That's why I chose the name of Francie. It reminds me of school, of you, your family bookcase. Good heavens, that huge illustrated edition of your father's!"

She clutched at my arm again with genuine emotion. I smiled with difficulty and tried to look her in the eye.

Original title: "Lermontov." Published in Michel Faïs (ed.), *Aroma vivliou* [Scent of a Book], Athens: Patakis, 2000, pp. 71-80.

Christophoros Milionis

The Find

"Keep it! It's your lucky find," I told her, without considering the consequences and without thinking at that moment that words like luck, lucky find, and so on, as we all know, are ambiguous.

We were returning to London after our trip to the north of England, and I insisted that we make a slight detour in order to go through Cambridge, where students flocked from all over the world—Man's one hope, with a capital "M" of course, as Kazantzakis referred to them when writing his *England* just prior to the Second World War. The same war that caused all hopes to fade and all men to grow suspicious.

All, that is, except me, who insisted on seeing the students swarming like ants in the streets and cobbled ways of the medieval colleges—all the tribes of Israel. Boys and girls, in jackets and jeans and satchels hung over their backs. They stroll in the parks and on the grassy pitches, sprawl in the greenery, loll beside the canal with the racing canoes—*Row, row, row the boat*, Mr. Murray recited rhythmically at the time. He was from a wealthy Scottish family who had their own castle and ghost—one of their ancestors who had been unjustly slain at the hands of Richard the Lion-Heart himself. And since that time, his spirit had been unable to find rest. Until, as Mr. Murray said, one of the Murrays would avenge him by killing a direct descendent of Richard, again with his own hands. And when we asked him, "Why, Mr. Murray, has that never happened throughout so many centuries?" he answered in all earnestness, "then the castle would be without a ghost!"

Daphne laughed and said: "It's amazing, mom, what that man remembers!"

✤

As we were wandering through the back lanes, we stopped before an old, two-story house with a marble plaque on its façade, which stated that Charles Darwin had once resided there. This very man, I reflected, who cut and removed the wings from the Spirit and made it walk on all fours and seek truth in the virgin forests of Africa and in the Galapagos Islands. Never mind, I later thought to myself. What Spirit and what Truth. Thoughts from before the war more suited to Kazantzakis when he wrote his travel book about England.

Suddenly, Daphne reached down to the ledge next to Darwin's front door and took hold of a small box, as big as a fist, inside a black plastic case. She opened it and discovered a camera.

We looked around to see who had left it, but there was no one else in the lane at that moment. We wondered where we might hand it in—"perhaps it contains souvenir snapshots," Daphne said. However, we decided it was pointless to look for the owner. It would be impossible to find him even if we went to the police.

"As if they'd even try," said my wife. In the end, someone else would keep it, we agreed. It was getting late, it would soon be dark, and we still had a long way to go before we reached London.

So I said:

"Keep it! It's your lucky find." And we headed towards the car.

✤

It was almost midnight when we arrived in London and, exhausted as we were, we went straight to bed—Daphne in her hotel room and my wife and I in ours.

Yet, as often happens after a tiring day filled with different impressions, I kept turning in bed, straightening my pillow again and again, and couldn't get to sleep. My mind kept following the same paths, again and again, till it stopped in front of Darwin's house and fixed on the camera that Daphne had put into her bag. And then I succumbed to what people usually succumb to during the hours of insomnia: the direst thoughts and, worst of all, the most horrific images began to pass through my fuddled mind, which was working and not working. It was working just enough to combine the images in absurd and monstrous associations and yet, strange to say, totally convincing ones. On the other hand, it wasn't working enough to come up with more reassuring and perhaps more rational combinations.

And so that black plastic box, in the shape of a camera, was actually an explosive mechanism, left there, supposedly by some absent-minded tourist, and was ready to explode and blow the head off the first person to look through it and press the button to take a photograph. And as this would most probably be Daphne early in the morning, as soon as she had recovered from the tiring journey of the previous day and began to examine her find—her *lucky* find, as I had characterized it—I was gripped by a terrible feeling of anxiety. Horrid, gory images passed beneath my closed eyelids. Rivers of red inundated my mind.

All the similar incidents that I'd read about or seen on the television, about bombs placed by Algerian Muslims in the Paris metro, by Irish Catholics in Trafalgar Square, by Basque separatists in Valencia, by Red Brigade terrorists in the Milan Railway Station, by downtrodden Kurds in the Frankfurt restaurant, by "Al Fatah" Palestinians in the Munich stadium, and by sheikhs at the Madras airport merged together creating a terrifying explosion that shook the universe.

I reflected, using logic that seemed to me to be completely sound, that Cambridge was actually the most appropriate place for such a deliberate act, given that there were thousands of students there from all over the world: Algerian Muslims, Irish, Basques, Palestinians, Red Brigade members, Black Panthers, dark and grim souls all of them, and fuelled by hate, desperation and fanaticism. An explosion of this sort in the heart of Cambridge, in this center of youth from all over the world, and exactly outside Darwin's house—Darwin, who had discovered the beast in Man, whatever this might mean—would spread with the speed of lightning to the ends of the world and *send a message* to both East and West.

❦

And yet, I kept saying to myself with a sense of grievance, but with the soundest of logic, what does Daphne have to do with all this? She'd happened upon a camera, the latest model, one of those that accurately captures reality. And since only I knew the truth and could stop things, I was overcome by anxiety and an urge to jump out of bed, run to her room, where she, unsuspecting, had surrendered to sleep and to her youthful dreams with her lucky find ominously lying beside her, and knock on her door and tell her—but while I was thinking what I would tell her, the fog in my mind cleared a little and I detected a hint of ridiculousness in all this and so I turned over, before continuing, after a short while, with the same grim thoughts but along different paths:

We were both apparently taking the black box out of her bag. With the utmost care, we carried it over to the window, opened it, looked down onto the street, to right and left—at that time no one is out in that part of London, behind Russell Square, apart from the damp and the dogs—and we let it fall onto the pavement, at the same time hurriedly closing the shutters.

At that moment, there was a huge explosion on the pavement in front of the entrance to our hotel and it shook London from end to end. Squad cars with revolving lights raced through the streets demonically. Fire engines woke the dead with their sirens. Fully armed police units sealed off the block and then ran up the stairs—no, no! That was no solution!

And I picked up the story again from the beginning. I took hold of the black box, put it in a plastic bag, one of those from our shopping, and went out alone into the street. I found the rubbish bin, looked around, not a soul in sight, just a dog—I remember that very well—that cocked its leg against the lamppost and then hurriedly went on its way again, keeping to the edge of the pavement and stopping at every tree to pee.

As indifferently as I could, I left my bag with the others, turned up my collar—it was horrendously cold—and I, too, hurriedly went on my way, behind the dog, supposedly making for the bus stop in order to catch the first bus that would take me to work, so as not to be late for my morning shift. And then it occurred to me that before long my leave would be up and together with all the other workers I'd have to get used again to the morning rush in the chill air, the morning breath of the passengers standing in the bus and blowing in my face, the bleary-eyed employees, some of whom I called colleagues and others superiors but who differed in nothing save for their sour faces. Apart from that swine, the director, who ranted and raved whenever he didn't see them poring over their documents. That's why everyone stood waiting for him, colleagues and superiors alike, each in front of his glass partition with coffee in hand and eyes fixed on the street, hoping to catch sight of him arriving.

Before long the sanitation men in their yellow uniforms would arrive, pick up the bags outside the bin—including mine—with their plastic gloves and throw them into the back of the garbage truck. Then, at precisely the moment that the limousine with that swine inside, reeking of his morning after-shave, would pass by the bin, then, precisely then...

But, of course, innocent people would pay the price too—as is usually the case in life—innocent and simple folk, poor wretches who had spent the night collecting the leftovers of a *voracious*—that's how I called it, I remember—and *insatiable* consumer society that was without mercy. And what's more they'd pay in such an inhuman way. And, even more, it was I who would be its instrument, I who every day etc. etc.—I don't quite recall my reasoning now, but it was sufficient to make me go back to the pile of rubbish and search through it for my plastic bag. I took hold of it and stood for a moment undecided as to what to do.

༄

Suddenly, with that bag in my hand, I felt all-powerful.

I remembered all those mythical stores in Oxford Street and Regent Street with their brightly lit shop windows displaying sparkling crystal and faience—which both my wife and I adore—and the jewelry and exotic artifacts that Daphne would gaze at for hours on end. Then I thought about all the homeless that I'd seen sitting over the grids on the pavement in order to keep warm, and with a bottle in their hands—in Paris, in London, in Madrid, in Munich. The foreigners and the down-and-outs in the underground passageways, the policemen looking awry at them, clutching their black truncheons, full of the experience they had obtained in their colonies—the United Kingdom as they call it, balderdash, that is: in India, Africa, and especially Cyprus that they surrendered to the wolves. And they said that when the war was over... And they said that they were fighting for their own freedom... And when the war ended, that black-hearted minister of theirs, who sported a twirling moustache like our own Roumeliots, said *never* through his rotten teeth..., and Karaolis, just eighteen years old, was hanged...and then there was Afksentiou, who was burned alive with petrol, like a rat in a trap... But now I had them in the palm of my hand..., I had them in my plastic bag...and I'd blow them to smithereens, so that all the world would know, in East and West, throughout the United Kingdom, what bastards they were...And the best place for the explosion to happen, so the whole world would know, would be where else but Cambridge, that center of youth from all over the world, and moreover outside the house of Darwin—who showed that man still has something of the beast inside him...so that if you scratch a bit below the veneer..., and, actually, the more veneer he has...

⌒&⌒

Eventually, I sensed that I was raving, in a sea of hate that was pouring out from my breast, as I stooped to place the black box once again on the ledge beside Darwin's front door.

Then I saw Daphne once more reaching down to pick it up, and I said to her: *Keep it, it's your lucky find,* and then again: *But what does Daphne have to do with all this? How is it her fault?* I kept saying to myself with a sense of grievance...

Of course, I reflected as soon as I'd calmed down, I could take it straight to the nearest police station, I spoke English of sorts, I'd explain to them how I came to be in possession of it—*don't touch it, don't touch it!*, I'd tell them. *I think it might be dangerous!*

But at that time of night, they'd think me suspicious. Yet even if I waited for morning, things might still turn out unpleasant...—and I began an endless interrogation process. I didn't understand any more what they were saying to me, nor could I think of the right words in order to explain to them. I tried in vain to bring to mind Mr. Murray and the conversations he organized in English, with the formality of the British Parliament: *This house considers...The debate...*Files were opened, former incidents were linked, personal incidents, that concerned no one but me—better not to have any truck with the police, whether for good or bad...

Around daybreak, exhausted now from my inner struggle, I fell into a deep sleep and had a dream that had no connection at all with what was causing me such anxiety:

I was in an open plain, seemingly a graveyard but without any wall around it, with bare trees here and there, like skeletons. One of these seemed to be a fig tree, also shriveled, with white plaster branches. Fallen figs were lying on the ground rotting. But I found one large round one, like an apple or pomegranate. I stooped and picked it up. I gave it to Daphne. She took hold of it carefully in both hands and slowly put it to her mouth. At that same moment, a light flashed across my face waking me. Opposite me were the grinning faces of my wife and daughter, who was taking a photo of me.

I noticed that she was using her find from the previous day and at last I felt relieved...A faint light, filtered by the curtain, was coming into the room through the window.

I pretended to be angry at them for waking me and I turned over, trying to calm my heart, as I could hear its beating on my pillow. They quietly closed the door and went out shopping—it happened to be our last day in London. I heard the sound of the elevator stopping, the closing of the doors, and then the elevator moving again.

⁓

I was still extremely tired from the previous day's journey and the night's restlessness and I didn't feel like getting up. This whole business had simply been about a camera that a passerby had left on the ledge, most probably in order to sort his bag out, and had forgotten it and gone on his way, something very common and not at all unusual. I saw it on the table, where Daphne had put it as she was going out.

I got up, took hold of it and examined it. It was a camera that was probably made in Taiwan, the latest model, and completely automatic. Acting like a child who wants to exorcise the object of his fear, I looked through it and took a photograph of the room—on the pretext of wanting a souvenir.

Yet it seems that a whole night of playing with the idea that it was a terrorist device had so influenced me that, although its use by Daphne had excluded any other possibility, the idea still hadn't left me completely.

No doubt—I reflected deep down—only a troubled conscience or some sudden event could explain why whoever it was had left it on the ledge. The light of the flash made my heart momentarily beat faster.

But in the end I regained my composure and looked at the tiny screen with the number of photos that had been taken. It showed ten. Minus the ones taken by Daphne and myself—so the film contained eight shots, which would no doubt reveal what things, what buildings and what people had interested its owner. I even reflected that in one of them I'd probably discover the owner himself; the one who had contrived the whole affair. It was impossible not for him to be in one of them. And I was certain that I would recognize him. All this would enable me to draw important conclusions when the time came.

For the time being, I reflected that there were still roughly another ten shots, supposing that the film had twenty-four exposures. I could go out and calmly take photos of the spots that had most aroused my interest before our trip to York. A state-of-the-art camera like that, with such hypersensitivity, would be able to capture and record even *the desert reflected in the eyes of the lions at the British Museum*, even the angels who had been dancing naked all day on the green grass at Hampstead:

> *On the green grass*
> *three thousand angels had been dancing all day*
> *naked as steel...*

It would even be able to capture the sentiments—these above all—of the poet John Keats in the photo of his house, of the house of his fiancée, Fanny Brown, that is, sweet Fanny Brown—as sweet as any middle-class English woman can be—who accommodated him in her house, in the adjoining lodge to be exact, from 1818 to 1820, before he left on his journey to Italy, where he had an appointment with death the following year, at the age of twenty-six. And Fanny's double bed with its pink canopy waited for him for years, till she departed too, leaving on the bed a cinnamon-colored cat, immensely fat and neutered, which tried to keep both sides warm, first one then the other, switching roles each time in its dreams.

So I photographed the bedroom and reflected that my sensitive camera would even record the cat's dreams, even the voice of the nightingale in the garden with its red tulips, where John Keats, the favorite poet of our own Sikelianos, had written his *Ode to a Nightingale*. I photographed the streets of Hampstead with its old houses, the naked angels dancing on the green slopes of the heath with its oaks, the desert in the eyes of the lions, at the entrance to the British Museum...The house of Virginia Woolf in Bloomsbury Street was my last snapshot. The camera automatically rewound the film, emitting a sound like a nightingale warbling. I found a photographer's in the same neighborhood, where I handed in the black box with all its secrets.

An hour later, I went and collected the snaps in an envelope on which was the photo of Virginia Woolf, with her melancholic gentility and the studio's logo. I sat down on a bench in the square and opened it.

The photos were arranged in order, with English scholasticism.

So the first ones were the ones someone else had taken. I avidly fixed my eyes on them in order to discover the truth at last, but there was another surprise in store for me. On a theater stage, boys and girls dressed in strange clothes, their faces painted like clowns, were enacting a play—which, I don't know. I tried to make it out, but not one play, farce, comedy or tragedy, Shakespearean or modern, came to mind. In the eighth snapshot, the last one that is, all the characters were on stage, the whole troupe: cute little boys and girls, but still in costume, exotic and unrecognizable.

I was unable to come to any conclusion and I had to be satisfied with the shot taken by Daphne of my own face, lying on the pillow, with all the night's restlessness reflected in it. And even more: to be satisfied with the dreams—my own and those of others—that the hyper-sensitive camera had recorded in the photos that I'd taken. My one truth.

Original title: "To evrima." Published in Christophoros Milionis, *Ta fantasmata tou York* [The Ghosts of York], Athens: Kedros, 1999, pp. 55-71.

DIMITRIS MINGAS

Memory

First, he lost his right leg. Not his whole leg to be exact, but a part of his shin just above the ankle. He had to do a lot of work before being able to put his foot down firmly and walk without limping. He found it hard because he kept forgetting, but he would immediately rectify it. He adjusted quite quickly. His trousers helped him to hide his infirmity and, given that he lived alone, there was no reason for him to take precautions as long as he was in the house. During the summers, of course, when the situation required that he wear swimming trunks, he would choose a deserted beach and go straight into the sea. He made sure he stayed there all the time without ever coming out to sunbathe. At work, however, he did meet with some problems at first.

Lefteris Seryanidis, a veteran footballer, capped twelve times for the national team, now worked as a coach for second-division teams.

At first, he had to give up his habit of training the team wearing only shorts and a T-shirt and was forced to wear a tracksuit. He felt uncomfortable and sweaty. During one training session, however, the last one before a crucial game, he took off his tracksuit and took part in the warm-up with the players. Of course, he made sure he kept running so that none of them would notice his infirmity.

He eventually managed to adjust his life and his habits in such a way that, after a few months, his peculiarity no longer bothered him. And he stopped taking any precaution whatsoever once he became convinced that no one was in a position to notice his physical imperfection.

As soon as he saw, however, that his skin was starting to wizen, he became alarmed. First blisters appeared, then—slowly but surely—the skin shriveled till eventually he felt it coming loose and peeling off. During the months preceding this loss, his skin had unexpectedly acquired an unnatural sensitivity on account of which running water was like a caress, woolen clothes felt like nettles and the mere touch by a woman was enough to sexually arouse him.

When he'd lost his skin completely, his body ceased to react to any stimuli. His cigarette burned out between his fingers while he was watching the match from the bench, and he washed himself in either cold or hot water without feeling any difference. For some time, he avoided any social contact and became withdrawn, though no one in his circle commented on the new loss. His hopes ran out of ever recovering. His disappointment was inevitably followed by resignation, by a life of seclusion and a tendency to self-destruction.

In the end, his longing to stay in contact with people prevailed. He set his memory to work and conducted himself more than adequately. He felt pain, cold, heat and sexual excitement using his memory. In love, the sight of a naked body in contact with his own triggered associations of similar scenes from the past and he would become aroused. The blunted powers of observation of others, his own determination, his persistence and, above all, his memory all played their part so that he was able to camouflage the signs of decay. He was worried, however; and not without cause.

He suffered the next blow during a match that was crucial to his then team's progress. There were only a few minutes to go to the end—the teams were drawing. In similar situations in the past he would have been tense, keyed up and, even further back in the past, his shirt would have been drenched with sweat. In the eightieth minute, he made two substitutions, smoked a cigarette and then (unexpectedly) sat down on the bench contrary to his habit; in the eighty-ninth minute, one of the players he'd brought on scored. The other substitutes ran onto the field and hugged the players, but Seryanidis remained motionless and expressionless. Very few noticed the composure of the usually demonstrative coach, and (in the joy of victory) no one thought anything of his eccentric behavior.

At the press conference that followed, he remained silent for a few seconds before his every reply, simply staring at the opposite wall. His mind was elsewhere; he wanted to know why the valuable win (and the justification of his match tactics) left him feeling completely indifferent. The journalists misinterpreted his long silences.

Of course, it was not the first time. Bringing to mind isolated incidents from the recent past, Seryanidis saw (with hindsight) that his emotional reactions and his modes of behavior were not normal. The news of a dear friend's death, professional successes (and failures), together with everything that came with them, the coming and going of some woman in his life, or a friend's thoughtless words did not trigger the expected emotions.

Things came about gradually. At first, he was deprived of the pleasures that joys bring to every person, though he experienced to the full anything unpleasant. As time passed, he even lost his capacity for feeling pain. He tried, unsuccessfully, to explain his behavior as the result of maturity and experience. As time passed, his initial feeling of vague discontent gave place to bewilderment, then to grievance, next (while he was still able to feel) to indignation and, finally, to indifference.

His ordeal tormented him and this annoyance could have been seen as a reassuring sign—it even motivated him up to a point—but in the end it degenerated. Seryanidis no longer reacted. Yet, insofar as he wanted to go on living and working and since he hadn't cut himself off from friendships, relationships and work, he had to respond to the stimulation they provided.

From experience he knew which emotional states and what kinds of behavior suited each situation and he took to acting the part. Often he miscalculated; sometimes excessive, more often restrained, he was misunderstood on many occasions, his conduct became a source of comment and he was treated with some suspicion even by friends. Having lost the measure of feelings and emotions, he also lost the ability to assess the consequences of his actions on the lives of others and his conduct was inconsistent and ambiguous. He conformed, however. He adopted those characteristics corresponding to the model that—in his opinion—would further his career and his personal life, and he took care to be moderate in his reactions and guarded in his words. In fact, in a very short time, he was able to act the part without any special effort. He had grown accustomed through continual repetition and, as happens with the talented actor who lives his role, he regarded his constant affectation as being normal.

The year that he lost his brother in a car crash, he was coaching Apollon Kalamaria (a team generally at the top of the second division). Financially secure and professionally established, he was living with a woman that he'd once desired, though he was no longer able to assess what he had or what he'd lost.

Keeping up appearances, he acted as the occasion required. He kissed his brother's cold brow for the last time without shedding a tear, then put on his sunglasses to hide from the onlookers. He did all he could the following day to appear grief-stricken, accepted his girlfriend's warm words and consoling kisses, and then got into bed with her and feigned incontrollable desire...It was a flat and undeviating life.

The team seemed to be making progress—it remained one of the title contenders. Half-way through the season, it went through a bad patch and lost ground, but it refound its form in the following games and went up to second place in the table, one point ahead of the third-placed team, Doxa Drama. The top two teams would be promoted into the first division and there was only one match remaining.

Apollon would be at home for the last match against a side with nothing to play for. The team had to win (a more or less safe bet) in order to gain promotion. Yet Seryanidis had a hunch that the match would end in a draw. This wasn't the usual attempt to avert a bad result, common among his fellow coaches, but rather a persistent premonition that, as the day of the match got closer, he tried to put out of his mind. He gave his team-talk to the players without letting his words and the tone of his voice be influenced at all by his gloomy thoughts. Then, expressionless, he took his seat on the bench.

The team got off to a good start. They had the better of the play and, just before half-time, they went ahead. Everyone was jubilant apart from the coach. During the half-time break, he made it clear to his players that they mustn't relax even for one moment and stressed that victory was theirs for the taking. He himself didn't believe it, but he was obliged to say what the others expected to hear. Despite all the encouragement and warnings, the team inexplicably fell back in defense at the start of the second half. Fifteen minutes later, the other team took advantage of this and equalized. The fans started to worry, but through two substitutions and a rearrangement of the players, the coach regained control of the center and strengthened the attack—tactics which won favorable criticism. Seryanidis watched the game without any show of emotion. His calmness was seen by the fans as a mark of composure and as proof of his belief in the team. Apollon was now on top, creating and missing chances and thrilling the crowd, but the goal needed wouldn't come. Everyone was on their feet—only the coach was still glued to the bench. He didn't get carried away even when he was told that Doxa was drawing too, which meant that their positions in the table remained the same, nor did he react on hearing from the radio, just before the end of the match, that the rival team had taken the lead.

The match finished in a draw, and in combination with the result of the other match, Apollon would remain in the second division. Disappointed, the fans took it out on the players and, in order to appease them, the chairman sacked the coach. Seryanidis accepted the inevitable outcome with dignity and without comment. He had foreseen the unhappy end of his association with this particular team and so it came as no surprise to him. Besides, he knew that he would be appointed almost immediately by Kastoria—a club with ambition and good promotion prospects.

This move signaled the end of his love affair. When they met for the last time, the two lovers didn't want to accept it. The woman stood silently at one corner of the bed, while he—supposedly in a dilemma—talked enthusiastically about their future, knowing there was none. He assured her that he would come back to Thessaloniki at every opportunity, while she promised not to forget him, but neither of them kept their word—she at least believed what she said, Seryanidis knew he was lying.

At the end of July, he moved into a very nice apartment overlooking the east shore of Lake Orestiada. Preseason training got underway at the beginning of August—important transfers had taken place and the team had been significantly strengthened. After three matches, Kastoria led the table. He met a microbiologist and she fell in love with him. He reckoned that if they had met in the past, he would most likely have felt something and would have responded. Kastoria remained constantly one of the leading teams. Seryanidis slept at the microbiologist's house whenever his obligations (away games and retreats to hotels) permitted it. In the second half of the season, the team lost ground due to some bad results. Fans, officials and players were all worried. Only the coach kept calm. And, in fact, a series of impressive performances in the following matches moved Kastoria into second place—one point ahead of the third-placed team. All that was needed was a win in the last home game and given that the other team was regarded as a pushover, they had already begun to celebrate promotion.

But Seryanidis saw his life and work repeating itself. He knew already that the game in question would end in a draw, that the team below them would win and that Kastoria would remain in the second division. He also knew that, without being held responsible, he would be sacked, that he would find a job at another ambitious club, in a new town, that he would meet someone new there...Besides, only a month before, he had again lost his brother in a road accident.

He was now convinced that his life was not a straight line, but a circle; that everything was being recycled in yearly intervals. In fact, after several such repetitions, he realized that, not only the major and significant events, but also almost all the everyday details in his life were repeating themselves. Looks, words, recollections, chance meetings kept repeating themselves, so that eventually he was able to foresee when he would come down with a cold, on which day following their first meeting he would sleep with his year-long lover, how many matches his new team would win and at which spot on the highway and at what time he would again lose his brother.

Each year he changed teams, towns, friends, lovers, yet everything remained the same. In every case, he knew exactly what would follow, whereas the others didn't. Nevertheless, he never gave in to the temptation to react by adopting different training methods or different match tactics, by saying a bit more or keeping silent, by making one less promise to his partner, by tactfully warning his brother, thereby helping things to take a turn for the better—even for the worse—by taking advantage of his experience. He yielded to the whirl of that repetition.

Till in the final decisive match of an identical football season— he was once again, after many years, back with Apollon Kalamaria— during the second half and while his team was still in front, he was deserted by his memory. He turned to his assistant and, smiling bemusedly, asked which teams were playing and what the score was! Taking his boss's question as a bad joke, the assistant confined himself to a shrug of the shoulders. Seryanidis went on watching a game which no longer held any interest for him, wondering at his presence on the bench yet reluctant to address any more questions to the stranger sitting beside him. Then, anticipating the end of the match, the disappointment of the fans, his sacking and separation and the consequent moves, he rested his head against the back of the dugout, closed his eyes and died...The usual substitutions never happened.

For the rest of the game, the Apollon players fell back and, not receiving any instructions from the bench, defended without any system. Yet, despite being in control of the game, the opposing team didn't manage to equalize. Not one of the substitutes, or the assistant coach, or the physiotherapist, or the trainer thought anything odd about the coach's inaction—they all had their attention focused on the game. As soon as the referee blew the whistle, they all leapt up from their seats yelling and screaming. Before long, the field was overrun with fans—the players were a tangled mass in the center.

In their enthusiasm and celebrations at their team's promotion, no one noticed Seryanidis get up, walk along the sideline dragging his right leg behind him and leave the stadium, bewildered and scarred all over his body.

Original title: "I mnimi." Published in Dimitris Mingas, *Tis Salonikis monacha...* [Befitting Salonica Alone...], Athens: Metaichmio, 2003, pp. 13-28.

Maria Mitsora

Halfpastdoom

Two months had passed since the arrest of Saddam Hussein and his name was no longer all over the media; the last piece on him in the *Herald Tribune* mentioned that the book found in his hideaway was Dostoevsky's *Crime and Punishment.* One evening they showed him again; they again broadcasted the shots of him submissively enduring having his mouth, hair and beard poked by someone with gloved hands and a shaved head, and once again opinion was divided with some saying they were searching for lice, or for scars from plastic surgery and others that these shots had as their main aim to disgrace the monster. The breaking news this time was not about Saddam, but about another international terrorist by the name of Viviano Vargas, also known as Viva, who had been found dead in a central hotel in Damacus, with a bullet fired at point-blank range in the back of his head. According to the scant information, Viviano Vargas was half South American and half Albanian. He had many faces. In the photographs constantly shown on TV, none of them resembled any of the others—he had a face that was thin, round, full and long, and eyes that were sometimes clear, eyes that were sometimes dark; he was the man of many faces, and the biggest mystery concerning his death was the reward of $30 million that no one had come forward to claim.

⁕

Anastassios O. Varangis never held surgery on Wednesday afternoons; he went down to his summerhouse at Sounion, an elegant stone building designed by Pikionis' devoted pupils, with a garden filled entirely with yellow roses.

The sea was calm, virtually silver, reflecting an overcast sky that had a strange luminosity about it. Just as he was unlocking the gate, the sun came out and he saw with delight that the frost of the previous days hadn't reached down to the sea and so his rose trees were untouched. He first went into the kitchen and made coffee and then sat in the leather chair behind his desk in the living room. For a while, he absent-mindedly opened and closed the bottom right-hand drawer in which was a particularly sharp paperknife. His sweetheart, with whom he had recently split up, had told him that his garden was the garden of a monomaniac—he opened and closed the drawer and thought of Nora's legs, her perfect legs with her rounded knees bent and relaxed as she waited for him to come out of the bathroom after her and, instead of lying beside her, for him to suddenly lean over her, feeling the same longing after eleven years. With some effort, he put this image out of his head and from his jacket pocket took the folded newspaper, got up, turned on the electric heater, sat back down again and looked at the photograph of the hotel in Marzde Square where Viviano Vargas had been found dead. There was no doubt, it was the same hotel where he had gone with his niece eight years before, when his passion for Nora had well and truly turned into an obsession. He continually tried to put her out of his mind but without success. He took Alienne's letter out of his pocket to read it again at his leisure.

"My dear uncle Anastassis,

It's my birthday today, I'm drinking champagne on my own, I'm now twenty-four. I'm in an apartment in Madrid and I'm writing to you on an olive-wood table—from an old Spanish monastery—where who knows how many people and loves were buried alive—and I'm writing to tell you that I am very well and passionate about the future after having settled my accounts with the past. I'm never going to see my father again. I'm never going to see my mother again. Even you, uncle Anastassis, though you were always kind to me, I don't know if I'll ever want to see you again. How and why? You're the one who taught me that by asking why, we're addressing the moral order of things, whereas by asking how, we're putting ourselves in the sphere of aesthetics. However, I want to start with another question, with an initial What? I have to start with this if I don't want to be another one of the inarticulate kids of my generation, created to press buttons. What's happening to me? What am I trying to tell you with this letter? Is it a settling of accounts with myself? And it's by no means a coincidence that I chose to spend my birthday alone without my boyfriend or my girlfriend.

In the past, I used to think that all that happened to me by chance was, at the least, bizarre, not to say intolerably grave. At that time, I believed that I was born to run—at that time I used to swear on the secret of my breathing, till coming down the steps of the plane on a flight from Damascus to Athens, I fractured a tiny bone in my left ankle. And even now as I am writing to you, I felt for a moment as if I were running over sharp stones—and perhaps at twenty-four I know only what I managed to touch while running.

I remember and feel angry, uncle Anastassis—that trip—I feel angry and become garrulous—because the words ease it—I who felt my body being transformed into a castle of air—I who would have won in the Olympics—if I hadn't come down to earth in front of an astounded crowd—falling so badly down the few steps following the bomb scare."

Anastassis O. Varangis stopped and lit a cigarette. Outside the clouds had gathered again, something fluttered in the tangerine tree, a trill was heard and then another, and he tried to drive Nora's lips out of his mind; it was a good period in their relationship after the short trip to Damascus, except that he'd become worried about his niece, for a moment he'd thought that Alienne was finished after that trip, finished forever in a world of her own. Alienne's fragmented speech following the trip to Damascus and Jordan with her father was an endless series of denials.

"I'm not called Alienne.
I'm not a female.
My mother is not called Julietta.
My father is not Viviano.
I'm not a human being."

And in the end, the one affirmation:

"We're all actors in one of the future's electronic games."

∽

I didn't hear the bang in the night, Anastassios O. Varangis thought, just like when he was a child, and then he thought how it would have been if one evening he had become autonomous and had rocketed into space in a bed with Nora in his arms, the deep blue of the sky darkened by her long eyelashes. The room had darkened, he turned on his green desk lamp and continued Alienne's letter.

> "I never wanted to come out with the details, you left me in the hotel and he picked me up, and in a taxi driven by a Palestinian, we crossed the Jordanian border and went as far as the ancient city of Petra. There, we lived for three days in secret, among the carved tombs—all of colored stone—yellow, blue and pink—we celebrated my birthday, my fifteenth birthday, with champagne and the full moon—and only I know the color of Viviano's eyes—they are green like the cypresses in graveyards under a full moon.
>
> During the day, a Chinese disguised as an Arab would come, and he did me the tattoo that I have on my left side, a black eagle with open wings, so close to my breast that I was ashamed, I wanted to disappear from the stone face of the earth and then I listened to stories about the conquerors and conquered, about the just and unjust, about the state that has the monopoly on legal violence, about the 327 lives of unknown people that my father and his people tried and sentenced. It was the first time that I didn't feel that he would have preferred me to be a boy, it was the first time that he spoke to me as if I were an adult. He spoke and became my hero, half avenging god and half human, and that's why I think I fell down the steps of the plane on returning to Athens,

subsequently spending an endless month remaining totally still and ceasing to believe that I would fly, slowly becoming human again. Limping at the beginning, I tossed letters into the letterbox with only his initials on the envelope and I swore that I'd kill him one day, preferably in the same hotel in Marzde Square, where I'd seen him for the last time, having breakfast with him, yogurt with cheese and olives and those very thin pitas in place of bread. Before killing him, I'd calmly explain to him that he had sealed my fate and broken my wings for good.

It was a traumatic period and was followed by my plummeting into the gray zone, a life that was gray and shallow. Now, things have found their color again—without any pain I recall that city with its minarets and the electronic voice of the muezzins—the marble fountains with the tin mugs—the voice of my father on the last night talking to me about the Übermensch. The following day when I fell down the airplane steps in the panic, in the unforeseen stopover in Limassol, I remembered that in his diaries Nijinsky divides people into eagles and little birds. I tripped in the panic caused by a phone call about a bomb on the plane. Obviously, I wasn't one of the eagles, I am quite simply a fragile bird.

Uncle Anastassis, at present I'm writing and about to finish a screenplay, the heroine is called Axana—she's a girl who believes that she was born to run. She runs in front of the café owner's young son—on an island where their yacht has moored with her mother and her frivolous women friends, who are more like high-class hookers. Her mother is referred to as DB, from dyed blond. It's clear that Axana has no communication with her, while, throughout the movie, the absence of the father is surrounded in mystery. In the lightweight pack that Axana carries on her back, she has a soozanie that her father had once given her, a mat with big orange suns. At first she liked the young lad because of the tattoo with the sea-blue wings on his arm and because, at some moment when she is still, he tells her that he wants to go to Amsterdam to become a dealer, because his god is Hermes, who is a merchant and the god of dealers. Hermes is Axana's god too, because of the wings he has on his feet. Running, they arrive at an old stone warehouse that recalls the age of the industrial revolution; the camera is more on her and has shown details from the route she's taken. She's sixteen but looks more like a boy of fourteen, short in stature and muscular with broad shoulders and feet with wings, almost visible wings like those of Hermes.

The little silver pack bobs on her back and her bright eyes hastily record the rocks, the soil, the plants and the trees—the numerous varieties, sometimes withered and sometimes blooming and content. And the plants of the underworld hear her soft voice. Panting, he follows behind her, his long brown hair flows loose and now, from behind, it is he who looks more like a girl. As she runs over discarded cans, her voice is heard off screen coming out with phrases like 'tiny fish, they removed you by force from your love for the water, eventually our loves end, that's why we die—now I can see my blood dyeing the sky red.' The blue of the sea from another distant shore hits her in the eyes and makes her lose a breath. They've come to another abandoned warehouse, this one too built with brick and stone. There, in front of the door and in front of the astonished eyes of the young lad, Axana does a somersault in the air like a sprite and fills her lungs; he sees her as a piece of rubber with blow-holes, motionless in the air, and then she comes back down to earth without losing her balance in front of the first of the five steps. She looks at the holes in the ceiling and asks without any sign of being out of breath, 'what time is it going to rain stones here?' and then she says to him, 'we could go on running for ever. No, because of you we couldn't.'

He is by now exhausted, whereas Axana is hopping up and down on a half-burnt mattress, testing it. She takes out the embroidered cloth and spreads it out and makes love with him for the first time in her life on the orange suns. Both of them are shy, embarrassed and hurried. Her voice is heard off screen, 'I swear on the secret of my breath that I'll forget him immediately, but it has to happen, to happen and be done with so that my body may function and become perfect.'

Once they have finished, she turns her back on him, and takes from her pack a tin box filled with rice with five toe bones made of clay. 'I baked them,' she mutters as she carefully spreads them before her on the earth. 'They're my father's,' she says off screen, not saying it out loud to him. 'I'll win in the Olympics and then I'm going to study sculpting. I'm going to make statues for roofs that will be visible from airplanes.' The young lad gets dressed behind her back, almost secretly. 'I hope you win,' he mutters, 'I think you should become a runner, you seem born to run.' She turns her head and stares at him in earnest, then she slowly gets dressed; he lights a cigarette and Axana, leaving the embroidered cloth on the burnt mattress, runs off again. The camera shows her in the distance crossing the landscape in reverse, making huge leaps. With the same momentum, Axana goes back to the shore where the yacht is—she sees it from up above and changes course. 'My father is a flying-carpet merchant in one of Hermes' towns,' she repeats the answer she had given earlier to the café-owner's son—'and I'm going to find him.' Running—flying, she reaches the harbor after an hour.

Here, there's a section, uncle Anastassis, with Axana alone on the boat, in a cabin with hospital colors, she's afraid of the water, she tries to sleep sucking on her finger and sucking on words such as run—want—arrive—afraid of nothing. I'm not going to tell you everything now in detail, nor about the harbor I mentioned to you, which is the harbor at Ermoupoli in Syros, but in the movie the town will be full of statues. The boat sails in the night, ablaze with light, and while Axana tries to sleep, frightened and mumbling future tenses of the verb to burn, we see the café owner's son leaping over fires in his village together with other smaller kids and his grandmother chasing him because he didn't go to work but also because she has good news for him. She has won, she tells him, a blue scooter in a television cooking contest. He distances himself from the village from which televisions can be heard with their volumes turned up loud. He walks alone along a path lined with pines. From up above, he sees that the yacht has left; he lies down and gazes at the sky and he can't understand, given his delight at winning the scooter, why he feels so empty beneath the heavy-metal moon.

So, that's more or less what happens, though I'm not going to set it all out in detail for you now, but the next day Axana is running past the flower shops in Vassilissis Sophias Street. She crosses Syntagma Square and, still running airily, she reaches Karayoryi Servias Street, amid the noise and glare as if having an appointment with the explosion, whose blast hurls her into the air. She hangs from an awning and her ankle is covered in blood. I don't know whether it should appear for a moment that she slows down before the flower shops to pick up a hyacinth or perhaps a rose so that even then an analogy might be drawn with the myth of Persephone.

A toweringly tall black guy snatches her from the scene of the explosion; she sees him as a giant whose head reaches up to the second floor of the buildings. Now he's the one who is running, holding her in his arms like a hostage. Why? Through dark underground passages they make their escape.

In the underworld, in a huge subterranean room, the indeterminable time of her captivity, the air, which was her element, is heavy and scarce. Her bed is separated from the rest of the area by semi-transparent curtains made of an unknown material; the bed sheets are white and coarse. She thinks of her previous life, of her father. They both have the same black eagle with the pointed beak and the penetrating blue eyes. In Petra, he'd told her that this tattoo could very well save her life one day. But now she hides it carefully. They haven't brought her anything to change into and she asks nothing of them; she's still wearing the same black pants and the same black T-shirt ripped in the explosion and she smells of sweat, prison and defeat. Limping, she goes to the bathroom and splashes some tap water on her face. Once, on coming out, she finds a packet of sanitary towels on her bedside table. The same black guy who snatched her brings her food twice a day. It is always olives, yogurt and bread like white pita cut into strips. Lying still, she stares at the foot of the bed, a TV screen showing only rain. The rain flashes but the time doesn't pass. She hears broken Greek and foreign languages and half-sees young men going in and out of the subterranean hideaway, the walls of which are lined with shelves of thick books. She doesn't attempt to escape, though she twice found herself alone. She doesn't want them to see her limping. Only the King of Yorumba, the black guy who brings her food, speaks good Greek; he was once a theology student. Now he's full of hate and he promises the monotheists death by fire. When she asks him why they are holding her, he laughs and doesn't answer; she just has time to see his blood-red tongue, sometimes he wears a hat of real leopard skin. Axana is ashamed of having to limp to the bathroom. It's a squat toilet and with the pain in her ankle, which is swollen and bruised, every movement is a crocked acrobat's nightmare.

Someone that she likes has twice come through the curtain, has stood there looking at her in silence. She's considered that perhaps he is their leader and for this reason doesn't avoid his gaze. The third time he comes, he asks about her father and Axana doesn't reply—though under her breath she mutters determinedly but without much confidence, 'my father will come to save me, he's not only a flying-carpet merchant, he's also an arms merchant and a souls merchant.'

Time passes like an illness, behind the mosquito net, the pyrotechnicians endlessly come and go. She often makes out the one she likes from his long brown hair. She thinks she can also make out a desire for destruction in his eyes. He is always naked from the waist upwards and the next time that he comes in and stares at her, he must be their leader, she reads in his fixed gaze that he must like her too because she looks like a boy, because she was born to win. Then she tries not to cry, she continually tries not to learn to think in the language of losers."

Shutting his eyes for a little, Anastassios O. Varangis tries to concentrate and to imagine his niece's life in Spain. Perhaps after all the girl won't end up a loser, perhaps there are many ways to fly. He looks at his watch, it was the time every Wednesday when Nora would arrive here always with mystery in her eyes, yet always impatient to fling herself into his arms and into his bed. With some effort, he continues reading.

"She had undressed from the waist upwards and with one hand was leaning on the dirty washbasin, while with the other she was splashing water under her arms and over her breasts, trying to wash herself as best she could, holding her T-shirt between her legs. The one she likes slowly opens the door, at first a man's bare foot appears, Axana notes how slender his toes are and then looks for his face in the cracked mirror, she remains perfectly still, without even breathing. His hair hides half his face; he suddenly lifts his eyes from her breasts and she hears her name; it's not at all like a voice over the telephone. His face changes, a mask has cracked and she sees in his look something other than desire. 'That's why you're my girl' and he touches the eagle next to her breast. Everything changes—the curtains are drawn back, she shows her breast, she thinks she can count twenty-nine pairs of eyes. Her father, Viva, is their leader! He's the one who has trained them! He's the one who supplies them with arms and explosives. The black guy has lifted her up, she almost forgets the pain in her ankle as the underground room becomes the scene of a big party, even a brown dog that would walk in and out and sometimes lazily doze at the foot of her bed stands on his hind legs and does circus tricks.

This is more or less how her captivity ends, uncle Anastassis, they take her out with eyes blindfolded, they take her out at dawn, to an unknown square that they tell her is called Prescription Square. The one she likes whispers in her ear 'we say nothing, but the dog knows.'

Just as plants live on balconies in pots, just as old items of furniture live in boarded-up houses due to be demolished, so pass the months after the operation. She wouldn't be able to run again, she was lucky not to have lost her leg, lucky that she would only have a slight limp, just an idea of a limp—the doctor assured her—but it was for just an idea that she'd lived up to now. Sitting still in an armchair in the garden, she watches the seasons changing. She pats the head of the brown dog that appeared in the garden one morning and DB allowed her to keep. Axana had given it the name Halfpastdoom. During this period of complete stillness, she had secretly condemned her father.

The fall came to an end, a chill enveloped the garden and it was a cold night when she got dressed and secretly went out of the house for the first time. Halfpastdoom has learned his name, leads the way full of joy and when she calls him he turns, stares at her and wags his tail. They walked a long time, perhaps two, perhaps three hours, and the cold became colder and the darkness darker...

I've got this far uncle Anastassis, they've passed the railway tracks and they are again in the circular Prescription Square. People dressed in rags have lit fires in barrels to keep warm; they toss half-eaten sandwiches to each other. 'Have a cigarette butt,' one of them says to her. 'Aren't you afraid they'll steal your eyes?' another wearing dark glasses and leaning on a white cane shouts to her. Halfpastdoom goes wild with delight at someone who takes off his hat, his long brown hair has grown longer and it now reaches down to his shoulders. The three of them get onto the motorbike. 'I want to see my father,' she whispers in his ear, feeling the gun in the pocket of his anorak. 'We have to get past the roadblocks,' he shouts to her. Just at the point where she thinks that the town is about to end, it starts again as an unfamiliar town, all the windows are dark and closed. 'Whatever happens, you'll always be my girl. Tell me yes,' he shouts to her. She whispers 'yes,' crying with a single tear, because sirens are heard approaching. She holds him even tighter round the waist. Two orange flashes light up the sky. They cross a filled-in river, making various maneuvers on the half demolished bridge with the concrete and iron girders gaping…"

Anastassios O. Varangis shuts his eyes for a moment, confused; so did Viviano Vargas die many deaths, he says to himself thinking aloud. He gets up and stands before the balcony door, it's blowing outside, the sky is full of stars. He can't get Nora's face and her perfect legs out of his head, that's why he feels so empty and the new moon seems so cold.

Original title: "Hafpastdoum." Published in Michel Faïs (ed.), *Thrimmatismenos planitis* [Fragmented Planet], Athens: Minoas, 2004, pp. 67-81.

CLAIRE MITSOTAKI

Pink and Black

As he was turning the key in the door, he felt, it seems, a slight dizziness. In trying to keep his balance, he must have yanked off the doorknob and, his strength failing him, have collapsed in front of the door, an uncommon and disturbing sight for the first tenant in the block who discovered him. Dead on the doorstep of his house. Before even crossing it. With the doormat under his feet and no pillow for his head.

~

Not yet sixty years old. With three kids, three descendants who, though resembling him in appearance, in no way resembled him in character, in ethos or in deeds. And a wife who did all she could to bring them up, and who did bring them up in the end. This was something he couldn't bear to see. To see these beings growing up. And so quickly. And resembling him. They had taken nothing of his wife's. Not even the hair on her head. They all had curly hair like his. They were all copies of him. An endless source of irritation. A veritable trap set by nature. With him unable to escape even for a moment. With him having to continually see himself in another time, another body, doing things that he himself was unable to do. He froze whenever he saw his three copies spinning like whirlwinds of ability around a mother who was somewhat hysterical, somewhat melancholic, not wicked, but unstable and difficult. Yet why should she care? It wasn't as if she could see anything of herself in them. She was short, with straight, permanently black hair, whereas they were tall, curly-haired beings, the eldest of which, aged twenty-eight, had already started to go gray. Naturally, he gave a lot of thought to it. But they'd told him it was better not to pester them with his thoughts. Perhaps later when the basics had been taken care of. For the time being, work was what mattered. They gave him a little pocket-money. He was ashamed but he accepted it. And he bought them little gifts. He took no care at all of himself. His mother still saw to his needs somewhat. Though she was old, of course, very old. However, in this incredible inertia in which he lived, even this seemed natural. Particularly because it was something that had never stopped.

One evening, less than a year ago, at a moment in the day characterized by the greatest amount of planned activity in the house, the mother in the bathroom, the daughter ready to go out and the youngest expected to come at any moment to grab something to eat and to watch a bit of news on TV before going out to meet his friends, the eldest one turned and said to him:

"Would you like me to rent a room for you, father? It's become like a transit camp in here. You can't get any peace."

His father froze. Froze. In a flash, he saw himself as he was then, when he was just like his son now, twenty-eight, tall with curly hair, a tiny clump of gray hair on his right temple, and his wife coming into the room with a baby in her arms.

"Can you hold him a while? I'm going to get some milk."

Latching onto her brother's words, the daughter in the doorway turned towards them.

"I'll help out too. I got a raise."

She walked over to him and kissed him.

"I'm off now. They're waiting for me downstairs. Goodnight."

He remained staring at his son with that look that no one could fathom and without saying a word. Behind the kitchen counter his son was preparing something with glasses and bottles. He wasn't interested to learn what. When his wife came out of the bathroom, he saw him give her a glass with a straw in it. A pink glass with a black straw.

His wife left and his son shut himself in his office to finish the accounts that his boss had saddled him with. The youngest still hadn't come.

He looked at his watch. It was gone ten. He was gone fifty-five. His own watch was his kids. Twenty-eight, twenty-five, twenty-three. At the next stroke, his personal time would be twenty-nine, twenty-six, twenty-four. Thirty, twenty-seven, twenty-five. And so on. Time for him was his kids and nothing more.

The key turned in the door. The youngest walked in. He came over, hugged his father and tweaked his cheek. The lights of the city appeared in the distance from the balcony. Perhaps he felt a special attachment to his youngest son.

He got up from his chair and went to fetch the youngster some watermelon from the kitchen. The youngster had parked himself in front of the TV and was glancing at the commercials. He sat down for a while beside him; at one moment he started to say something but stopped. It was now almost eleven. He'll soon be going into the bathroom, he thought. But the youngster didn't go into the bathroom. So he'll be going out without taking a bath. But the youngster didn't go out at all that night. He stayed at home, sitting in his room and writing something. His father stayed in the living-room, switched channels and started watching a film. At one moment, he heard talk from the bedrooms. His sons were talking to each other. A rare thing. They didn't have a lot to say to each other. No doubt the "matter" of what to do with him had provided the occasion. He put his head in his hands. It was now too late for him to say anything. And what could he say after such a long period of silence and inertia? The best thing he could do was to do nothing. He went on watching TV till he felt tired, then undressed and went to sleep on the couch.

No one before death can know whether he was a hero or a windbag. And no one after death can find out. So, only the person who lives and departs remains forever in complete ignorance about something that should only be of concern to the person who lives and departs. What is conscience, then? Is it the voice of others, and even more, the voice of others within us?

His friends began to arrive early in the afternoon. By coincidence, the first to come was the owner of the studio that his son had rented for him. He was immediately notified by the tenants of the apartment block and he, in his turn, notified the others. It was of no consequence that they hadn't seen each other for years. They saw Mina from time to time at her house in Aigina and got news about Grigoris. What news, that is? The news was always the same. How's Grigoris doing? As always. Those who knew him in his youth, at his best and at his wildest, put together everything they heard with what they knew "as always," and in their imagination presented Grigoris as a rebellious, withdrawn family man, a house-husband, always at home, bringing up the kids with a man's apron and a woman's devotion. The truth is that he himself did nothing to contradict their own expectations of him in the role of Mother Earth. They laughed at him. Cybeles, they called him, with kids sprouting everywhere, from his embrace, his shoulders, his trouserlegs. Cybeles.

❦

Now they are all standing, on the balconies, in the hallways, in the apartment doorway, smoking or not, pensive and sorrowful. The eldest one arrived first. They hadn't seen him since he was a child. They were all amazed. The image of Grigoris! Build, head, hair. That characteristic hair. Then the youngest one arrived. It was remarkable! The same beautiful eyes. As if they were seeing Grigoris at twenty-five, when he got married, somewhat restrained now, somewhat resolved, somewhat disciplined. A captive of advertising and of Mina. And though advertising didn't last, Mina proved to be a mine. Except that he was the ore. He gave of himself and it was himself he got back.

When his daughter arrived with her boyfriend, the amazement exceeded all bounds. She was CYBELE. They simply had to admit it. Grigoris had the gift of producing copies of himself, doubles of himself.

The funeral took place the next day. In less than twenty-four hours, the silent, withdrawn, irresolute and inactive man became the founder of a family, the head of a dynasty. Those kids, who in no way resembled him and whom he in no way resembled, had become indisputable proof of his strength. The eyes of all of them embraced these three beings with an unbelievable familiarity, given the few seconds of contact on which it was based. Yet their appearance had driven out all thoughts of analysis that the mind could come up with, and the uniformity led to identification, with all the reverse processes and the permutations of characteristics and features that could be made between individuals so very different from each other.

The elder son was very moved. The love he felt for his father suddenly found support beyond his own personal feelings. All these people, all these middle-aged people who recognized him, though without knowing him, caused huge tectonic movements in his soul. He wanted to go up and hug them all, to kiss them, as if they were soil, the soil of a homeland from which he'd been exiled and to which he'd now returned, steeped in solitude and salt-spray. He looked at them standing there, wearing or not wearing their dark glasses, and he saw that incalculable distance that takes you miles and eons away from the other person, for no other reason than that you can look at him and see him not in his uniqueness anymore but as a unique object, as an aggressively unique, closed object, and then all this distance is abolished for no other reason than that the other person turns and stares at you with a look of recognition. On that day, Grigoris' elder son came into his birthright.

Mina was as she always was. Few words, and all in order. This somewhat nervy presence managed never to disturb the waters. Did she have some well-hidden instinct? At any rate, this woman, who was hardly noticeable, maintained a strange harmony with the environment; she never caused conflict. But, how strange, her daughter was unable to communicate with her at all. Perhaps this was what had led her, in such a short period of time, to marry that rather bland and rather plain young man who had been with her the last few months. And so they stayed at home, the mother with her two sons, who, so it seems, had nothing keeping them apart, but who, on the contrary, had a person who clearly brought them together. The elder virtually adopted the younger and, besides the drinks that he made for Mina when she came out of the bathroom, he also served fruit and whatever else to the youngster when he came back from the television. The meetings of the friends in Aigina continued; sometimes the elder son went with her. One of them had the brilliant idea that the group should buy a boat. They called it Cybeles. Whoever asked where the name came from received the pregnant response: "we had a friend, a good guy, who we lost. That was his nickname because he produced kids identical to himself."

༺

This, more or less, was the story of Grigoris from law school. We had really lived it up in our youth. Twenty years old and we'd painted the town red. Now who remembers and why should anyone remember? I remembered it because of the death, the other day, of our friend Nicolas, who was also from the Zografou district, and their graves happened to be side by side. As I was standing, then, and looking at the headstones, I saw engraved on the marble:

GRIGORIS ZAPHEIROPOULOS,
1949-2007

Original title: "Roz kai mavro." Published in Michel Faïs (ed.), *Okto thanassima amartimata* [Eight Deadly Sins], Athens: Patakis, 2001, pp. 83-87.

Sophia Nikolaïdou

How the Sting Hurts and It's in Deep

He took her to the school bus each morning. A father at thirty-eight, he drove to the top of the road in his little car and reached the Eptapyryio turn at precisely eight-twenty. Below, the city stretched out in the morning light, a chick with worn-out patent-leather shoes, bruised knees and a mini skirt with a crooked seam, still pretty but, well, as if sucked dry by all too many and ill-treated by life. He never even looked, but went straight on, as far as the dip in the ring road, where those waiting to be picked up and taken to their work were standing. They both sat there and waited. He looked at the traffic through his rear mirror, in case he saw the school bus coming. She rocked her body back and forth, the blonde ponytail swung wildly, the blinds were down on her world. She was an attractive girl, blond and blue-eyed, with teeth like a hare's. The school bus came at eight-twenty-five; he opened the door for her, took hold of her hand and walked her to it. "Autistic Children's Unit," it said on the outside.

His day passed at work, hers at the special school. The other kids revealed their unique natures immediately, all it took was a look. Something in their faces betrayed them; something wasn't quite as it should be and the others understood. A slight disfiguration, something to do with the eyebrows or the forehead, a twitching of the mouth together with saliva running down the chin, unexpected jerks. But Corina was of a different sort. "Now, there's a picture of a girl," thought passersby when they saw her. She had a blank look, which was part of her charm. As though she were looking opposite her, but not focusing, as if a cloud of dust were in the way. "Don't be fooled by her eyes," the specialists told her father, "you think she's watching you, seemingly understanding. She's lost in her own world. We don't know what goes on in there. Let's just say that in the course of a year, there may be a few occasions when your worlds come close together, like cracking two eggs, but hers is made of wood, just remember that. It doesn't break."

He tried. With words and games. What did the doctors know, anyway. All they could reel off was advice, big words and references to books. What did they know about Corina. Had they seen her in her cotton pyjamas with their bear and rabbit designs when she woke up in the morning with the sleep still in her eyes? Or when she was drinking her milk and spilled it down herself because the greedy little thing couldn't get enough into her mouth? What did they know; they had children who could read books, who went for holidays and went swimming, who had their favorite programs on TV and ran into open arms, who had friends to play with. But Corina was alone. He sometimes saw her on the school bus as she sat quietly inside her shell, when she hadn't begun that wild swaying, back and forth, or those cries, shrieks more like "aiiiiiiiiii..." He'd hear them and lose years from his life. So many times he'd begged for a miracle.

In spring, he began taking her to the children's playground. At the times when most children weren't there and the voices and cries of joy were fewer; if they were really lucky, they found it empty. They played in the sand, on the swings and the slide. They went up backwards, from the bottom to the top, stepping on the aluminum. The girl shrieked, her shoes slid, she loved it. Different shrieks now, shrieks of joy, but somehow lugubrious, as if they were coming from untold depths. Then he sat her in the sandpit; some of the sand went into her shoes and tickled her, dirtying her socks with their tassels. Sometimes she put her finger in the sand and then stuck it in her nose or mouth. "Ooooo," she shrieked, enjoying the delicacy and her game.

One day, it was well into May, pleasantly warm and for short sleeves. Her father picked her up at three in the afternoon in order to go to the playground. All the other children were at home eating. They found themselves alone. Corina was wearing a yellow romper, her father had chosen it for her from the closet and it suited her like a dream. Her ponytail was held up with a ladybird hairpin. Her father wore his tracksuit too so that they would match. And without more ado, they set off on foot.

The park was close by, they were soon there. Corina went straight to the sandpit. She never even turned to look at the swings. Her father stood to one side watching her. She had sat down next to an anthill and was shoving her finger inside the hole. She poked her forefinger in and out of the hole, then her little finger, then the forefinger again. For a long time. In out, the hole gradually got bigger. Crazy, the ants ran to get out of their nest, to right and left in the sand. Corina laughed and laughed. Then her finger was inside again, up and down. It was the first time he'd ever seen her like that. He got up and went and stood in front of her. "Corina," he shouted. Laughter and giggling. Again, "Corina." She lifted her head and looked at him. As if understanding that he was calling her. As if understanding who he was, what he was to her. "Corina," he said to her, softly and gently. He showed her his hand. He was squeezing the wings of a bee between his thumb and forefinger. "Look," he told her. The bee was humming like crazy, he let it sting him. He didn't let out as much as an "ouch." He knelt down beside Corina and, without any sound, showed her the swollen thumb and the mark of the sting. He continued to hold the bee carefully by its wings. In less than a second, he had removed its wings, taken Corina's forefinger out of the anthole and quickly pushed the wingless bee inside. Corina pushed it deep inside with her finger and patted the sand down over the top. Then she opened her mouth and her father placed the wings on her tongue for her to chew them. She looked at him while she was swallowing them.

Then she returned again to her own world. Presently, he took hold of her hand and they went back home. Once home, she shut herself once again inside her cocoon. He called her, talked to her, but no response. Months went by like this. A whole year went by from that happy day. And even more days, many days, in silence and in her walled-up self. Till one afternoon, her father heard a bee buzzing in the kitchen. He didn't give it a second thought. He trapped it between the curtain and the windowpane, the poor thing went crazy. Then he squeezed it in his finger, his thumb turned red, swelled up, hurt him. He quickly turned to his daughter, "Corina," he shouted. No response. Again, "Corina, Corina." Again no response. She was bent over the carpet, looking at its flowers. She neither heard nor spoke. He rushed up to her waving his swollen finger and shoved it in front of her face. "Look," he said. No response. None, none, none.

And suddenly she turned to his finger and enthusiastically licked the wound. His thumb joint was covered with saliva. Corina began to laugh. She didn't look at him, but remained bent over licking him. Wrapped inside her cocoon. She was enjoying herself, laughing on her own. It was as if the heavens opened and the black hole gaped over his world. It was as if the stars' wounds appeared. His mind flashed and he understood. He saw her walled-in world. With him on the outside, now and forever. The lights in his mind faded, he looked at his daughter with compassion. He again held his swollen finger before her eyes. "Oh, my little poppet," he said, hardly able to get his words out. For a long time he squeezed the wound with his nails, trying to get the sting out, to show it to her.

Original title: "Poso ponaei to kendri ki einai vathia valmeno." Published in Sophia Nikolaïdou, *O fovos tha se vrei kai tha 'sai monos* [Fear Will Get You and You'll Be Alone], Athens: Kedros, 1999, pp. 145-150.

DIMITRIS NOLLAS

The Old Enemy

*Always in my sleep I'm hounded by
the third window a merciless eye*

NIKOS-ALEXIS ASLANOGLOU

It was during a long walk that I wondered if perhaps I were in a genre tale and not in one of Piraeus' older neighborhoods, through the back streets of which I'd been aimlessly roaming for some time now. My suspicion became a certainty when I realized that I'd spent the greater part of my time following in the footsteps of a hawker who for some time now had held me captivated so that I was walking around an invisible center, which was becoming ever more distant, ever more indistinct, as I followed him in a daze.

It was obvious that something was drawing me to this man. I must have made his acquaintance, have met him in the past for me to be stuck to his heels and to be following him like a hound its prey. I couldn't remember who he was, but I was sure about one thing: I must have met him in the distant past when nothing had boded his present sorry state.

Without being really aware of it, I had gone with him into two cafés and a bakery, where I'd bought a kilo of rolls in order to justify my presence, and now I was in a grimy tavern, full of barrels that were hanging ominously over the heads of the few customers and that I suspected were part of an illusory setting, as the tavern-keeper filled the cup of wine ordered by the man from a demijohn behind the counter and not from one of the barrels decorating his dingy establishment. He did the same for me just afterwards when I collapsed into a chair, resolved at last to put an end to my tortuous wanderings.

As far as I could tell after having lost a whole morning with him, this man was trying, with little success, to sell Bulgarian perfumes. The way he walked, his battered shoes, which at every step looked ready to leave their heels on the asphalt, the dragging of his left leg, and in particular the way he pronounced a double "l," as though he wanted to drown it in saliva every time he shouted "Colognes, Bulgarian colognes," was what made me glue myself to him. It was all this that had made me wonder if perhaps I was skipping through the first lines of a genre tale.

He sat down at the facing table, and if his gaze hadn't been so tired, his eyes would no doubt have passed through me, given the way he had them fixed on me.

"Only four hundred," he said. Without moving from his seat, he showed me the sample bottle that he displayed to everyone and drew his chair over to me without my inviting him. "We must have met somewhere before," he added with a tone of familiarity totally befitting the place, and mentioned the name of some miserable suburb in a scorched Attica, the bowling center of which we had supposedly frequented in the past.

I was quick to deny it, as if not wanting to allow him to be the one to recognize me. Hell, I thought to myself, no, not when I'm the one who's been following him for so long.

I poured him some of my wine and began going through the past, quickly passing from the white to the black squares of memory, and I wondered whether we'd perhaps gone to the same school, if we'd been together in the army, or perhaps we had worked together in Perama, where for a few years I'd been employed in the accounts department of a company that dismantled old ships. This seemed to me to be the most likely.

Full of apprehension, I waited for him to answer, because, I could see it now, I could swear that I knew that gaze. Perhaps it wasn't the warmest look I'd encountered in my life, but I recognized it, I certainly recognized his look. And I was waiting for confirmation.

He began with a rather interesting introduction, but excessively long and quite irrelevant to the matter, as it seemed to me at first.

"I am," he said, and faltered as if thinking better of it. "I have the opportunity, every day, because of my work, to come into contact with everything anew. I go everywhere and so I can walk in streets I've often walked and see again old acquaintances who thought I'd forgotten them. I encounter everyone and everything from the beginning and in new ways. Last time, however, I saw someone I felt I'd been looking for all my life but he escaped me at the last moment. I recognized a man, an old friend of mine, who had hurt me a long time back. He'd wronged me and I hadn't been able to forget it. Though a great deal had happened in the intervening years that should have softened the pain of the hurt, I still remembered it, though not of course as vividly as at first. So I followed him and kept asking myself why I couldn't forget him. The harm he'd done me hadn't been so great, the proof being that I only vaguely remembered it, but what started to scare me more was the thought that perhaps all my encounters with random people from the past were not accidental, but were in fact the agonizing hunt for one man alone: the one who was now walking in front of me. And if anyone were to look at us, given the way I'd coordinated my stride with his, they'd see that not only our step but also the swinging of our arms was identical, so much so that we must have both looked like a projection of each other. And I kept wondering what it was that was gnawing inside me and not letting me break free of its memory, which had turned into a nightmare."

At this point, he took a deep breath and I got the impression he wanted to check the effect his words had had on me. I tried to hide my annoyance and reluctantly ordered another half-kilo of wine. I was once again on the dark border of a state into which I'd begun to slip and from which I'd find it difficult to emerge, unless I too, in my turn, decided what it was precisely that I was looking for.

He got up as if about to leave and, before I was able to understand how difficult these things are, he began humming, accompanying the song coming from an invisible cassette recorder. The nasal subterranean melody accompanied the words of that strange song, the murmur of which sounded like a hymn of repentance:

> *I'm not playing dice again*
> *or rummy or any cards*
> *if only they'd promise me*
> *the sky with all its stars.*

At that same moment, as if he'd lost something valuable, which he may have dropped, he turned slowly round himself looking carefully at the floor beneath his feet. This entire ritual acted as a smoke screen for the song, for it was obvious that his feet were saying one thing and his heart another. His voice had such heartache that he undermined the whole message of the song at the same moment that he was singing it. It sounded as if he were again ready to do the same things about which the song complained. As if he longed for them—even worse, as if he were planning to do everything brought by the night as it approached *with its own counsels*, and was already dreaming of how it would turn out.

No one had noticed his dance step and he immediately came and sat down again next to me. He went on as though the dance-music interlude hadn't happened, while I still couldn't get the words of the song out of my head.

"And then the strangest thing of all happened," he said. "The more I followed on his tail, certain that there was no way I would lose him, but without going up to him to make his acquaintance, pretending to be a stranger, the more clearly I recalled another event that had happened in the time since his disappearance and to which I'd been a witness. It was a calm discussion between friends that came to an unhappy end, and perhaps it was the memory of this other interpolated story, during the time of his absence, that was the reason why I delayed going up to him, the reason why I avoided going up to him. And, in any case, to do what to him? God only knew. Anyway, this little episode happened as follows: Sitting and chatting at a nearby table were two acquaintances of mine, one of whom had actually worked with me as a shipmate for some time. They were close buddies and I'd never seen them in anyone else's company. In fact, they were annoyingly close. And suddenly, while they were discussing something quite insignificant, one of them, I don't recall which one, got up and, after letting out a scream of pain, took out a knife and plunged it into the other's chest. Murdered him just like that. It took me days to recover, and the reason that I delayed going up to my old enemy and remained constantly behind him at a steady distance must have had something to do with that shock."

He had no intention of letting me get a word in or make any comment on his tale. Meanwhile, we were getting down the half-kilo of wine at a pretty fast rate. In his case because his throat must have been dry from his endless narration, and in my case to ease the boredom caused by his two unlikely tales.

"Because we, too, my good man," he said with renewed familiarity, "sitting as we are like this, have every opportunity, with every word that slips out from between our teeth, to lead the conversation to a bad end. Our every word might give rise to something bad. And that's why we're careful, just like everyone who approaches another person for the first time. But those two had already said everything there was to say in life, everything that might have divided them. And yet one word, a word that perhaps still hadn't been said, woke the other self that they'd had hidden inside them for so many years and whom they'd struggled to satiate with other conversations."

He suddenly stood up and, without another word, went out and stood in the tavern doorway, undecided as to which direction he should take. A chill had penetrated the afternoon languor and I felt the oxygen that I was breathing piercing my nostrils. I didn't even think of suggesting he pay his share of the bill, or of asking his name, since I'd begun to suspect, as a result of his narration, just what dangerous surprises might be concealed in the words of the poet, *take my word, give me your hand.*

He stood in the doorway and discreetly managed to restrain himself from swaying. He started anxiously searching in his pockets and, with a ponderous air, sometimes feeling them and sometimes thrusting his hands into them, he very carefully pulled out various bits and pieces of paper, notes with faded addresses and telephone numbers, receipts and bills and orders for fines, which he perused with excessive attention. He was absorbed in this pile of crumpled papers and profoundly studied them one by one in the mauve light as if he were about to make some major decision or settle one of the bills at that very moment. He made himself appear extremely busy, pretending to be the sober type with endless jobs to do, perhaps because he believed that there was always someone watching us, who is following on our heels, and who we have to mislead.

Original title: "O palaios ehthros." Published in Dimitris Nollas, *O palaios ehthros* [The Old Enemy], Athens: Kastaniotis, 2003, pp. 67-76.

NIKOS PANAYOTOPOULOS

The Strength of Materials

She's sitting beside the bed and smiling at me as though welcoming me. She reaches out and pulls the cover up over my chest. She touches my forehead as though wanting to see if I have a temperature. I recall how my mother used to kiss me on the forehead. I want to tell her that she looks a little like my mother, but, before I'm able to open my mouth, she puts her finger to my lips and prevents me. Seconds before I fall asleep again, I wonder what this angel is doing beside my bed...

I open my eyes and shut them more or less immediately as the room is now flooded with light. I open them again to confirm that she is no longer there. To my great disappointment, her place has been taken by an incredible head—a head that is all corners. The cheekbones are so prominent that the cheeks below seem like huge, dark caverns. This is enhanced by the five or six days' growth of the blackest stubble. The image is completed by two enormous blue eyes and two comical hairy ears, which are turned in my direction and which stick out almost vertically from the angular skull that is covered in very short gray hair.

The unfamiliar face makes the round of the bed. I follow it, moving only my eyes, as my head is held fast by some invisible clamp. A hand with long fingers and pronounced joints rises and noisily scratches the short hair on its right temple. Raising its eyebrows, the unknown face turns around and addressing one or more people that I'm not able to make out, says "he's awake," or "he's come round," or some such thing.

A few seconds later, a second unfamiliar head enters my field of vision. I'm overcome by panic. For just a few moments it occurs to me that I've woken up in a Laurel and Hardy movie. Because the preponderance of corners on the one head are completely absent from the other. Where on the one there were two hairy caverns instead of cheeks, on the other there are two fleshy balloons sticking out. Beneath the chin there's an enormous second chin, which might easily conceal another head inside it. The eyes are barely discernible through two slits. The scalp is bare. The ears nowhere to be seen.

The hairless face turns and casts an anxious glance at its hairy partner. When it looks at me again, it has a forced smile, which transforms the slits of the eyes into infinitesimally tiny lines.

"You're awake at last," it says and I'm certain that the voice I heard belongs to the second head, the one that is concealed in the rolls of fat under its chin.

It turns again to Laurel.

"Do you think he can hear us?" it asks.

Laurel does no more than raise his eyebrows in two huge arches of wonderment and then, with a nod that brooks no objections, indicates to Hardy that they should leave. And they vanish as I strive to make them understand that I could hear them.

With slow, hesitant movements, I raise my arms and note that what is preventing my head from moving is a metal contraption, the base of which is attached by belts to my chest. Two thin, metallic rods stretch from this base to just below my chin, where they are joined together with a wider metal plate that is wrapped in a protective layer of foam material. Something similar must also be the case behind my back as I can feel the rigid presence of metal rods between my body and the mattress, together with the constant rubbing of the foam material at the base of my skull.

Before I'm able to formulate any hypothesis concerning my situation, a new face makes its appearance. A female face, plain and expressionless. If not for the white nurse's cap, it would be a completely unremarkable face. No comparison with the other that had spent all night at my bedside.

The nurse comes in with a rush and stands over me, looks hurriedly at her watch and leaves with a rush. Instinctively, I try to turn my head in the direction in which she left. The scaffold stops me immediately and a momentary stab of pain in the back of my neck gives me some idea of the reason for my enforced immobility.

Laurel's head again enters my field of vision. He laughs restrainedly and this is one of the funniest sights I've ever seen. The smile seems clumsily stuck to that conjoining of corners that is his face. It struggles to accommodate itself between them, struggles to stand out between the thick hairs and the deep caverns and, at the same time, struggles to conceal the void left by a missing molar, though without any great effect.

"Are you feeling better?" he asks.

I try to nod and he seems to understand because a wave of anxiety spreads over his face.

"Don't move! You mustn't…" he says, reassuringly placing his hand over my chest.

"What day is it?" I ask him, achieving the impossible, speaking, that is, without in effect opening and closing my mouth.

"Friday…" he answers with some surprise.

"How many days have I been here?"

"Since Wednesday afternoon."

༄

Leaning over me this time is a young man, with thick, gold-rimmed glasses, no doubt a forced attempt to add a note of maturity to a childlike face.

"How are you feeling?" asks the child with the academic's glasses.

"I don't know…" I reply with a burst of sincerity.

The child purses his red lips in evident displeasure. It wasn't the reply he was expecting.

"Are you hurting anywhere?" he says, starting again.

"No..."

"That's good..." he says, and his lips return to their original position, while, at the same time, he mechanically pushes his glasses back up to the top of his nose.

"Do you know how you came to be here?" he asks.

"I've no idea," I reply.

The child-doctor nods affirmatively and as if pondering.

"It's not unusual... But don't worry... Your family has been notified... The fact that you've come round so quickly is a good sign..."

It's already afternoon. Laurel explains the commotion in the corridor.

"The resident, the one who came to see you previously, gave the wrong medicine to someone in the next ward and was taken to task by the director. Naturally, he maintains that it was the nurse who made the mistake, but who can say?"

I close my eyes and let the sound of his voice lull me to sleep.

❦

I'm woken by a light touch on my forehead. It's impossible that I imagined it because, on opening my eyes, I see her face so close to mine that she must have stooped to kiss me. On the forehead. The way in which I look at her must cause her consternation as she begins to talk with incredible jitteriness, coming out with incoherent phrases, something about my having woken up at last, and how she knew that I could hear her and she believed it wouldn't be long before I recovered and I shouldn't worry, everything would be okay, I shouldn't ask for details for the time being, the important thing was that I'd woken up...

All this time I've been focusing my gaze on a mole just under her chin—I thought it so unusual for there to be a mole there. As the woman is talking and her jaw is going up and down, the mole first appears and then disappears. The more I stare at it, the more it seems like a bug playing at hide and seek; a little more and the hairs growing out of it will turn into legs.

I again close my eyes with revulsion and almost simultaneously the woman falls silent. It was so simple after all. I open them again and see her looking at me in astonishment.

"It's me," she says.
I don't know what she means exactly.

⁂

He points with the chalk at the diagram on the board behind him. *Up to this point*, he says, *the deformations suffered by the body are elastic. Once the deforming stress is no longer applied, the body returns to its previous state. This point is known as the elastic limit.*

⁂

I wake up with a tune playing inside my head. The tune is dragging its echo behind it. I open my eyes wide, but the tune doesn't go. Nor the echo. On the contrary, it grows louder, wells up. The words come into my mouth like vomit. Can you stop vomit? Too late. An angry shhh is heard from the far end of the darkened room. I swallow the last two lines of the verse. I close my eyes and unfamiliar voices that leap into my head continue the song. Children's voices. The tune gets mixed up with their laughter. I feel a pleasant warmth enfolding me. What must I do to make it last?

⁂

She must have been there for some time. She looks at me with that smile that negates the darkness. I smile back at her. All day I inwardly begged for night to fall so that she might once again be beside me.

"What time is it?" I ask her.

"After three," she says, without looking at her watch.

Her white blouse emphasizes the paleness of her face. She emits a fragrance. I'm surprised by the fact that she's not wearing a white cap like her unattractive colleague in the morning. I ask her name.

"Joy," she says and smiles.

A smile of Joy, I reflect.

⁂

I hear their mutterings. Hardy insists that they look alike. He lists the points that constitute their likeness. Laurel answers condescendingly that they are a couple. They start coming out with incredible arguments and soon grow tired. They fall silent for a while.

Hardy appears first. He smiles. On seeing that I'm awake, he lets out a feigned apologetic "oh," putting his chubby little hand to his mouth.

"So you heard what we were saying, eh?" he says.

I nod in affirmation, but he is unaware of it. My head remains clamped.

"Don't think it indiscreet of me, but... I started the conversation because it seemed to me that...The way I saw you together, that is, these last few days and particularly yesterday afternoon..."

They had been talking about me. About me and the woman who woke me by kissing me on the forehead. Suddenly, I realize the significance of a gesture like that. The woman with the mole under her chin kissed me on the forehead and tried to comfort me. She looked particularly happy at the moment when she said "the important thing is that you've come round." She seemed relieved...

"He's right, she's my wife," I tell him, only becoming aware of it at that moment.

His smile suddenly fades. The skin beneath the right slit twitches nervously, very briefly. He tries to smile, but it won't come. He turns away with evident disappointment and walks off. He says something to Laurel that I can't hear.

The ride on the stretcher put me in a good mood. From the stretcher you see completely different things from those you would see if you were to make the same journey on foot. Now they've got me in a strange machine—I feel as though my breath is going to give out at any moment. It's dark and my nose is almost touching the curved metallic cover. They only tell me the essentials.

"Remain completely still... It won't take more than a quarter of an hour..."

I want to tell them that I am still, completely still, and I have been for the last four days, but I don't have time. The nurse disappears before I can even open my mouth.

Again the child-doctor. He's holding something that looks like an x-ray—but somewhat smaller—and he's looking at it with a ponderous expression. He speaks to it.

"The situation is exactly as it appeared from the x-rays. It's fortunate that the nerve wasn't damaged... You were very lucky... Very lucky..."

Now he turns to me.

"You can't even begin to imagine..."

I don't know what to say to him and so I fix my eyes on the ceiling. I see the image of Joy smiling at me. Night is slow in falling. I smile too.

"Now you're smiling and you're right to smile but you're not out of danger yet..."

The child-doctor talks as he walks away. I turn my eyes and see Laurel.

"He's not bad deep down..." he says, nodding towards the door closed by the doctor as he goes out. "And the mistake with the medicine was the fault of the nurse," he tells me. He hesitates. He makes up his mind. "How was it?" he asks eventually.

"Suffocating," I answer. "I thought my breath was going to give out... They told me fifteen minutes but it must have lasted over half an hour."

He looks at me puzzled. He reflects.

"No... I mean... The accident..." he ventures.

"What accident?" I inquire.

A conspiratorial psst is heard from the far end of the room. Laurel suddenly turns and smiles at someone I can't see.

"Come in," he says and makes room for her.

This time my wife kisses me on the cheek. She's holding a little girl by the hand. Momentarily, my mind rings with the sound of children's voices and laughter, but nothing specific. She pushes the little girl towards me. The girl hesitates. It's only then that I see she's holding a daisy in her hand.

"Aren't you going to give daddy a kiss?" she says, leaning over her head and kissing her hair, encouraging her to come up to me. The little girl turns and stares at her.

"Why is he wearing that iron thing?" she asks.

"Because he's hurt himself and he has to remain still," she replies, pushing her gently.

The girl advances reluctantly. With a sudden movement, she leaves the daisy beside me and, slipping away, goes to hide at the foot of the bed. I search for the daisy with my hand. My wife comes over, takes it from the bed and holds it over my chest.

"She picked it from our garden for you," she tells me with a forced smile.

"Ask her to come here," I tell her. "So that I can see her…"

"Come here so that daddy can see you," she says to the foot of the bed.

The little girl comes out hesitantly. I hold out my hand and motion to her. The girl passes at a distance of half a meter from my fingers and sticks her head out from behind her mother's waist. I assume it's her mother, that is. Given that I'm her father… I observe her face. Does she look like me I wonder?

"What's your name?" I ask her, and the girl bursts into tears. My wife stares at me seemingly terrified.

⁓⁓

As I have nothing better to do, I try to remember. Anything. All that comes to mind are plans. Plans for an apartment block. I can see the concrete floors and the beams and the pillars and the walls of the elevator shaft. I can see the armature, marked in every detail. I can see the sign marking the building's orientation. I can see the board with the outline of the plans. The scale, the date the study was submitted, the names of the engineers. Stamps and signatures underneath. Then I recall thinking about this same plan while driving. But nothing else.

⁓⁓

He's standing as always before the board with the diagram. He's explaining. *In this area* (he indicates which with a circular movement of his hand) *the deformation is plastic. Which means that some deformation will remain even if stress is no longer applied to the body. The second point on the diagram is called the strain limit. Beyond this point, the slightest increase in the amount of stress causes disproportionately large deformation.*

This time, too, I don't manage to be awake when she comes. The moment I open my eyes, she asks me how I'm feeling.

"Fine," I reply.

"The first days are always difficult," she says. "Then you get used to it...", she says, pointing to the metal collar, "and you won't even be aware of the time passing...".

"I can't remember anything," I tell her.

"That's understandable," she replies and appears to mean it. "After a shock like that..."

"I try to remember but the images that come into my head are from way back... A teacher at school, a song that my mother used to sing to me when I was very small, things like that..."

"It will all come back to you... In time..."

"I remember my father's face... On the day of the office opening. He was so proud that day. Takis..."

"Who is Takis?"

"My partner... We were students together and became friends..."

She just nods affirmatively.

"Takis," I continue, "was very fond of him...My father, I mean... On the day of the opening, he'd told him to see to all the flowers that were brought...I recall him putting the flowers in a row, changing their places, not being happy with the way they were and starting again from the beginning... I remember myself being in a bad mood... and Takis nodding to me to follow him onto the balcony... and saying to me, *'don't walk around with a face like that, you twerp... it's not as if he's trying to do you any harm, is he?'* And then he went back inside the office and helped him to arrange the flowers properly. As for me, alarmed by their alliance, I remained alone on the balcony."

Hardy informs me that he'll be discharged tomorrow. Laurel doesn't know how long he'll still be in. He thinks that he's completely healthy and that the doctors don't know whether they are coming or going. Hardy takes my yogurt, after first reassuring himself that I'm not going to eat it.

This time she's come without the girl. She tells me that on the previous occasion the girl had gone away upset. She falls silent.

"Her name's Stella," she continues eventually. "Like your mother."

Again she falls silent. She looks me in the eye. A worried expression suddenly spreads over her face.

"What is it?" she asks me, alarmed.

"Stella," I say simply, without continuing.

"Stella," she repeats and immediately changes the topic. "The doctor told me that you'll be out in a couple of days. Of course, you'll have to remain at home for some time…"

※

"I don't want to go home," I tell her, and Joy stares at me as though not understanding.

"Why?" she asks.

"I don't know," I tell her. "It's a thousand times better here…"

She smiles.

"I'm sorry, but I can't believe that," she says. "No one wants to stay here…"

Her certainty sets me thinking. There's no way that Joy would lie to me.

※

The child-doctor gazes at me sullenly, waiting for my answer. Looking at the ceiling, I tell him that I can't remember anything recent. The child-doctor follows my gaze. I tell him that talking to Joy helps me to remember some things; old things from the past.

"To Joy?" he asks, looking at me suspiciously.

"Yes," I say. "The nurse who comes at night."

He nods his head condescendingly.

"Don't worry," he tells me.

"About what?" I ask.

"Listen," he says. "The shock was a profound one. It's not an unusual phenomenon. It's called cerebral stimulation. It's temporary… A matter of days… Nothing to worry about…"

"Elastic deformation," I mumble.
"What was that?" he says.

❦

She explains to me that the car is for the scrap heap.

"If you'd been wearing a belt…"

"What happened? How did it happen?" I ask her.

She stares at me sorrowfully. She lowers her head. The bug under her chin disappears. She speaks without looking at me.

"You were on your way to Corinth because they were going to lay the concrete for the third floor…"

She lifts her head and looks at me.

"At Douvis' construction site, do you remember?"

"Go on," I tell her. I don't want her to know that I don't remember.

"A driver who witnessed the accident says that the other motorist crossed over into your lane…He was the one who notified the police and the emergency services…"

"And the other motorist?"

"He got away with just a few scratches…"

"And me?"

"What about you?"

"What do I have?"

"Your vertebrae's broken in two places…Smashed. The doctor says that…" she hesitates.

"What does he say?"

"That if the nerve had been damaged…Anyhow…God's good…"

"What would have happened if it had been damaged? I want to know."

"You'd be paralyzed, even…"

"Even what?"

"Drop it, will you…Forget it…It's over…You're going to get better, that's what counts…"

❦

Gradually, the images grow clearer. Faces, most of them still without names, smiles, the odd few words, nice places and others simply nondescript, some dates, a photograph. Takis and I standing in front of the concrete skeleton of a three-story building. Our first job, I remember that.

Strange he hasn't come to see me. Business can't wait. And business is going well. Thanks be to God. And times are difficult. As if I can hear him. He hasn't changed at all from back then. From university. I still recall the day when Takis introduced me to his sister. My wife. The day when we announced to him that we were getting married. We didn't tell him anything about the pregnancy. I recall the day when we made the decision to open the office together. I recall how I'd believed then that Takis was the most suitable person. He liked the work. He went out looking for it. With him I'd be sure to come out ahead. I hoped that he would carry me along...

Joy listens patiently.

"What did you want to study?" she asks me.

"Nothing...Besides, he never allowed me any space to even think what I'd like to study...I studied what he wanted...In his time, engineers got rich by buying up old houses and building apartment blocks in their place. Now, whenever I talk to him about the crisis in the profession, his raises his eyebrows and says, '*there's always work for those who are good at their job*,' and the conversation ends there. He was always like that. He always knew best. What I ought to read, how much I ought to read...The right profession, even the right woman for me...He never liked my wife. He thought I was too young for marriage. He came out with fiery speeches about the valuable experience of those older and how the young would do well to profit from it in order to avoid the mistakes that they would regret all their lives...For once he was right..."

Three or four doctors are standing over my bed. The child-doctor is one of them. He is talking to someone older, who is constantly staring me in the eye. When the child-doctor finishes, the older one simply nods affirmatively and leaves. The others follow him. They stand a few paces further off. They whisper conspiratorially. The child-doctor tells them about a woman who I talk to at night.

"She's a nurse," I say to help them. "And beautiful like an angel…"

The older doctor turns and smiles at me.

"Obviously the stimulation, though there are signs of normal recall," says the child-doctor with a smug smile.

Strangely the older doctor nods in assent and walks away towards the door of the ward.

※

Takis puts a box of chocolates down on my bedside table. Pity Hardy left. He jokes about the metal collar.

"Nice bit of scaffolding they've put round you, partner," he says. And then: "So, I'm letting you have a week's leave but not a day more…You won't believe it but the whole affair has brought us luck…Two jobs have come in since that day so get yourself sorted out….I can't manage on my own…"

I smile because I don't know what to say.

"Don't laugh," he continues unperturbed, "there's the big match next Sunday…You don't expect me to go alone, do you?"

"You'll find someone to keep you company…" I tell him, though what I really want to tell him is that I won't be going to the stadium again. That I never wanted to go to the stadium.

※

"So why did you go?" she asks me with genuine surprise.

I'm ashamed to tell her what comes to me by way of an excuse.

"I don't know. Because he always had free tickets," I eventually say to her.

"I thought Takis was your friend…"

"Yes, he was…It's just that…"

"Just that what?"

"From the moment I married his sister, something else happened…Partner yes, brother-in-law yes, but friend…Takis turned out to be a trap…"

She stares at me almost sorrowfully. It makes her look even more beautiful.

"We were in our final year when his sister came to Athens. He introduced me to her. I married her because she got pregnant. I hated him then. Except that I never told him. After coming out of the army, we opened the office together. It was more or less taken for granted. I never really wanted any of it. Any of it at all..."

"There's always time," she said as she got up. "I'll see you tomorrow."

∽

I'm dreaming that I'm running along a beach, like the characters in the romantic American movies that I watch on video with my wife. In my dream, Joy is running ahead of me over the sand. I can hear her laughter and I reflect that it's the loveliest thing I've ever heard. Joy turns and looks behind her. But her gaze doesn't come to rest on me. It goes beyond me. She's looking behind me and she obliges me to turn.

I am awoken by an acute pain in the back of my neck. Awake now, I follow the rest of the dream. Sitting on a small rock at the end of the beach is my wife. She's not looking in my direction. She's looking out to sea. It's that time when she lost the child. Four months after our wedding. After that she suddenly changed. She shut herself up and left me on the outside. She was verging on the strain limit, as I'd call it now. Things got better when Stella was born. They were never as they were before. She held onto her daughter, protected her like a shield, nothing else mattered. I remained alone. Takis was overjoyed. *'I've never seen you work with such enthusiasm,'* he'd told me.

∽

The third point is called the fracture limit. I don't think this requires any explanation... He makes a show of breaking the piece of chalk that he's holding in his hand. He leaves the pieces on the desk and rubs the chalk off his fingers. *We're finished for today,* he says. *I'll see you all again next week.* Takis, who is sitting beside me, is watching me looking at Antigone. He nudges me and I'm compelled to turn round. *She's not for you, pal,* he says. I never understood what he meant. Many years later,

I bumped into Antigone at the Association's elections. She was the one who came over and spoke to me. She remembered me! I don't know where I found the courage to tell her that she was as lovely as ever. '*I liked you too,*' she told me. '*Of everyone in our year, you were the most likeable.*' That's what Antigone said. Then we started talking about work, about our marriages, we exchanged telephone numbers. I tore her card up when I got back home. Takis had lied to me.

～❧～

The nurse insists that I leave in the wheelchair. I explain to her that I'm capable of walking, but she is adamant. My wife begs me to comply. I refuse. I go out into the corridor. They follow me. I turn round and ask the nurse where I can find Joy, to say goodbye to her.

"Joy?" she asks, grimly.

"One of your colleagues," I tell her. "She's been coming at night and…"

"I'm sorry," she says. "There's no Joy working here so far as I know…"

My wife leans towards her and whispers something in her ear. The nurse steps aside and my wife pushes the wheelchair in my direction.

"Come on," she says. "They're waiting for us at home…"

"I want to have a few words with Joy," I say to the nurse.

She looks at my wife.

My wife touches me on the arm.

"Listen," she tells me. "I've discussed it with the doctor… he says that sometimes, in such cases that is…Well, our minds play strange tricks on us…Because of the shock, the jolt…That woman you've been seeing at night is just…"

"I am not going to sit in the wheelchair unless you promise me that you'll convey to her what I say to you…" I tell the nurse, who is looking at my wife. My determination, it seems, makes her turn to me.

"By all means," she says, smiling. "Tell me…what do you want me to say to her?"

"Tell her that you can't always do as you like…You mustn't have passed the strain limit…It's a law to do with the strength of materials…"

⁂

We come out into the hospital forecourt. She holds me tenderly by the hand. She tells me that she's brought Takis' car. Takis is waiting for us at home with Stella. And my father too. And Takis' wife and their kids. All waiting for me at home with joy. I walk with slow steps.

We get into the car. She sits in the driver's seat and fixes the mirror. She helps me put on my seat belt. As she is bending over to fasten it, she tells me that a doctor told her that she could easily have the mole under her chin removed.

"Why?" I ask.

"What do you mean why?" she replies. "It's horrible, isn't it?"

"I don't know," I say. "Perhaps I've got used to it."

She starts up the engine and we set off. The collar round my neck prevents me from turning. I have to look ahead.

Original title: "I antohi ton ilikon." Published in Nikos Panayotopoulos, *I enohi ton ilikon* [The Materials' Guilt], Athens: Polis, 1997, pp. 113-136.

ALEXIS PANSELINOS

Arrogance

The rain had been falling constantly all week; rubbish of all kinds was racing through the gutters at the side of the road. Filth, Pericles thought, and felt the spectacle clogging his mind. Decades of filth. A century of grime; that was our city. What city? Athens is the whore of all us provincials who haunt it.

The clock on the taverna wall still said eleven. The time had stuck too. It wasn't moving.

In recent years, his time passed ever more slowly; it dragged, seemed to stick. As a child he was never still. His old friend, Yannis, used to call him a fidget. He had stayed behind in Preveza together with the poetic jackdaws, repairing cars and, in the evenings, cleaning the stains in the sink so that he'd get something to eat from Fani, Pericles' high-school sweetheart, who had, however, preferred Yannis, the certainty of a regular job and the prospect of giving birth to and raising three little brats with him. He had a repair shop just outside town. And with a view of the "place of sacrifice"—as Pericles called it—close to the sea.

In the summer, they'd go swimming on this beach, which as they'd learned at school was something of a monument. His schoolmates had their minds more on the girls sunbathing there, on cigarettes the brands of which they changed regularly and on practical jokes played on the principal. A shiver ran down Pericles' backbone whenever he looked at the place. The place of sacrifice... The shore of the young poet.[1]

He had decided not to stay in Preveza, with its jackdaws and with the *place of sacrifice* getting stained from all the suntan oil. A theology teacher had told him that he was destined for other things. Not for the fields, like his folks. In Thessaloniki, he worked in a souvlaki bar, a shoe shop, and for a company that cleaned apartment blocks. He didn't get on with any of his employers and moved down to Athens. He never went back to Preveza. Just telephoned. His mother—while she was alive. His sister, who'd been married for years—at festive times. And not always. And Yannis—or rather, Fani—whenever he dreamt of the town and its evening strolls. Which was less and less. His dreams, too, had changed. It was I who killed Preveza, he'd say. That's what the poet wanted to do—and he killed himself.

He worked as a dishwasher and studied accounting. There was money to be made in that profession; he'd been told by those who knew. Even his boss at the club was looking for an accountant—one with his wits about him and a head for figures. He was hungry. But he was sustained by the idea of poetry, rooted deep inside him since he'd first heard about the poet who had died on the beach in Preveza and was considered unrivalled in Greece today. He, too, had been a clerk, working as a state employee. You see so many in the tax offices, the registry offices, the courts and the land registries, who perhaps write poetry when they go home in the evenings.

On graduating as an accountant he took the position in the club where he'd been working as a dishwasher. His salary was a joke. His boss gave him half the normal rate. He ate very little. He read a lot. And in the evenings he wrote feverishly, throwing away, tearing up, biting his nails, relighting the extinguished butts in the ashtray with its advertisement for beer.

His crowd of friends in Athens, The Guys, were a group he'd met

---

1. Reference to Greek poet Konstantinos Karyotakis (1896-1928), who committed suicide in Preveza by shooting himself after having made an unsuccessful attempt to drown himself.

three years before in Vyronas, in a little café full of aged refugees bent over their card and dice games, with their sleeves rolled up and their gazes vacant, lost in the past that smoldered beneath the dense recollections of old age. The Guys had stood by him in difficult times. They had found some junk to furnish his tiny room; they had chipped in to help his wretched finances when they had seen that he didn't have the wherewithal for the movies or for a Sunday excursion by motorbike to go swimming at Oropos. They'd even brought him books—particularly the oldest one in the group, a former nurse at the Tzaneio Clinic, who had now given it all up and preferred to study history.

Pericles would bring him some of the verses he scribbled. The other one laughed, told him that he still had a long way to go before he would produce a poem like those that he knew by heart and could recite to him. "We need poetry," he told him, "that speaks of people's dreams. But if the poet hasn't first embraced life with open arms, he'll write only twaddle."

All this changed one day when he woke up and set himself to writing down one of those dreams that at first you don't realize are over and aren't continuing now that you're awake. One of those that fill your days with their fragrance and with the feelings they aroused in you. Without it being very clear how or why, that dream clearly opened up the way for a poem. A poem that would come out powerful and memorable, like those of the great poets, such as the suicide in Preveza, with that look of an aged child and with the high forehead that had been kissed by the Muses. He set himself to writing it.

From that day on, he called himself the Slave of the Deity. To distinguish himself from the slave of Preveza, the slave of hunger, of fasting and prayer, the slave of the leash, of exploitation, of necessity. He was now the servant of a higher force; he belonged to a world that was special. He struggled and wrestled, writing and tearing up, trying to bring back into his mind the magic of the dream that didn't seem to want to come back to him and transport him with its wings.

In the third year of his acquaintance with The Guys, Pericles was still in his job as accountant at the club and still wrestling with the poem he had dreamt of on that night. He could now think of the others in the group as "my brothers." The Guys were no sentimentalists; they all worked somewhere from time to time, they all had strong opinions concerning what went on around them, the things that affected them. They often talked about the unions selling out, the parties compromising, the crude foreign intervention. But none of them had any open accounts with the police as others had. He saw them all as people with sharp minds, clear hearts and sound views. But there were several occasions when the conversations were cut short whenever Pericles went to sit with them. They changed the topic. It was as clear as day: they had some other kind of relationship, a different one. Just like professional people who stop talking shop when someone else joins them, and turn to topics that everyone can talk about.

That year, Pericles had begun to despair. The poem slipped away from him like a live fish, like the water from his hands. He'd begun to sink. Where was the Slave of the Deity? The Deity had had its back turned to him all those years, didn't deign to look his way, to reveal its secrets to him, to embrace him as its own. Why am I struggling? he asked himself. Why am I forcing myself? The poem won't come, I'm never going to succeed. I've got nothing. Zilch…

One day, he spoke to the former nurse.

"What's eating you, son?" the other asked.

"It's more like a love poem," said Pericles. "I wanted it to be political. But I can't get away from the image that's stuck in my mind. I don't want to alter it. But I can't move forward… take it any further."

"What image?" he asked.

Pericles reached in his pocket and took out the papers, which he now had with him all the time, in case the inspiration came to him while he was doing additions in the club, while hanging from the rail in the trolley or getting up to go for a pee in the taverna. He wanted to be prepared at every moment. The despair at drying up had disguised itself as enthusiasm for creation, pretending to be the inspiration that was ready to spring forth and sweep him away like a sudden storm. I'll be ready, he thought. I'll take hold of it by the hair and bring it to its knees. I'll stand out from the others, as befits me. He took out the paper, straightened it and read what he'd written.

"Listen!"

Fair and gracious lady, again I find you
Running joyfully, laughing, singing,
In the garden of my dream.

Hitherto bowed, I now stand on tiptoe
Behind the fence to see your tender
Glow which ever haunts me.

Secretly I'll ascend to the bedchamber
That radiates around the rosy body
Of your youth like a veil.

Kneeling beside your virginal bed
With lips all awe I'll touch
The skin of an uncovered thigh.

"I'll tell you something," said the former nurse, leaning over with the tufts of hair on his head like long-faded paint. "Can you keep a secret?"

"Yes," said Pericles.

It was that night in the taverna, when the rain had been falling constantly for days. The stunted trees outside were swaying this way and that in the wind and rain, the leaves glistened and rivers spurted from the drainpipes onto the sidewalk's broken slabs.

"Eleven," said the other. "An hour before the day changes... Are you ready to start a new page?"

"I haven't finished the first one yet," said the accountant with a forced smile. "I tear them up and go back to the beginning."

"I'll tell you something. It concerns me and some of The Guys. If you want, fine. If not, forgot what I've told you and go your own way... your brothers have to count on you... Not a word, that is! You won't even repeat it in your sleep—do you hear?"

The former nurse began talking, trying not to shock him, ready to change tack if he thought that he'd chosen the wrong person. Even though he was sure.

He wasn't mistaken. The Slave of the Deity knew how to listen and kept looking straight into the other's eyes. You knew that he wasn't hiding anything. And so, feeling at ease, he got down to detail. The plan had been drawn up for months. There was no danger. It required some coordination, two visits on the spot before the job, for a rehearsal. The getaway was secure: one waits in the stolen car, another watches the street corner, the third on the stairs of the apartment block, on the top floor, to give the signal as soon as the target came out of his office. They would split up in the commotion, then disappear in the crowd in the main avenue into which the back street led.

"Unknown. Unrelated. No knowledge, no involvement, no relation. Some of us had worked for him in the past and were fired by him. They might follow the thread as far as our little circle. But for them to get to *you*, they'll first have to sift through four million others without any knowledge of or any relation to the man. In others words, they never will. You've seen all they've achieved so far."

Pericles felt the blood racing in his veins, warming his temples.

"You'll earn a place in our hearts. You'll be one of those who dared. You'll never again have any involvement in any business like that. You won't leave any trace and they'll never find you out. It will be a secret all your life. The target is one of those that it would be better if they weren't around. I don't need to tell you. You know him, you read the newspapers, listen to the news. One of those who swell up like the ticks behind a dog's ear. Just him and nothing else."

"Him and *something else*," said Pericles, as though distracted.

"What else?"

"The poem. I'm talking about the secrets I'll be carrying from now on..."

"Waiter, more wine... Listen here. The poem may never come. If it comes, why should it remain a secret? You publish it... There are plenty who do it. But tell me... who ever learned anything about the dream of the one who wrote it? No one. Do you see? They're alike— the poem and the job. People will hear about it, but how and why... never!"

"You could write poems too," said Pericles, looking him in the eye.

"I have."

"You!"

"Yes. But not that kind... The other kind."

The rehearsals took place the following week. The first on Monday. The second on Wednesday. The job took place on the Friday evening, at eight-thirty, when the streets were busy with people and traffic, and the rain seemed to be letting up somewhat. The Meteorological Office had promised sunshine for the weekend. The Guys had planned a trip to Salamina. Pericles could go along with them if he wanted.

For the Friday evening, he wore his work trousers. In his left pocket, the unfinished poem no longer rustled, the paper had become soft, had become one with his lining. Yet he felt it touching the skin of his thigh and burning him; the words were going round in his brain like the image of a sweetheart who had married someone else. Just like Fani had with Yannis…Unrelated…Unknown…You can go up to him, get close to him, pretend you stumbled, accidentally, apologize, say you're sorry, lean on him supposedly to stop yourself falling. These things happen on the stairs, in doorways in the city's streets. No one has any reason to look at you, to remember you. An unknown, unrelated face, one you see everyday, common, a nonentity, zilch. A non-existent enemy who springs up before you like a nightmare, takes his hand out of his threadbare pocket, out of an ordinary jacket, and raises it to your head, with a movement that might be simply a greeting, a joke, a gesture of apology for the inconvenience…And everything ends in the darkness of sleep.

The Guys left on the Saturday for Salamina with their wives. The nurse took the plane to Thessaloniki. Pericles shut himself inside his house. He planned to go in late to work to finish off the books for the quarter. Sleepless from the previous night, he walked up and down in his room and pitted the words that had remained, floating in the air. At an interlude in this feverish movement between the four walls, he washed his trousers, which had a dark stain at the knee. It was a momentary contact that he was unable to recall. But it must have happened. Otherwise, where had the blood come from? Then, with his hands still wet, the flesh of his fingers dyed with a faint red from the stain, he rubbed his temples hard trying to cool himself. He pulled the crumpled papers from his pocket and set to. Everything went dark round about, and nothing remained but him and the table with his paper upon it, lighting his face like a reflector.

With the Biro that was coming to its end so that its ink was flowing thick and fast, he continued, changing the word "awe" in the last tristych. And then, all of a sudden, as if he were copying it, the rest of his poem was ready:

> *Kneeling beside your virginal bed*
> *I'll touch with lips all hatred*
> *The skin of an uncovered thigh.*
>
> *And with a sharp knife I'll open*
> *A new mouth there, equally rosy.*
> *And only your new mouth will I kiss.*
>
> *From the bloodied cavity I'll drink the Ichor*
> *From your unblemished soul, my Virgin,*
> *Aloof forever a stranger,*
> *In the intoxication of your bestial Beauty.*

For the first time in weeks he slept like a log. He woke up on Sunday afternoon another man. A High Priest of the Deity, he said as soon as he opened his eyes. And he laughed to himself.

Original title: "Alazoneia." Published in Alexis Panselinos, *Tesseris ellinikoi fonoi* [Four Greek Murders], Athens: Polis, 2004, pp. 23-34.

I. H. PAPADIMITRAKOPOULOS

Rosamund

I am often asked by friends (recent ones in particular) how I came to get involved with the army and how I served in it for so many years, albeit as a doctor... I"ve tried, at times, to give various answers (the suffering we endured during the Nazi Occupation, the poverty that followed, the Civil War, and so on—I have even hinted as much in an entire short story), but usually what I say falls on deaf ears. The others listen mechanically, not so say indifferently, most have no idea what I am talking about. And so, after a whole string of attempts, I settled on an answer of more or less one word:

"Rosamund," I say.

The effect is really rather impressive. Their faces light up, they smile meaningfully, nod their heads knowingly, show consent (approval even), while some go even further.

"Girl?" they ask.

I vaguely nod my head—and everyone thinks what they want. Who knows what they imagine, not to mention that one colleague once asked me in a somewhat offended tone:

"Where did you find her, you old rogue, and with a name like that?"

I smile with satisfaction: let them imagine what they want. Once, though, being a little foolish and feeling in a somewhat confessional mood, I added:

"Rosamund is Andreas."

The person I was talking to looked at me with scorn and, before I'd had time even to finish, said dryly:

"A curse on your balls for having us believe that…"

Anyhow, I gradually forgot all this—together with the recourse to Rosamund, and Andreas. I only remembered him last year when (after many years) I went back to my hometown to vote.

I was wandering late at night through some deserted streets, badly lit as ever, but now asphalted, without mud and puddles (though it had rained heavily), when I suddenly found myself before Andreas' family house.

It was a fine stone house with a huge enclosed yard, of marble, where once carriages, horses and the like must have drawn up. I halted. The house was closed, abandoned, crumbling. When, in the past, I would visit Andreas (we were pupils together), he would never come to the entrance, but would receive me in a dim living room, with a strong musty smell, and after first talking of everything under the sun, he'd eventually make his way over to the piano, supposedly indifferently, and looking deeply into my eyes, almost imploringly, would ask me if I would like to hear something—at the same time pointing out to me the risk involved in the undertaking, given that his father was resting, his mother suffered from migraines, his brother was studying for the University and so on.

Andreas never managed to learn to play the piano, but highly energetic, highly optimistic and impetuous as he always was, he had managed to learn to play (with many mistakes, of course) an excerpt from Schubert's *Rosamund*. I recall him sitting at the piano, unassuming at first, hesitant, but as time passed gathering momentum, tuning himself, till he reached the inevitable point, where (now upright), frenzied and beside himself, he pressed all the keys along the whole length of the keyboard with dizzying speed, first with the tip of his right forefinger, and then (in reverse) with that of his thumb, and with tremendous force and strength, thus achieving two blood-curdling chords one after the other, at the same time feverishly pressing the pedals alternately—and that's where he stopped, suddenly turned to stone, and apparently exhausted, though ready for a deep bow if the audience applauded with the corresponding passion.

This performance (because it was a performance) was given on every occasion and at every opportunity, and always with the same excerpt from *Rosamund*, whereupon (inevitably) it wasn't long before Andreas became scoffingly identified with Rosamund.

We were by then in the final year of school. We were starting to feel the pressure: what were we going to do now? We had no money, no prospects, no opportunities. The Civil War was still dragging on. One morning while we were loafing around in the schoolyard (we rarely went in for the lessons), Andreas waltzed over to me.

"I want to talk to you," he whispered.

"What is it?" I asked.

"This afternoon at five," he said.

And leaning over closer to my ear, he added with due gravity:

"I've come up with a solution to our problem. We've got it made!"

I was kicking my heels outside his house from three o'clock, without daring to touch the doorknocker. His father used to sleep until four-thirty and he was strict about time. At five to five (I kept asking passersby what time it was), I knocked on the door. It was opened by his elder brother, a medical student at the time, who said to me in a formal tone:

"Andreas is awaiting you in the living room."

Andreas was jumping up and down in tremendous excitement. I waited in vain for him to sit down somewhere, even at the piano. Eventually, amid vagaries and generalities, in a conspiratorial and evasive way, he came out with the secret, just as his brother had revealed it to him. Namely, that there was a Military Medical School in Thessaloniki; we'd sit exams in August, get in, study at the University, all expenses paid by the School, where we'd eat, drink and sleep for free, have a blue uniform with gold buttons for the evening, a sword, leave, girls, etc.

"We've got it made, Ilias, my friend," he said to me finally, almost in tears.

We sat the exams. Andreas didn't pass. After that I lost touch with him for decades.

I bumped into him quite by chance yesterday morning while sitting in the office of the director of a private clinic. At first I didn't recognize him given the way he was walking slowly, carefully, almost demurely, wearing an impeccable gray checked suit and carrying under his arm a doctor's bag. As he was about to leave, I said his name quietly, almost in a whisper.

He turned hesitantly.

"Did you call me?" he asked.

I got to my feet. He recognized me, but he wouldn't sit down or wait.

"Nice to have seen you," he said to me. "I've a lot of doctors to see; unfortunately, they only allow us in here every other Friday."

He halted. He came back—and in his eyes I saw something of that old spark.

"Life came to an end for us," he said to me. "After what happened to my brother and his daughter, you must have heard of course, we don't speak any more, our life ended, we died."

He stopped and, with an almost imperceptible bow of his head, said:

"With all due respect, it was nice to have seen you, goodbye."

He left.

I had indeed heard—but I'd already forgotten about it. The daughter of his brother, the doctor, a student in her final year at University, had attempted to commit suicide and had ended up as a vegetable. She had been in the intensive care unit for months. After a year of fruitless efforts, her father, wearing his doctor's coat and accompanied by the usual staff on his morning visit, unplugged the machine keeping her alive (so to speak) with his own hands and in an atmosphere of deathly silence and astonishment. They buried her in one of the capital's cemeteries with only a close circle of family and friends present.

The next morning, the doctor was found dead in his bed—having died, so it was said at the time, of a heart attack.

Original title: "Rozamoundi." Published in I. H. Papadimitrakopoulos, *Rozamoundi*, Athens: Nefeli, 1995, pp. 19-27.

DIMITRIS PETSETIDIS

Away Ground

For a moment I thought of asking her, given that she smiled as she greeted me, "Do I know you?" But then I felt embarrassed because of my memory and walked on, between the café tables, stumbling and tripping as if drugged; I was playing on an away ground, I found the cigarette smoke annoying, not even the music, which seemed as if it were coming out of the ceiling, was to my taste.

She was wearing a short miniskirt and her smile painted an image of audacity on her harsh face, her unkempt bleached hair made her seem like a caricature, the pupils of her eyes appeared hugely dilated. I thought to myself "You can go fuck yourself too," but where did I know her from? Had we met years before, had we chatted, what if I'd confided in her any of all that tormented me and still torments me night and day, to hell with my memory, I need to exercise it, start doing crosswords. I strive to recall a poem by Embiricos that I'd once learned by heart, little egoistical twerp, what you did to try to impress, and all I can think of are some lines by the poetess: "*In their ostensible nonchalance there's always the horrible suspicion.*"

There's plenty of time, I thought, we have time, leave it for later, why rush, and if we lose out on meeting some new chick or lose out on acquiring a new position, what's the big deal. We've taken care of all three of our dimensions—that's care for you too!—and we've acquired a belly ignoring the fourth dimension, the treacherous one, that pervades us and slowly erodes us, the one that is the flesh's canker. And we never realized when the body-beanpole, when the body-cypress became like that, so that you pee and you can't see your willy, you hear tell of beanpoles and cypresses and your mind turns elsewhere, a shudder runs through you.

Three boys are smoking and drinking their coffee; one of them can't be more than fifteen, a deep scar on his face, disfiguring him. A car accident, even so he was lucky, his friend who was with him on the speeding bike is in the hospital, a vegetable, and his folks don't want to pull the plug.

I keep going and arrive at a chair in front of the bar's marble surface, I'll order an ouzo, no cooked meats in the meze, maybe I'll have a second. Once upon a time, I used to come here with Angeliki, how the years had passed, thirty, maybe more, it was a café then, but there was always ouzo and fresh tomato and cheese for the meze. Angeliki and I used to drink ouzo, she'd been accepted into the School of Architecture. "How much can I possibly mean to you now?" I said to her, "you're going to become an architect, what am I?" Someone looking for a job in a newspaper, at least let me get into an advertising agency, ideas for sale. Angeliki's eyes filled with tears and, moron that I am, I never gave it a thought, I pretended to be the tough guy, I must have seen some film earlier that evening at the cinema, the hero was speaking through my mouth, not to mention that I was convinced I looked like him, as I came out with all that supposedly gallant bullshit, all that worthless drivel.

And as the time passed, you'd park yourself every other day in the café drinking your ouzo, you asshole, you avoided looking in the huge mirror on the café wall, like "*someone sick who prefers not to see how his appearance is constantly deteriorating.*"

A young lad is talking loudly with one arm round his girl and a cigarette in the other hand; the girl, like the lad, is smoking like a chimney; he's saying something to her about an old man, he turns towards me and in a loud voice continues to relate the business with the old man, continually stressing the words *old man*; he sees another lad who has just walked in. "Over here, dude," he shouts.

The girl stares at me, I detect in her gaze more of an inquisitive air than a disapproving one, that's it! As if she were grinning while drawing on her cigarette and blowing the smoke in my direction.

The barwoman is an acquaintance of mine, I knew that she'd married a lackey of the ruling party, I was amazed to see her working in a café. "We split up," she tells me, "in a few days I'm starting work at a fast-food restaurant in Tripoli, to get away from this lousy city, and I'm never coming back." Don't you know, poor Danae, that the city will always follow you, better for you that you don't know or perhaps heaven help you that you don't? No they hadn't had children, I remember those dreadful scenes when my folks announced they were splitting up, the deafening sound of that word *divorce*.

"It's fortunate you don't have kids," I told her, without her hearing me, she had moved away and was serving a group of soldiers in civvies who were saying various things to tease her, I'm alone again with my ouzo.

Now on the wall where the huge mirror used to be, there are bare stones, strange-shaped electric lamps and some wooden contraptions that don't seem to have any use, that must have been the decorator's idea.

I reflect that we've remained kids. I could fall in love with the girl opposite who continues to stare at me inquisitively, her boyfriend is still sounding off about old men. I reflect on love, loves, long-lost desires, desires linked to faces and bodies, all covered in the mist of a memory that gets weaker by the day.

I try to work out how many years are still left, but I've resigned myself to it from my youth.

From nothing to nothing and however long you live in between. How have so many years gone by already? Spring, summer, autumn, winter and again spring, summer, autumn, winter, again spring, summer, autumn, winter, I feel dizzy, it's also the fault of the two ouzos I've downed.

I get up to leave the café with the American name, once it was the "Cosy Spot" café, now I find it difficult to walk with a steady step in the direction of the door, I recall that I didn't say goodbye to Danae and turning round I wave to her. I look at the table where the girl was sitting with her friend who was railing about that old man, they're hugging and kissing, I can only see their backs. I open the door and as the cold wintry air hits me in the face, I mumble to myself: "*We're like the old man who supposedly doesn't know...*"

Original title: "Se xeno yipedo." Published in Dimitris Petsetidis, *Se xeno yipedo*, Athens: Patakis, 2003, pp. 45-50.

Yorgos Skabardonis

Mussels in the Flower Vase

There must have been around six or seven fishermen, ranging in age from thirty to sixty, unshaven and dirty. They were sitting on gas cylinders and frying mussels in a round sheet-metal tin with a little blue primus stove underneath. Then they'd take them while they were steaming, squeeze lemon on them and eat them whole, drinking ouzo from mini-bottles, laughing loudly, joking, jostling each other.

A hundred meters further off, the sea glistened with its moored boats, its plastic waste, its seabirds. And on this side was a curve in the Nea Krini public highway, which is where I lived, in a new apartment block, and where I'd just arrived by car in the middle of the day and in high summer to park in the usual spot.

But in the place where I usually parked, the carousing fishermen had left four three-wheeler jalopies loaded with fish boxes and with a reasonable space between them but not enough for a car, nor was there any other space for parking. If they moved two of the three-wheelers closer, I would easily be able to tuck it away. Otherwise, I'd have to continue on for about five hundred meters to find another spot and walk back, not something I wanted to do, because I was tired, wet with sweat and the sun was beating down.

I'd gotten out of the car and was watching them with eyes half-closed because of the intense light; I looked at them, envious of their merrymaking. At a momentary lull in their revelry, when they quieted down, I braced myself and called out to them from ten meters:

"Hey, can you move the three-wheelers over a bit so the rest of us can park too?"

A menacing silence descended upon the group, the fishermen froze, as if momentarily embalmed, then one, the heftiest, two meters tall, raised himself to his full majestic stature, and shouted provocatively:

"You want to park, do you, asshole? Take your jalopy and put it up there in that open space."

The others laughed, muttering something among themselves, while I, after the first wave of anger that I felt right down to my feet, tried to remain calm. I was in no position to take on that hulk, and then there were the others as well who would make mincemeat of me. I turned and said in a steady voice:

"So that's it, is it pal? Instead of inviting me over for an ouzo, you hurl abuse at me."

The hulk was taken aback; he remained speechless, swaying upright in the sun, like a Cyclops who has just had a stake suddenly thrust into his only eye. The others got the message and tugged at him from behind, made him sit down, and shouted to me:

"Come on over, friend, come and have a mussel with us."

I stood there a moment and then proudly walked over to them, with a somewhat labored step and expression. Before I knew where I was, two of them nipped over and moved the three-wheelers, another took my car and parked it, while I found myself sitting on an upturned gas cylinder with a mussel in one hand and a mini-bottle of ouzo in the other.

Presently, the other three came back after the parking, flushed from the effort, staggering from the ouzo and the sun, and sat down. The tall one who had hurled abuse at me got up, came over to me, squatted next to me, clinked his bottle against mine, and said:

"Sorry, pal, if I offended you. Come on, drink up, and I hope you'll always find plenty of mussels waiting for you. You know what kind of mussels I'm talking about, right?"

"I know, I know," I replied, raising my bottle so it gleamed in the light.

More mussels were put in the pan, giving off a delicious smell as they cooked. With small, tender counterattacks, the sea caressed the sand, the sun beat down on us diagonally, every so often I squeezed lemon juice on my hands to clean them, the ouzo made the eyelids droop, while the cars gliding over the shining asphalt and the huge apartment blocks nearby seemed no longer to exist; they dissolved in a strange undulating tremor of light, vanished, vaporized.

The ouzo had made me dizzy, I downed one mussel after the next with absolute inner confidence that there was no way I was going to get poisoned, I joked with the fishermen, we'd all become one in spirit, we were in another time, beyond normal time, in another town, in another strange and lovely place.

Eventually the ouzo ran out, someone got up to go and fetch some more, while another, who noticed my smooth hands and saw the wedding ring, turned and said to me:

"Married?"

"Married."

"Say no more ..."

We kept going, everything was spinning now, sea and sun, cars and gas cylinders, all in the air, mussels and female mussels were all rotating, and in the opposite direction to that of the planet. I couldn't take any more, I got up staggering, steadied myself, took a deep breath and said:

"Guys, thanks but I'm going. I have to be off because my wife's expecting me."

"You're going? Wait a moment," said the man who had sworn at me at first. "Wait while I put a few mussels in a bag for your missus."

And he reached out, grabbed two handfuls of cooked mussels, thrust them into a crumpled paper bag and handed them to me.

"Thanks," I said to them, they acknowledged me by raising their bottles, "thanks and I hope we'll never come to any worse."

"So long," they shouted, "so long and come back any time. Bye."

Dizzy, tripping, holding the mussels with great care as though they were flowers, trying hard not to fall over and make a fool of myself in front of my fishermen friends, the only friends I had, doing my best to avoid the sun, I eventually reached the apartment block and went inside. I pressed the elevator button and leaned against the wall, breathing heavily. Strange shapes flashed and vanished in the hall mirror, while the ceiling first approached me menacingly and flattened me, then raced off screeching to a fathomless depth.

I got into the elevator and went up, feeling as though the apartment block was sinking into the ground following a silent explosion; I felt that, floor by floor, it was passing away and that I was radiantly ascending and vanishing into the heavens.

The sudden halting brought me round for a moment, I got out, bumping the door with my back, holding the mussels in one hand and turning the key with the other, I fell sideways into the apartment, proceeded with great difficulty into the living room, holding onto the walls, and dropped the mussels into a large glass flower vase in the middle of the table. The mussels "for my wife." What wife—it had been three months and seven days since we'd split up for good. What wife, I mumbled to myself and fell headfirst onto the sofa, remembering that I'd left the keys in the car, that I'd left it open but I didn't care, and gazing at the bookcase in which the books had been replaced by hundreds of mini bottles of ouzo, or so it seemed to me; my stomach was churning, I could feel it turning like the innards of a washing machine, I turned, leaned over the edge of the sofa and vomited violently on the floor, I began to cry, to cry, and I knew that my wife would come out of the other room, might come, must come, and I fell into a stupor, into the black depths of the sea, into the blackest blackness.

Original title: "Midia sto anthodoheio." Published in Yorgos Skabardonis, *Mati fosforo, koumando yero* [Eye Peeled, Firm Command], Athens: Kastaniotis, 1992, pp. 49-55.

Ersi Sotiropoulou

The Assistants

It was the day before I was leaving for New York, no, three days before. I took the electric train and went to the new shopping mall near Kifissia. I looked in the windows of the first two floors and then got into the elevator to go up to the top floor. I found myself in a huge area with thousands of people and deafening music. The ceiling was made of glass and as the light shone through it, its rays bent like broken lances and streamed to the floor forming strange patterns on the dark mosaic tiles.

I walked through the crowds. Opposite the escalator was a space arranged like a park, with a few benches and some plastic blooms in flowerbeds. On a screen on the wall, an invisible video projected the sign "Merry Christmas," in red children's letters on a green background. The letters flashed several times, the sign darkened for a fraction of a second and suddenly the screen turned silver and the names of well-known makes of children's clothes, toys and so on began dancing on it before eventually becoming fixed. The place had something fanciful about it; people were going to and fro, gesticulating and shouting, while the same Christmas carol was played first in English and then in German. There were plastic palm trees, snow-covered firs and also pink bougainvilleas, a midget Father Christmas and a small fountain with water that kept changing color.

"Hey, Sting!..." I heard a voice beside me and I turned round.

A girl had fallen down and was trying to get up, supporting the weight of her body on her arms. Her legs were scrawny and she was wearing black roller skates. She was flushed and her face had an ambiguous expression, so you couldn't tell whether she was crying or laughing.

"Sting!...Sting!..." she shouted again.

The one answering to the name was racing and doing stunts in front of the escalator, preventing people from getting off. He was a boy with long hair and an earring.

"God, what an asshole," the girl said.

She had managed to get up and wobbled a little before finding her balance.

I sat down on one of the benches and stretched out my legs. It was a carefree day for me and I congratulated myself on having had the inspiration to get out of the center. Throwing my head back, I gazed at the glass ceiling and beyond it at the pale sky. Tiny clouds suddenly appeared, quickly crossed the glass dome and disappeared at the opposite side. In the distance, a thick black cloud hung motionless like a hot-air balloon. I looked again at the illuminated sign. The children's letters were so clumsy and messy that they provoked repugnance rather than feelings of tenderness. Further off, at the edge of the park, I saw a tiny train that I hadn't noticed earlier. Four or five carriages painted in bright yellow were doing the round of the floor on fake tracks. Mothers could get rid of their kids for a while and stare into space, smoking a cigarette. Others took their shopping lists out of their bags and studied them with due care till, whistling, the tiny train came back round, whereupon they got up with a sigh and unenthusiastically went to take their kids.

I, too, lit a cigarette and watched the sign. I got the impression that the clothes advertisements remained on the screen longer than the "Merry Christmas" and, what's more, that before they faded, they suddenly grew brighter and the background filled with small black spots. I looked at my watch, trying to time them. Before long, the children's letters were dancing before my eyes and I gave up. My attention focused on the expressions of the people around me, but before long that made me dizzy too. They all appeared to have a very specific goal in life. The clothes, the plastic bags and the purses were all in their proper places. Every mouth seemed to say "two plus two equals four," without making a sound. If you looked at them more closely, however, they were all washouts, I knew. At that time, this was the keyword for me. Washout. Women managed to hide this degradation better. The panic nestled in their spinal column. This is what stopped them falling as they walked, burdened with kids and shopping. But what did I care? That day I felt carefree right down to my very marrow. All I could dream of was a hamburger with French fries.

Carefree from head to toe. I didn't want to think about anything. Even the desire for a hamburger acted like a brake on the free flow of insouciance. A new beginning, I kept repeating to myself. I'd quit my job, I was still young and I was preparing to leave for New York. It was then that something happened that ruined my mood for the rest of the day and that, today, even at this very moment, still makes me feel depressed. A woman came and sat down on the other end of the bench. I looked at her out of the corner of my eye. She must have been around forty and was dragging two bulging supermarket bags with her. She put the one bag down, rested the other on her knees and began searching impatiently and hectically, scattering a pile of rubbish about her. Too young to be mad, I thought. She was rummaging with her right arm, searching blindly because the bag reached right up to her shoulder, while with the left, she was trying to hold the bag steady on her belly. I started to feel strange; I was overcome by a kind of irritability as though I, too, were looking for something that I'd lost. I stood up and went across to the kiosk to buy an icecream.

"Strawberry and pistachio," I said, immediately regretting it.

The girl operated the machine and the icecream began to flow, whirling into the cone. I wasn't in the mood for icecream and, what's more, I hate the taste of pistachio. I glanced at the woman on the bench, but she was bent over her bag and I couldn't see her. So I paid and, holding the cone, I looked around me for another place to sit. The only free seat was two meters further off and I made for it. As I walked past her, the woman raised her head and gave me a momentary look. It was a vague look, expressionless. But something bothered me about it. It crossed my mind that she may have thought I was trying to avoid her. I went back.

The moment I sat down next to her, she stopped searching. She hugged the bag with both arms, held it tight to her and remained totally still. Every so often, her left leg moved ever so slightly, without her lifting it up, as if she wanted to touch the other bag that was on the floor. I licked the icecream on top and slowly began to eat the cone, biting it symmetrically. But all my attention and all my thoughts were focused on her. After a while, Sting and his girlfriend skated past us. I watched them as they gathered speed towards the far end of the floor, behind the escalator. That side of the store hadn't been decorated, it was an empty space with an arch formed by some beach umbrellas that had been there from the summer. Sting did a few pirouettes there while the girl waited for him with her back against the wall. Then he held out his hand, pulled her to him and they whirled round together a few times, till they disappeared from my view. For a few minutes nothing happened. Then they passed in front of us again. Now, their movements were coordinated and their bodies glided harmoniously on an imaginary straight line. Sting was holding the girl round the waist and was leaning towards her slightly. They were both looking straight ahead with a steady gaze and had the same expression on their faces, slightly taunting, slightly innocent.

"I won't let them," said the woman.

I turned towards her. She seemed completely absorbed in the spectacle of the two youngsters as they skated away.

"I won't let them," she sighed, "they've attached wires to them..."

Suddenly, she turned and looked at me.

"Can't you see them with the wheels?" she said in an irritated tone as if I hadn't understood anything. "If they talk to me, they'll blow them to pieces, they've got wires attached to them..."

There was a noticeable asymmetry about her face; her nose suddenly grew thicker above her left nostril and veered toward her earlobe. Her eyes were on a different level, the one much smaller than the other.

"What's wrong?" I asked.

"They're bringing me a message..." she explained, nodding in the direction where Sting and his girlfriend had disappeared. "I wait for them here every day... But they've attached wires to them, they don't let them."

"Who?" I asked.

"The assistants. They're hidden everywhere..." she mumbled and suddenly lost all interest in me.

She remained silent for a while, hunched over the bag. Her clothes were threadbare but reasonably clean, she didn't look as if she were homeless. It was now late afternoon. The crowds, rather than thinning out, got thicker and thicker. Sting and his girlfriend were nowhere to be seen. For no reason at all, I began to imagine myself in five, in ten years time...Imagine myself in this woman's place. I wasn't thinking of anything specific, simply that I'd be sitting on a bench on Christmas Eve, that I'd be carrying all my belongings and that I'd be imagining sinister plots involving shop assistants.

"Would you like a biscuit?" said the woman suddenly, smiling for the first time.

As she looked me in the eye, I saw that the asymmetry had vanished from her face.

"Thank you," I said.

She leaned over the bag and began rummaging in it furiously.

"What's your opinion on the rumors that are circulating?" she asked without raising her head.

"I don't know..." I mumbled.

"Rumors about Christmas!" she said, apparently becoming annoyed. "They want to run it into Easter... That's what the assistants say..."

"I've no idea..."

"In that case, I can't help you," she said condescendingly. She stopped her searching and tied the tops of the bags in a knot.

I wanted to leave. I wanted to get outside and walk in the fresh air.

"And there's AIDS too..." I mumbled just to say something and I immediately felt even more stupid. Another wrong move, I thought.

"Don't worry, I know..." she said. "Eat your biscuit."

She hadn't given me any biscuit.

"Thank you," I said, and got up.

There was a line for the elevator. I went down using the escalator. On each floor, the crowds were milling around the stands with the bargain items. In front of the entrance, a group of youngsters were arguing and among them I thought I saw Sting and his girlfriend. I walked outside and the cold air hit me in the face. I walked aimlessly around the mall. I walked until my legs were numb. I kept thinking about that woman. I kept thinking what I'd do in her place and if I'd be saying the same things.

Original title: "Oi ipalliloi." Published in Ersi Sotiropoulou, *O vasilias tou flipper* [Pin-ball King], Athens: Kastaniotis, 1997, pp. 149-158.

Antonis Sourounis

His Last Role

With eyes half closed, Harissis stared at his face in the mirror. Goddamn it, even like that, still befuddled from sleep, he was a good-looking guy. For his part, he was the most good-looking guy he'd ever set eyes upon from so close up. Everyone had told him so from the time he'd first started exercising his pecker. His mother, his schoolmistresses, he himself—above all, he himself—the women who'd approached him. It was the men who needed their eyes testing. We're not talking about the punks and pansies who fawned over him in the hope of getting laid, but about the others, those who hold the keys to important doors in their hands. And who open them to you only if you become a faggot like they are, only if you "wave a white flag," like they once had. All his life Harissis had been waiting for them to ask him to surrender, so he could say no, could fight and win, but no one ever asked him, no one dragged him into war; they left him alone in his corner to slave away at whatever he thought best. And he fucked. He fucked and aged. Even today, if his luck crumbled and confronted him again, asking this and that from him, Harissis intended to say no, but not by shouting it from the rooftops as he'd dreamt of in his youth. He was still determined to wave a white flag to the bitch if it asked—and a piece of ass if it insisted. He would surrender this and more, just so long as he could exploit his good looks a little, in order to improve his life. There's no sight more degrading than an aged good-looker who ended up a loser. Men take delight in it—"we got the better of you in the end pretty boy, you asshole"—but women, who miss nothing and stand by you, now begin to feel pity for you, because they sense that you've begun to feel pity yourself. And so they too close their doors to you and you no longer have anywhere to lay your heads. Harissis was approaching forty and he'd learned the fucking lesson by heart.

In the other mirror, his cousin was drying his hair with the dryer. Six o'clock, he said, it was six o'clock when the dickhead had woken him. He'd already shaved and washed his hair. He shaved and washed his hair every morning. Then he'd go to the landing where, from the night before, the clothes he would wear had been hanging over the wooden rail. Clean underwear, starched shirt, pressed suit, matching tie, polished shoes and clean socks. So far, the whole thing seemed quite reasonable; the real madness began when the cousin, wearing this fancy attire, didn't go off to get married, but to shut himself up in an office till late afternoon. In the evening, he came back, took the dogs out to pee, watched whatever was on television with his wife, and then had a warm shower in order to relax and be able to sleep. Sometimes not even the warm shower had any effect and then he would jog five or six kilometers in the dark wood, so as to be able to get to sleep and go on doing all that he did.

"I'm going down to make the coffee…I'll turn on the middle shower for you so you don't get water all over the floor. You'll have to bend a bit. Go downstairs if you want to crap."

During the twenty years that Harissis had lived in Germany, he hadn't met any other Greek who lived in a house with two floors and two bathrooms. His cousin had done all right for himself. Apart from the two floors and bathrooms, he also had two cars, two dogs and two mirrors in one of the bathrooms. Whether he still had his two balls, Harissis couldn't say.

He remained upright watching the water striking his belly and running down his legs. For the first time it went through his mind that perhaps his pecker had started to hunch. When it appeared to the world, it still seemed as though it were on parade, but who knew how it lived like that for so many hours all alone in its cave? Harissis took it in his palm and caressed it. "Old pal…" It remained bent and quiet like a tired dog that had aged along with him. If it had had a voice and if things had been somewhat different, it should have been day and night at the State Pension Offices demanding a retirement pension. Why should your old age depend on how many days you'd worked and not on the all the fucking?

He emerged from the shower, dried himself and sat on the toilet. He could hear muffled sounds downstairs as his cousin was getting the breakfast ready. His wife woke up around noon. The bugger had got it all worked out. At carnival time, when the company turned into a whorehouse, he even screwed around.

Suddenly, he heard him coming upstairs and, flushing the toilet, leapt to his feet. His cousin came into the bathroom to tell him something but, alarmed, he smelled the stench and said something else that he couldn't keep back:

"You took a crap!"

"No, on my life!"

"What do you mean no, you asshole, it stinks in here!"

He went to look in the toilet.

"Look, there's still shit in it. Didn't I tell you to go to the downstairs one? Not even I crap in here."

He cleaned it with a plastic sponge, flushed it and opened the windows as far as they would go.

"We'll wake Karin and all hell will break loose! Come on, finish up, we have to be off."

Harissis remained alone with Harissis facing him in the mirror. Old pal, and with the shit still on his ass, it reminded you of Hollywood. He was the spitting image of those guys who showed on the screen what a bitch society is so that your average person would take comfort and not cause trouble. "They even got the better of Paul Newman, so who am I to think I can escape them?" Harissis had seen his life at least a hundred times on the screen up to then—or was it that he lived in keeping with the script. But to live the Passion of Christ without being filmed by a camera, you must be Christ himself, or, if you make it to forty alive, you end up being told where to wash and where to crap.

Harissis recalls that night when his dream approached him, kissed him and left him, and leans on the washbasin. Just once, if only it would come again just once! Though he's well aware that this is out of the question, his dream died sometime before him—it's gone, finished, asshole. A good few years have passed since then, but he feels as though what happened happened only the previous evening—what were you doing there, then?

He was sitting at the bar and quietly drinking his whisky, waiting for some woman to sit down next to him, but this time it wasn't just any old whore who came, it was Madam Fortune who sidled up to him, the high procuress in person. She was dressed as a man.

"We're making a film and you're just what we need for a minor role that's in it. You don't have to speak; it'll be easy."

Harissis was neither surprised nor taken aback. Leaving the house each day, he fully expected someone to stop him and say precisely that to him and it was as if he'd heard it a thousand times.

"What kind of role is it?"

"You'll be the client of an aging whore. He has to be an emigrant worker and I think you're just right."

The fact that it was only a minor role and the fact that the whore was old didn't bother Harissis at all. He reflected that when he'd eventually give his interviews and he'd relate all he had to endure, his thousands of admirers would smile. They told him to wear something to make him look like a bum and Harissis wore his Canadian jacket with its big checked pattern so familiar to all his friends. The director was pleased.

It was a night when the cold froze your ears off. The scene was to be shot outside town, beside the railway tracks. He climbed into a truck with two or three others and throughout the journey listened to them cursing the writer, the director and the weather. Nevertheless, he understood that the scene was quite important, the key—KEY!— to the whole plot. When they arrived, the director gave him his final instructions.

"As the train passes, you'll pretend to be fucking. You know how to do that, eh? Ha ha… The camera will be on the other side and will shoot you under the wheels. By the time the last car passes, you'll have finished, but you'll remain still, till the woman here says to you: 'You paid to fuck, not to sleep.' Then you'll get up, spit at her, zip up your pants and head for the hill. But while you were fucking, your wallet fell out—you don't need to know the rest."

So this, then, was the writer's big invention. The old woman found the wallet, found a couple of chicks and made her fortune, while Harissis made his at the same time. Beneath the bordello make-up, Harissis recognized an actress who had got on his nerves years before.

"Let me see my client in the light…"

They brought Harissis to her and shone a spotlight on him.

"Mmm… You're a good-looking boy. I'm glad it's you who's going to fuck me."

The others laughed. Harissis looked her in the eyes and told her that he was now living his big dream, and he wasn't lying.

They set up the lights and the machines and wrapped the supposed (supposed?) whore in a blanket, in case she caught her death. They didn't wrap up Harissis. Any time now the train would pass and someone with a flashlight went up the hill to signal as soon as it appeared. Ten minutes passed and the flashlight started flashing. The woman threw off the blanket and, lifting her dress up to her waist, she lay down on the ground.

"My ass is frozen already… Come on, dude, get down and keep me warm…"

Harissis lay down with great care and began moving.

"Not yet!" the camera crew shouted.

He felt just like when he was in the elevator with strangers. Then, after a while:

"Let's go, now!"

For Harissis, there was nothing easier in the world. It was, let's say, as if his whole life hung on one question and he'd been asked what his name was. He wriggled, as he'd done in reality a thousand times previously, opening shallow holes in the walls, till he reached the bottom where he crushed the horny monster. When there was quiet and he heard from the whore what it was he was supposed to hear, he got up, did what they'd told him to do, and headed up the hill. But they had omitted to tell him how far he should go and, in order to be sure,

Harissis went all the way to the top and came back, approaching them from behind. The lights had been turned off and he heard his partner shouting, shaking from the cold and from her anger:

"Anyway, I, for one, am not getting down there again. If you want to shoot the scene again, bring me someone who knows how to fuck and not that asshole. You've got half an hour to find someone before the next train passes."

Harissis retraced his steps in the darkness and went back to town on foot. He stayed three days and nights in bed trying to understand what he'd done wrong. He'd pretended to fuck, pretended to spit, zipped up his pants, walked all over the hill—what the hell else did they want?

He got dressed and went down to the kitchen. His cousin had finished and was now washing up everything he had used.

"You don't have time to eat, we have to go."

Harissis poured himself a cup of coffee and as he was putting it to his mouth, the dog leapt at him and tried to reach his face. He pulled back.

"Don't worry, the bitch only wants to kiss you…"

He remained still and the dog licked him till it got tired and left him alone. He drank some of his coffee, amazed at the taste that the dog's tongue had left on him. He reflected that plenty of tongues far worse than the dog's had passed over him.

They got into the car, which moved off by itself and took its place among the other cars. His cousin was talking. Harissis was looking out of the window at the schoolgirls and women waiting at the bus stops. He didn't have time to even distinguish them clearly.

His cousin stopped the car, but not his chatter.

"Like we said; you'll act the saint, because I've vouched for you and also to show the Germans that we haven't just come out of the jungle. This is your card, you'll take it out, clock in and put it in the slot next to your number.

Harissis did as he was told and there was no bugger around to tell him that he didn't do it well.

Original title: "O teleftaios tou rolos." Published in Antonis Sourounis, *Meronihta Frankfourtis* [Days and Nights in Frankfurt], Athens: Kastaniotis, 1999, pp. 25-35.

Petros Tatsopoulos

A Smelly Weakness

With the exception of pain, which I could never get used to—apart from smacks on the backside or a few gentle slaps across the face—I am open to every kind of sexual invitation provided that the person doing the inviting is wearing panties and isn't hiding anything peculiar inside the panties. With these few reservations, old-fashioned but indispensable ones—short reckoning, as they say, makes long friends—I am prepared to try even the humblest hors d'oeuvre from pleasure's dish, to scavenge even the last crumb of debauchery. I don't have any moral hang-ups. My only limits are to do with taste.

With the passing of time, I too acquired certain foibles. Today, having reached fifty, with three marriages round my neck and an equal number of divorces, a now sworn divorcé, it's too late for me to deny them, even limit them. Naturally, I don't compare my innocent vices with the filth that covers the front pages and oozes out of our TV latrines. In comparison with their perversions I seem like a choirboy—though an odd choirboy, not one of the best. I share the disgust at incest and bestiality. It goes without saying that the former don't deserve any share in the family's warmth, nor the latter any shelter in the pen. Though were I obliged to try the practitioners, I'd take into account certain extenuating circumstances, I wouldn't send them straight to the firing squad without more ado. Let the one without sin cast the first stone. Brave words, exact ones. And not words uttered by just anyone.

To get back to my own sins. As for my weakness for drink, I don't think I need to expand on that here—though, without this weakness, it would be hard for the others to find fertile ground. From time to time, my liver sounds a warning. And until it quiets down, I take care to abstain—so as to return even more rigorously. It hasn't escaped my attention that during the days of abstinence, my conduct is irreproachable. Without question, it's the second and sometimes the third glass of whisky that provides the necessary fuel in order for my engine to start up. With the fourth glass, it begins to race and with the fifth—I'd rather not think of it: with the fifth it cuts out.

I managed to harness an early tendency towards urophilia before finishing high school. I attribute it to adolescent experimentation, side by side with the group masturbations in the construction sites, with peeping at the literature mistress in class—this is how I explain my scoliosis—with the evening trips to the bordellos and with smoking joints to appear cool. From the experiments with my bladder, I've retained the stink of urine as a pleasant memory, its steam as something arousing—but the ensuing cooling and the smell on the skin as off-putting. If not for these irritating disadvantages, I may have had a career in it. As regards coprophilia, I don't recall having any characteristic inclination towards this after the age of four and even though—needless to say I don't have any recollection of that lost paradise either—as an infant I must have shown unusual zeal and have given my family some very unpleasant surprises. If we are to believe my mother's testimony, I never lost any opportunity to oblige them to take part in an exceptionally smelly treasure hunt, to race wildly from room to room and search in the most improbable hiding places. As we lost our infantile sense of humor a long time ago, the cathartic combination of Bourville and Pasolini, I won't go on with other spicy details. Suffice it to note that the distant reverberations of these weaknesses (two dormant weaknesses throughout my adult life) paved the way for and kept alight the flame of my present quirk.

I admit it straight out. I take pleasure in toilets. I'd like to believe that this confession of mine acquires additional value given that it's not signed by a normal fifty-year-old, one who's recently begun suffering with his prostate or his intestines, one who's made a virtue of necessity and has reached the sad point of taking pleasure in his own relief. Despite my excesses and the periodic liver pains, my digestive system works marvelously, my kidneys may one day very well be exhibited as models at a urologists' conference and never—touch wood—have I been personally aware of either internal or external hemorrhoids. As such, my fetish for toilets is totally disinterested and the only return I expect from it is of an aesthetic nature. Above all, I'm addressing art lovers because it's their vision that I espouse and their sacraments that I receive. I stand before the toilet bowl as I might stand before a sculpture. I pull the flush as I might pull the sash to unveil a painting. I probably don't need to add that the sound of the water is one of my favorite melodies.

Unfortunately, it's not often that I find any response—at least, not as often as I would like. My soul mates (souls with panties, as we said, otherwise there are lots) are scattered all over the globe, hard to find and hard to approach. Before maintenance payments started to eat away my income, I'd travel regularly in search of them—but for some years now, the courts have decreed that I should pay only those women that I don't encounter. And then again, our own local women are cautious, faint at the thought of public humiliation or the opinion you'll form of their person, tremble at the slightest suspicion that—behind your audacious proposal—the testing of their virtue may be lying in disguise, that lurking beneath your underpants is not an upright friend, but a stern and sullen Mormon. There are very few who don't follow the beaten track, the safety of the bed, hot water and clean towels.

In the toilet—they complain—everything happens clumsily and hurriedly. Even if some nosey parker doesn't catch sight of you going in, even if he doesn't notice the tetrapod that—with a spectacular leap—vanishes from the face of the earth, he is not going to miss the debauchery on your coming out, he'll smell it in the air, he'll discern it in your flushed cheeks, in your disheveled hair, on your dress or your trousers. Not that they're entirely wrong. A sperm stain—invisible to any naked eye other than my wife's—cost me my first divorce. Open flies the third. The second was by mutual consent. Enough said. She was a saint.

Now we come to the difficult part. Even if you hit upon the right circumstances. Even if you meet up with one of these rare women, even if you find you have something in common with her, even if you weaken her last reservations in whisky, unfortunately, this doesn't mean at all that your troubles are over. The suitable women may be very few, but the suitable toilets are even fewer. Those that usually meet the hygiene standards—disinfected, scrubbed, fresh—are also off-limits. As soon as you cross the threshold, some surly Cerberus steps out and—on the pretext of a penny or two—polices you as you go, keeping watch in case you stray. At the other extreme, in those cases where the regulations are slack or nonexistent, it's not long before a total lack of restraint prevails. With your belt undone and your underpants round your knees, you're obliged to balance between used condoms and filthy syringes, while at the same time using your back to replace the broken door latch. Under such circumstances, it's more or less the same to you whether you copulate or defecate.

Perhaps that's why I believe that I touched upon perfection tonight. My engine started up with the second glass, the woman beside me turned out to be amenable, and the barman pretended not to notice that we both made for the toilet only a minute apart. Three months of research in the wider area had led me to the safe conclusion that only this particular joint met all the prerequisites for a successful outcome—and today, at last, I found the opportunity to put it to the test. I walked towards the Garden of Eden without any hurry, certain that there would be no Cerberus to block my way. A young girl was washing her hands in the bowl and I bided my time till she was gone. I knocked three times on the door. The woman was quick to open, to pull me towards her and, equally quickly, to again turn the key in the lock. Oh, that lock that immediately stole my heart—no more latches, no more backs to the door. I quickly glanced around and for the umpteenth time saw that the surroundings, the cleanliness of which was nothing to shout about, at least didn't put me off. The first flush, like the third bell at the theater, encouraged me to stoop and raise the woman's curtain. Another five flushes followed in order to conceal our groans—and only at the seventh did we take our final bow, now completely exhausted. The woman straightened my tie and I arranged her hair. With a silly smile of contentment, I turned to unlock the door.

 I wasn't at all disconcerted when I felt the key sticking. I tried again, with more dexterity, but with the same results. I let the woman try, certain deep down that a woman who knows how to lock a door must also know how to unlock it. I was proved wrong and I undertook the task once more. When at my fourth attempt I failed, I began to lose my composure; I threw technique to the wind and forced the key with all my might. I would never have imagined myself capable of bending it. Amazed at my feat, I stared first at the key, then at the woman. She was about to burst into tears.

 "Don't worry, dear," I whispered. "Be patient. Someone will let us out."

Original title: "Mia disosmi adinamia." Published in Petros Tatsopoulos, *Komedie* [Comedy], Athens: Kastaniotis, 1999, pp. 69-76.

Vassilis Tsiaboussis

The Doll

Every day, Filio's new doll paraded in the neighborhood. Her uncle, who worked at sea, had sent it from America. It was blonde and an arm's length in height, with a shiny red dress, black shoes and short socks. Underneath her petticoat, so the girls said, she wore white lace panties.

"Now that's a doll for you, you get horny just by touching her!" mocked Symeon, the biggest rascal in the gang, and someone I couldn't stomach, firstly because I sang in the church choir and I didn't like the way he talked and, secondly, because I loved Filio and I wanted, when I grew up, to make her my wife. But one afternoon, he brought a few penny chocolates and said to her: "I'll give you one, if you let me touch your baby." She wouldn't consent at first because she didn't do favors like that not even for her girlfriends, but in the end not only did she let him but, with their mouths full of chocolate, they marveled at the doll's little thighs beneath the petticoat and giggled like little scamps. Then I got angry, I left and took a long walk to the far side of the neighborhood so the other kids wouldn't see that I was on the verge of tears.

Filio lived with her mother next door to us, but they were from Piraeus, which is why her uncle had become a seaman. He would send a postcard from every country in the world where his ship docked; Filio had them in a pile tied with a gold ribbon and we were all envious. England, Russia...she even had a photograph of the Aurora Borealis from Alaska; she brought it to the geography class and the teacher showed it to us. But apart from the postcards and the rare stamps attached to them, their uncle also sent them checks in the mail, because her mother didn't work though she was young and blonde, but sat all day in the backyard and smoked as if she were some old Gypsy woman, which is why the neighborhood talked about her. Even my father said to me one afternoon, "That Dora woman dolls herself up like she was a streetwalker," but my mother defended her, "The woman is from Piraeus and you're comparing her with us. From the day you marry us, you shut us up in the house like slaves." On another occasion, however, the conversation was reversed. "Talk about a sinful woman," said my mother, while my father said, "All you women in the neighborhood are jealous of her because she's modern and shapely." From that time I realized that there are a lot of things that couples don't agree on.

Anyhow, I loved Filio, not only because she was pretty and spoke like someone from Piraeus, but also because she had the mother that she had, and I thought that this was the kind of woman I'd like to marry one day, the kind who dolls herself up, who smokes, who dresses in fancy clothes, not like my mother who washed dirty linen from morning to night.

Anyway, what's a cigarette? Not long ago, when Symeon had taken us to the old hospital, we smoked too. At first, I was afraid in case my parents found out, though I knew that smoking wasn't a sin, because even old Demosthenes smoked, and he was a saintly man and a cantor in church, though he was also a diabetic. Always, after vespers, he'd send me secretly to buy sweets from the grocer's opposite and after we'd satisfied our craving, he'd smoke, though he always cut the cigarettes in half.

But at the old hospital, where we'd all been born, before they built the new one outside the town, Symeon wanted us all to do other things, not just smoke, but I refused. "Think what we'll have to say in a few days when we go to confession," I told him. "Whatever we say, the priest has sworn not to reveal it to anyone," he replied, trying to persuade me. In the end, I held myself back, because there was another reason why I didn't want to stoop to such things. I was in love with Filio, and only with her, when the time was right, would I do what was necessary. Besides, Father Spyros was wellknown and had appointed my father church counselor, which is why I had to be very careful. One day, he'd expelled Filio from the catechism class because, he said, she's been giggling in church, though I later heard from an aunt that he'd been looking for an opportunity and he'd done it on account of her mother. Because Dora, being a modern woman, didn't go to church; all she did was drink cups of coffee and then read her neighbors' fortunes, but that was a sin. A couple of times, my mother went to her house, but then she got into trouble with my father who, being a counselor, was very strict.

With all these things happening, I loved poor Filio even more, because she had the pain of her father, who had abandoned them a long time before and was living with another woman, and if it wasn't for her uncle at sea, she wouldn't even have had a doll.

About this doll then. One Saturday afternoon, they asked me whether I wanted to baptize it, and I had to answer within half an hour, because it was already four and they had to send out invitations for five. "If you refuse, then Symeon will play the priest," said the wily Sevastoula, who was the neighborhood matchmaker and whose backyard was next to the street where we played, so that when our ball flew over the wall and broke the lettuces, she would give it back to us, if her father wasn't home, because he was the angry type and once he'd slashed Panayotis' new leather ball with a penknife. Then Panayotis had burst into tears and in the end had shouted, "I'm finished with that hag," because before this he'd loved Sevastoula, and from that time on we all called him the "divorcé."

At four twenty-five, I sent Dinos to tell them that the baptism would take place and to prepare a bucket of water, a little oil and some scissors. Then Filio said, "You're mad, you'll ruin my doll," and when my assistant, who always carried the cross in church because he was the tallest and a year older than all the others, returned with the news, we agreed to perform a baptism by air.

They invited the whole neighborhood and the godmother was Vassoula, whose father was a lawyer. I brought along with me a book with Byzantine music that my brother had at home, a censer and the New Testament. We sang "Those baptized in Christ" and then I read from the Gospels. Dinos sang flat, so twice when he was out of tune I trod on his foot. We christened the doll "Alice," though when I heard the name I was taken aback as it wasn't a Christian name. Then, Dora gave us some candies and Symeon said under his breath, "The daughter's nothing compared to the mother!" Towards the end of the celebrations, Filio came up to me and I offered my best wishes, "Congratulations on your daughter's christening," but then Dinos said, "And here's to your wedding," and I turned as red as a beetroot. I later learned that he'd been put up to it by Symeon and on account of their underhandedness I didn't speak to either of them for a week.

The time passed; Filio was the bottom of the class in her lessons and all our classmates made fun of her, but I loved her all the more. One day when she hadn't come to school because she was sick, she turned up at our house in the afternoon so that I could tell her what we'd done. My parents were out and we sat at the kitchen table. It was an opportunity for me to tell her everything, but she only had her mind on schoolwork. At one moment, our legs touched under the table and in my turmoil I minced my words. When she had gone, I lay on the couch face down with my arms hanging to the floor and said the "Our Father" forty times.

Summer was approaching when I decided to reveal my feelings to her. It took me a whole week to prepare myself emotionally for this confession. On Sunday morning I took communion so as to have God's support, though I also had to ask Sevastoula's help. I went and found her in her backyard, she was eating hazelnuts but she didn't give me any. I tried three times to turn the conversation to the topic that concerned me but without success. At the fourth attempt and before I'd even started, she told me that there was no need for me to tax myself because as the matchmaker that she was she had known about it all from way back, but that I didn't have a hope in the matter. "Filio loves Yorgos, Vasso's brother, because his father is a lawyer and they have an encyclopedia in their house and, whenever she wants, they let her go and write the biographies that our teacher assigns us. They also have an icebox and in summer they give her vanilla and cold water."

I left, running like a madman. I couldn't believe it! Filio with that lump who couldn't even pronounce his "r"s. With Yorgos? So that explains why Vasso was the doll's godmother, because Filio's best friend was Mary and they didn't talk to each other for two weeks after the baptism. And the doll's name? Alice was the name of Yorgos' mother, her mother-in-law. Yet all these airs and graces were no doubt the work of her mother, Dora, of course! She was the one who thought so much of herself, who wore fancy clothes and who smoked with her coffee... "We're almost in-laws...our children..." she'd say to the lawyer and his wife. "But take care, you stuck-up mother and daughter, I'll fix you."

⁂

How often the Devil had tested me! How often I'd restrained myself at the last moment before committing sin!

Our bath-house was adjacent to theirs at the end of the backyard. They were separated by a two-meter wall of stones and earth. Higher up, the gap was closed by planks. On Saturday afternoon, as soon as I saw the smoke, I went and informed Symeon. Without making any noise, we climbed up on the firewood and glued our faces to the slits.

We didn't have to wait very long. Dora came first and tested the water in the tub. Then came Filio. They got undressed and began bathing themselves. The soapsuds rolled slowly over their breasts, bellies, navels, over "there"... "Now that's a mother, look at the hair she has there!" whispered Symeon. Though I could hardly breath—as if a dwarf were sitting on my lungs—and though my heart was beating like a drum, not to mention that I was trembling lest they get wind of us, nevertheless it was the first time I admitted that he was right. "Now that's a mother!" I whispered in turn.

That afternoon, my love for little Filio was completely cured. Anyway, I couldn't marry her from the moment that my best friend had seen her naked.

Meanwhile, summer had arrived, the schools were closed, and we, just the boys that is, led by Symeon, went every evening and played various games in the ruins of the old hospital.

Original title: "I koukla." Published in Vassilis Tsiaboussis, *I vespa kai alla eparhiaka diiyimata* [The Scooter and Other Provincial Tales], Athens: Nefeli, 1990, pp. 111-118.

THANASSIS VALTINOS

Addiction to Nicotine

I smoked my first cigarette at the age of eleven, in 1943. At that time, we were living in Karavas, a place on the west bank of the Eurotas River. We'd settled there temporarily at the start of the Nazi Occupation. The story is as follows:

On his way back from the Albanian front, one of my mother's brothers, a pharmacist with literary interests and an adventurous inclination, instead of going on down to Tripoli and from there making for the village, followed his buddies—buddies from the front—and ended up in Sparta. A few months later, a doctor friend of his, with whom he'd shared experiences in the same mountain surgery, got married. Part of his dowry was an estate, four kilometers outside town, with olive groves, citrus trees and pastures. This was Karavas, and the doctor, who intended to farm the land systematically, was looking for an overseer. My father, a master mason, immediately accepted our uncle's proposal. All the signs pointed to the harsh winter that would follow. So, though mountain people from Arcadia, we suddenly found ourselves down in the valley.

The estate covered an area of about seven hundred and fifty acres. I can describe the place with relative accuracy. At the foot of a mountain slope were some imposing ruins. Two low, narrow storerooms and, between them, without any windows or roof, were the thick stone walls of a two-story tower. Every night at first, the owls in this empty shell froze our blood with their hooting. Widow Spyraina, of whom only the echo of her voice remains, had said to my mother: "They're souls cursing. You'll get used to them."

The tower had been built by a descendent of Barbitsiotis Zacharas. A local tradition provided ample information. This son or grandson of the first Klepht* to revolt had stood one day atop the hill of Yatrissa, opened his arms wide and called his own whatever area he was able to encompass in this way. It seems that in his shadow there were people to witness this. None of the poor band of small farmers dared to question this arbitrary act, and it seems that, apart from the toughness that was characteristic of his generation, this rugged man also had other less-common leanings flowing in his blood: The mothers who went to collect their bloodied daughters stood far off, heads lowered and murmuring: "The owls will be hooting." But not one of them had ever said it out loud.

On the edges of the estate, where the thinnest soil was, there were other smaller holdings. We thought of their owners as our neighbors.

At first the whole family worked exhaustively. Our father cut down a tree that was growing behind the tower, dried out the one storeroom, put in new beams, laid floors, and made two rooms. The other one he turned into a stable. The sharecroppers, who came down from the neighboring villages of Mount Taygetus, marveled at his competence. These were people who were fatalistically bound to the cultivation of the land. It rained—they reaped; it didn't rain—they tightened their belts. Their relations with the boss were based on the principle: "half of the half." Each year, a quarter of their crops, whatever that was, was gone in advance from their hands. Some of them, with the inherited guile of the liberated, tried to win over my father. He greatly disappointed them. He never turned a blind eye, not even in the most difficult times for them. Stealing meant disgrace. And he believed in work.

---

* Klepht. Member of irregular armed bands formed during the period of Turkish Rule. Initially they operated as brigands but later as the main forces of resistance against the Turks. They were distinguished for their brave exploits during the Greek War of Independence.

I remember him—I remember his body, the movements of his hands, at whatever he turned to. I ask myself now just what dream he was pursuing. He wasn't only relentless with himself, but with us too. There was no school in the area and so he forced us to go to Sparta on foot. Four kilometers every day, summer and winter. And Martha was still almost a baby, in the first class of junior school.

The doctor came to the farm regularly, to check up on things. He usually brought company with him. In front, he himself with his wife, in an old convertible, behind, two light carts, painted capriciously. Their wheels were red, the wooden rails golden. Every time this procession appeared, the estate was filled with merriment. The sharecroppers gathered to welcome the bosses. The first to jump from the carts were the men—our uncle among them—in order to help the young ladies climb down. Nice days, imbued with the scent of those women. When it was especially hot, having discreetly paired off, they would all go down to the river to swim. While our mother was preparing the meal—almost always free-range duck,—our father, using the boards from our beds, set up a large table in the shade of the walnut tree, next to the waterhole. Still innocent as we were and excited by the strangers' euphoria, we helped him. Without our ever suspecting it then, we were the quaint décor for this idyll.

Of all the people in that period, only their names have remained in my memory. Bachaviolas. Beynikolas, with his two Swiss cows. Louis—Louis who?—who was the same age as me, the Kastanis family. Damian Kotsarelos. Sharecroppers and neighbors. Ambelia from Sparta: a prewar provincial miss and later mistress of the Italian garrison commander. Sesamis, also from Sparta. During the intervals, in complete contradiction to his nickname, he sold us nougat bars, made exclusively from carob syrup. Mister Takis: the boss. Anna-Maria Vladet: daughter of our religion teacher, whose father, abusing his authority, put her in the boys' section. It was the first eight-grade school, 1942. Her friend, Sophia Pikrou: my one secret love. In my free time, I'd fill my exercise books with sailboats in her name. Now, in sleepless hours, I sometimes torture myself trying to reconstruct their faces, but it's impossible.

The summer of '43 was a rough one. Karavas had become a kind of neutral zone. At night, units of the ELAS* reserves would come down to get food or burn the houses of any "reactionaries." During the day, bands of security militia went around scrounging. In mid-August, on the eve of the feast of the Assumption, the guerillas set up a daring ambush below Analypsi—a place of execution on the outskirts of the town—and wiped out the detachment that was taking some hostages there. The Germans were furious. By proclamation, they tightened the curfew for the whole prefecture, from eight to eight. For us in the neutral zone, these restrictions had never been enforced.

Four days later, at daybreak, special units of "hunters" made a quiet sally into our area. They rounded up all the men they found "on the streets" and, continuing their operation up the Eurotas River, they took them with them.

The news spread immediately. They were all our neighbors and two sharecroppers who had been caught out by the night close to their vegetable patches. Our father was lucky to get away. Deep in the second storeroom that he'd turned into stables, he was struggling to castrate a wild boar, and amid the animal's screams, he didn't even realize that the Germans had passed by. At around nine, six tearful women gathered in our yard. I don't know whether in their choice of gathering place, the presence of a man had unconsciously played some role. In vain, our father tried to calm them. Presently, some of the sharecroppers, who had meanwhile come down from their villages, also arrived. As the turmoil that prevailed showed no signs of letting up, one of them had the bright idea to shout out loud, "shut up!" Startled, the women fell silent. The big-boned farm hand, bandy-legged too, no doubt with similar memories in his blood, knew how to lie. He stood beside my father and stared grimly at the women.

"They've taken your men as guides," he said. "Before sunset, you'll have them back."

His words fell on fertile soil. A deep sigh of relief went round, as though a knot had been loosened. Yet the women didn't disperse. They remained there, sharing their waiting. One or two things were said that were comical.

---

* Ellinikos Laikos Apeleftherotikos Stratos (National Popular Liberation Army).

"My man had gone outside to relieve himself. They took him as he was, in his shorts."

However, as the sun gradually came up, the sudden euphoria abated. Midday found the women sitting in the shade of the tower in silence. Our mother took them water, bread and tomatoes. They didn't take so much as a bite. The farm hand's effective argument was gradually undermined by its own logic.

Two hours later, a cry was heard. "They're coming." The women leapt to their feet. From the west corner of the house, Bachaviolas could be seen running. Clutching the spade used for watering like a scepter and with his trouser legs rolled up above his shins, he was pointing downwards. Between the river and the tower, at a distance of about two hundred and fifty meters, there was a deep ditch that irrigated the plain from one end to the other. Its left embankment, trodden down over the years by both men and animals, had been turned into a path.

With their gray-green uniforms and in a single column, in the clandestine silence of their step, interrupted in places by foliage that was equally gray-green, the Germans were returning along that path. When the last of the party disappeared, the speechlessness that had accompanied their passing lasted a little while longer. Just as long as was necessary to quash the hopes that, perhaps lagging behind, were the neighbors and sharecroppers who had been snatched. A cry, which began as a lamentation, quickly turned into a shrill scream and, without reaching a crescendo, put an end to that unnatural inertia.

Dry, grim, barefoot, the wife of Vlachos Karmiris suddenly put her hand to her mouth and looked in alarm at the other women. Then a strange commotion began. These women, who from the morning had been ruminating on the calamity, repressed it now that it was upon them. They stared at each other, held each other, shook their heads in a daze. Widow Spyraina and our mother went up to them, trying to calm them. Silent, together with our brothers and sisters and widow Spyraina's twins, Michalis and Spyros, who were older than us, we watched their pain that refused to burst forth. It didn't have anything to do with us directly, but it upset us. This anguish didn't have any direct connection with death, it was more the anguish of love. And vaguely, instinctively, we grasped this. Fully aware of his inability to do anything, my father stood on a stump and tried to say something.

"Women..."

One or two stopped and, motioning to the others, waited for him to open his mouth. There was an embarrassed silence. Our father was unable to think of anything to say. Then, suddenly, another voice, shrill, almost cold, filled the void.

"Why are we hanging around here?"

Beynikolas' wife, Angelina, a forty-year-old, double-chinned, stood facing her women companions. She stared at them gravely and, without another word, she turned to leave. Bachaviolas rushed to stop her.

"Where are you off to, woman?"

He stepped in front of her and did all he could to try to convince her that their men folk had got held up somewhere. That they would come and that they ought to wait for them. Like a bear from the rear, Angelina hammered his shoulders with her fists all the while that he stood there not letting her pass, saying again and again: "No, no, no!" Then she began jumping up and down, screaming with a comical intensity. She raised her eyes, stared at the sky and ran her nails down her cheeks. She stared at the ground, lifted her dress and tore at her thighs. The other women stood stupefied. Widow Spyraina darted forward and grabbed her by the wrists.

In the end, Angelina surrendered, caught in her net. Hanging from her armpits, she dropped her head and, as Spyraina and Bachaviolas dragged her, she groaned deep inside her bosom. They sat her down on the stump that our father had stood on just before, and our mother ran to get some water.

"She's come back, let's go," Michalis then said as if inspired.

He jumped away from the wall he'd been leaning against and we followed him. We didn't know just what exactly he had in mind, but it was as if we'd all decided on it together. We took the path that went to the right from the tower. A little further up, it disappeared into the small macadam road that linked Sparta with the northern villages of Mount Taygetus. Undecided, Martha started to come toward us. She was clutching an improvised doll. Yorgos had made it for her out of a tender cane root. I stopped and told her to go back. Embarrassed, she burst into tears. I left her and ran to catch up with the others.

We really didn't know where we were going. We emerged onto the road. The sun was low in the sky but the scorching heat didn't seem to be getting any more bearable. And so we wandered on like that for some time. The desolation of the landscape, its punctuated stillness alarmed us deep down inside. Yet at the same time, also deep down inside us, we felt a tremendous sense of freedom. We reached the big bend in the road. At this point, the road, hanging vertically over the river, looked across towards Vordonia. To our left, on the top of a low hill, was Boutsikakis' hut. Notwithstanding his age, he lived alone, grazing a dozen or so sheep. He also had a stud ram, a huge beast, and every August, for the whole of the month, he would keep it tied up outside, beneath a vine-arbor. Those neighbors who had she-goats for mating sent them to him, always paying the tupping fee in kind.

"Let's go and see him," said Michalis, going up first.

The door to the hut was a canvass sheet. The goat, tied to its stake, "laughed," lifting up its chin and peeing on its legs.

"He's not here," he said.

Up against the wall was a low-built bench. Some dry corn leaves, cut symmetrically to the size of cigarette paper were pinned under an old, worn knife. Others had been scattered by the wind. In a small wooden platter there were two or three fistfuls of tobacco and beside it a box with tinder.

Michalis stood there with his hands in his pockets and looked around.

"He must be somewhere around," he said.

The goat was in heat and its smell stuck to our hides. Michalis slowly paced around the hut and then came back out to us.

Below on the other side, Boutsikakis' sheep were grazing freely. Michalis bent down, picked up a corn leaf, put some tobacco inside it, straightened it with his finger and rolled a cigarette with remarkable dexterity. He licked the tip of it and gave it to Vassilis. He rolled a second, and Spyros immediately imitated him. They lit them and the three of them began smoking one after the other. They held the smoke in their mouths for a moment and then they let it out in successive puffs. Then Vassilis said something to the twins. What he wanted was to involve us in the game too, so we wouldn't tell on him. Spyros held out his cigarette to Yorgos, but Yorgos declined. Spyros went up to him threateningly.

"Leave him alone," said Vassilis.

Michalis stood before me, rested his hand on my shoulder, like equal to equal, and showed me what I should do.

"Squeeze your stomach with your other hand and inhale deeply."

I took hold of the cigarette and did what he told me. I suddenly felt my throat burning and my eyes popped out. I dropped the cigarette and, choking myself coughing, I began spluttering saliva without being able to stop. The twins burst their sides laughing and began chasing each other, leaping in the air like goats. Vassilis followed suit. Through my tears, I saw them race down to the meadow, where they began wildly goading the sheep. Yorgos came over to me, to console me.

"Shells," we heard them shout all together.

Yorgos immediately left me on my own. At that time, shells had replaced marbles. It had a value as a game. Following the general system, you could swap ten of them for a variety of things. I immediately forgot my crying. But we didn't have time to charge down the slope. We saw the three of them down there, on all fours, having frozen. Then they slowly got up, stepped back a little and, suddenly, they got up and began running towards us. They came up to us out of breath.

"They're there," said Michalis, beside himself. "In the brambles."

And they dragged us with them in a wild dash to get away.

༄

I smoked my second cigarette five years later. Following the liberation, we went back to the village. We had survived and my father wanted to go back to his old trade. He said that with the devastation that had taken place during the Nazi Occupation, business would pick up again. Personally, I think there was also another reason. The valley wasn't for him; he was used to the successive horizons of our mountains. In the meantime, Vassilis had entered the university. Yorgos, who was also getting ready to take the entrance exams, had gone to be with him. I stayed to finish high school in Tripoli.

In January 1948, a passing division of commandoes used our school building as temporary accommodation. We were transferred to the high school for girls. In the same classrooms, at the same desks, "alternately," we in the morning, the girls in the afternoon. This "cohabitation" added an even sharper edge to our provincial adolescent lust. Nikos D., who sat at the same desk as me, often used to claim that he felt a strange warmth passing from the wood of the desk and into his thighs, and creeping pervasively into the area of his kidneys!

One morning, during the French lesson, while the teacher was writing on the board "Pavlos and Virginia felt happier day by day," one of the boys in the front row got up and, turning towards us, started waving, like a trophy, a pair of girls' panties. He'd found them under his desk. All hell broke loose, and as it was impossible to find the perpetrators, our uproar was punished with a three-day expulsion, by lot, of five of our classmates.

Nikos D. is now a radiologist. Married for years, but without children, he owns a penthouse in a classy neighborhood and is a director of Panathinaikos Football Club. What's known as "making good." After high school, our paths separated. If, as sometimes happens, we bump into each other, we exchange a few words and, naturally, always talk about that time with nostalgia.

At the time, Nikos D. had been going through a crisis. Urged on by his pervasive warmth, he eventually got up the courage to write a message in ink on top of the desk. "Fair reader, you are the object of my dreams." Anonymously. We'd thought up the message together, but the "fair reader" was his own doing.

The next day, there was an answer. "Dreams!…" Nothing more. But with an exclamation mark and lots of dots. Nikos was crazy with delight. The messages continued feverishly and in the same lyrical style. Before long they were regularly exchanging notes. It was progress. They'd leave them in the toilets, in a crack over the door. Always anonymously. I tried to persuade Nikos to reveal his identity and to demand the same from her. He eventually gave in, and disaster struck the very next day. His correspondent was a fat girl who wore glasses. One of those studious pupils that we called "bookworms." Nikos was devastated. In his notes, he'd not only invested his ideals concerning beauty. His investment was even deeper and more serious.

I tried to console him. We went for long walks. I tried to turn his attention to other things. That winter, the reputation of the "African Queen" plagued us like the 'flu. The "African Queen" was the new star in Kazamias' brothel. Nikos wouldn't listen to me. He only once showed any interest when I told him that various well-to-do men, from as far away as Argos, were hiring taxis together on her account. He stared at me full of suspicion, supposing actions on my part that I'd been keeping secret from him.

"How do you know?"

"From Koularmanis."

Koularmanis was a scoundrel who rented us bikes.

At the beginning of February, they had handed us the program for the tests during the semester. We wasted the first hour on this and during the break, at the order of the principal, we lined up in the schoolyard. This surprised us somewhat. It was the common practice and we had supposed that we wouldn't have any lessons afterwards.

Our principal got up on the rostrum and, coolly and formally, presented the "national poet," Mr. so-and-so, to us. Beside him stood a skinny man wearing military boots and a scarf. With some delay, the school janitor put down several piles of poorly printed pamphlets on the concrete, next to the man's boots. Following the recitation, we had the "option" of buying his poems. I don't remember the monetary scale of the time, but the price of those pamphlets was equal to that of our morning doughnut.

Nikos gave me a meaningful nudge as soon as the poet began and we moved, taking care not to be seen, to the back of our line. From there, it was easy for us to slip away. It was a cold but clear day. The sun was fierce. We skirted round the court house and came out in Areos Square. The square appeared deserted at that time of day. Deserted and huge. At its far edge, a trash collector was slowly pushing his cart and a few bare tables had been put out in front of the *Mainalon*. Nikos still hadn't got over the fiasco of his correspondence. We were standing at the entrance to the park and talking about love. Then we heard the sound of a car and from the corner of the *Serayou*, there appeared an old dump truck, like those used by contractors. It mounted the square's curb, reached the middle, turned right round on the spot and stopped, with the engine still running. A sergeant with cartridge belts and a Tommy gun got out of the front. The back of the truck started to slowly rise and, when it reached the necessary height, we saw corpses falling out of it.

We were the first to go up close. Naturally, the circle soon grew. The truck remained with its back end tipped up and before us there was a tiny pyramid of dead men. The only woman among them, lying face down, completed the top of the pyramid. Her dress was pulled up as far as her buttocks and on the outside of her left thigh there was a gash made by a bayonet. Despite the chill of death on her skin, which was intensified by the winter sun, I felt a rush of excitement.

Various conjectures were already circulating. The commandoes had wiped out the small band of guerillas in a night-time ambush. Another version was that they had taken them captive. Then one of them had attempted to escape and they had all been executed.

The following day, we were due to have a history test. I shut myself in my room and tried to study. Nikos came round early in the evening to get me. He couldn't concentrate either. History, in the shape of a sexy curve of dead buttocks, mocked at us from the top of that morning's pyramid.

We went out into the streets and eventually found ourselves near the station. Beyond the tracks, on the old asphalt road to Tegea, was Kazamias' official brothel. The house was surrounded by a low wall and, though it was still daylight, a small naked bulb was lit out front. Hesitant, we stood outside. We didn't dare admit that we lacked the courage to enter. In the end, a second door, beyond the low wall, got us out of our impasse. It suddenly opened to reveal the national poet, head bent, with his scarf and military boots.

We leapt smartly to the left, went round the wall and ended up at one corner of it round the back. We stood on the wall. Before us was a ditch with greenish water. Hundreds of used condoms were rotting inside. While waiting for the poet to walk away, Nikos took two cigarettes from his jacket pocket. He'd begun smoking on the day of the fiasco and, so as to avoid any "evidence," he bought them loose and always in twos. He handed one of them to me and this time I didn't refuse. I lit it, inhaled the smoke carefully, held it for a moment in my mouth and then let it out in puffs.

∽

The end of the story is as follows:

My father died in May '69, at the age of seventy-two. He remained a hard man till the end of his life—and till the very end was a firm believer in work. He had chiseled marble staircases. He had sculpted lintels for churches. In Karavas, he had dug ditches, planted trees, brought animals back to life. For others. Later he had kidney problems and for a while worked as a vendor in a kiosk, selling gum and newspapers. He died with a deep sense of satisfaction as to his integrity. He was a dreamer—for good.

I never returned to Karavas after that, never. Recently, I heard that the estate, divided into building plots, had disappeared on paper.

As for that uncle of mine from the beginning, he's still living, on a coast deep in the Peloponnese. His adventurous inclinations came to an end with his marriage to the heiress to a pharmacy. The only pharmacy that still emits the old smells. Sometimes I go by there to see him. With diabetes and the like, having had to stop smoking years ago. An aged lion. Though he still has his literary interests. From his student years, he's been buying the literary magazine *Nea Hestia* without fail and, without opening its pages, he binds the copies in yearly volumes.

I hope he proves to be as much of a Methuselah as the journal.

Original title: "Ethismos sti nikotini." Published in Thanassis Valtinos, *Ethismos sti nikotini*, Athens: Metaichmio, 2004, pp. 11-36.

Zyranna Zateli

The Ivory Buttons

They were nineteen brothers and sisters, of four lines. Seven from the same father and an unfortunate woman who had died together with her newborn in her eighth childbirth; the other seven were the three from the first and the four from the second marriage of the second wife he had married, who had been widowed by her last husband while she was pregnant—though without knowing it—with her eighth child, a stillborn.

She gave birth to it, buried it and, on the evening of the following day, she received an offer of marriage from the widower Theagenes. She took her seven children and went to his house with the other seven. He talked to her conspiratorially and plainly from the very first:

"I've heard that you're a good mother for lots of children but a witch when it comes to men. Take care not to get it into your head to become a widow for a third time or you'll be a goner."

Their children were of more or less the same age with a difference of only a year or two, perhaps only months or weeks. Two and two happened to have the same name and two more to have been born on exactly the same day in the same year—the midwife had gone from the one house to the other.

At first, all they did was glare at each other without saying a word or eating. Afterwards, they argued as to who would be the first to hold and nurse the baby born exactly nine months after the coupling of Theagenes and Penelope. Whoever managed to get up first in the morning, at first light, ran unwashed and with the dreams still hanging from his eyelashes and grabbed hold of the wooden cradle of the baby, who woke up from the jolt and with a deafening scream burst out crying. Then the other children realized that someone had already got there first, in other words, had been the first to grab the cradle, which meant that he would be the lucky one that day: he wouldn't have to go to school, or to the fields, or to their father's sesame-oil mill and, in general, he would be spared the endless daily chores that the children were obliged to do—usually half-heartedly and with their mind on playing, apart from the two elder girls, who were already thinking of marriage, but who also vied for the cradle, more so even than the younger ones, because being older they had heavier responsibilities on their shoulders, even though they were still only adolescents' shoulders.

So it was the baby's cradle, probably more so than the baby itself, that united the three—and now four—lines of siblings as if by magic and smoothed over or covered over their hostile feelings; the outbursts of jealousy became fewer—they now had another incentive, another goal—the angry looks somewhat softened, and they turned to other means in order to express their desires and claims.

The lucky boy or girl of the day took up the position and attitude of a guard beside the cradle, and before long took up a stool too because being on your feet is tiring, and they were happy that in this way they secured for themselves a long respite from doing chores for the grownups, yet a little unhappy too because they were also missing opportunities for escapades. As for the whining newborn, there were some days when it didn't cry at all, whereupon Theagenes and Penelope called the child guarding it to come out and do some work. But that happened only two or three times: if the wailing didn't spring spontaneously from the baby's innards, its little guard would provoke it with innocent and unexpected pinches or warm kisses that ended in bites.

Finally, it was a great temptation for the lucky child if one of the other children came up to him with a small coin in his palm or an ivory button, or anything else that shone or smelled strange, was sweet, colored or juicy. He would open his fist and show it to the guard, hold it out timidly or boldly, and the other one would weigh the pros and cons of such an exchange and act accordingly. He would accept the offer and give up his rights or refuse, clutching the rope of the swinging cradle and waving it like a banner, so that the other either fumed or pitied him, and if he had come with a handful of damson plums or a quince, he'd stay and eat them in front of him with due care and delight, sucking the pips and the peel, before spitting them out all around. But we learned how the guard too found a way to keep not only his position but also his dignity. "Look," he'd say to him, "I'm not looking at you!" And he did have his eyes shut and squeezed them tight—so that even if the other one was eating cake, he didn't see and so didn't suffer. Yet the subtle torment didn't end there. "I'm not looking at you, no, I'm not looking—so how do I know that you're not looking at me and turning green with envy?" said the other one who was eating. "I said I wasn't looking at you first and as I'm not looking at you," said the guard, "how do I know that you're not looking at me not looking at you?" There were occasions when they even came to grips, they rolled round and bickered, no longer on account of the quince or the cradle, but about who was looking and who wasn't looking at the other.

Meanwhile Penelope was expecting their next brother and half-brother.

And so another five children were born to the multifarious family, in addition to two more stillborns, and Theagenes and Penelope decided that it was time to put an end to the perpetuation of their species, given that the eighth birth was generally regarded as an accursed one. Besides, this exceptionally fertile woman was unable to escape from melancholic thoughts every time she gave birth:

"We keep on having children…Whether they're sent to us by God or the Devil I can't say, but the earth takes them sooner or later."

Focusing on the last child of Theagenes and Sophia, his first wife, who had another name but who everyone called Benjamin, perhaps because he was the youngest before the younger ones were born, perhaps because he had a weakness for biblical stories and the joke he never got tired of telling was "Who was the father of the children of Zebedee?," we see him at the age of eleven having amassed ten ivory buttons—a veritable treasure trove for a child at that time.

One day, while searching for hours for something else, he found a green velvet jacket belonging to his little and late departed mother. He spread it on the bed, took two steps back, one forward, half a step back again, half-closed his eyes and imagined how much it would suit him without the sleeves and collar, as a waistcoat. If he asked his other mother, Penelope, to alter it for him, he was afraid that she would find that such a garment would be more suited to one of the girls. So he asked the help of one of Sophia's sisters, who was a seamstress. She found Benjamin's idea wonderful, after seeing that the dead woman's jacket was far too tight for her, and given that she didn't have any daughters.

So just like Archibald's grandmother, that implacable grandmother in Cronin's *The Green Years*, she sat down one evening and sewed an indescribable parrot-green suit for her little grandson, tearing up a velvet curtain from her house, so that the next day Benjamin donned—and shone from head to toe—a green waistcoat with a double row of ten ivory buttons. And, unlike Archibald, he wasn't at all embarrassed about appearing in such a garment at school or on the street. On the contrary; from the moment he got it, he never wanted to take it off. Besides, it wasn't bright green so the boys didn't poke fun at him. It was a faded olive green, the color of an unripe bitter olive tree, an ideal background for the shiny buttons with their white and gold hues, on account of which he learned how to hold his body upright, chest out and back straight.

However, the others dreamt of these buttons too. At least one of the boys, Toulis, had his eyes on them from the start—"And if you don't get them from him," he warned himself, "you won't be worth as much as fly spit." He was three years older than Benjamin, very tall and lithe like a shoot—in a play at school, an original sketch in which all the roles were plants, Toulis had played Mrs. Rye.

One day, after planning it with two others, he lay in wait for Benjamin on a lonely road and at a quiet time. And he leapt in front of him like a huge famished locust.

"You see this, my fine young lad?" he said, showing him a gleaming blade that made Benjamin's heart jump out of his body. "I want your buttons, my fine young lad."

The other two leapt out, encircled the boy, who didn't dare let out a sound, and Toulis, bending his one knee like a swordsman and throwing his other leg back, in order to somewhat reduce his height, placed his forearm on Benjamin's chest without any ado and, with a smile of restrained triumph, cut off the ten ivory buttons one by one with the blade. He played with them in the palm of his hand like florins…

"Thanks, my fine young lad. Say hello to your redheaded sisters for me," he said, turning and leaving with the other two and jumping for joy.

Beneath the missing ivory buttons, Benjamin's heart returned to its usual place, but tearful and degraded.

"Farewell lads, bye!…" he shouted, full of humility and yearning, in the great hope that they might pity him and throw the stolen treasure back to him. But they didn't hear him so as to even ignore him; they had already vanished out of sight.

And now…ah, now. Now he wanted to aim all the stones in the world at Toulis' head! All of them! He considered what had happened unfair, very unfair, he was overcome by grief, anger, despair, and the most unbearable thing of all was that he recalled how passive he had remained while the others had robbed him. He swore on his mother's bones to avenge himself, and he found consolation in this—having nothing else.

He didn't want his waistcoat with any other buttons, common ones, ordinary ones, and after all the ivory ones he'd had, but had no longer, he didn't have the inclination or patience to start again from zero. It was just like a philatelist being robbed in an instant of all his stamps, the fruits of a whole lifetime of collecting.

The anger clamored inside him, hissed, bellowed and rose up—it wasn't ordinary anger—whenever he saw Toulis passing by with those large gawky strides of his and moreover with the heartlessness to grin at him or shoot him a sly wink. He got someone to tell him that the buttons were magical and that whoever stole them would, within three weeks, or at most three months, lose their hair, nails and teeth, but Toulis paid no heed. And one afternoon when he came upon him in a deserted spot, with Toulis looking for something in the earth and with him up on a rise, hidden by bushes and clouds of vengeance, he picked up a stone, took a deep decisive breath and threw the stone straight at Toulis' head. He fell on the spot, collapsed in a heap, and Benjamin didn't wait around to see whether he would get up or what he would do—he took to his heels like a hare, not knowing whether the feeling that inundated him was delight or panic.

He arrived home and, entering through a secret door, went up and shut himself in the attic. He crouched under an old black dress, full of pleats and dust, belonging to some huge grandmother and hanging from a long butcher's hook. The dress reached down to the floor, trailed over it...If he heard footsteps on the staircase, he stood on a chair that he had placed beneath the dress and hung from the hook. When he heard nothing, he sat on the chair, with his head in his hands, surrounded by the black garment and by even blacker thoughts.

He spent the entire night there. No one looked for him, no one cared and he didn't know whether he should see this as something good or bad.

The morning filled him with anxiety. A dark commotion had begun to spread throughout the house, creaking as though drawers were being opened and hearts were being closed, children's voices that someone cut short, Penelope's sobs, sometimes heavy and sometimes ethereal footsteps, every so often Theagenes' voice, though you couldn't understand what he was saying...He felt the sudden urge to find a rope and hang himself from the hook! Something told him that only he could be the cause of all this: *he had killed Toulis!*

And if he didn't hear his name at all, or thought he didn't, it was because in such a serious matter, they would have called him by his other name, his real one, which in his fear he had completely forgotten and nothing that reached his ears—even though it seems incredible—reminded him of it. More trouble now: he had to discover what he was called! How had they christened him...He mumbled the names of his brothers and sisters one by one, the individual ones and the double ones, he faltered over some, got confused, but they existed in his memory, were going round, never mind if they escaped him at this moment—but not his, it wasn't there. Such an ordeal for ten ivory buttons!

"Toulis...Toulis," he heard the lament, which reached the limits of madness when he heard priests arriving in the rooms below, and his nostrils filled with the smells of incense and lighted candles. There were moments when he wished that all this was in his imagination, that it wasn't really happening, that it was all an hallucination, a phantasm—he shook his head to make everything go away and stamped his foot on the floor, at the risk of being discovered—besides since when has the murder victim's funeral taken place in the house of the murderer? He emerged from the dress concealing him, went and put his ear to the attic door, was even bold enough to open it slightly...

It wasn't a lie. It was a mixture of hymns and incense that cause hilarious wheezing, people kept arriving at the house, stifled crying, sniffing, sighing—and the bell that had been missing until that moment also began to toll...He froze, and it never occurred to him to return to his hiding place or to come out from the attic. Totally absorbed, he gazed at the hundred and one disparate objects that had remained silent in there for years and that had been happily embroidered by the spiders: jugs, sacks, old clothes, saws, scythes, a horse's saddle, arms from rag dolls, a pot full of horns belonging to rams and deer, watering cans without any bottoms, a plate with tinsel at the edge of a broken table, sieves, beams, tobacco leaves in sacks, mousetraps, brooms, scales, chair legs, a spinning-wheel and some red yarn ravaged by moths and with its ends hanging like tassels, three wire baskets for eggs, two torn cushions, white cuttlefish bones on a dish... He gradually sank into their silence, into the world of obscurity; he sat down somewhere, he felt everything—his body, mind, eyelids—as though immaterial, and he forgot them all. He fell asleep.

He was found by his aunt, the seamstress, when they got back from the funeral and Penelope had sent her to the attic to get something.

"That's right, he wasn't there," she admitted as soon as she saw him at her feet, a ball of clothing on the floor.

The child jumped. He had a wild expression.

"Don't be afraid," she said, stroking his head, "you have other brothers and sisters, you're not alone."

"And Toulis?" whispered the child.

"Which Toulis?"

"Toulis! The tall one...the ivory buttons..."

"O, Toulis. I don't know—why? You mean you didn't come to the cemetery because you didn't have the ivory buttons? I told you to let me put on other ones, but you didn't want to..."

He saw Toulis the very next day, with a white bandage round his head, boasting to a group of children about how he'd come to blows with some cattle-thieves...But he never again saw one of his redheaded sisters, the smallest and sweetest of all, who had fallen into some scalding milk that morning, burned herself and expired as if she were a butterfly.

Original title: "Ta fildisenia koumbakia." Published in Zyranna Zateli, *Stin erimia me hari* [In the Wilderness with Grace], Athens: Sigaretta, 1986/Kastaniotis 1995, pp. 15-26.

BIOGRAPHICAL NOTES

EVYENIOS ARANITSIS (1955–) was born in Corfu and is a poet, prose writer, essayist and critic. In 1976, he founded and is the managing editor of Akmon Press and, since 1978, has worked regularly for the Greek newspaper *Eleftherotypia*. He was awarded the 2000 Greek State Prize for his study *To Whom Does Corfu Belong?*

SOTIRIS DIMITRIOU (1955–) was born in Thesprotia. He studied economics in Athens, where he now lives. He has published a collection of poetry, four collections of short stories and two novels. He has won the Diavazo Prize three times, the last time being in 2002 for his collection of short stories *Good's Slow Pace*. His novel, *May Your Name Be Blessed* (translated into English by Leo Marshall and published by the University of Birmingham) was proposed for the European Aristeion Prize. A number of his short stories have been made into films and arranged for the theatre.

MARO DOUKA (1947–) was born and raised in Chania, Crete. She studied history and archaeology at the University of Athens and has lived in Athens since 1966. She has published three books of short stories, six novels and a collection of literary essays. In 1982, she was awarded the Nikos Kazantzakis Prize for her first novel, *Fool's Gold*, and in 1984, the Greek State Second Prize for *The Floating City*. She was also awarded the 1995 Greek State Prize (which she refused) for her novel *Come Forth King* (translated by David Connolly and published by Kedros).

MICHEL FAÏS (1957–) was born in Komotini. He studied economics at the University of Athens and is a literary critic and editor for various publishing companies. His books include the novel *Autobiography of a Book* (Kastaniotis 1994), the collection of short stories *From the Same Glass and Other Stories* (Kastaniotis 1999), for which he was awarded the 2000 Greek State Prize, the novella *Aegypius Monachus* (Kastaniotis, 2001), the biographical novel *God's Honey and Ash* (Patakis, 2002) and the novel *Greek Insomnia* (Patakis, 2004).

RHEA GALANAKI (1947–) was born in Heraklion, Crete and studied history and archaeology at the University of Athens. She has published four novels, two collections of short stories, four collections of poetry and a book of literary essays. Her first novel, *The Life of Ismael Ferik Pasa*, was the first Greek novel to be included by UNESCO in its Collection of Representative Works. She received the Nikos Kazantzakis Prize in 1987. She was awarded the 1999 Greek State Prize for her novel *Eleni, or Nobody* (translated into English by David Connolly and published by Northwestern University Press), which was also shortlisted for the Aristeion European Literature Award, and the 2003 Kostas and Eleni Ourani Foundation Prize for her most recent novel, *The Century of Labyrinths*. Her most recent collection of short stories *An Almost-Blue Arm* was awarded the 2005 Greek State Prize.

E. H. GONATAS (1924–) was born in Athens, where he worked as a lawyer. As a writer, he has particularly cultivated the short prose piece and has published six slim volumes: *The Traveller* (1945), *The Crypt* (1959), *The Chasm* (1963), *The Cows* (1963), *The Hospitable Cardinal* (1986) and *The Preparation* (1991). He has translated, among others, Ivan Goll, Antonio Porchia and Pierre Bettencourt and was awarded the Greek State Translation Prize. His own works have been translated into English, French and German.

TASSOS GOUDELIS (1949–) was born in Athens. He studied law at the University of Athens. In 1982, he co-founded, together with Kostas Mavroudis, the literary magazine *To Dendro*. He works as a critic and teaches film studies. Since 1990, he has published five collections of short stories. In 2003, he was awarded the Diavazo Prize and the Greek State Prize for *The Woman Who Speaks* (Kedros, 2002).

VASSILIS GOUROYANNIS (1951–) was born in the village of Granitsa, in the prefecture of Ioannina. He studied law at the University of Thessaloniki and works as a lawyer in Athens, where he has lived since 1977. He has published books of poetry, short stories and three novels.

CHRISTOS HOMENIDIS (1966–) was born in Athens. He is a graduate of the Law School of the University of Athens. He made an impact in Greek letters in 1993 with his best-selling novel, *The Clever Kid*. He has subsequently published three more novels, *Up to the Occasion* (Hestia, 1995), *The Voice* (Hestia, 1998) and *Past Perfect* (Hestia, 2003), and two collections of short stories, *I Won't Do You a Favor* (Hestia, 1997) and *Second Life* (Hestia, 2000).

NIKOS HOULIARAS (1940–) was born in Ioannina. He is a graduate of the Athens School of Fine Arts and is wellknown as both an artist and songwriter. He began writing in 1962 and published poems, prose works and art criticism in various magazines. He has subsequently published books on art criticism, several novels and a number of collections of short stories. His novel *In My Enemy's House* (Nefeli, 1995) was proposed by Greece for the 1996 Aristeion European Literature Prize. A number of his short stories have been translated into French, Italian, English, Swedish and German, while his collection of stories *Bakakok* (Kedros, 1981) and his novels *Lousias* (Kedros, 1979), *Life Next Time* (Nefeli, 1985) and *In My Enemy's House* have been published in French by Hatier. Several of his short stories have been arranged for television and his novel *Lousias* was made into a TV series broadcast by Greek Television (ET-1) in 1989.

YANNIS KAISARIDIS (1959–) was born in Veria. He studied politics, Greek literature and theatre. He has published two collections of short stories: *The Chronicle of a Premiere* (Exandas 1997) and *Encounters and Guiltfeelings* (Kedros, 2000).

DIMITRIS KALOKYRIS (1948–) was born in Rethymnon, Crete. He studied modern Greek literature in Thessaloniki, where he founded the literary magazine *Tram* (1971–1978). In Athens, he published the art and literature magazine *Hartis* (1982–1987) and also served as managing editor and art editor of the cultural magazine *To Tetarto* (1985–1987). He works as a graphic designer and an illustrator of books, and has staged four exhibitions of his collages. He has published numerous books of poetry, prose and translations and has twice been awarded the Greek State Short Story Prize (in 1996 for *The Discovery of Homerica* and in 2001 for *The Numbers Museum*).

IOANNA KARYSTIANI (1952–) was born in Hania, Crete. She studied law. She started work as a cartoonist and has published two books of cartoons. She has written a book of short stories, *Mrs Cataki* (Kastaniotis, 1995), and three novels: *Little England* (Kastaniotis, 1997), for which she was awarded the 1998 Greek State Prize, *Suit in the Earth* (Kastaniotis, 2000), for which she was awarded the Diavazo Prize, and *Saint of Solitude* (Kastaniotis, 2003). She also wrote the film script for Pantelis Vulgaris' film, *Brides* (Kastaniotis, 2004).

MENIS KOUMANDAREAS (1931–) was born in Athens and worked for insurance and shipping firms. He published his first book, *Pinball Machines*, in 1962 and has subsequently published a number of novels and collections of short stories. He received the Greek State Prize for his novel *Glass Factory* in 1975, and again in 2002 for his novel *Twice a Greek*. He has also received the Greek State Prize for his collection of short stories *Their Smell Makes Me Cry* (translated into English by Patricia Felisa Barbeito and Vangelis Calotychos and published by the University of Birmingham). He has translated into Greek works by, among others, William Faulkner, Carson MacCullers and Lewis Carroll.

ACHILLEAS KYRIAKIDIS (1946–) was born in Cairo. He graduated from Law School in Athens and worked as a bank employee until 1988. He has published nine books of short stories, prose and essays (on cinema and literature). He is the author of three screenplays for films and has directed seven short films based on his own screenplays. He has published over forty-five translations of works by such authors as Borges, Perec, Queneau, Sepulveda, Jarry, Crumey and others. He was awarded the 2004 Greek State Short-Story Prize for *Artificial Breathing* (Polis, 2003).

PAVLOS MATESIS (1933–) studied theatre and music and is a noted playwright, novelist and translator. His thirteen plays to date include *The Ceremony* (1966 Greek State Prize), *Biochemistry*, *The Ghost of Mr. Ramon Novaro*, *The Plant Carer* (1989 Karolos Koun Award), *Towards Eleusis*, *Roar* and *Guardian Angel For Rent*. His prose fiction includes two collections of short stories and the novels: *Aphrodite* (1987) *The Daughter* (1990, translated by Fred A. Reed and published by Arcadia Books in 2002), *The Ancient of Days* (1994), *Ever Well* (1998), *Dark Guide* (2002) and *Myrtos* (2004). In addition, he has translated works by Aristophanes, Shakespeare, Ibsen, Brecht, Pinter, Orton, Genet, Miller, Mamet, Ackroyd and numerous others.

AMANDA MICHALOPOULOU (1966–) was born in Athens. She studied French literature in Athens and journalism in Paris. Since 1990, she has worked as a columnist for the Greek national newspaper *Kathimerini*. She first appeared in Greek letters with a collection of short stories, *Life Is Colourful Outside* (Kastaniotis, 1994), the title story of which won the short-story competition organized by the journal *Revmata*. She has since published five novels: *Wishbone Games* (Kastaniotis, 1996), which won the Diavazo Prize for best novel, *As Often as You Can Bear It* (Kastaniotis, 1998), *Foul Weather* (Kastaniotis, 2001) and *I Killed My Best Friend* (Kastaniotis, 2003). Her latest book of short stories is *I'd Like* (Kastaniotis, 2005).

CHRISTOPHOROS MILIONIS (1932–) was born and raised in Epirus. He studied classics at the University of Thessaloniki and worked in secondary education. He has contributed to major Greek literary journals and for ten years, was a columnist for the newspaper *Ta Nea*. He has published numerous short stories, novellas, novels and literary studies. His collection of short stories *Kalamas and Acheron* was awarded the Greek State Prize in 1986 and has been translated into English by Marjorie Chambers (Kedros, 1996). He was also awarded the 2000 Diavazo Prize for his collection of short stories, *The Ghosts of York*.

DIMITRIS MINGAS (1951–) was born in Messinia. He studied physics at the University of Athens and works as a secondary-school teacher in Thessaloniki. His first book of short stories, *Of Those At Rest* (Polis, 1999) won the Diavazo prize for best first-time author. This was followed by his novel *It Rarely Snows in the Islands* (Polis, 2001) and another collection of short stories *Befitting Salonica Alone* (Metaichmio, 2003). *Not Playing For Real*, his latest novel, was published by Metaichmio in 2005.

MARIA MITSORA was born in Athens. She studied sociology in Paris (Sorbonne and Vincennes). She has traveled widely, from the Arctic Circle to Haiti, and from Beijing to Santa Fe de Bogota. She has published a collection of short stories, *Anna, There's Another* (Akmon) and the novels, *Scattered Power* (Odysseas, 1997), *Summary of the World* (Kedros, 1999) and *The Sun I Set* (Odysseas, 1997). Her most recent novel is *Fine Weather/Movement* (Patakis, 2005). She has also written numerous short stories and travel essays that have been published in newspapers and magazines.

CLAIRE MITSOTAKI (1949–) was born in Heraklion, Crete. She studied classics at the University of Athens and medieval studies in Paris. She has worked as a contributor to various journals and newspapers, as an editor, and is also a notable translator. Her first book, *Princess Tito and I* (Diatton) appeared in 1989. She has subsequently published *The Strange Words of Madame Bovary* (French Institute, Athens, 1993), *Metals* (Ikaros, 1993) and *Flora Mirabilis* (To Rodakio, 1996).

SOPHIA NIKOLAÏDOU (1968–) was born and lives in Thessaloniki. She studied classics at the University of Thessaloniki, teaches literature at a drama school and writes for *Ta Nea*. She has published two collections of short stories: *Blonde* (Kedros, 1997) and *Fear Will Get You and You'll Be Alone* (Kedros, 1999) and a novel, *Planet Prespa* (Kedros, 2002).

DIMITRIS NOLLAS (1940–) was born in Adriani, near the town of Drama. He studied law, sociology and cinematography and worked as a scriptwriter and TV program consultant. He is currently president of the National Book Center of Greece. His first collection of short stories was published in 1974; he has published thirteen books including short stories, novellas and novels. Awards for his work include the 1983 Greek State Prize for Best Short Story Collection, the 1993 Greek State Prize for Best Novel and the 1997 Diavazo Prize.

NIKOS PANAYOTOPOULOS (1963–) was born in Athens. He studied technical engineering. Between 1989 and 1992, he worked as an arts correspondent for newspapers, magazines and television. Since 1992, he has written screenplays for television and the cinema. He has published a collection of short stories, *The Materials' Guilt* (Polis, 1997) and three novels, *Ziggy from Marfan*, *The Diary of an Extra-terrestrial* (Polis, 1998), *Benefit of the Doubt* (Polis, 1999) and *Hagiography* (Polis, 2003).

ALEXIS PANSELINOS (1943–) was born in Athens. He studied law and worked as a lawyer. He first appeared in Greek letters in 1982 with the novellas *Stories with Dogs* (Kedros). His first novel, *The Great Procession* (Kedros, 1985) was awarded the Greek State Second Prize. He has since published three more novels, *Ballet Evenings* (Kedros, 1991), *Zaïda or The Camel in the Snows* (Kastaniotis, 1996) and *Lame Angel* (Kedros, 2002), a book of essays, *Test Flights* (Kedros, 1993) and a book of short stories, *Four Greek Murders* (Polis, 2004).

I. H. PAPADIMITRAKOPOULOS (1930–) was born in Pyrgos in the Peloponnese. He studied medicine at the University of Thessaloniki and worked as an army doctor. His first book of short stories, *Toothpaste with Chlorophyll*, was published in 1973 and he has since published a further five collections together with numerous essays and articles. He was awarded the 1997 Greek State Prize for best Chronicle-Testimony.

DIMITRIS PETSETIDIS (1940–) was born in Sparta. He studied mathematics and has worked as a teacher in private education. He has published six collections of short stories: *Twelve on a Dime* (To Dendro, 1986 / Nefeli 1999), *The Game* (Nefeli, 1991), *Epilogue in the Snow* (Nefeli, 1993), *Sabates Lives* (Nefeli, 1998), *Tropic of Leo* (Nefeli, 2001) and *Away Ground* (Patakis, 2003).

YORGOS SKABARDONIS (1953–) was born in Thessaloniki. He studied French literature at the University of Thessaloniki. He has worked for newspapers and magazines, television and radio and has written scripts for television documentaries and films. He has published one novel, *I'm Aging Successfully* (Kedros, 2000), and four collections of short stories: *The Textiles' Passage* (Kastaniotis, 1992), for which he was awarded the Greek State Prize, *Sharp Eye, Firm Control* (Kastaniotis, 1992), *The General's Embroidering Again* (Kastaniotis, 1996) and *The Eucharist's Soft Centre—Outer Lane* (Kastaniotis, 1990).

ERSI SOTIROPOULOU (1953–) was born in Patras. She studied philosophy and cultural anthropology at the University of Florence and later served as cultural attaché at the Greek Embassy in Rome. She is the author of eleven books, which include poetry, short stories and novels. She is also a regular contributor to the national newspaper *Eleftherotypia*. Her novel *Zigzag Through the Bitter Orange Trees* (Kedros, 1999) won the Greek State Prize and the Diavazo Prize for Best Novel in 2000.

ANTONIS SOUROUNIS (1942–) was born in Thessaloniki. He worked variously as a bank clerk, sailor, hotel boy and professional roulette player. Since 1969 he has published thirteen books consisting of short stories, novellas and novels. He was awarded the 1995 Greek State Prize for his novel, *The Dance of Roses*.

PETROS TATSOPOULOS (1959–) was born in Rethymnon, Crete and grew up in Athens. He studied economics and politics. He has worked as a social worker, a journalist, a scriptwriter, a publisher's reader and a TV book program presenter. He has published twelve books including three collections of short stories, *Cartoon* (Hestia, 1984), *Light Stories* (Hestia, 1995) and *Comedie* (Kastaniotis, 1999) and five novels, *The Juveniles* (Hestia, 1980), *The Painkiller* (Hestia, 1982), *The Heart of the Beast* (Hestia, 1987), *The First Appearance* (Hestia, 1994) and *Complimentary Copy* (Kastaniotis, 2004).

VASSILIS TSIABOUSSIS (1953–) was born in Drama. He studied civil engineering at the Thessaloniki Polytechnic School. He has published five collections of short stories: *The Scooter and Other Provincial Tales* (Nefeli, 1998, 1990), *Away Game* (Kedros, 1993), *Cherubim on the Roof-tiles* (Kedros, 1996), *Sweet Bonora* (Kedros, 2000) and *May Life Love You* (Patakis, 2004).

THANASSIS VALTINOS (1932–) was born in Karatoula, in the Peloponnese. He is president of the Greek Film Center and president of the Hellenic Authors' Society in Athens. He studied cinematography and has written screenplays for the cinema and has translated a number of ancient Greek tragedies. In 1984, he was awarded the Cannes prize for best screenplay for Theo Angelopoulos's film "Voyage to Cythera." Since 1972, he has published numerous novels and collections of short stories. In 1990, he was awarded the Greek State Prize for his novel *Data from the Decade of the Sixties* (Stigmi, 1989). This book, together with *Deep Blue Almost Black* (Stigmi, 1985), has been translated into English by Jane Assimokopoulos and Stavros Deligiorgis and published by Northwestern University Press.

ZYRANNA ZATELI (1951–) was born in Thessaloniki. She studied theatre and worked as an actress and for the radio. She has published two collections of short stories, *Last Year's Fiancée* (Sigaretta, 1984/Kastaniotis, 1994) and *In The Wilderness with* Grace (Sigaretta, 1986/Kastaniotis, 1994), and two novels, *And in the Twilight They Return* (Kastaniotis, 1993) and *With the Strange Name Ramanthis Erevous* (Kastaniotis, 2002), for both of which she was awarded the Greek State Prize.

ABOUT THE TRANSLATOR

DAVID CONNOLLY (1954–) was born in Sheffield, England. Since 1979 he has lived and worked in Greece and became a naturalized Greek in 1998. He is currently Associate Professor of Translation Studies at the Aristotle University of Thessaloniki. He has written extensively on the theory and practice of literary translation and has translated over twenty books by leading Greek authors. His translations have received awards in Greece, the United Kingdom and the United States. Recent translations include Rhea Galanaki, *Eleni or Nobody* (Northwestern University Press, 2003), Yannis Kondos, *Absurd Athlete* (Arc Publications, 2003), *The Dedalus Book of Greek Fantasy* (Dedalus, 2004) and Petros Markaris, *The Late-Night News* (The Harvill Press, 2004).

A CENTURY OF GREEK POETRY 1900-2000

Selected and edited by
Peter Bien, Peter Constantine, Edmund Keeley and Karen Van Dyck

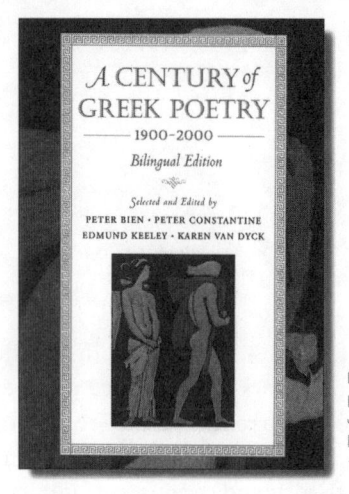

DE LUXE EDITION
HARDCOVER WITH DUST JACKET
PAGES 1,024
17 x 24 cm

This bilingual anthology presents the achievements of Greek poetry in the 20th century. Included are 109 poets and 456 poems, with the Greek original and the English translation on opposite pages. Many of the poems and the translations are published for the first time. Also, included are Kimon Friar's unpublished corrections/modifications to his original translations.

"...If Homer, Sappho and Euripides live on as household names, Seferis and Elytis, both Nobel laureates, are still little known to the wider public. The poet and scholar Constantine A. Trypanis refers to Greek poetry as that 'with the longest and perhaps noblest tradition in the Western world,' and concludes that 'in the last hundred years greater and more original poetry has been written in Greek than in the last fourteen centuries which preceded them.' With the exception of Cavafy, whose poetry earned him international recognition as one of the most important poets of the twentieth century, no other major Greek modern poet has been able to attract more than a limited readership. Yet modern Greek poetry is neither marginal nor minor.
It is the constituent part, and a very important one, of the literature of modern Europe. The 20th century poets, including the two Nobel prize winners, that appear in this anthology will be bringing to light a massive and splendid achievement of modern European literature and will underline its continued vitality and originality."

—Haris Vlavianos

www.greeceinprint.com

LIFE IN THE TOMB
By Stratis Myrivilis

PAPERBACK
SIZE 14 x 21 cm
PAGES 356

Life in the Tomb a war novel written in journal form by a sergeant in the trenches, has been the single most successful and widely read serious work of fiction in Greece since its publication in serial form in 1923-1924, having sold more than 80,000 copies in book form despite its inclusion on the list of censored novels under both the Metaxas regime and the German occupation.

Published in nearly a dozen translations, it is the first volume of a trilogy containing *The Mermaid Madonna* and *The Schoolmistress with the Golden Eyes,* both of which have been available in a variety of languages.

"*Life in the Tomb has moments of great literary beauty and of more than one kind of literary power. In 1917, Myrivilis was twenty-five. 'Before I entered the trenches I had not the slightest inkling of life's true worth. From now on, however, I shall savour its moments one by one...' This... truthful fiction... [makes] one see... It is antiheroic and completely convincing.*"

—Peter Levi

"*[Peter Bien] has turned a Greek masterpiece into something not much less than an English one.*"

—C.M. Woodhouse, Times Literary Supplement

www.greeceinprint.com

THE COLLECTED POEMS OF NIKOS KAVADIAS
Translated by Gail Holst-Warhaft

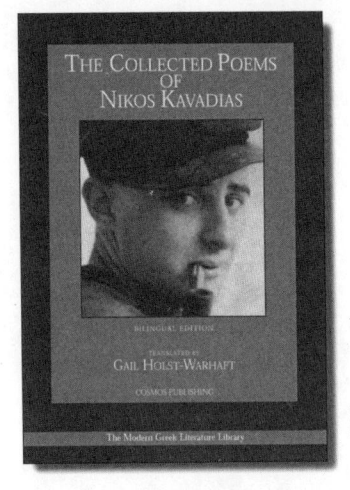

PAPERBACK
PAGES 240
14 x 21 cm

"Modern Greeks dominate the world's merchant marine; ancient Greeks like Homer's Odysseus sailed the Mediterranean and beyond. But what do we know about shipboard life? Not much. Reading Kavadias fills this emptiness. He spent his adult life sailing world-wide and writing poems about monsoons, cats dying on shipboard, masts snapping in two, dream-girls or disgusting whores on shore, and fleas jumping off one's pubic hair. "In this fo'c'sle," he laments, "I ruined my calm self / and killed my tender childhood soul. / But I never gave up my obstinate dream, / and the sea, when it roars, tells me a lot." Scrupulously translated, these accessible poems will tell landlubbers a lot about life on the winedark sea."

—Peter Bien, Translator of Nikos Kazantzakis and Stratis Myrivilis

"It is from the open sea's horizon that he draws his inspiration. The anchor, the fo'c'sle, the marabou and brothels in various exotic countries, excite his imagination to the point that the world of the sea becomes a metaphor for his poetic philosophy. "A mad dog's howl./ So long shore and farewell tub./ Our soul slipped out from under us./ Hell has got a brothel too". (Fata Morgana). His erotic ideal is Fata Morgana, a beautiful woman in Celtic myth, heralding disaster; just like the sea that seduces and drowns. Kavadias turned his profession into poetry. Does this explain the unique charm of his poetry? It certainly suggests the added difficulty that it must have presented for the translator, Gail Holst Warhaft. The translation is very successful."

—Katerina Anghelaki-Rooke, Poet

www.greeceinprint.com

THE PASSPORT AND OTHER SELECTED SHORT STORIES
Translated by Andrew Horton

PAPERBACK
PAGES 112
14 x 21 cm

Antonis Samarakis (1919-2003) was modern Greece's most widely translated writer after Nikos Kazantzakis. He published four collections of short stories and two novels beginning in 1954. His novel, *To Lathos (The Flaw)* has been translated into over twenty languages. Graham Greene called this novel, "A real masterpiece. A story of the psychological struggle between two secret police agents and their suspect told with wit, imagination and quite outstanding technical skill." Arthur Miller wrote that, "*The Flaw* is a powerful work. I only wish some people who profess democracy would read *The Flaw* and see what it is they actually support. We are living in a time when words and their substance are very unrelated-to the point of meaninglessness. And this is not only in the question of Greece."

Samarakis's short stories were equally well received at home and abroad, and this collection brings together eight of his finest stories including "The Last Participation", "Mama", "The Knife", and "The Passport" which he wrote during the period of the Dictatorship of 1967-75 when he was denied a passport to travel abroad.

www.greeceinprint.com